REDEMPTOR DOMUS

Companions true and gallant my young Crusader had,
(Fired for adventure were the souls of them),
But bravelier than they fared forth my Galahad
To seek the jasper-citadeled Jerusalem.

REDEMPTOR DOMUS

GAMELYN CHASE

Matador
9 Priory Business Park,
Wistow Road, Kibworth Beauchamp,
Leicestershire. LE8 0RX
Tel: 0116 279 2299
Email: books@troubador.co.uk
Web: www.troubador.co.uk/matador
Twitter: @matadorbooks

ISBN 9781789010091

British Library Cataloguing in Publication Data.
A catalogue record for this book is available from the British Library.

The quatrain opposite the title page is taken from the poem
Boy Galahad by Henry Green Barnett

Printed and bound by CPI Group (UK) Ltd, Croydon, CR0 4YY
Typeset in Adobe Garamond by Troubador Publishing Ltd

Matador® is an imprint of Troubador Publishing Ltd

Contents

Author's Note

Decades ago, I came across a book in a ship's library. It was Roger Peyrefitte's *Special Friendships,* translated from the French by Edward Hyams. The book remained at the back of my mind in the intervening years for three reasons: the boldness of its subject matter, the elegance of its writing and the fact that I'd never managed to reach the end of it for stress of shipboard duties.

Curiosity eventually got the better of me and I ended up searching for the book on the internet. Having thus been re-acquainted with it I found myself once more enthralled by Peyrefitte's prose but disappointed by a rather unimaginative, not to say improbable, ending. Although I'd never contemplated writing a novel myself I felt I could at least arrive at a more credible outcome; after all, we've all been to school and can draw on and enlarge upon our experiences. I could not hope to match Peyrefitte's encyclopaedic knowledge of antiquity and religiosity, nor the elegance of his prose, but, be that as it may, as I proceeded the work 'just growed'. The key characters acquired Bunyanesque attributes, the plot gathered its present ramifications and the impending denouement became more and more Wagnerian such that at times the tail was in danger of wagging the dog. I sometimes wondered what a *proper* novelist could have done with it.

Of dramatic necessity this work encompasses a celebration

of that span of the male human condition that lies between the nursery and adolescence; but what may have been bold in Peyrefitte's day has since become something of a melodramatic cliché. Accordingly I have trod lightly in that direction, such that the apprehensive reader will encounter more *eroica* than erotica.

Otherwise, a telling that retains an enduring capacity to shake even the author himself obliges me to consider what it might do to others. I did not deliberately set out to construct the spiritual experience that *Redemptor Domus* seems to render; as a lifelong sceptic I'm no fit person to so proselytize. It's just that the course of the work took on a directionality of its own, my own part but that of a helmsman under orders. Should some readers find themselves swept along in the wake, let them not look to me for a lifeline...

Devotees of *Special Friendships* — if indeed there are any left — might detect the echo of certain phrases. I have also in deference retained the same name for the hero of my work, for, try as I might, I could not conjure up a more heroic name than Alexander.

Gamelyn Chase, 2010

Author's Note to the 2018 edition

The coruscating light that is *Redemptor Domus* has been languishing under a metaphoric bushel ever since its original publisher ceased trading back in 2014. Recent research has indicated that the work is ripe for a renaissance.

So here it is again under a new imprint, unabridged and unexpurgated. Apart from some opportune syntactical tweaks, the only change of substance is that I've given one of the leading characters better recognisance at the closing catharsis.

Gamelyn Chase, 2018

Prologue

August 1949. A father despatches his young son from the turbulent Far East to the comparative certainty of an education at an exclusive Roman Catholic school on the North Wales coast. It is the same school where the father himself had been a pupil between the wars. On the voyage west the young boy learns that his family — parents and younger sister — have perished in an aircraft wreck as they were fleeing before the advancing communist army in north-eastern China. The boy arrives at the school in austerity post-war Britain as a stateless and destitute orphan. With only one year's fees prepaid, his future is uncertain. Furthermore, his father has prepared him for the school as he knew it — not as it has since become...

CHAPTER ONE

Confessions and Insurances

The two clerics became aware of the insistent ringing of the telephone. It was the internal telephone, the one in the corridor; the one that connected with the lodge at the town gate. The ringing pattern on the obsolescent telephone system was not automatic; it was at the insistence of the intending communicator and this particular communicator was indeed insistent. The lateness of the hour and the frantic urgency of the signal indicated that it was an emergency of some kind. Of the two clerics, the first, Canon Pynxcytte, bade the second, Father Fillery, to answer it. As was their occasional wont, the two clerics had been working late in the presbytery house of the Roman Catholic College of St Michael Monsalvat. It was now after midnight. The college was closed for the Christmas holidays. The dormitories were empty. The date lay between Christmas and New Year's Day and the New Year would be 1946.

Father Fillery duly took the call and reported back to his superior: "It's Bringsam at the town gate lodge. He says there's a man outside who has been battering at the lodge door and won't go away. He says the man's hysterical and incoherent. Bringsam thinks he's a German trying to speak English; probably an escaped prisoner of war. Bringsam has threatened him with the police but all he can get out of him is 'confess, confess'. He seems to want to make confession. He says he won't go away until a priest has heard his confession."

"Then he must think he is in imminent danger of death. Has Bringsam opened the door to him?"

"No, he's calling down to him from the bedroom window."

"Very wise. How's your German, Fillery?"

"Er... not good enough to take confession, I fear."

"Then it devolves upon me. Let us take ourselves to the lodge and appraise this strange fellow who has turned up out of the night. Make sure you lock the door after us."

"He could be dangerous, Rector."

"Indeed he could — and so could I."

Canon Peter Pynxcytte, Rector of the Roman Catholic College of St Michael Monsalvat, was indeed a person of formidable presence. Well over six feet in height, of athletic build and still young enough at fifty-six to put himself about if necessary. Father Fillery, pastoral priest of the same establishment, forty and tending to fat, could not match him in all that but had enough weight to put about nevertheless. The two put on storm cloaks and sallied forth into the frosty night. It was a short walk up the drive from the presbytery to the lodge. As they approached they could see Bringsam, silhouetted against the night sky, leaning out of the window in his dressing gown. Below him, in the light of the gatehouse lantern, they could see the importunate stranger cowering before the closed door. He was of average build and was dressed very shabbily in what appeared to be second-hand clothes. He had no overcoat and was clearly suffering from the cold. He was also hysterical and possibly drunk. He had a tenor voice that was lapsing into a pathetic falsetto in his apparent pleas for urgent absolution. The Rector called up to Bringsam:

"Put some clothes on, Bringsam, and get yourself down here.

Whatever this fellow's up to, we can't turn him away on a night like this. I see no harm in him. We can put him up in the old bothy. Break out some blankets and a fresh mattress, the ones in the old bothy will be damp. There's kindling and coal there, give him some matches, he can make a fire in the stove. Fillery, telephone the police in case someone's looking for him. I doubt they'll be much bothered, he hardly looks like a top Nazi to me."

At the word 'Nazi' the man visibly flinched. The Rector noticed. Otherwise the other listeners were impressed with the Rector's knowledge of the minutiae of domestic arrangements in such obscure interstices of the college estate as the old bothy. What else might he not know?

"Perhaps Mrs Bringsam would be so kind as to make the man a mug of tea."

Bringsam retreated inwards, shut the window and made arrangements accordingly. The college caretaker and his wife would do well to comply with the wishes and whims of the Rector of St Michael Monsalvat. Father Fillery was similarly instructed to conduct the provisionally refreshed man over to the confessional booths in the college chapel while the Rector himself returned to his quarters in the presbytery house to accoutre himself to take confession. While he was doing this the telephone in the corridor rang again. This time the Rector himself answered it; it was Bringsam at the gatehouse again:

"There's another German here. A very different kettle of fish, this one. Very composed and correct. He speaks excellent English. He says he's looking for his friend. He says his friend is much troubled in mind. Apparently they're both interned merchant seamen. They're from a prisoner-of-war camp on the outskirts of Liverpool."

The location given was some seventy miles distant from Pencadno where the college was situated. The Rector told Bringsam to conduct the newcomer to the old bothy on the same terms as his predecessor but without the intervention of absolution.

Father Fillery escorted the earlier man over to presbytery and left him in the ambulatory outside the south transept door of the chapel to await the arrival of the Rector. He had no qualms about leaving him there unescorted; there clearly was no harm in the wretched fellow. Then he did indeed telephone the police and the police in turn telephoned the duty officer of the P.O.W. camp at Longview in the outer suburbs of Liverpool. The duty officer responded that the two missing men, being merchant ships' stewards, were of no particular interest as to security and that he would send transport to collect them "in the morning". It was already morning.

Confession was duly taken and absolution presumably given to the supplicant. By this time Bringsam was hovering on hand in the chapel to conduct him over to the old bothy, there to be reunited with his concerned compatriot. When the meeting did take place Bringsam noticed a certain apprehension on the part of the first arrival. He was no longer in fear of his life but he seemed to be resigning himself to whatever else fate might have in store for him. The second arrival, who gave his name as Christoff Waliser, reassured Bringsam that he would look after his friend until the P.O.W. camp authorities came to pick them up. As for the Rector, while he clearly could not disclose the secrets of the confessional he was able to vouchsafe the general information that the first arrival was one Heinrich Daser and that he and his compatriot were indeed merchant seamen. Apparently they had been crew members of a vessel called the *Cap Frio*, which had been under refuge in Vigo in northern Spain for the duration of the war. The *Cap Trio* had been intercepted by the Royal Navy, shortly after the unconditional surrender of Germany, while making a dash from Vigo to some undisclosed South American port. According to Daser, after several transfers on the high seas and elsewhere, the crew had been brought into Liverpool for internment. The Rector independently checked the narrative of Waliser with that of Daser and the two accounts appeared to tally. It did not escape the Rector's notice that 'Waliser' was the German for 'Welshman' and that it seemed highly coincidental that this particular German had fetched up in Wales. Furthermore, even in his ill-fitting prison uniform and a hand-me-down overcoat, he gave the impression of being an erstwhile authoritative man who seemed to be underplaying his hand.

The morrow came and went and no transport arrived for the two absconders. It being the time of the Christmas holidays and the two absconders being of low security risk, the camp commandant at Longview was quite amenable to having some other institution hosting his aberrant charges in the meantime. When some meaningful communication *was* established after the New Year, the authorities were quite amenable to leaving the absconders where they were if the hosts could find a use for them. It was a time when ex-prisoners of war who had yet to be repatriated were generally employed on low risk, high priority work, such as in agriculture. Furthermore there were plans to grant residency rights and work permits to those prisoners who, for some reason, did not wish to be repatriated. There were many who certainly would not wish to be repatriated to the political rigours of the Soviet zone or the economic rigours of a devastated homeland. There were others whose next of kin had been wiped out in the hostilities and for whom return would merely exacerbate emotional stress. There were also a few who had formed compelling emotional attachments in the United Kingdom.

As it so happened, Monsalvat (as the Roman Catholic College of St Michael Monsalvat was colloquially known) had much need of cheap labour at this time. Prior to the war,

Handel Trefor, the head gardener and groundsman, had had no fewer than six young assistants, the erstwhile inhabitants of the old bothy. These had gone off to war and had not returned. The gardens, hothouses and greenhouses were in a state of decay. Among other things, the contents of the steam heated peach house, lately the pride of college, had died off for want of attention. There was work to be done and the two Germans expressed a willingness to do it. Thus did it come about that Wali Waliser and Heinrich Daser were temporarily taken onto the staff of the college. The college Bursar, Father Qnedda, was tasked with normalising their status as to remuneration and the requisite residency and work permits.

For the time being they were to remain accommodated in the old bothy. The old bothy was the upper floor of a two-storey brick structure abutting the long, high free-standing rear wall of the peach house. The peach house itself was a long lean-to structure constructed along a gentle but increasing gradient leading down to the sea and thus aspected to maximum sunlight.

In the ensuing years the two Germans remained in the old bothy, although they were free to find accommodation beyond the college estate if their modest remuneration so allowed. They had running water and could boil a kettle. The college supplied them with linen and they were taken onto the ration strength, eating with others of the lay staff in the college refectory, albeit at a lowly table. Father Quedda drafted a work routine for them. They were to come under the general direction of Handel Trefor for outside estate and horticultural work and they would also assist the Sisters who ran the messing arrangements, providing muscle power where needed around the kitchens on such chores as hauling trash and swill bins. As for their spiritual needs, whereas Heinrich Daser continued to be the committed Catholic that he had demonstrated, Christoff Waliser rather belied his name by being somewhat tardy in that regard.

After a few months however, he did start desultorily making Confession and taking Holy Communion; but many gained the impression that he regarded these divine offices as an insurance more of his employment than his soul. Be that as it may, it was the Rector himself who was to remain their exclusive Confessor throughout.

* * *

Some six months after the events of Christmas week 1945, Third Former William Wesley Wepper had become something of a bone of contention among the pastoral Fathers. His name cropped up ever more frequently, both in general convocation and in pastoral conclave. For a start, the boy was the child of a mixed faith marriage contracted under the Tridentine canons and related prescripts; not a satisfactory state of affairs in itself and not a model profile for a pupil of the Roman Catholic College of St Michael Monsalvat. The latent tensions in such a union had become manifest; the Rector had received information that the parties were separating and each was abrogating responsibility for their son in an anguish of disparity of worship. His parents lived in Ireland, although they were not overtly Irish. They were prevented by Irish law and the tenets of their faith from divorcing. Then information was received that Wepper had been consigned to a guardian of indeterminate faith in London. Thus did Wepper, in the vernacular of Monsalvat, change from being an 'upliner' to a 'downliner'; for which an explanation is requisite:

The college looked down from its foothill onto the main railway line between London and the packet port of Holyhead. The line ran along the foreshore and the local station serving the college was that of Pencadno, a modest seaside resort and quarrying centre. According to railway convention in mainland

Britain, directionality is referenced to London. Accordingly, those pupils who had come across the Irish Sea from Dublin to Holyhead arrived by the 'up' line. Conversely, those arriving from mainland points of origin arrived by the 'down' line. It is pertinent to add that within the cloistered confines of Monsalvat the direction from which one arrived had connotations beyond the merely geographical.

Lately it was the Bursar, Father Quedda, who had been complaining in general convocation that Wepper's school fees were late in arriving. Even more lately he was complaining that a contingency arrangement to have them paid in instalments was not being kept up. The now fifteen-year-old Wepper himself was unaware of these concerns. His guardian was remote, both geographically and familially. And he was a naturally mischievous schoolboy. Consequently he fell victim to an evil conspiracy of events. The first event was that his guardian was declared bankrupt; the second event was that, in ignorance of the first, he wrote an essay. Either event gave the Rector sufficient grounds to terminate the boy's pupillage at Monsalvat. As to fees, Monsalvat was not a charity; as to essays, that written by Wepper was palpably heretical and against all the tenets of the House.

Wepper had written it in parallel with another essay, which he had routinely rendered as part of a scholastic task. However, he had not rendered this parallel essay to his tutors; rather he had published it anonymously throughout the college. He had given a title to this parallel essay; a title consisting of a quotation of Voltaire, to whom he gave due recognition. The quotation ran: 'Religion began when the first scoundrel met the first fool'. The essay thus so scurrilously titled continued in similar vein, citing numerous other quotations from similar luminaries, all calculated to undermine the True Faith to the promulgation of which Monsalvat was dedicated. Despite the frantic efforts of the Fathers and their goading of their lay staff members, in the ensuing weeks all the boys, junior and senior, had become exposed to this gross abnegation of the True Faith. Wepper had had his heretical testament hectographed so that multiple copies could be made available. As soon as one was torn down by the irate hand of authority, another would appear.

Every day for several weeks did the priests search frantically through their pupils' effects in the hope of flushing out the perpetrator. Every morning did the Rector rail from the chapel pulpit against this 'bold contemner' and against any who would be complicit in the posting of the essay or in concealing the author's identity. Thus did the essayist, in his anonymity, accrue the opprobrious title of 'The Bold Contemner'. This appellation proliferated on the lips of every boy and staff member; the nuns who ran the kitchens and laundry, the janitors, the gardeners, the night staff. Even the monks of nearby Basingwerk, who occasionally helped out at Monsalvat, had learned of the scandal of Monsalvat's Bold Contemner.

For weeks, the question 'who is The Bold Contemner?' was posed, albeit with varying degrees of gravity. Out of earshot of authority the question was bandied about in dormitory and refectory in typical schoolboy badinage. All this time the hectographed copies of the essay were surreptitiously being passed from hand to hand. They were traded for such various schoolboy considerations as collectible stamps and jazz gramophone records. The wags were putting it about that faggots were being prepared ready for a public burning at the stake on the great parterre for when The Bold Contemner was eventually flushed out.

It was only when the news of his guardian's bankruptcy reached him that Wepper realised the extent of his predicament. His tilt against authority had come unstuck. He knew he would be flushed out eventually as the writer of the essay, but he had reasoned that when that happened he could look forward to being transferred to another school, one with a secular and more liberal regime within which he would continue to flourish. That prospect was dashed with the news of his guardian's bankruptcy. Contemptuous though he might be of the tenets and mores of Monsalvat, at least the school was providing him with an education and, catechism aside, an excellent one at that. His issue was with the ordained priests, not the academic lay staff. Without tuition fees he now faced being expelled and consigned to the uncertainties of publicly funded education — which funding terminated at precisely the age he was at — and at fifteen he was too old to try for a redeeming scholarship. For a promising scholar with an otherwise assured future, this was a disaster. He could see himself being consigned to the status of a mere artisan and a life of comparative penury.

Furthermore, when Wepper first set out to promulgate his heretical views among his schoolfellows, he had reckoned without the consciences and sensitivities of his confidants. Thus did his principal confidant come to him in an anguish of doubt and remorse about his complicity. Wepper was sympathetic but he also realised that his confidant had now become a threat. He averted that threat and assuaged his confidant's conscience by telling him that he would admit to authority that he was The Bold Contemner. He duly did make that admission, but, ever the schemer, he played the Fathers at their own game. He made his admission under the Seal of the Confessional. His confessor, Father van Reldt, found himself the custodian of the revelation.

Within hours Wepper found himself consigned to Monsalvat's bell tower. The bell tower, a most prominent feature of Monsalvat's roofscape, rose from an isolated block that housed, among other things, several guest suites for lay visitors. It was also a place of isolation for those awaiting expulsion. Although he had no evidence, Wepper knew that the Seal of the

Confessional had been broken. The Fathers were not playing the game according to the rules.

It was the boys, collectively astute as ever, who made the connection between the published heresy and their relegated schoolfellow. Of course they were not privy to Wepper's straitened circumstances nor to his confessional testament, but it was the swiftness of his relegation to the bell tower several days before end of summer term that confirmed their diagnosis.

Nor was The Seal of the Confessional being observed within the confines of the priestly presbytery. At the express command of the Rector, the pastoral Fathers in conclave were made privy to the boy's disclosures by Father van Reldt himself. The Rector was also much exercised by the sudden declaration of impecuniosity by the boy's legal guardian, *videlicat:* "I'm not sure of the legal position of a guardian who finds himself in Carey Street. One who has palpably failed in one respect might be deemed to have failed in the other."

"Not only his guardian but also his godfather," interjected his erstwhile confessor.

"Well, he has certainly failed in that respect."

Another observed: "What can you expect of someone whose middle name is Wesley?" These remarks elicited modest chortles from the array.

The upshot of the meeting was the aforementioned relegation to the bell tower. Thus it was that William Wepper was obliged to observe, from a virtual *cordon sanitaire,* the departure of his schoolfellows for the summer holidays.

Priests and lay staff, gardeners, caretakers, nurses and nuns and indeed all spare hands were deployed for this evolution. There would be a loading of handcarts with baggage for the short trek down the hill to the station. Here, by prior arrangement, the scheduled stopping trains would pull in, some with an additional coach attached 'reserved for scholars'. By these means the 'downliners' and 'upliners' — their directions upon departure now being reversed — were respectively despatched towards Chester and Crewe for onward rail connections, or towards Holyhead for the steamers to Ireland. Since its founding in the 1840s by a high-minded caucus of Liverpool merchants, the college had built up a considerable connection with Ireland and a significant number of its pupils hailed from that direction.

Confined to his lonely room in the bell tower, William Wepper could picture the departure platforms bustling with high-spirited pupils and with the station staff busying themselves unlocking reserved compartments and loading baggage into guards' vans. The college made a significant contribution to the revenue of Pencadno station and the railway was duly solicitous of its custom.

As to the evil conspiracy of events bearing upon William Wesley Wepper, a third event was needed. It duly presented and Wepper seized it. In so doing he set in train a sequence of events that would have significant consequences for the Roman Catholic College of St Michael Monsalvat.

* * *

It was the second occasion upon which Wepper had seen the flashy American car parked in the *porte-cochère* at the rear of the presbytery. There were not a few of these cars to be seen at the time. American officers stationed in Britain brought them over in preference to driving the rather more modestly proportioned and underpowered products of the British motor industry. When their owners were posted elsewhere the cars came onto the domestic market and some thus fell into the hands of the more flamboyant and well-heeled natives. As an object, the car was decidedly out of place in the Puginesque surroundings of Monsalvat.

Exactly a year ago, as a Second Former, Wepper had been

in the same place at the same time and had observed the same scene. It elicited his curiosity then and it intensified it now. Then, as now, he had remained a hidden observer. It was not that he was purposefully hiding; it was just that he was passing unseen through the thicket behind the presbytery as a short cut between the town gate and the bell tower. Then, as now, he was returning from an excursion into the little town of Pencadno after spending a few pennies of his dwindling pocket money on a bottle of Sparkling Special and a batch cake. Most of Monsalvat's pupils had gone away to the homes of their guardians or, if they were fortunate, their parents. Those many boys who had to stay with the college because their parents were abroad had gone away to summer camp. But summer camp costs money and money had lately been scarce in the home of Wepper's guardian; and furthermore his guardian was in London, some two hundred miles away. The upshot was that he had to stay on the premises and, because the dormitories would be closed for painting and other such maintenance, he had been relegated to the bell tower.

Except that on this occasion this was to be his last stay in the bell tower. William Wepper would be leaving The Roman Catholic College of St Michael Monsalvat for good. He would depart for the station as soon as his guardian in London had forwarded the money for his rail fare. The college was reluctant to cover that expense. For them to have done so would have been tantamount to admitting that they were expelling him. The illusion had to be maintained that he was being withdrawn by his guardian. That which had been admitted to under the Seal of the Confessional could not be used in evidence against him. The Fathers were playing the game at least to that extent. Having regard to future consequences, better had it been for the Rector had he paid the rail fare out of his own pocket.

* * *

Then, as now, the man who parked the flashy car wore a pencil moustache and a camel hair coat. Even in August. The coat seemed to go with the car. Neither went with the location. Such flamboyant ostentation seemed out of place in the environs of a Roman Catholic boys' school. The man had all the appearances of a spiv, the word then current for a man who lived by his wits by engaging in dubious trade. Wepper also detected a well-contained air of menace in the man.

It was now Wepper's turn to learn to live by his wits. As it was, he turned out to be a quick study. As previously, he saw the man put an attaché case in the boot of the car. Indeed he seemed to recognise the case from last year. He saw the man lock the boot lid, turning the key most carefully and checking the handle to test the lock. Wepper distinctly got the impression that there was something very valuable in the attaché case. He saw the man hesitate then turn and re-enter the presbytery. If he was the cockney Wepper surmised him to be, then he would have a long drive ahead of him. Wepper also surmised that the man had re-entered the presbytery in order to use the lavatory facilities. That meant the man would have to walk along the lower corridor to the staircase at the front of the building, go up to the first floor, find the guest bathroom, complete his ablutions then walk back down again. All of which took time. Time enough, thought Wepper, for him to act.

Wepper ran across into the shadows of the *porte-cochère* where he tried the handle of the car's rear passenger door. It was not locked. Wepper flung himself inside and pulled forward the back cushion of the rear seat. It came forward and folded down as he expected it would. He dived over the displaced cushion and went head first into the darkness of the boot space. A few moments of frantic scrabbling among other items of luggage and he had his hands on the attaché case. Then he scrambled out of the boot space and returned the rear seat cushion to its place as if it had never been disturbed. The next critical task was to close the rear door without any noisy slam. He accomplished this by pushing it to and then butting it with his hip. Slight as he was, the car rocked on its springs and the lock clicked. It remained for him to sprint over to the thicket and out of sight. Breathless, he watched as the man re-emerged. His estimation of the lapse of time had been accurate. He watched as the man got into the driving seat and sat studying his maps for a minute or so. At last, to Wepper's relief, he turned the key in the ignition and drove slowly out of the *porte-cochère*, did a U-turn on the asphalt apron and turned back onto the main drive. Wepper listened for the tell-tale noise of the engine dying away as the car moved towards the town gate, turned left onto the main road and headed towards Chester and the south. He reckoned it would take less than five hours before the attaché case was missed. He was right.

* * *

Clutching the attaché case, Wepper skulked his way by a devious route behind the chapel and the bell tower, crossed the bridge over the stream that ran through the grounds and fetched up among the utilities and out-yards of the college estate. Beyond lay the playing fields and open country. He was making for the old bothy. Here he was hoping to meet 'Wali' Waliser and confide in him over this, his latest and most serious misdemeanour.

By this time, Christoff Waliser and Heinrich 'Heini' Daser had both declined repatriation and had acquired work permits and leave to stay in the United Kingdom. They were now employed as assistant gardeners and had their work cut out restoring the estate of Monsalvat to something approaching its pre-war condition. They were still housed in the old bothy next to the peach yard and the greenhouses. Both had struck up a special affinity with the boys. They had many stories to tell of the sea and the war and Wepper considered he had acquired a good and faithful friend in Wali. In his several adversities he had rejected the pastoral care of the priests and it was to Wali he would turn for advice and assistance. Heini on the other hand was not of the same calibre as Wali — and was rather too fond of the bottle, to boot.

Wepper was relieved to find Wali on his own at the old bothy. The German was appalled at his young friend's theft of the attaché case. He turned it over and over in his hands. It had seen better days but was of excellent quality leather, and felt heavy enough with its contents. He shook it tentatively; what sounded like card impinged upon its inside. He recognised the case as an item of the ubiquitous 'war surplus' that was spilling onto the markets at the time. It had evidently been intended to carry important despatches, for there were two robust lockable latches on it. Gingerly, Wali tried them. They were both locked.

Understandably, Wali wanted none of this. Wepper's action in bringing the case to him was tantamount to implicating him as an accessory to theft. Clearly it would be safer for all concerned if the case was removed from the college estate altogether, to some place beyond the remit of the Fathers. He advised and assisted Wepper accordingly; to that extent he did become an accessory. He sent Wepper off on another skulk, this time down the hill towards Pencadno station, still furtively clutching the attaché case. A few minutes later Wepper was walking confidently back up the hill again, unburdened by anything other than a 'left luggage' receipt.

* * *

In the ensuing twenty-four hours, in the refectory and about the grounds, the lone schoolboy's path crossed with those of the Fathers several times but he was surprised and relieved that no-one had taxed him on the matter of a missing attaché case.

Perhaps the case and its contents were not of much consequence after all. But his relief was to be short-lived.

That evening Wepper returned to the bell tower only to find that his effects had been turned over in a frantic search for something. That something could only be the missing attaché case or its contents. Wepper immediately repaired to his late dormitory only to find the same evidence of a search. There was no effort to conceal the searches; in the bell tower his effects were left in disarray; in his late dormitory lockers and wardrobes had been left agape. Clearly he was the prime suspect, the case was of import and the Fathers were wise to him. More disturbingly still, he was uncomfortably aware that there must be other men of other persuasions in other places who felt a concern for the contents of that attaché case.

* * *

Down at Pencadno station, stationmaster Evan Thomas received a telephone call from Father Fillery up at the college. Father Fillery was inquiring if an attaché case had recently been lodged in the station's 'left luggage' facility. Thomas was able to confirm that indeed there was such a package in railway custody. Up at the college the Fathers had been searching for an attaché case whereas they should have been searching for a receipt. Thomas volunteered no further information as to the depositor. Surprised he was then when Father Fillery arrived just a few minutes later, demanding the surrender of the attaché case. The Father was rather put out to be told that without the official receipt the package could not be surrendered.

"Very well then, Mr Thomas," came the priest's imperious response, "I'll be back presently with the receipt."

But, as previously mentioned, the stationmaster had volunteered no information as to the depositor. There was no need. Where else to look for the receipt but to the college's Bold Contemner languishing in the bell tower? For sure, there were no other pupils on the premises. But as Father Fillery was going uphill in his car for the receipt, the receipt was going downhill by the path across the sheep meadow in the pocket of The Bold Contemner himself; along with the single fare to London and cash enough for subsistence on the journey, all moneys courtesy of Wali Waliser.

* * *

Within twenty-four hours those other men of other persuasions in other places had arrived at Pencadno to take up the initiative. Their mode of address differed substantially from that of Father Fillery: "Come on, Taffy, ante up. Just give us the keys to the left luggage and we'll leave you alone."

Evan Thomas's apprehensions had been realised. The two strangers hanging around the station after the last train had gone were indeed up to no good. They had waylaid him just as he was locking up the booking office and turning down the gas lighting for the night. There was nobody about who could raise the alarm. There was a signalman in the box at the end of the 'down' platform but he was in 'mid turn' and wouldn't be aware of what was happening in the station buildings anyway. They had him tied to a chair in the booking office. A smack to the side of the face had loosened a tooth and a trickle of blood had started from the corner of his mouth. These men meant business. They were not locals; they spoke with cockney accents. Furthermore, they hadn't come by train. Thomas knew there was a lone automobile still parked on the station frontage. A flashy American automobile.

Furthermore, if robbery was their motive it was a strange robbery. They expressed no interest whatever in the day's takings in the booking office cash drawer. As for left luggage, that part of the station's business was minuscule. It usually consisted of a few cabin trunks sent on ahead for the desultory trickle of visitors to Pencadno's scattering of hotels and guest houses.

Thomas was in shock now and readily relinquished the keys. What price somebody else's personal effects when liberty, safety and possibly life were in danger? Thomas had to think of his wife who would be preparing his supper just a few steps away in the station house, unaware of his predicament. But if he was delayed much further he knew she would come looking for him and the situation might get a lot worse. The trick was to get the matter done with quickly and without provoking his assailants to further excesses.

One of the men took the keys and went out onto the platform and along to the station's modest left luggage depository. A few moments later he was back in a state of some agitation.

"It's not there. It's gone."

The other thug rounded upon Thomas. This time, their enquiry became more specific:

"Where is it, Taffy? Where's the fucking attaché case that was here yesterday?"

Thomas had already been offered a fifty-pound bribe for it, several times his weekly wage. He had refused it, knowing better than to jeopardise his secure railway job for short-term gain. But now he found himself with a loaded revolver pressed to the side of his head. The steel of the muzzle felt cold and hard. Time to end this now. Thomas suddenly became nervously garrulous.

"It's been collected. You can look in the book for the description and the ticket number. You'll find the receipt on the spike. It was one of the boys from the college who deposited it. Sam Rowlands the porter told me. He was the man on duty. He said the boy collected it yesterday afternoon and got on a train. Sam said he was booked through to Euston. He thought it odd out of term time — but some of these boys stay behind during the holidays. Their parents are abroad and that sort of thing. That's all I can tell you — honest."

"Whoa, Taffy, slow down. We believe you."

The first thug made a show of inspecting book and spike but both knew from Thomas's demeanour that he was indeed telling the truth. There was no more to be done here.

"Untie 'im," the one said resignedly.

The other moved behind the chair and slackened the bonds enough for the stationmaster to struggle free. "Okay, not a word, Taffy — or we'll be back. Understand?"

"Yersss," added the other, "just tell the wife you slipped and banged yer 'ead on the door post. That's all she needs to know. Got it, Taffy?"

Almost as an afterthought the thug reached into his jacket and brought out his wallet. He peeled off twenty pounds from a wad of notes and flung them on the desk top. He put an ostensibly reassuring hand on the stationmaster's shoulder. "That'll cover the dentist's bill. Otherwise no 'arm done, eh, Taffy? No need to call out the rozzers, eh?"

Thomas nodded compliantly and murmured something to the effect that he had indeed 'got it', and with that the men were gone. He waited until he heard the car start up outside and take off up the hill towards the main road before he considered it safe to wriggle free. He picked up the discarded bunch of keys and went about locking up the station. Mrs Thomas did indeed come looking for him. He had no difficulty in getting her to accept his explanation for the delay. His agitated state could easily be attributable to a fictitious fall, notwithstanding the decidedly factual injury to his face.

"You'll have to enter it in the accident book, Evan. Come into the kitchen; that face of yours looks as if it could do with a cold compress."

But Thomas decided not to carry the deception forward. Ever the stickler for propriety, he did report the incident to the police and to his superiors at Bangor station. The incident accrued some notoriety in the sleepy little town and was made the subject of a brief mention in the local papers. But Thomas did not tell them the whole story. It was the earlier involvement of Father Fillery that caused him to truncate his account of the incident. The college loomed large in the affairs of Pencadno — and it didn't do to upset the college. As it was, the police and his employers seemed content with his attenuated version of the incident; but he remained puzzled nevertheless. There was clearly more to this attaché case than met the eye.

* * *

The boy followed Waliser's advice regarding London's main line termini. Instead of lodging the attaché case at Euston left luggage office, he took it across town somewhat and lodged it at Kings Cross. He then doubled back to Paddington and took a local train to where the home of the uncle who was also his guardian was situated. Confronted by his guardian, he clearly had some explaining to do.

His guardian's telephone had been disconnected at the behest of the receiver in bankruptcy. His guardian arranged for him to telephone from the office of an erstwhile business colleague. Wepper called the number of Wali's lady friend at her lodgings in Pencadno town. Her name was Yseult. It was from Yseult that he learned of the extraordinary events at Pencadno station. Realising he was in over his head, he decided to tell his guardian everything he knew about the attaché case. He handed over the receipt from Kings Cross left luggage depository.

Thus it came about that his guardian made a telephone call to Canon Peter Pynxcytte, the Rector of Monsalvat himself.

When he came off the telephone he called his nephew before him and addressed him formally, confidently, confidentially and thus: "You are to go back to Pencadno tonight and you will resume your residence and studies at Monsalvat. You are to stay there until you take and pass your university entrance exam. At the beginning of each term the Bursar will give you ten pounds by way of spending money. Your safekeeping and welfare are guaranteed. I cannot speak for your future conduct but whatever happens, you must not abscond again."

He then handed Wepper a piece of paper with a London telephone number written on it and continued: "It's imperative that you memorise that number and destroy that piece of paper. Every Thursday at 6pm you are to telephone that number entirely without fail. You are not to speak of this arrangement to anybody, understand? Anybody." And then: "Failure to follow these instructions will bring this arrangement — and much more — down about your ears. Do you understand?"

Wepper affirmed that he did. But his guardian had not finished. "This Waliser fellow... Get him to call that same number as soon as you get back. It's imperative I speak with him most urgently. Do you understand?"

Once again Wepper affirmed that he did indeed understand. Later that day, guardian and charge set off for Euston. There the guardian put his charge on the next northbound express that connected with one of the local trains serving Pencadno. His guardian had managed to borrow the money for his fare and dinner for the two of them in the station buffet. He also gave Wepper another two pounds by way of pocket money; a considerable sum for the time. His guardian seemed unconcerned now at the prospect of having to pay back the money.

Having seen his young charge off thus, the next morning Wepper's guardian retrieved the attaché case from Kings Cross left luggage depository and took a taxi to a safe deposit in the

West End. The attaché case, still locked and unopened (for neither guardian nor charge had keys), was to remain in the safe deposit for the next three years. Beyond the denizens of the presbytery house at Monsalvat and its thwarted recipients in London, only four other persons knew of its existence; Waliser, Wepper's guardian, Evan Thomas and of course Wepper himself.

In the intervening three years Wepper was to grow from a callow schoolboy into a handsome young man. He came to seek solace and company beyond the cloistered confines of Monsalvat, often in defiance of authority. He was to develop a liaison with Rhiannon ap Gruffydd, the daughter of a local solicitor. Eventually, in his last year at Monsalvat and without seeking the blessing of the Fathers, Rhiannon and he became betrothed.

Within the college hierarchy he was significantly denied a prefecture. This was reasonable enough; it would hardly do for Catholic authority so to elevate its Bold Contemner — for the opprobrious appellation had pursued him through the rest of his school years, not that he was overly anxious to deny it. By way of an attempt at rehabilitation and as a public example of forbearance, the Rector appointed him sacristan of the chapel, thus putting him in charge of the holy vessels and accoutrements. Wepper performed this office assiduously enough, regarding it as a necessary burden on the way to achieving his academic goals.

* * *

Before the normalising of his social preferences Wepper had, like so many boys consigned to the hot-house atmosphere of boarding school, formed amorous liaisons with other boys, some older than himself, some younger. All these liaisons had been fleeting and matters of instant gratification; with the exception of one, a certain youngster then in the Remove. Intelligent, athletic of body, easy of address and exceptionally fair of face, Wepper had first come into serendipitous contact with him when, as a lightweight Removite, he had been drafted in to cox Wepper's racing four on the Conway river. Their relationship had been intense and long. Indeed it had been sealed in blood in a hocus-pocus ritualistic ceremony in the peach house. The relationship endured until the older boy began to seek that more orthodox solace outside the walls of Monsalvat. The affair inside had become ostensibly dormant; it was on the younger side however that the embers still smouldered and could be fanned into flames in unpredictable directions. Rhiannon, for one, could not be the most popular person in the eyes of Wepper's erstwhile paramour.

In the autumn of 1948 Wepper entered for a valuable scholarship entitling him to study French Literature and Philosophy at the Sorbonne, and he was successful. He also became sponsored by Tegid ap Gruffydd, Rhiannon's solicitor father who had his practice in Pencadno. Wepper had been welcomed into the ap Gruffydd household and in later months had become virtually a day boy at college; this with the ready connivance of the Rector, ever mindful of expense. Here at last was a welcome release from the chill penury that had dogged Wepper's later school years. Accordingly he was scheduled to leave Monsalvat for the Sorbonne at the end of the summer term 1950.

As for the attache case lodged in the London safe deposit, eventually a party of men would call to seize it for the authorities. The party would consist of a chief inspector of police, a special branch detective in mufti armed with a magistrate's warrant, and two uniformed officers of military intelligence.

CHAPTER TWO

The Boy from Manchuria

At the appointed time Father Laskiva made his way to the common room in the presbytery where a general convocation of pastoral and secular staff was scheduled to order the affairs of Autumn Term 1949. He was the last to arrive and as he walked into the room he was confronted by an array of upturned faces. He still felt some unease at his constant impression that he was an outsider in these concerns. At least he was no longer having to remind the others that his name rhymed with 'diver'. The others were all seated on one side of the great oak table in some order of precedence, the more senior nearer to an ornate chair set at the head of the table. Father Laskiva moved towards the only other vacant chair that was set opposite the others at the bottom end of the table.

Footsteps were heard in the corridor, rapping on the parquet with a palpably authoritative beat. There was an urgent scraping of chairs as all present rose to their feet. They visibly stiffened as a tall figure in clerical purple and black biretta strode purposefully through the doorway. The new arrival had a commanding presence. Unbidden, one of the priests left his seat and went to close the great oak door behind this august personage. Canon Peter Pynxcytte, Rector of the Roman Catholic College of St Michael Monsalvat, had arrived.

Canon Pynxcytte was known to staff and boys by various appellations, depending upon circumstances. Officially he was of course the Rector but many habitually referred to him as the Cardinal. By now, Father Laskiva knew this to be a retroversive title deriving from Pynxcytte's pastoral duties as head of the Cardinal's Men, the name of one of the four 'Quarters' into which the pupils of the college were gathered. Less deferentially, and decidedly out of earshot of authority, some referred to him as Peter the Painter, this last being an erudite Latin schoolboy pun on his name.

The Rector took his seat at the head of the table, bade the others to be seated, and began imperiously rapping out orders to all and sundry as requisite as he went through the agenda. Among matters under consideration were the new boys, all of whom were consigned to the Removes. A bundle of files lay at his elbow and he started to leaf through them.

"Here's one for you, Laskiva." Clearly he was not one for priestly protocols. "Take a note. Arriving Liverpool Landing Stage the day after tomorrow, s.s. Antenor, Blue Funnel Line. Call Central 5630 in the morning and ask their passenger department for the time of disembarkation. The boy's name is Alexander Fragner Vudsen. He will be twelve years of age on his next birth-day, June twenty-ninth 1950. That will make him the youngest boy in the college. Unaccompanied, no escort presumably due to the urgency of his despatch. A most tragic case; both his parents and younger sister missing, presumed dead. His whole family. They were in an aircraft flying between Dairen and Tsingtao across the Yellow Sea. It never arrived. According to the local British Consul some identifiable flotsam was found, seeming to confirm the aircraft went down with no survivors. The boy was lately at the *Mission Catholique Francaise* in Mukden, although he seems to have moved about a bit. His parents had sent him down to Hong Kong to embark for the

UK. I understand the sad news reached him via the consul when the ship reached Singapore." He paused while this melancholy information impinged on the array; then: "Better take the Super-Snipe and Sister Gloria."

Father Laskiva was intrigued by the Rector's idea of precedence.

"Until the dorms are ready he'll have to go in the bell tower. Have Godred prepare a room for him." The Rector returned his eyes to the boy's file and continued: "Not the usual colonial caste. Immigration status uncertain. Born in the Far East, never been to the UK, neither he nor his parents have British passports but it seems his father is — or rather was — an Old Monsalvation. They were in shipping. I gather from the records that the family were émigré Lűbeckers. Clearly not Lutheran Lűbeckers, then. They had been documented by the Manchukuo government...provisional government of Manchuria..." he added helpfully, for the benefit of the more cloistered. "Probably on the strength of their German connection. What with the Japanese, the Kuomintang and the Communists, I could understand a definitive nationality being an embarrassment, especially for a businessman. It says here the boy has been granted 'British Protected Person' status in Hong Kong and presumably he comes with documentation as such. No guardian in this country; his parents didn't nominate one, presumably because they intended coming here themselves. We find ourselves his guardian by default until someone comes forward to claim him. As we know, the situation in that part of the world is very volatile at the moment, with Europeans decamping in droves. I expect some friend of the family will come looking for him in due course when they've found their bolt-hole — but we shouldn't hold our breath. As a preliminary I think we should contact the Society of Saint Vincent de Paul with a view to arranging a local adoption."

At this point, concerned at the boy's plight, Father Laskiva felt emboldened enough to intercede. "Has he no uncles? Has he no aunts?"

"If he has, they are not in this hemisphere.., apparently," was the Rector's curt response.

The Rector looked along the table at the line of concerned faces to his right. His gaze stopped at the Bursar.

"Father Quedda, have a word with Davies & Co. as soon as possible about his status and see if they can assume provisional guardianship. The rules prevent the college assuming guardianship except in an emergency — and because of the passage of time this can no longer be considered an emergency. Also, find out from them the implications of the new Children Act. I believe it comes into force in January. He'll need a ration book and clothing coupons too. See to those things. The letters tell me he's been outfitted in the Far East with the help of American and Australian military, but he'll still need specific uniform items when he gets here."

Father Laskiva had been at the college long enough to know that Davies & Co. officiated as the college solicitors and that they had an office in Bangor. The legislation referred to by the Rector had its origin in a fatal case of child abuse in 1945. The O'Neill children, three boys and a girl, had been in local authority care since 1939 under the auspices of Newport Borough Council in South Wales. In 1944 Dennis, the eldest child, along with his younger brother, Terence, were fostered out to Reginald and Esther Gough on their remote farm in Shropshire. Unbeknown to the social services of the day, Reginald Gough had a conviction for violence and their marriage had not been a stable one. In the ensuing seven months both boys were subjected to systematic whippings and neglect at the hands of the Goughs, so much so that Dennis died from a combination of main force and neglect on January 9th, 1945. The case attracted such notoriety and revulsion throughout the country that its reportage took precedence over the closing stages of World War Two. The subsequent inquiry elicited a tale of dilatoriness and lack of communication between the supervising authorities. The wider inference was that England, and Wales for that matter, would be no 'land fit for heroes' until the contributing official negligence had been excised. It was, but to an inadequate extent, as the subsequent history of child abuse in the United Kingdom will give evidence.

Like others of his generation, Father Laskiva committed the O'Neill case to the background memory of his mind; to be disconcertingly recalled when certain matters in pastoral care arose. Now the priest contemplated the hapless, friendless orphan at the gates of Monsalvat and, for some reason he could not fathom, found himself recalling the graphic reportage of the O'Neill case and musing upon the fragility of childhood. He consoled himself with the thought that the new boys now homing in on Monsalvat for the start of the new term were from a far different social mould to that of the unfortunate O'Neills. He was also certain that, although they might not make the immediate connection, none of the participants at the meeting would be unaware of the abominable case upon which the legislation was founded.

The priest was jolted out of his dark reverie by further developments of the moment. The Rector was pushing a sheaf of papers towards the Bursar and saying: "You'll find there a bankers' draft for one year's fees plus estimated outfitting expenses and pocket money. After that — who knows? Make out a letter in triplicate for Laskiva to produce for the ship-owners and the Immigration. Presumably they'll let him in on a student visa. As it is, he's on our doorstep and there's nowhere now he can be deported to."

The Rector then addressed another of the priests: "He'll be

with you of course Fillery. Remove 'A'. As for Quarters, his father was a Cardinal's Man so I shall gather him unto myself."

A 'Cardinal's Man' was a member of the Cardinal's 'Quarter'. Unlike most public schools thcre were no 'Houses' at Monsalvat because the boys' accommodations were segregated according to age, with each age range being supervised by one of the pastoral Fathers. Instead, in order to promote "healthy competition in academics and games", the pupils were mustered into 'Quarters'. Each Quarter was headed by a 'Quarter Captain' appointed from among the senior prefects. Three of these Quarters were known by their colours, variously, as the Reds, the Light Blues and the Dark Blues and, as divulged, the fourth Quarter was known, eccentrically, as The Cardinal's Men. The Cardinal's Men wore mauve neckties and mauve hatbands on their straw cadies. A boy was assigned his Quarter on entry and kept it throughout his pupillage. Assignment was arbitrary unless influenced by considerations of alumnus. This new boy was being assigned to the Cardinal's Men because his father had been in that Quarter. On games shirts, the Quarter colours were actually quartered with gold (yellow), the generic colour of Monsalvat.

Father Laskiva knew that segregation by age was purposefully fostered at Monsalvat as a guard against illicit liaisons across the age range. The only in-house institutions that transcended this segregation were the Quarters themselves and the usual school clubs relating to pursuits and pastimes. The clubs found themselves subject to considerable surveillance in that specific.

The Rector continued, still addressing himself to Father Fillery: "I see our long-absent friend Barden Sender will be back with us this term. It is to be hoped he has got over his indispositions. Ask Sister Gloria to put Vudsen next to him in the dorm; he'll benefit from the older boy's experience. And ask her to sort out another steady boy to flank him. It might be as well if she had a discreet word with them about Vudsen's... err... delicate situation."

Father Laskiva thought this to be most considerate of the Rector vis-à-vis his new charge. He did however wonder how Sister Gloria was expected to sort out 'a steady boy' from an influx of unknown quantities.

The Rector pored over the new boy's school reports. "A diligent and promising scholar — and something of a linguist I see, fluent in three European languages *and* the local Chinese. Some knowledge of Japanese too. He's an accomplished soprano soloist, reputedly used to performing in public. One for the dome, I trow. Clearly one does not trifle with a boy partly brought up in Tsingtao."

The faces round the room smiled deferentially. Father Laskiva noted that the Rector was inclined to such impromptu condescensions.

As each new boy's case was considered the papers were passed to the Bursar. In addition to a large Irish contingent, Monsalvat recruited many of its pupils from military, colonial and consular families and expatriate business communities. Thus they came from the four corners of the world and many of them had no homes in Britain. For this reason, apart from the long summer break and the Christmas holidays, the incidental holidays were taken in-house. During the longer holidays most would be claimed by their appointed guardians but there was always a significant number who were unassigned. The college had an arrangement with local summer camps to accommodate and entertain these pupils.

Father Laskiva noted that most of the new arrivals were ex-prep school of some sort and would not have much difficulty in adjusting to boarding school routine. As the files were passed from hand to hand he also saw that each boy's file included a note of physical characteristics and a medical report, attached to which were chest x-ray plates and full-length photographs of the candidate, nude and aspected anteriorly, posteriorly and in profile against a graduated background. Such detail would necessitate the employment of a professional medical photographer. The priest thought this requirement rather extreme but, not having had much to do with schools, he had little to compare it with. He discreetly strained to see the photographs as the documents passed to and fro but from his perspective they were upside down and largely too far away.

Father Laskiva had not envisaged ending up in a boys' school. He had approached the assignment with some trepidation. He was a diocesan appointee assigned to Monsalvat for some reason not vouchsafed to him other than a remit to 'Observe and Report' as he thought fit; but up to the present he had found no reason to so 'Report'. He could only assume — and took it that others would assume — that the diocese was not entirely happy with the present regime at Monsalvat. Certainly he was aware of a certain reserve, short of actual hostility, among the pastoral Fathers and certain staff members.

Otherwise, he considered himself fortunate to have been consigned to Monsalvat. The location on the North Wales coast was superb and the regime seemed benign and progressive apart from the rather stringent entry requirements — none of the bizarre customs that some public schools seemed to go in for. There was no ignominious 'fagging', whereby juniors had to perform menial tasks for seniors, or compulsory cold showers or any of that nonsense. True, there was a morning run along the beach to wake up the juniors for the day ahead. This morning run could be decidedly chilly, especially in the winter months but the ensuing showers were hot enough. As specified and provided for by the founding fathers in the 1840s, cleanliness was indeed next to godliness. Father Laskiva had expected to take issue with corporal punishment but he was relieved to learn that, unlike in other public schools of the day, it was no longer the prerogative of prefects or masters generally, indeed neither was it the prerogative of the pastoral Fathers. There was no barbarous birching, as at Eton or Harrow. Only the cane was used and that was awarded only after due investigation and administered on formal notification under controlled conditions in a prescribed place at a prescribed time by an appointed official who was presumably skilled in its application. The possibility of excess or injustice seemed eliminated. The one anomaly was Sister Gloria's tawse, but that functioned more as a deterrent than an actual sanction. It seemed all very satisfactory, having regard to the tenets of the times.

In the greater dimension Father Laskiva felt content with his priestly station. Its necessary privations largely did not reach him. Indeed his faith was his refuge. In his philosophy of life those who seek instant gratification are like amoeba. They extend their pseudopoda in enticing directions. If what they encounter is too hot or too cold they withdraw and extend in another direction. Instant gratification is forever out of reach. If it is reached, it fails to gratify. Life is a long siege and satisfaction goes to the impregnable. His faith made him impregnable — or so he liked to think.

In the present dimension he was intrigued by the way the boys' minds seemed to crackle and fizz. Clearly these were the sons of the likes of consuls and colonels, taipans and technologists, agents and artists, librettists and landowners, bankers and barristers.

Other pressing matters were tabled and, after satisfying himself that his staff was suitably apprised of the business at hand, the Rector rose to make his exit. Once again all present rose to their feet in deference to his departure. As his footsteps died away, someone closed the door behind him and the company visibly relaxed. Father Quedda shuffled the documents before him, looked down the table, and held forth confidently: "The Cardinal knows how to pick 'em, eh, Fillery? All good Aryan specimens again, eh, no round shoulders or knock knees. Care to have a look through the photos? A nice new crop of peaches, I'd say."

The priest thus addressed shifted uneasily and ventured: "We must trust to the Rector's good judgement in these matters."

Father Laskiva distinctly got the impression that there was more than met the eye at Monsalvat. The conversation drifted on and a few minutes later Father Fillery was holding forth on the propensities of his charges.

"Boys are like cats. Everything they do is in their own self-interest. They have neither love nor consideration for their fellow creatures."

Father Laskiva thought it time to assert his presence and found himself querulously taking issue with Fillery's negative philosophy. "That's a sweeping generalisation. I suppose if you crowd them into barrack blocks and leave them largely to their own devices and only look down on them from above, they're bound to seem like that. I'd venture to say the boy in the family is a different animal."

He wished he could cite examples of gratuitous kindnesses and considerations, but his experience with the species was sparse to say the least. He could only draw on his own experiences of school and seminary; and that, in the context, was not inspiring. Embarrassed at his inept interjection, he tried to retrieve the situation with some mild humour: "Anyway, methinks you do cats a disservice too."

All that got him were funny looks along the table.

* * *

There were two distinct levels of staff conference at Monsalvat. The present had been 'general convocation', which included all the priests and those lay staff members who might be interested or involved in the matters minuted. Then there was 'pastoral conclave', which was restricted to the pastoral Fathers — those who took confession and were in charge of the dormitories. Even Father Quedda was excluded from pastoral conclave by reason of his office of Bursar. Father Laskiva certainly was, but there was an anomaly. He was not considered to be a pastoral Father because he had not been assigned to supervise a dormitory but, as a priest, he could not turn away any boy who elected him to be their confessor. He distinctly got the impression that the Rector and the pastoral Fathers resented him this sanction but there was little they could do about it under ecclesiastical law. The same applied to Father Quedda but his duties as Bursar were full-time, which meant he rarely came into pastoral contact with the boys.

* * *

So it came about that early on a sunny late August morning, Father Laskiva found himself at the wheel of the Humber Super-Snipe, one of the college staff cars, with Sister Gloria by his side. The A55 was busy with holiday traffic but most of that was coming the other way. They crossed the border into England at the Queensferry bridge and headed along the Wirral peninsula towards Birkenhead and the tunnel under the Mersey river. The car's two occupants took the opportunity to compare notes. Sister Gloria's remit was to marshal the Removites and Second Formers. In the college hierarchy it was her duty to deliver her charges to their scholastic duties in the rig of the day, bodies washed, underwear changed, teeth cleaned, noses blown, hair brushed, shoes polished, laces tied, socks up and neckties straight. In truth, much of this was a sinecure, since most new boys were experienced prep school boarders and were finished products in those particulars; but she remained on hand to coax the occasional inadequate along the flowery path of good order or deal discreetly and sympathetically with the occasional wet bed.

Otherwise, she was an old hand when it came to the propensities of young boys. She habitually took the aforesaid leather tawse with her when conducting them to the bath house, but prided herself on the fact that she had never actually had to use it; having such a fearsome instrument in such proximity to so many bare bottoms was sufficient enough to ensure that the proprieties were observed. The boys knew she was not to be trifled with but they also knew they could rely on her for sympathy and discretion when needed. Significantly she was the one staff member at Monsalvat who habitually addressed every boy, be he little Removite or august Quarter Captain, by his first name.

Father Laskiva had been at the school for only a few months. As divulged, he was a diocesan appointee, whereas the rest of the pastoral staff had been recruited under the auspices of the Rector. Canon Peter Pynxcytte had acceded to the office of Rector of the Roman Catholic College of St Michael Monsalvat during the war years. He was hurriedly drafted in from abroad to replace the eminent and well-respected Canon Drage, who was retiring. It was Canon Drage who had had the Vudsen boy's father in his charge in the 1920s. None of the pastoral priests survived from the Drage regime. As soon as Canon Pynxcytte assumed office he began replacing them with his own men whom he brought in from all points of the compass.

Father Laskiva's role was not clearly defined and the Rector tended to use him in a peripatetic capacity; hence his present assignment. He had no dormitories or forms to supervise and therefore found himself taking a disproportionate number of the masses. He was ostensibly a confessor to any boy who would choose him but so far none had looked beyond their form priests for that office. He was a Divinity graduate and was qualified to teach Religious Instruction, English and History. However, when it came to teaching, Monsalvat largely relied on suitably qualified lay persons living off the premises.

He took this opportunity of taxing Sister Gloria with the vexed matter of the senior pupil William Wepper, whom everyone knew as The Bold Contemner. This very senior boy had a commanding presence, sufficient indeed to captain the school, yet he had not acceded to the status of prefect. This itself was no wonder because, as was common knowledge, for the past three years he had never made confession nor taken Holy Communion. Yet he appeared to be immune from the sanctions attaching to these omissions, omissions which would normally result in expulsion. For term after term he had apparently exhibited this thoroughly bad example to his peers and juniors and had got away with it. Whenever he deigned to attend chapel he usually sat at the back on his own behind the other seniors. Furthermore, Father Laskiva noted that he never genuflected nor availed himself of the holy water.

On the other hand, he was academically gifted and an accomplished athlete who had, among other things, represented the college at swimming, rowing and boxing. He was due to leave next year to study at the Sorbonne. Sister Gloria agreed that his situation was anomalous but sufficient, according to her, that the Rector's judgernent be relied upon in such matters.

"The Rector is inclined to do good by stealth," she reasoned. "The continuing presence among us of this Bold Contemner is perhaps the supreme example of the Rector's forbearance. Surely, Father, his appointing of Will as sacristan is an example of this. Perhaps Will's duties as custodian of the sacred vessels will prick his conscience and help to return him to the faith of his fathers. I've no doubt the Rector hopes to land this big fish as some kind of grand finale to his pupillage and as an example to all others that the Word of God shall triumph in the end."

Her mitigating homily was mildly castigating of the priest, but somehow Father Laskiva did not feel convinced of its message.

By this time they were in the Mersey Tunnel and the exigencies of urban navigation discouraged any further putting to rights of things at Monsalvat. Father Laskiva brought the Humber out onto the city streets at the dock exit of the tunnel system and headed towards the landing stage. After a cursory exchange with the policemen on duty he was waved onto Princes Parade alongside the boat train shed. The policeman had told him he would find a parking space there while they went to collect their young charge. The ship-owners had told him on the telephone that the *Antenor* would not be going alongside the landing stage. Instead she would be lying off the Gladstone entrance downriver, waiting for the tide to enter the dock. This meant that her passengers would have to be transferred to the Dock Board tender, which would bring them to the landing stage for port health, immigration and customs clearance.

Priest and nun hurried down one of the flying-bridges and across the deck of the stage to where the tender was moored. The weather being mild and calm, the boarding party, readily identifiable by their proliferation of briefcases, had gathered in small groups on the wide upper deck of the tender. Some were in civilian dress, others wore the uniform of HM Customs. Once on board, the two representatives of the Roman Catholic College of St Michael Monsalvat made their way to the upper deck and made themselves known to the shipping company's boarding clerks. At the appointed time the tender cast off and made her way downriver and into a developing heat haze that blurred the horizon. The tranquillity was shattered when the tender started to sound fog signals on her steam whistle. Startled at the first blast, the priest and nun looked at each other and laughed nervously.

As the tender proceeded downriver, priest and nun took in the panorama of the north docks of Liverpool, a veritable forest of cranes, masts and funnels evincing trade from all over the world. At the entrance to Huskisson dock a bevy of tugs fussed about a great Cunarder, preparing to conduct her to the landing stage to embark passengers. As the tender neared the river mouth it ran into a slight lop and started to lift perceptibly. A slight but chilling breeze was blowing now and Sister Gloria had to look to her headdress and habit. Out of the haze emerged a dark shape which eventually crystallised into the profile of the s.s.*Antenor*. As the tender made its approach, figures could be clearly discerned about the steamer's decks. Several young children were running excitedly about the upper decks. Father Laskiva and Sister Gloria fixed onto a small group standing apart from the others at the after end of the short promenade deck.

As the distance shortened they could make out a mature couple standing side by side and dressed as for disembarkation. Standing directly in front of the lady was a young boy in a tweed overcoat and matching peaked cap. The eyes of all three were fixed on the approaching tender. The lady had her arms straight down in front with her gloved hands resting on the lapels of the boy's coat, pressing him to her in a protective manner. The breeze eddying round the angle of the deck housing was lifting the skirt of the boy's coat, showing glimpses of a pair of sturdy bare knees over a pair of those powder blue stockings much favoured by planters and the like in the East. Even at a distance it was evident that the boy was incredibly fair of face and that the expression on that fair face was one of enduring melancholy. Both priest and nun instinctively knew that the boy was Alexander Fragner Vudsen.

'The two vessels converged, the waters roiled and thrashed between them, fenders were put out, messenger lines were thrown, mooring lines passed and the tender was secured in position alongside. A short gangway was run out from the upper deck of the tender and secured by the ship's deck hands just forward of the superstructure. Slings of baggage had been made up on the adjacent cargo hatch and the deck hands made ready to transfer them to the deck of the tender by means of the ship's derricks. On the passenger decks blue uniformed stewards busied themselves with bringing down pieces of hand baggage. The port health officer was the first to board and there was some delay until the yellow 'Q' flag was struck and the rest of the boarding party, including the priest and the nun, were ushered along the gangway. Here they were greeted by a smart young apprentice who shepherded them to the forward lounge where immigration inspection was to be conducted.

It was in the forward lounge that the captain of the *Antenor* made a special point of introducing Alexander to Sister Gloria and Father Laskiva. The boy gravely shook each hand and responded with a formal 'how do you do'. On re-entering the accommodation he had doffed his cap and unbuttoned his overcoat to reveal a smart lightweight knicker suit in terracotta linen. The captain also introduced the couple they had seen with the boy on the promenade deck. It transpired that this was a Mr and Mrs Edgar who had also embarked at Hong Kong. The captain discreetly explained that the Edgars had especially looked after Alexander on the passage west and had done their best to comfort him when the news of the death of his parents and sister had been notified to the ship at Singapore.

The priest took the Edgars to be in their late fifties and it was clear they were people of substance. At an opportune moment Mr Edgar confided that he had written to the school from Colombo offering to adopt Alexander if no-one came forward to claim him; and that the offer included an undertaking to pay his school fees for the duration of his pupillage. Father Laskiva was obliged to tell the Edgars that if any such letter had been received at the college it had not been brought to his attention.

It also transpired that Alexander had been issued with a passport by the Swiss consul in Hong Kong and on that and other evidence he had acquired the status of 'British Protected Person'. This however did not give him any right of abode in the United Kingdom. The Immigration officer was agreeable to granting him entry on a student visa but this would not protect Alexander from deportation when his school fees ran out. Father Laskiva realised the boy was on a year's grace. His situation was precarious and unresolved but there was nothing that could be done about that for the moment.

The boy remained diffident and reserved towards his new acquaintances but that was not the case with his fellow travellers. At every opportunity, busy though they were with the disembarkation, the ship's officers, the stewards and all the other passengers crowded round to say goodbye to the boy from Manchuria. When the passengers proceeded to the foredeck to join the tender, the apprentices and deckhands all had an encouraging word for him. The chief cook vociferously made it known he was losing the best galley boy he had ever employed and, in his turn, the chief engineer made it known he was losing an excellent supernumerary stoker.

The *Antenor* was one of the Line's surviving coal burners and it seems Alexander had done several stints in the stokehold, bare to the waist and helping to fire one of the furnaces. At one stage, to the amusement of the ship's company, he had even taken to wearing his belt buckle back to front in the manner of men who had to bend and labour in the sweaty purgatory of stokeholds. Although the young boy's puny efforts did little to hasten the vessel along her track, the men on watch had to acknowledge that he worked with a will. Alexander and the *Antenor's* Liverpool-Irish 'black gang', normally a sullen and truculent lot, were from very different backgrounds yet somehow his predicament had managed to touch even their calloused hearts. The firemen had sensed an incipient empathy with the young boy. Perhaps they saw him as a future politician or labour activist sympathetic to their condition.

There were many in that ship who would make a fuss of the orphaned boy from Manchuria. The one exception was the boisterous clutch of children. Their demeanour towards Alexander was one of polite deference, presumably, Father Laskiva surmised, because they associated him with death.

Eventually the transfer was complete and the tender pulled away, its upper deck now crowded with passengers and slings of baggage. The Purser of the *Antenor* came off with them, escorting the ship's box on its way to the company's head office near the waterfront. He made it known to Father Laskiva that he would be retaining the keys to Alexander's steamer trunk until it was presented for customs inspection at the landing stage. On the tender's deck Alexander now stood alongside Sister Gloria holding her hand but, significantly, he still glanced longingly towards the Edgars standing just a few feet away. Father Laskiva feared it was going to be a particularly painful parting when the tender got back to the landing stage.

But more was to come. As the tender passed round the stern of the *Antenor* where the firemen's accommodation was situated, a bed sheet could be seen hanging over the taffrail. Painted on it was the semi-articulate legend 'All The Best Alex'. Furthermore, those of the stokehold crew who were not down below on watch crowded the rail and gave him a rousing cheer. Alexander raised his right arm and gave a slow and prolonged wave in acknowledgment. Priest and nun noted the effect this sad little boy was having on the most improbable people.

But this sad little boy knew he was passing now from his familiar bustling eastern world, the world of his late father, a world of merchants and ships and captains and pilots and stevedores and friendly officials; passing into the cloistered confines of academia with all its attendant uncertainties. Little wonder the fair face remained wan and reserved.

There was an incident in the baggage examination hall at Liverpool landing stage. Alexander's steamer trunk had been placed on one of the low platforms and the Purser of the *Antenor* had come forward with the keys. The lid of the trunk had been raised and Alexander found himself looking upon an array of home comforts packed with a loving care on the other side of the world by a dear hand now dead. Laskiva noticed his lower lip beginning to tremble and saw him bite his knuckle and look away. In an instant the Purser leapt over the low baggage platform and knelt before the boy. Grasping the boy's upper arm with his left hand, he placed his other hand over the boy's heart and gently intoned the words: *"Courage, mon p'tit brave, courage."* Alexander stiffened and swallowed and his distress seemed to pass away. Perhaps the language used was significant, Laskiva did not know. Neither did he know that Alexander had spent time in the Purser's office making a real contribution to the endless paperwork necessary to progress the voyage. He did know that long sea voyages are like no other human interactivity; they give one the opportunity to look into the soul of another. The customs officer, for his part seeming to sense the boy's distress, peremptorily closed the lid, made his sanctioning chalk mark and proceeded to the next passenger without more ado. Priest and nun again noted that Alexander seemed to have that effect upon people.

* * *

On the return journey Alexander sat in the back of the Humber with Sister Gloria. His cabin trunk and valise were stowed in the boot. As Father Laskiva had expected, at the landing stage there had been tears at the parting with the Edgars. Mrs Edgar had been particularly upset. The mutual anguish was only slightly assuaged by their promise to write to Alexander as soon as they were settled back in England. It seems they had sojourned in the Far East for decades and must needs set up home again in Britain.

On the return journey Father Laskiva deliberately kept up a sort of running commentary on the passing scenery, for he knew Alexander would be in no mood for conversation. He could see the boy in the rear-view mirror and saw that Sister Gloria was keeping a protective arm about him. He seemed to perk up as they entered the old walled town of Conway. Father Laskiva assumed this was because he was now beginning to recognise features that his father had described to him.

They crossed the Telford suspension bridge and passed under the grim walls of Conway castle and the priest could see the boy craning his neck up at the crenellations. Father Laskiva ventured a sentence: "Tis Conway castle, Alexander. I've no doubt you'll be visiting it with your form fellows in a week or so."

The boy made no reply. The car passed through the Penmaenbach road tunnel and he began to take a renewed interest in the features of the rural landscape on the other side. This was country his father would have known well. The road ran alongside the railway for some distance before veering off to the left. To the right green pastures fell away to the silvery expanses of Conway bay. The road signs indicated that they were approaching Pencadno by the Holyhead road. To the right, the extensive sports fields of the college came into view and the priest pointed out the 'country gate' — little more than a field gate, the easternmost extremity of the college estate. Alexander knew from his father's account that they would soon be arriving at the 'town gate'.

The approach to the gates of one's new school can be an

intimidating experience, especially when one is approaching them in the company of strangers and after a journey of ten thousand miles. Father Laskiva was acutely aware of this and was duly solicitous of Alexander's disposition, doing his best to put the boy at ease as much as possible:

"Of course the best way to approach Monsalvat is by rail. You don't really get much of an impression of the place from the road. It's all just railings and a screen of trees until you reach the town gate. From the railway you really get a good view of the place, looking uphill towards it and seeing it against the backdrop of the mountain. First you get a glimpse of the chase gate, then comes the sports field; and the kitchen garden with its greenhouses; you can pick out their water tower and the chimneys of the stove houses. Then comes a grove of trees and after that the college proper. Through the trees you can see the gable end of the big L-shaped dormitory and classroom block extending away into the rear. This is the start of the long colonnade that connects all the main buildings." He checked in the rearview mirror that the boy was paying due attention to his disclosures. "Next comes the bell tower. It's a kind of campanile with some buildings around its base. That's where you'll be staying, Alexander, until the term starts. There's another chap staying there at the moment, a Sixth Former. But I doubt you'll see much of him; he'll probably be off and about with his girlfriend most of the time."

The priest checked himself at this last utterance and again looked in the rearview mirror, this time for any sign of disapproval on the face of Sister Gloria. She was no prude but thought her youngest charges needed shielding from any gratuitous mention of the corporeal propensities of her older charges. He saw her lips pucker slightly, possibly portending some later verbal admonishment. By now he knew Sister Gloria to be a doyenne of the college and not to be trifled with. For the moment at least, the priest continued unscathed.

"The bell tower's where the sanatorium is... and the night station. It's there you'll meet Godred and Geddington. 'They're the college male nurses; they run the 'san', amongst other things. They'll be looking after you until the dorms open. Next to the bell tower comes the chapel. It's angled off the colonnade on an east-west axis so the first thing you see is the dome. There's a great gold cross atop the dome, vying with the bell tower for height. Then comes the chapel facade with its great west door, interrupting the run of the colonnade. After the chapel comes the presbytery house. That's where the Rector has his chambers and where the Fathers stay out of term time. The presbytery house has two *porte-cochères;* one at the rear and a much grander one at the front, extending out over the grand terrace. That *porte-cochère's* got a balcony on top overlooking the great parterre. That balcony is where some day the Holy Father will stand. He'll be able to look down on the whole school assembled on the great parterre and give us his blessing. Some day, Alexander... We live in hope..."

The priest fell silent for a moment before continuing: "Beyond the facade of the presbytery house is the end of the main drive-way running down from the town gate and on the other side of that there's the gable end of a run of outbuildings; but all that's largely hidden in another grove of trees. The wood marks the end of the panorama and the college estate. After that you start seeing the houses and hotels of Pencadno but by that time your train's running into the station and the view gets shut off."

Alexander knew all this from his father's descriptions of the college. He knew that between the two groves of trees and below the *grand terrace* lay the great parterre, a liberal expanse of ornamented garden where the boys, the Fathers and the lay teachers were wont to stroll and dally in spiritual introspection or academic discourse. He knew that a carriageway, known as the *aditus maritimus,* led up to the great west door of the chapel, thus bisecting the great parterre; and that the great parterre was separated from the pasture land below it by a deep and dry ditch, a declivity faced on the uphill side by a brickwork revetment. This form of cattle-proof boundary between pasture land and formal garden was a landscaping *trompe l'oeil* quixotically dubbed a 'ha-ha'.

The ha-ha was spanned in way of the *aditus maritimus* by a mason-work bridge ornamented with balustrading, its piers surmounted by cressets. The thus embellished bridge was a curiously isolated structure in a landscape otherwise laid open by means of the ha-ha. Between the balustrades a cattle grid prevented the ubiquitous flocks of sheep from invading the great parterre. From the bridge an unmetalled track wound downhill towards the railway station.

Father Laskiva had also omitted to mention that hidden in the first grove of trees were the wartime air raid shelters; and that next to it, on the downhill side of the grand terrace, was an unprepossessing corrugated-iron-clad, wood-lined structure known as 'the old gym'. Alexander knew the old gym had been there in his father's day. Of the air raid shelters he could have no knowledge.

* * *

Back on the Holyhead road thorn hedges gave way to a long dwarf wall surmounted by wrought iron railings. There was a screen of trees behind it through which the varied and Puginesque buildings of the college could be discerned. This was the public face of Monsalvat to the passengers on the road. The Humber swung into the 'town gate', the main entrance with its lodge and its imposing freestanding sign board proclaiming 'The Roman Catholic College of St Michael Monsalvat' complete with escutcheons and mottos. Father Laskiva took the opportunity of taxing Alexander on the two Latin mottos, *Secura nidficat* and *Quis Ut Deus.* At the priest's gentle prompting Alexander had no difficulty in rendering translations of both.

The driveway led all the way down to the grand terrace, but the car took a turning to the right halfway down, passed behind the presbytery and then behind the domed east end of the chapel. Beyond the dome the driveway turned left again to fetch up alongside the accommodation block at the base of the bell tower. Father Laskiva switched off the car's engine. Fortuitously, it was Geddington who was on hand to open the car doors and take charge of the new boy's baggage. Just as Alexander was stepping out of the car there was heard the rumble of a distant explosion. The boy froze and looked perturbed. The smiling Geddington patted him on the shoulder reassuringly.

"Just the granite quarries blasting again. It goes on all the time. After a while you won't notice it." Alexander unfroze and responded with a wan smile of his own.

Priest, nun and boy followed the baggage into the two-storey building, past the night and first aid station and up the staircase to the several accommodations on the first floor. The boy from Manchuria had arrived at The Roman Catholic College of St Michael Monsalvat.

CHAPTER THREE

Idyllic Interlude

It was now some five days before the start of autumn term 1949. There was temporarily no hot water in the bell tower accommodation; Bringsam the caretaker had the boiler shut down for servicing. Wepper found this an annoyance because it meant him having to make his way to the big communal bath house in slippers and dressing gown, a journey that took him down a flight of stairs and out along the colonnade. To make this excursion he slipped his bare feet into an old pair of unlaced gym shoes. Fortunately it was high summer and this particular morning the weather was mild enough as he approached the wide double doors that led into that part of the long, echoing building that was reserved for seniors. Both leaves were propped wide open. The bath house was set alongside the swimming pool, the hot water plant being common to both amenities. There was a connecting door in a cross corridor behind the plant room, normally kept closed but now also wide open. Bringsam was getting the facilities ready for start of term and the sybaritic Wepper was reassured to see a wisp of smoke coming from the boiler room uptake. He continued into the bath house.

The great echoing shed was tiled around with glazed white tiles and was furnished with duck boarding. It was lit by a range of horizontally aspected windows set well above head level. Bringsam had set several of these on the cant and, what with the open doors, the bath house was a veritable temple of the four winds. The range of windows was almost continuous, punctuated only by buttresses supporting the flat roof and several extractor fans set at strategic intervals. To the left was a set of tiled bays, each fitted with a sextet of shower heads. Scattered about were several long benches upon which tins of medicated talcum powder had been placed. There were no individual partitions between the shower heads; unlike many Catholic institutions of the day, Monsalvat seemed to make no effort to conserve corporeal modesty. To the right of the central walkway were several W.C. compartments. Wepper knew that this layout was repeated in mirror image in the junior section beyond the connecting door aperture.

As Wepper entered he could see that the connecting double doors between junior and senior sections were also wide open. As a result he could see right through the building. The juniors normally approached the bath house from the opposite end. As he walked through the double doors he was stopped in his tracks by a sound emanating from beyond the connecting door aperture. The sound was that of a soprano voice. It was a voice of great clarity and immaculate purity:

> *"Come again,*
> *sweet love doth now invite,*
> *thy graces that refrain*
> *to do me due delight."*

Then the lilting voice paused. Wepper waited expectantly but there was no more for the present. The singer had undoubtedly been encouraged by the acoustics of the place. Not wishing to deter or distract him, Wepper stealthily advanced a few more steps over the duck boarding. Then it came again with the continuation:

"To see, to hear, to touch, to kiss, to lie..."

That last note transfixed Wepper as a lepidopterist's pin would a moth to a board. The unknown, unseen singer sustained the long high note on the word "lie" with seeming effortless ease, swelling it perceptibly and with the clarity of a well-tuned bell. He sustained it to the point where the tension was almost unbearable, then just as effortlessly he brought it down and resolved the tension and the stanza:

*"...with thee again
in sweetest sympathy."*

Wepper was hearing no run-of-the-mill hooting choirboy trying his luck in the prevailing acoustics; this was a trained and rehearsed singer, albeit a very young one for Big School. Wepper was totally intrigued now. He felt inexorably drawn towards the open connecting doors, notwithstanding it was a point beyond which seniors would not normally go. He felt he had to seek out the origin of this sublime sound. Then it came again, clear, measured and confident. The singer commenced a new verse:

*"Gentle love,
draw forth thy wounding dart:
Thou canst not pierce her heart;
For I that do approve."*

The singer paused again. He was not doing a public performance and was in no hurry to consummate his stanzas as he presumably went about the mundane task of bathing. Furthermore, not that

Wepper knew, but he had elected to omit the second verse. Wepper found himself poised expectantly, frozen lest some creak of the boards might put off the singer from completing the verse. Eventually it came:

> *"By sighs and tears*
> *more hot than are*
> *thy shafts..."*

There it was again; that sublime climactic note echoed down the bath house, attained, sustained and relinquished with consummate ease. It remained for the singer to complete the verse:

> *"...did tempt while she,*
> *while she for triumph laughs."*

The impact of John Dowland's melancholy plea of excruciatingly unrequited love seemed all the more poignant by its being rendered by a juvenile, one as yet unscathed by the vicissitudes of life and love.

Determinedly now, Wepper approached the door aperture, intending to make his presence known to the creature from whom this immaculate noise was emanating. "Full many a flower is doomed to bloom unseen," Wepper mused, "and waste its sweetness on the desert air." And here was this performer 'wasting his sweetness', as it were, against the tiled walls of an old school bath house.

He was on the point of emerging into the junior section when once again he was stopped in his tracks. The singer was repeating the last stanza but this time he daringly increased the volume and lowered the timbre, going for the *sforzando:*

> *"By sighs and tears*

more hot than are
thy shafts..."

'The resulting sound on the protracted note was that which only a boy on the threshold of pubescence can produce, the pure soprano giving way to a riper, lower register. It was truly the *pourriture noble* of a boy's singing voice, that most elusive and fleeting of attributes. As the now-enriched sound fell upon his ears, Wepper could feel the hairs on the nape of his neck stand on end.

"...did tempt while she,
while she for triumph laughs."

With that, the tension became resolved. The singer had pulled off an artistic master-stroke. His boldness could easily have gone wrong; could, in a public performance, have ended in ignominious embarrassment. But there was no diminution in quality and the effect was electric. What unknown, unseen creature, thought Wepper, was presuming to have this effect upon such an urbane fellow as himself? He crept through the doors and into the junior compartment.

The sight that met him was as arresting as the sound that still seemed to echo round the building. Facing him was a young boy. The boy remained oblivious of Wepper's presence because he was busy towelling his hair, his head buried in the vigorously flapping towel. He was using one of the college swim towels; Wepper assumed this was because Sister Gloria had not yet unpacked the boy's things. The creature was *in puris naturalibus* and decidedly wet with it. The wetness clung to his perfect skin not as droplets but as an all enveloping and enhancing sheen, setting the creature glistening sensually, like an animated marble statue. As he stood towelling his hair, his right foot had become elevated slightly, which cast his form into a classic *contraposto* stance. As if by divine intervention, a ray of sunlight shot in over the boy's shoulder and illuminated his dorsal aspect. The consequent sudden reflection in the glazed tiling of the adjacent partition showed that dorsal aspect in all its callipygian perfection. Aspected any way, the immature perfection of such a form was sufficient to command the attention of a Praxiteles or a Phideas. Wepper was put in mind of the famous *bas relief* of the Apotheosis of Polydeukion. The creature before him was veritably a juvenile god. Surely it was too much to hope that the still unseen head was in as noble a cast as the body it surmounted?

The creature before him was also a natural boy. Not quite. The effort of towelling the hair had set things a-jiggle somewhat; Wepper could not help but notice that the boy had been circumcised. An imperfection? Hardly, thought Wepper; beyond medical imperatives it was the fashion of the day. But otherwise a natural enough boy. Indeed the eternal boy. A gatherer of conkers, a tickler of trout, a scrumper of apples, a carefree, running, laughing, gambolling, caprioling creature; a creature whose domain was the verdant lea and whose oyster was the big wide world. The repository of, rarely, the most sublime sound the human condition can produce. A creature the like of which Wepper realised, with a tinge of regret, he himself no longer was and now could never be.

Then Wepper also realised that the duration of his reverie might be construed as improprietous. Accordingly he gave a diplomatic cough. The startled boy instantly drew the towel down so as to hide his pudenda. And there, looking at Wepper, was the fairest of faces in the noblest of heads crowned by the most exquisite tumble of rich wheaten locks. Those locks were truly the herald of latent fecundity and surely the secret envy of every balding senior. And the ears that discreetly nestled in the wheaten swirls, backlit as they were by the August sunlight, were carnelian convolutes of the most exquisite diaphaneity.

This was no ordinary boy. He had already demonstrated a most unique and developed talent. One such talent must surely garner a myriad others. And again, that face... It was a face that was going to be handsome at any age.

The image was complete. Wepper's heart missed a beat and his breath stood bated. He was nonplussed as to whether his perception of such beauty was subjective or objective. Whatever it was, he instantly and instinctively felt protective of this 'peach of peaches'.

But by his intervention the confident nude god had become instantly reduced to a naked and apprehensive child; a child who felt compelled to hold his towel so that it hung down to mask his genitalia. Whether he did this in response to his own pudicity or with some intention of sparing Wepper the concomitant embarrassment was not clear. What was clear was that he was a schoolboy, bare, wet, small, junior and new, and that he was confronted by another schoolboy, clothed, senior, tall, authoritative and old. The boy reasonably assumed that such a commanding presence must be a prefect. He looked up at Wepper apprehensively, fixing him with piercing blue eyes. At this point Wepper noticed that there was in fact some adornment on the boy's person: a gold medallion on a slender chain round his neck. Seeing his discomfiture, Wepper moved quickly to put the boy at his ease. Setting his bathing things down on an adjacent bench, he held up both hands, palms outwards, in a conciliatory gesture.

"Oh I'm so sorry; I didn't mean to startle you. I just had to know from whom that sublime sound was emanating."

A faint, uncertain smile flickered across the boy's face. "Master A.F. Vudsen, I presume. It's all right, I saw the name on your cabin trunk. You and I are both in the bell tower until term

time. I'm in the room next to you. My name's William Wepper."
He paused before adding helpfully: "You call me Wepper and I
call you Vudsen. That's the way of things here at Monsalvat."

Alexander gauged that some response was now requisite.
"Oh, I see. Thank you... Wepper," he ventured tentatively. Even
from that brief response it was obvious to Wepper that the boy
spoke with seemingly perfect modulation and articulation.

"Not at all... Vudsen," he replied, amusingly mimicking
Alexander's hesitant response and reinforcing this with a
reassuring smile. "Where on earth did you learn to sing so
beautifully?"

'At my prep school. We had a very good music master."

"Very good you say? He must have been a genius to bring on
a singer like you. And pray, where was this most favoured prep
school?"

"Tsingtao."

Alexander evidently did not feel the need to qualify the
location. Wepper was not dismayed; he was reasonably familiar
with the geography of the Far East.

"Tsingtao's a long way from Pencadno. You'll have some
adjusting to do."

"Not completely... Wepper."The hesitant pause was still
evident. "My father was here before the war. He told me all
about Monsalvat... and Pencadno."

"Yes, I thought I recognised the name. Later on I can show
you his mentions and contributions in some of the old school
magazines. They're in the library."

He paused to allow Alexander to reflect on this opportunity.
Knowing something of the confused situation in the Far East
he then went on to venture what, in the circumstances, was a
reasonable enough question. "And are your people back in the
UK with you now?"

At this, Alexander's eyes became ominously downcast.

Wepper sensed that the subject might be delicate. There was a moment of silence before Alexander responded. The Edgars had tutored him how to respond to inevitable questions of this nature, but now the moment was upon him and he must gauge his response according to the questioner. In the present circumstances he gauged that discreet evasion would not do. His erstwhile lilting voice shifted down to a lower, quieter register and he spoke in a flat, palpably controlled tone: "My papa is dead. And my maman is dead. So is my little sister. They were on a plane crossing the Yellow Sea. It never arrived, they are all presumed dead. The captain gave me the news when the ship reached Singapore. They say I'm an orphan now."

The words fell as drops of molten lead might fall upon the bound soul. Wepper visibly recoiled at this devastating bombshell. Little wonder the boy could convey such poignancy in his singing. What price schoolboy urbanity in the face of this? And Alexander's instinctive, inadvertent shift in terminology from the formal to the familial hit him hardest. He turned away and paced the duckboards for a few steps before attempting any kind of response. Clapping a hand over his mouth, he made to stifle a sob but it escaped nevertheless and momentarily echoed round the empty bath house in an embarrassing falsetto. Eventually gathering his wits in this unprecedented predicament, Wepper purposefully decided to eschew pointless platitudes. Struggling to regain his composure, he responded in another vein. His words came out in staccato bursts: "I know something — just a little — of what you're going through. My father and mother's marriage has failed. They live apart and neither wants me. It's been like that for three years now. I do have a guardian, an uncle, but he's down in London. And he's bankrupt. If you know what that means. He has no money. I've nobody else."

"Oh, I'm so sorry to hear that," said Alexander, rather graciously, considering that he had by far the greater hurt of the moment.

"Not at all," ventured Wepper, "as I said, it's been some three years now." He paused again before adding apprehensively: "I can't begin to imagine the grief that must be upon *you* now."

To Wepper's relief the boy retained his composure. But he was visibly shivering now, and from a more proximate cause. The draught running through the bath house was chilling the boy's naked, wet body. Wepper, belatedly becoming aware that it was he who was delaying the boy's ablutions, moved to assuage his discomfort.

"Oh but you're cold. How damned inconsiderate of me, keeping you talking. Here, chuck that silly little towel aside. I've two big bath towels here, you can have one of mine."

With that he picked up one of his great bath towels and began to unfold it. Diffidently, Alexander cast his own small towel aside onto an adjacent bench and momentarily stood facing Wepper quite bare. Perhaps he was thinking that this was the way of things at Monsalvat and that the modesty of junior boys was of no account. In his turn Wepper was thinking that the boy before him was indeed the very reincarnation of Polydeukion — but, if such were possible, yet more noble of head and more handsome of visage.

Wepper moved towards him, holding the great bath towel open invitingly. Alexander advanced tentatively. Wepper went down on one knee before him and, reaching out, totally enveloped the diminutive figure in the towel. Only Alexander's face remained visible. Their gazes locked, each upon the other's. Wepper continued: "Oh, and we can chuck this Wepper-Vudsen business. My first name's William. You can call me Will. What's your first name?"

"Alexander."

"That's a noble name. I'll be honoured to call you Alexander. That is... if you'll let me," he added guardedly.

"Of course I will ...Will," Alexander responded warmly, smiling faintly at the juxtaposing of the two homophones.

"Mind you, Alexander, this is for when we're alone together or out of school. While we're in school we'd better stick to Wepper and Vudsen.That's the way the boys — and the Fathers — prefer it, especially between seniors and juniors. But you and I will know it's only a necessary formality between friends." Then he added tentatively: "That is, if you will consider me your friend. I don't wish to impose. I would consider it a privilege to be your friend." Without waiting for a response, Wepper continued: "And you're going to need friends here, Alexander. Oh, of course you'll make plenty of friends among your form fellows — but you're going to need friends in higher places. I'm afraid Monsalvat isn't *quite* like it was when your father was here," added Wepper cryptically. Then, dismissively: "...but never mind that for now."

This puzzled Alexander but he did not feel bold enough to pursue the point.

Now that he was close up to the boy, Wepper reached into the enveloping towel and gently took hold of the medallion between forefinger and thumb. He saw that it depicted a lamb with cross and banner; an *Agnus Dei*.

"You're a Child of Mary?" he asked.

"Yes," Alexander replied, "my mother fastened it round my neck when we were saying goodbye." Wepper thought it best to say nothing for a while and stayed fondling the medallion. Eventually he found himself constructing a suitable homily. Gently replacing the medallion onto the boy's fair skin, he reached out and caressed the boy's cheek with the back of his hand and spoke softly but purposefully:

"God has taxed you most severely, Alexander. His alone

was the hand that plucked your parents' plane from the sky and dashed it into the sea. It is clear He has singled you out for something special. Whenever that will be we cannot know. But you must hold yourself in readiness."

An improbable statement coming from a non-believer but this was no occasion upon which to question the faith of the boy's fathers. Thus did Monsalvat's Bold Contemner put himself in thrall to the small golden god that happenstance had placed across his path.

Instinctively, paternally, proprietorially, Wepper began to dry Alexander's still damp hair, using a vigorous rotary motion with his hands over the big bath towel. Then, without further thought, he moved his hands down onto Alexander's towel-clad torso and, standing up himself, swung the still-shivering child easily up onto one of the benches, landing him there like a rubbery doll. By this time Alexander was holding the big bath towel about him with arms crossed at shoulder level. Without a word passing between them and as if it were expected of him, Wepper commenced to towel the boy's torso, buttocks and thighs by rubbing his hands over the towelling. It was more an act of warming rather than drying. He became acutely conscious of the developing and exquisitely-contoured young musculature beneath the thickness of the luxuriant fabric.

And instinctively, paternally, proprietorially, Wepper moved his right hand down to the intercrural area and began to gently massage dry the immature pudenda through the fabric of the towel. It seemed the natural progression of things and Alexander responded with nothing more than a feigned grimace at some momentary discomfort; he gave no hint of pudicity whatsoever. Only at this point did Wepper realise that his intentions and actions might once again be open to question. He was minded to look round apprehensively but the only evidence of any other presence was the distant sound of

Bringsam noisily working away in the adjoining swimming pool hall. As for the boy, he was demonstrating total innocence and it was clear he trusted this obtruding senior completely. Then, incredulously, it dawned on Wepper that he was taking the place of the boy's *amah*. How many times in the Far East, he thought, had a succession of *amahs* lifted the nude child out of the bath to envelop him in a towel and dry him off, just as he was doing now? He was minded to ease his own discomfiture by throwing in some jest accordingly, but thought better of it. Acutely aware of his young charge's delicate circumstances, he did not want to risk stirring some latent, poignant memory and thus cause Alexander further distress. Gently, dutifully, he concluded the proceedings by drying the sturdy young thighs and calves with the drape of the towel. At this point he felt confident enough to smile reassuringly and construct a sentence.

"Of course you'll have to do all this for yourself in term time — but of course you'll manage," he added reassuringly. The boy smiled back confidently. The big towel had fallen from his head and was resting on his shoulders now. There was no question that he would manage; perhaps it was just the thought that he would not have an *amah* — or someone like Wepper — on hand to attend him hereafter. Wepper contemplated the deprivations he had endured when he was Alexander's age; here was a meeting of two innocent victims of circumstance... two casualties of life seeking momentary solace in each other's chance company. That and the boy's trust and confidence in him caused tears to sting his eyes. All the poise and urbanity of an eighteen-year-old was evaporating in the presence of this unfortunate and vulnerable eleven-year-old. He made to avert his gaze but Alexander had noticed.

"Oh, are you all right?" he asked

Wepper was devastated by the boy's solicitousness. Precipitously he blurted out: "It's just that... I wish I could have you for a little brother."

"Oh, that would be nice."

At this, Wepper broke up completely. Drawing Alexander towards him so that the boy's feet were lifted off the bench, he enfolded him in a powerful, rocking embrace that went on for several seconds. The normal nexus of schoolboy, junior and senior, had been blown away by mutual appreciation of their respective adversities. Lost soul had found lost soul, momentarily at least. The encounter had completely disarmed Wepper and his guard was quite down.

Thus was it that Monsalvat's Bold Contemner came to meet the boy from Manchuria.

* * *

Later that morning Wepper, composure duly regained and urbanity duly restored, took Alexander on a tour of the college and its estate. Alexander was shown over his dormitory. It seemed comfortable enough, all dormer windows and oak panelled dadoes. Heating pipes ran around the periphery and there seemed to be plenty of radiators. Each bedspace had been labelled with the name of its intended occupant. Each was furnished with a wardrobe and locker and an oblong of coconut matting. From the name on the wardrobe he discerned that his own bed was second from the end and was flanked by those of one Gyles-Skeffington, T.C., and one Sender, B. Just names now, but Alexander wondered what they would be like and how he would get on with them. At the far end was a separate room that projected into the dormitory area. It was accessed from the corridor and from it a window, curtained on the inside, overlooked the boys' bedspaces. Wepper explained that this was the accommodation of the priest in charge of the dormitory, in this case Father Fillery. He spelled out the name. "Rhymes with dairy," he added helpfully. Opposite the priest's room was a range of wash-hand basins separated from the bedspaces by a wooden partition. Adjacent was a W.C. compartment signed 'For use in emergency'. Alexander noted that another 'spy' window over-looked this utility area. There were no body bathing facilities at hand; for those, the boys had to go down to the big bath house in the angle of the L-shaped block.

The form members were spread between the four 'Quarters' and Alexander noted from the name labels that, like himself, both his flankers were to be Cardinal's Men. Wepper mentioned that the Sender boy had been there last year.

"He got sick and missed a lot of the year so he's back in the Remove again. He'll be a year older than the rest of you so he'll know the ropes quite a bit. I suspect Sister Gloria has put him next to you on purpose."

The silence of the dormitory had a pregnance that seemed to anticipate the hurly burly of arrival day. There were seventeen beds in the Remove 'A' dormitory, two of which were spare. The other fifteen had been made up by Sister Gloria. Wepper explained that this was just for arrival day and that thereafter each boy would be making up his own bed and looking after his bedspace. He explained to Alexander what the daily routine would be and what to expect on arrival day and the busy day after when all the textbooks were issued and the daily schedules and other scholarly evolutions fixed for the term. Paramount among these apparently was one's choice of confessor. Wepper told Alexander to opt for Father Laskiva. It really was a matter of choice, apparently the only constraint being whether a given Father-confessor had enough slots. "He already knows you and you'll have a head start on the other fellows. They'll have to make do with Fillery. Fillery's the priest responsible for the pastoral care of you Removites," Wepper added helpfully. It all seemed satisfactory to Alexander.

The tour included the extensive college library, all leather-

topped tables, sound-deadening carpeting and mahogany glass-
fronted bookcases. The only noise was the ticking of the clock.
It was here that Wepper introduced a most curious subject. He
took Alexander over to the music section where he extracted a
songbook. Opening it at a particular item, he advised Alexander
to learn the song by heart so that he could sing it when anybody
asked him to sing a song. Alexander wondered why anybody
would want to do that but Wepper was insistent without offering
any explanation. Alexander was not familiar with the song —
it seemed to be a hymn about St Patrick — but he could read
music and he promised to copy the verses and commit them
to memory. He presumed it was needed for some sort of test
imposed upon new boys and he otherwise did not question
Wepper's insistence.

Alexander felt reassured to find the layout of the estate
exactly as his father had described it to him back in the Far
East. The layout of the college estate was largely rectangular,
particularly at the townside end where the main buildings lay.
The one exception was the chapel; in order to aspect it due east
it sprang off the grand terrace at an acute angle. The west gable
end however still marched with the grand terrace, thus giving
it a wider elevation than the ground plan would otherwise
warrant. This eccentricity allowed the chapel's great west door
to appear as a particularly imposing aperture. It also accounted
for a rather unique triangular garth between the chapel and the
presbytery. It was the hypotenusal ambulatory of this garth that
gave access to the chapel on its south side via the south transept
door.

Marching with the grand terrace was the colonnade, which
gave covered passage linking, from the townside end to the
country end, the presbytery, the chapel, the bell tower block
and the classroom/dormitory block. One stepped down from
the colonnade onto the grand terrace, which served variously

as a promenading place and a ceremonial — or emergency —
vehicular access. From the grand terrace one again stepped
down onto the great parterre; an area of formal lawn and
ornamentation. Here was the giant chess board and the lily
pond. As we have learned, the great parterre was divided by
the *aditus maritimus,* a wide pathway that led from the bridge
over the ha-ha up to the great west door of the chapel. Below
the bridge the *aditus* reverted to an unmetalled track winding
over the sheep meadow and down towards the railway and the
shoreline. Alexander felt comforted to know that wherever he
walked, his father had walked before him.

The chapel building absorbed the colonnade at this point,
ensuring that passers-by would either have to transit the chapel
and make due obeisance to the high altar in so doing, or step
down onto the grande terrace and possibly into inclement
weather in order to make passage. Passage through the chapel at
this point was between what were known as the north and south
transit ports.

As previously mentioned, the chapel followed the east-
west line. This meant that, as viewed from the foreshore, it met
the grand terrace at an angle of forty degrees, thus putting the
dome considerably to the left of its west facade. Apart from this
eccentricity, the ground plan of the chapel followed convention.
There was a clerestory nave with side aisles and a stub transept.
The adjacent ambulatory had been extended to run the full
length of the south side. This afforded weatherproof access
to the south transept doors and the chevet (the rectangular
space circumscribing the circular chancel plateau). The chevet
accommodated the confessional booths and the sacristy
cabinets. Over the chancel platoon soared the magnificent dome
topped with a gilded lantern like a golden sun. The drum of the
dome incorporated two high galleries from which the voices of
choice sopranos and altos would echo down to grace the vespers

and the masses. The rest of the choir occupied two opposed semicircular stalls on either side of the high altar, inside the supporting columns bounding the chancel plateau. The north transept door opened into a porch which gave onto an open space between the chapel and the bell tower.

Again as viewed from the foreshore, the bell tower lay to the left of the chapel and its golden weathercock vied with the golden cross on the lantern of the dome for ascendancy in the magnificent roofscape of the college. To the left of the bell tower buildings the colonnade made a right angle uphill to march with the L-shaped classroom/dormitory block. The other wing of this block gathered in various outbuildings like a protective arm: bath house and swimming pool, gymnasium, kitchens and refectory, laundry and the various necessary lesser offices.

Beyond the gable end of the main building the grand terrace downgraded into a utilitarian carriageway which led back to the main road at the country gate. Other than the groundworks of the great parterre with its bridge and ha-ha, the only building of note on the seaward side of the grand terrace was the structure known as 'the old gym'. Built out on brick piers over the gradient and partly hidden in a remnant of the great fox covert which gave Pencadno its name, the old gym was a wood-lined corrugated-iron-clad building. It had long been superseded by a more modern facility sited in the angle of the L-shaped main block. The old gym was largely given over to storage of furniture and other movable college appurtenances. There was also an adjacent toilet block, now in some state of neglect and disrepair.

Also adjacent to the old gym and fully hidden in the bosk were some rows of World War II air raid shelters. These shelters were 'out of bounds' to the boys and were supposed to be kept locked — but that was not always the case.

Wepper conducted Alexander beyond the end of the formal grand terrace and along the access road — which it had now become — to the college greenhouses. These had become neglected during the war and were semi-derelict now. Arriving at the peach house, Wepper introduced Alexander to Wali Waliser, the ex-P.O.W. assistant gardener. It was Wepper's turn now to stand diffidently by while Wali and Alexander had a spirited conversation in German. Then Wali showed them over the old bothy (not that Wepper was unfamiliar with it), a two-storey brick structure adjoining the back wall of the peach house. The upper floor had contained rather spartan living quarters for the six gardeners' boys who had gone off to war and never returned. Wali occupied these quarters now, although he lately had begun to share more comfortable accommodation in the town with Yseult, his local lady friend.

At an opportune moment, Wepper discreetly took Alexander aside and explained that Wali used to have a fellow P.O.W. working with him but that Heinrich Daser had decamped last September, along with one of the college staff cars.

"The police found the car at Llandudno Junction next day. Heini must have taken a train from there. Never been heard of since." Then he added, as if his presence might have changed matters, "I was in London taking an exam at the time. I only found out when I got back. I miss old Heini. He didn't seem to quite hit it off with Wali — but he was quite a character." Alexander absorbed all this without comment.

Wali led them from the old bothy, past the entrance to the peach house boiler room — long disused — and to the double door aperture in the long back wall of the peach house. Here he unlocked a wicket gate in one of the door leaves and let them into the peach house. Wepper took this opportunity to explain to Alexander the significance of the word 'peach':

"It was the idea of one of the benefactors when they were building the place. He wanted the pastoral Fathers' diet to include an exotic fruit and the gardeners were charged with producing, of all things, peaches. Of course the gardeners were local and the townspeople got to know about this indulgence. That's why you'll sometimes hear the locals calling us peaches. It's not necessarily meant in a disparaging way. Old Monsalvatians call fellow Old Monsalvatians peaches. But there are other.., err... less favourable connotations of the word, into which we'll not go at this time."

This was the second cryptic statement Wepper had made, about which Alexander had thought best not to ask for further clarification.

Wepper explained that all the gardeners had been called up during the war and the contents of the peach house had died for want of attention. There were four other hothouses further down the slope and these had suffered from the same wartime neglect. For the time being these were rented out to local contractors. These contractors and their deliveries came onto the estate via the country gate at the easternmost end of the property. It was a temporary and unsatisfactory arrangement but it supplemented the college income and had to be put up with for the time being.

As for the peach house, it was evident that the impressive structure was presently just used by the college for storage. There were bags of fertilizer, produce, stacking chairs, garden furniture and other items stored along its length. The long, slatted bench running along the front under the glazing of the sun-facing facade was largely given over to potting plants. There was some three-tiered staging to one side of the double door aperture in the rear wall. On it was a cluster of large pots containing white lilies.

Inspection complete, Wali locked the deal wicket gate behind them and the pair went off elsewhere. As they walked, Alexander noticed that Wepper looked pensive. Eventually he opened up.

"Err... Alexander?"

"Yes, Will?"

"If you need to contact me any time, leave a note with Wali. Oh, it's alright, we have an arrangement. He acts as a *poste restante*. But you must be very discreet. The Fathers must never know. You'll be passing the old bothy at least twice a week on the way to and from the games pavilion. Just dodge in when there's no-one looking. And just remember.., there's others who use this facility too. No names, no pack drill, as they say."

"What shall I put on it then?"

Wepper thought a moment then replied: "Just put an 'E' with a circle round it. It's the second letter of my name, that should be vague enough." Wepper paused, then went on: "And I'll need an identifier for you as well. Let me see... what was that song you were singing? Who composed it?

"John Dowland."

"That'll do. Just put 'JD' on it."

"Got it," said Alexander conspiratorially. He was intrigued at the prospect of all this clandestine passing of notes. He wondered who these other note-passers might be. Maybe Monsalvat was going to be a more exciting place than he had first thought.

Eventually their tour of the college estate brought them back to the bell tower. Wepper borrowed the keys from Godred at the 'first aid and night station' so as to show Alexander a particular feature of the estate. The bell tower stood alongside a brook running down from the mountain into the side of which Pencadno was cradled. The bell tower supplanted an old candlewick mill and the brook had been dammed to provide the mill pond. The mill machinery was still in place but had been adapted for another purpose unique to Monsalvat. Alexander found himself on a control platform which gave access to an array of hand wheels. There was the sound of much rushing water close at hand. From the platform he could look down at the main axle ponderously turning in its pit. Wepper walked across the control platform and opened a side door leading onto a footbridge over the canalised brook. Alexander followed him and found himself looking down into the tail race of the slowly-turning water wheel.

"Now you're looking at *Y Felin Alaeth Chlychau.*" Alexander looked understandably puzzled. "The mill of the sorrowing bells. You'll hear them on Good Friday and on martyrs' days. Oh, and if someone dies important to the school."

The tail race disappeared under the stone arch of a culvert. Wepper explained that the mill brook was canalised below the tail race and was taken underground to serve as the main sewer of the college complex. Alexander thought it a shame that such a sparkling natural feature tumbling down from the mountain should be banished from the light of day and consigned to such an ignominious usage. According to Wepper the brook finished up as a submerged sewer outfall several hundred yards out to sea, "so only go sea bathing on the ebb tide". Alexander made an appropriately deprecating face.

The two went back into the plant room. Wepper raised his voice so as to be heard over the noise of the idling wheel axle: "You can see the water wheel drives a take-off shaft geared to the main axle. It's engaged by means of a clutch which is let in by turning that big wheel." He indicated a wheel larger than the others. "The other wheels control cams on the secondary shaft. The cam followers haul on bell ropes so as to operate the hammers up in the tower. By manipulating the wheels each bell can be rung separately. Otherwise it's a carillon which will carry on for as long as the clutch is in. The mild pun brought a fleeting smile of acknowledgement to Alexander's lips. "There's only four bells but it's as sombre a peal as you'll ever hear. They say the notes reflect those selected by Richard Wagner for one of his operas. He's that noisy German fellow; you know — *Ride of the Valkyries* and all that."

"Ah," replied Alexander, "he also wrote the bridal chorus from *Lohengrin*. That's not particularly noisy."

"And where did you learn all this?"

"From my music master at Tsingtao. He used to describe himself as 'an unreconstructed Wagnerite.'"

"And I suppose he ear-bashed you with Wagner?" Wepper ventured.

"No, he didn't actually," was the reply he got. "He said there was no need. He said that everybody comes to Wagner sooner or later. Those that never do simply don't live long enough."

Wepper was impressed. Such erudition from one so young! Clearly one did not trifle with a boy partly brought up in Tsingtao.

"How old are you?" he asked with feigned incredulity.

"Eleven and a half," replied Alexander. He exaggerated just a bit.

"Well you did indeed have a very good music teacher."

From the plant room they went into the shaft of the tower. Alexander found himself looking up into a square stairwell. In the well the four bell ropes soared upwards from four snatch blocks and disappeared into timber staging high in the tower.

The bell tower performed another function vital to the running of the college. It elevated the header tank for the college water supply. The tank itself was supplied via a pipe which bled off some of the water of the brook from a point higher up the mountain side. As well as for normal domestic purposes, the header tank primed the fire hydrants throughout the college buildings.

Now that they were free of the noise of machinery, Wepper took this opportunity to test Alexander on his language skills. Firstly he rehearsed him in the pronunciation of *Y Felin Alaeth Chlychau*. It was clear that Alexander was a natural linguist and he quickly became adept at rendering this snippet of Welsh.

"How many other ways can you say 'the mill of the sorrowful bells' then?"

Alexander responded firstly with German, then French, then Spanish and finished with vernacular Chinese. As far as Wepper could tell, apart from that last, of which he had no knowledge, Alexander's renditions, fluency and pronunciations were instantaneous, exact and totally convincing. Actually, linguists were no rarity at Monsalvat because boys came to the school from the four corners of the world.

"And how old did you say you were?" Wepper asked, this time with some not entirely feigned incredulity.

"Eleven and a half and seven minutes," the boy replied mischievously

Wepper felt prompted to lecture Alexander as ponderously as the machinery they had just viewed. "While you're here you mustn't let your languages lapse. The college teaches French and Latin but not those others. Oh, I forgot — they've started to teach German now; to the later in-comers. Something to do with post-war reconciliation or some such. You'll be able to put the German master right on his grammar. He won't like that. He's new; I think his name's Bell. The lay teachers all live out, by the way. Only the Fathers live on the premises.

"As for self-improvement, we're not allowed into the town library — it's considered too worldly and sinful a place for us peaches. For your Chinese you'll have to make do with going to Liverpool and hanging around an opium den or somesuch."

At this, Alexander got a fit of the giggles, the conversation descended into farce and the idling pair addressed themselves to the more pressing matter of lunch.

Out of term time, meals were still taken in the refectory but without ceremony and together with the estate workers. Those of the Fathers who were still in school had their own table on a dais at the top end of the room. Being the only two pupils present, Wepper and Alexander found themselves consigned to one of the lower tables. Wepper took this opportunity to tell

Alexander about Rhiannon, and that he and she were planning to go to Llandudno the next day. He suggested that, unless other matters were pressing, Alexander was welcome to come along. Alexander said he would check with Sister Gloria. At this Wepper warned, "Just ask Old Glory if you'll be free. Don't tell her where you're going or who you'll be going with. Remember, I told you they don't particularly like unsupervised contact between seniors and juniors."

He purposefully omitted to mention that 'they' certainly wouldn't like any contact at all between a new boy and Monsalvat's infamous Bold Contemner.

* * *

Later that evening Wepper informed a reluctant Rhiannon that he had committed her to a threesome on the morrow's excursion. Realising he might have been presumptuous, he hastened to explain.

"There's this new boy just in from the Far East. I'd really like you to meet him."

The unconvinced Rhiannon now looked decidedly askance. Understandably, she was hoping to have Will all to herself in these last few precious days before the start of term, and she made it known to him that she felt highly miffed at this unexpected imposition. Furthermore, she was worldly enough to know the supposed propensities of public school boys, and responded mischievously: "I would have thought you were past all that stuff by now — cultivating little peaches. And this peach turns out to be a bloody gooseberry as well."

This pomonal persiflage set Wepper chuckling. "I had the pick of the peaches in my day," he responded, accompanying this scandalous boast with a conspiratorial wink. But Rhiannon was still not assuaged. She continued in similar vein, mischievously goading Wepper into being more specific as to his illicit dalliances in lower school.

"Now it can be told," said Wepper expansively, emulating the style of a newspaper announcement. It transpired that Wepper's erstwhile 'prize peach' was also known to Rhiannon, at least by sight. Wepper pointed out that she had already seen him on the Conway River, rowing 'bow' in the middle school racing eight.

"Ah yes, now I remember; that dishy blond at the front of the boat. You pointed him out to me but you didn't tell me his name. You had excellent choice, William Wepper, now he's free I wouldn't mind setting my cap at him myself. What did you say his name was?"

"I didn't. And you'll find him a bit young for an old boiler like you. Anyway, his name's none of your business. He's in the Shell now."

Ignoring Wepper's counter-persiflage, Rhiannon persisted. "And by the way, what's this blood-brother mumbo jumbo you fellows get up to? Did you make this dishy blond your blood-brother, Will?"

Wepper put his thumb alongside his nose and declaimed, "No names, no pack drill." Rhiannon chortled knowingly. Then, shifting to a more serious mode, he continued: "But I think you'll find this one rather special."

He then went on to explain Alexander's unfortunate circumstances. He deliberately made no mention of the boy's other attributes, preferring that Rhiannon find these out for herself. She did at least know that Monsalvat was picking its 'peaches' rather carefully these days and that this boy would not be overly tall or short, or black, brown, fat, ugly, spotty, lame or any other such thing. She did express commendable concern at his predicament and resigned herself to doing her best to entertain him on their proposed excursion to Llandudno.

And on the next morning it was to Llandudno the trio duly went, armed with bathing things and a packed lunch. They were attired for the balmy August weather and Alexander was resplendently all white in shirt, shorts and ankle socks. They strolled along the promenade of the elegant resort, went for a ride on a tram and had a swim in a flat calm sea. By now Sister Gloria had unpacked Alexander's steamer trunk and he was no longer short on bath towels and other things. For swimming, he was equipped with a snazzy pair of ice-blue Speedos, very probably the first of that brand to appear on a North Wales beach and which caused not a few envious glances. Wepper noticed that Alexander was a competent swimmer, adept at all the strokes. He even ably demonstrated some abstruse new American evolution called 'butterfly' that he had learned in the Far East. Clearly one did not trifle with a boy partly brought up in Tsingtao. Wepper, no mean swimmer himself and with his nose now severely out of joint apropos swimming strokes and apparel, opined that, as it was slower than front crawl, he didn't see the point. Watching from the beach, he railed impotently: "Look at him go, the bloody little show-off, in his speedsters or whatever it is they're called!"

"Sour grapes!" riposted Rhiannon triumphantly

They took the cable tramway to the summit of the Great Orme and ate their packed lunch among the heather on the short sheep-cropped grass. In the all round panorama, the buildings of Monsalvat could be seen away to the west. Beyond Pencadno, the quarries indented the hill side and occasionally an upsurge of dust told that blasting was in progress. As if in confirmation, the dull booms of the explosions came across on the still air. The smoke of a train could be seen puffing its way along the rim of the bay and there was a coaster alongside the ballast pier. Wepper cursed that he had not brought a camera to record the view.

Returning to sea level, they regaled Alexander with ice cream on the pier. It was a short walk from there to Happy Valley, an open air entertainment arena on the slopes of the Great Orme. It was a by-day for performances and entry into the enclosed area was uncontrolled. Rows of seats had been left out from the weekend performances but today they faced an empty stage. The stage was a low platform canopied over and flanked with chambers either side which served as dressing rooms and props stores. The trio walked purposelessly into the railed enclosure. Alexander took stock and quickly took charge. The little charmer ostentatiously conducted the couple to a pair of seats in the centre of the front row. Having got them seated, he scampered the few yards onto the stage. Rhiannon prepared to be embarrassed on the boy's behalf but Wepper knew better. She need not have worried. The boy was quite the little professional. He struck a pose and launched into an animated song which he very evidently thought appropriate to his two companions:

"Man, man, man is for the woman made,
And the woman made for man
As the spur is for the jade
As the scabbard for the blade,
As for digging is the spade,
And for liquor is the can,
So man, man, man is for the woman made,
And the woman made for man.

As the sceptre to be sway'd,
As for night the serenade,
As for pudding is the pan,
And to cool us is the fan,
So man, man, man is for the woman made,
And the woman made for man.

Be she widow, wife, or maid,
Be she wanton, be she staid,
Be she well or ill arrayed,
Court ward or harridan,
Yes man, man, man is for the woman made,
And the woman made for man."

It was a short, succinct, amusing and polished performance. It stemmed from his days in Far East expatriate society, where he had been in much demand as page at weddings. Unbeknown to Alexander, behind him and out of his view a small group of men, presumably the regular troupers of Happy Valley, issued out of one of the side cabins and stood under the canopy. They clearly wanted to know who was usurping their performing prerogatives. Wepper and Rhiannon were apprehensive but the men did not interfere. When Alexander came to make his final expansive bow, they spontaneously broke into a round of genuinely appreciative applause. A surprised Alexander wheeled round and swiftly recovered his composure by taking a further bow in their direction. At this they intensified their applause and it was smiles all round as the boy scampered off the stage. It was only infrequently, if at all, that they heard Purcell performed at Happy Valley.

Long before reaching this climax of the day, Rhiannon had become totally won over by Alexander. Her earlier misgivings and incipient jealousy had been totally swept away by the handsome boy's deportment and demeanour. Out of his earshot she upbraided Wepper: "You told me he was an orphan but you didn't tell me he was an angel as well."

Wepper turned to Rhiannon, suddenly looking pained. "Do you realise, that boy will have no one to embrace or caress him in innocence for the rest of his minority?"

This melancholy observation brought a determined

response from Rhiannon: "He has me now. And he is assured of *my* innocence."

The afternoon was well advanced by this time and they repaired to a cafe where Alexander was introduced to what Wepper described as traditional English fish and chips. Alexander was not to be so easily persuaded.

"England's forty miles that way." he said, nodding his head in the approximate direction of the Dee estuary.

"Bloody smart-arse!" Wepper responded, feignedly *sotto voce*. From fish and chips of any nationality it was to the station to take the Holyhead stopping train back to Pencadno. Wepper needed to smuggle Alexander back to the bell tower, ostensibly without his agency.

On the train Alexander found himself seated next to Rhiannon with Wepper opposite. The train was comfortably crowded and there were three other passengers in their compartment, a mature couple sitting next to Wepper and another middle-aged gentleman. As Wepper and Rhiannon engaged in conversation, the warmth of the compartment combined with the activities of the day began to take their toll and Wepper could see the boy's eyelids beginning to drift down. His body gradually slumped over and the sleepy head lolled against Rhiannon's breast. Feeling the contact, Rhiannon looked down at the wheaten curls. She could feel the warmth of the small young body through her thin summer dress and could sense an aura of sea salt and sun-kissed skin. Instinctively she put her arm over the boy's shoulders as if to gather him protectively to her side.

She mused that were things different, she could envisage taking him into their putative family, adopting him in effect. But Alexander was no longer a passive, mewling infant. The head that lolled against her bosom was that of a natural boy, a dynamic, bounding, leaping, gambolling, shouting, screaming, fighting, contrary creature with all that capacity for cruelty and inconsideration and need for guidance and direction that comes with the species. Not that Alexander's demeanour had not been impeccable throughout the day, but then he was probably on his best behaviour. A formidable challenge. Nevertheless, this child of another was indeed evincing all her protective maternal instincts. Tears threatened to well up in her eyes. She looked away, out of the window, but her protective arm had not escaped Wepper's notice. Within each self, neither could escape the thought that for the day playful diversions had shut out the realities of life, and for the moment merciful sleep was banishing the ache that must for ever lie on the brave little heart of the Boy from Manchuria, the grief that will not go away, that inexorably must return upon each awakening. But such melancholic thoughts could not be manifested at this time, in this place. More diversions seemed appropriate.

Wepper saw his chance. Feigning a mischievous grin, he gently chided his fiancée *sotto voce,* "Well, you've certainly changed your tune since last night. Why, I do believe you've come over all broody."

This visibly amused the other passengers and they smiled indulgently. They would have taken the pair to be indulgent parents had it not been for their obvious youth.

Realising she had been caught off-guard, Rhiannon reacted with an embarrassed smile and could only expostulate: "Oh, get on with you."

A few moments later, more composed, she elected to retrieve the situation with some barbed badinage. She looked up from Alexander's wheaten locks, fixed Wepper with a now more mischievous smile and hissed: "As far as I'm concerned, *you* can get out at the next station. This one'll do for me."

In deference to the sleeping boy, the compartment stifled its guffaws. All in all a most successful day. Would that we could say they all lived happily ever after...

CHAPTER FOUR

Compacts and Columbines

First day of Autumn Term 1949; all spare hands are deployed to the station to meet the scheduled incoming trains and to work baggage up to the college. Alexander was drafted in to help under the direction of Father Laskiva. Down at the station he espied William Wepper similarly deployed but was circumspect in not acknowledging his presence in accordance with the advice Wepper had given him about familiarities between seniors and juniors.

Alexander learned from the jargon that pupils arriving were categorised into 'upliners' and 'downliners'. The upliners arrived from the direction of Holyhead, the downliners from the direction of Crewe and points beyond, but mostly from London, Euston.

The upliners tended to arrive by one local train that connected with the arrival of the Dublin day mailboat at Holyhead. Compared to the downliners they were relatively few in number, which was fortunate because they, and more pertinently their baggage, had to pass across the main line from the far platform. There was a footbridge at the west end of the station for passengers but heavy baggage had to be worked across the rails by the station staff on a flatbed trolley on an unprotected level crossing. Use of the crossing was restricted to railway staff and there was no access for road traffic. When using the crossing, the station staff had to be mindful of express traffic and they worked under the direction of the duty signalman in the box which overlooked the crossing. The crossing itself was just a run of levelling timbers laid parallel to the rails and which traversed the line at an oblique angle just beyond the sloping platform ends. Unless baggage was being worked, both platform ends were gated off under the footbridge to prevent passengers getting access to the crossing.

Out on the public road a pick-up truck and a small charabanc had been hired for the day and both were kept busy running boys, cabin trunks and other baggage up to the school. The notional complement of the school was four hundred boys but attrition from various causes had whittled this down to about three hundred and seventy. Not a few people surmised that the resultant loss of revenue in fees must jeopardise the economic feasibility of the college — but it seemed to soldier on nevertheless.

The bulk of the boys arrived in an afternoon slot but there were the inevitable stragglers, particularly among the seniors. As for his fellow Removites, Alexander had no difficulty picking them out; they were conspicuous by their extra smart appearance in brand new uniforms. The Second Formers, on the other hand, conspicuously affected such casualness as the dress code and propriety would allow.

Alexander himself had been fitted out with a smart new blazer, dark grey flannels and straw cady. All cadies came with a length of black lace fixed to the brim and which could be led to a lapel buttonhole, the purpose being to prevent the hat being carried away on a capricious gust of wind. Sister Gloria had taken Alexander to the local outfitter in Llandudno for the purpose a few days before. He had also been equipped with less formal wear and all the sartorial trappings of public school life as allowed or demanded by the regulation list. As an 'old hand' of some ten days' standing, he was exempt from all the bustle of registration, medical inspection and deployment to dormitories. He himself had been moved from the bell tower into the Remove 'A' dormitory that morning.

One Removite, seeming older than the rest, had arrived in mufti and he seemed to be greeted with some familiarity by the staff. Alexander took a peep at Father Laskiva's clipboard and saw the boy's name ticked off as 'Sender, B.'. He recognised it as the name newly affixed to the wardrobe in the bedspace next to his own. Alexander wasted no time in introducing himself. This Sender fellow was a stocky type with black hair, brown eyes and dark complexion. Alexander thought he looked a bit like a basset hound. He responded to Alexander's overtures with confidence and a clipped manner of speaking. He wasted no time on trivialities and departed to the business of checking in with a cheery "Righto, see you up on the hill." Alexander was impressed by his seeming urbanity and ease of address. Removite he might be but it was clear he was not a new boy.

* * *

The next few days were given over to textbook issuings, Quarter 'pep' meetings, medical inspections, lectures on personal hygiene, voice trials, first confessions and the general minutiae of induction. Club secretaries canvassed for memberships among the new boys and prefects ordered them about authoritatively but seeming sympathetically. The perspective of the new boy at big school is that of the minnow swimming in the bottom of a very large tank and looking up at the bigger fish shadowing it from above — some trout, some salmon perhaps, some pike, some sharks and barracudas... What their hunger?

* * *

The new boys of Remove 'A' were a cosmopolitan lot and Alexander found he would not be the only linguist among them. There was French-speaking Jouvet from Leopoldville and Spanish-speaking Rivadavia from Uruguay. Loxley was reasonably proficient in Italian, his people being in the consular service. The formidable Haroldsen was an émigré Dane — albeit he became routinely referred to as 'the big Swede'. Most of the rest had come from all points of the compass and had accrued language skills accordingly. No German speakers though; so soon after World War II it was not a popular language or teaching subject in the United Kingdom. Notwithstanding, Alexander never encountered any prejudice as to his Hanseatic antecedence, the Monsalvatian ethos and community being far too urbane and cosmopolitan to harbour any such mean-spiritedness. Elsewhere in the less esoteric schools of the land it might have been a different matter. In one major respect Alexander differed from his contemporaries in that, if not parents, they at least had guardians in the United Kingdom. This meant they had somewhere to go during holiday breaks.

* * *

Soon after induction, Alexander, Sender and Gyles-Skeffington, Alexander's other bedspace flanker, were drafted into the choir by Parry-Jones the music master. Parry-Jones's primary duty was to provide the appropriate musical honours for the Masses but this was not the limit of his remit. He was a qualified voice coach and, as he was fond of saying, he "looked for singers, not choirboys". He found Alexander to be largely a finished product in that regard; the coaching he had received in the Far East standing him in good stead at Monsalvat. His voice had a special quality and his vocal delivery was pure, unencumbered as it was by any defects in diction and pronunciation. He had no discernible accent, an attribute which Parry-Jones thought a refreshing change from the languid patrician drawl affected by so many of his schoolfellows. However, like any growing boy, his voice was developing in pitch, timbre and endurance and Parry-Jones kept his ear tuned accordingly. He gave the boy particular attention and rehearsed him assiduously for solo concert roles and interventions in the Masses and Vespers.

After further voice trials and rehearsals, Alexander and Gyles-Skeffington (who soon accrued the nickname 'Farmer') learned they were to be part of an elite soprano quintet that would sing from the upper gallery of the chapel dome. Sender was already a part from last term, although his soprano voice was now on the developmental limit somewhat. The other two sopranos were from Remove B. The boys were shown how to get to the upper gallery via an external iron staircase accessed by a door in the hypotenusal ambulatory. A head for heights was needed and each boy could take a weatherproof 'storm cloak' from a locker near the foot of the staircase if the weather was bad. They re-entered the chapel through a door at the height of the upper gallery. The gallery was narrow so that the singers had to pass around it in single file. There was an optimum position from where they could look down over the guard rail in order to take direction from the music master who would position himself alongside the choir stalls down on the chancel plateau. A quintet of altos, largely from the Second Forms, was similarly stationed on the lower gallery. His elite songsters now having been selected, it remained for Parry-Jones to rehearse them to the standard of perfection their elevation demanded.

* * *

In the ensuing weeks Alexander and his fellow songsters learned and intoned the chants, anthems and orisons that embellished the masses and offices of the Catholic ministry. In between responses they had ample time to study the architecture and decoration of the hexagonal dome in which they were ensconced. Now that they were closer to the underside of the dome itself, Alexander was intrigued to discover that the apparent 'coffers' tricked out in blue with gold stars were nothing other than a *trompe l'oeil* on an otherwise plane surface. He wondered what other subtle subterfuges might reside within Monsalvat's architecture.

Around the base of the lantern was a narrow storey of ventilation louvres that trimmed on the prevailing wind. One day Alexander became aware that a white dove had walked through the open louvres and was perching on the adjacent rim. Then he was surprised to see it flutter down onto the guard rail opposite, where it sat preening itself and apparently enjoying the updraft of air warmed by the proliferation of candles down below. It was a handsome snow-white fantail and seemed to conduct itself in the deferential manner that the venue demanded.

The dove subsequently made an appearance every day. Ever mischievous, the boys started smuggling morsels of bread and breakfast cereals up into the dome and flaking them out along the guard rail in an effort to entice the bird over to where they were stationed. As the days went by the bird became bolder and bolder, advancing to where the group was stationed, taking the bread from the flat of the handrail. Alexander was stationed on the right extremity of the quintet, making him the most opportunely placed to entice the dove. Within a week it was taking food from his hand and was happily perching on his wrist while doing so. A few days later and it took to perching on his right shoulder. Here it would sit, nuzzling his ear with its beak and forehead while he sang the responses. Parry-Jones, from his conducting position alongside the choir stalls down below, never troubled himself to look up to see these untoward developments; as long as the responses from on high came on cue and in the requisite perfection, he restricted his field of vision to the main choir on the chancel plateau.

In the ensuing months the dove became a permanent feature of the boys' duties in the upper gallery of the dome. As the term advanced they decided it merited a name. Alexander took to calling it Colly, this being a diminutive of the Latin *columbinus,* meaning dove-like.

* * *

Wednesday and Saturday afternoons were given over to games and the new arrivals were tried out at the cricket practice nets and in scratch games as a preliminary to selection into Quarter teams. In addition to cricket there was also tennis but this was largely the preserve of the seniors. The college was equipped with a fifty-metre swimming pool constructed just before the late war and all boys were required to be proficient in swimming and water safety. Sea bathing was also practised when the weather allowed. The college had a pontoon moored some distance offshore which all the boys aspired to reach with their newly coached swimming strokes.

In addition to games, all juniors were exercised on a morning run along the beach under the direction of Mauger the college P.T. Instructor. Mauger was lately out of the military and a bit of a martinet — and not very intelligent with it. It was Mauger who officiated at the feared 'eculeations' — the college term for corporal punishment formalities. Eculeations were customarily scheduled for Saturday mornings and each weekend seemed to throw up a handful of miscreants and others who had inadvertently fallen foul of college protocol. The sanction seemed to be rigidly regulated as to time, place and extent and was not unduly severe, having regard to the tenets of the times. Unlike in many other establishments there could be no gratuitous administering of corporal punishment by such as prefects, lay masters or even the pastoral Fathers. Canon Pynxcytte appeared to run a tight ship in that regard.

There was an early issue with Alexander's *Agnus Dei* medallion. Mauger considered that it could be hazardous for the boy to be so adorned when engaging in physical training or swimming. He had a point of sorts. At first he demanded that Alexander surrender the device into the custody of Father Fillery for the duration of the term. This distressed Alexander; the medallion had been blessed by the Metropolitan of Shanghai and fastened round his neck by the loving hand of his dear, dead mother on the point of his departure for Hong Kong and the *Antenor*. It was a surviving shred of a life now irretrievably lost to him. He appealed to Father Laskiva, who intervened on his behalf. A compromise was reached whereby Alexander would surrender the device into Mauger's hands prior to the period at hand and Mauger would lock it away in a convenient drawer in the gym or pool office for the duration. Of course Alexander was inclined to cavil at the precious token having to pass through such unworthy hands. The compromise seemed to work well enough but he was always mindful that the return of his medallion might be overlooked in the busy traffic between periods.

* * *

On the third day of the Autumn Term Alexander received a summons. "Vudsen to the Cardinal's chambers right away, sir." The messenger, young as he was, had knocked and entered and made his announcement with the confidence and authority that the originator of the message imparted to him. The intervention had come during a maths lesson and Mr Calthrop, who taught mathematics and physics, duly despatched Alexander in ready compliance. Clearly one did not lightly disregard such a summons.

By the time Alexander had got to the door the messenger had gone on his way and was not available to give him directions. Alexander set out, trying to remember his way through the unfamiliar labyrinth of corridors and walkways that would take him to the presbytery and the Cardinal's chambers. He made his way along the colonnade, a route that took him through the west end of the chapel via what were known as the transit ports. As he made the transit, he made the obligatory genuflection before proceeding further along the colonnade to where it marched with the façade of the presbytery. He tried an auxiliary door which he first came to but it was evidently locked. He had no option but to carry on until he fetched up in front of the ornate main door at the *porte-cochère*. There was nobody about.

With some diffidence he entered and made his way up the main staircase where he found himself in a soft-carpeted and oak-panelled corridor lined with framed photographs of Old Monsalvations. He knew his father's face would be there somewhere, looking down upon him, but this was not the time to search out such detail. One of several doors seemed more imposing than the rest and Alexander felt drawn towards it with mounting trepidation. The great oak door was ajar and Alexander could partly see into the room beyond. Great expanses of purple carpeting beckoned. He rapped his knuckles on one of the door panels with what he gauged to be due deference. An imperious voice boomed out: "Enter."

The tall and imposing figure that Alexander had seen taking morning assembly was standing behind a vast and ornate desk. A leather-finished chair was placed somewhat towards the farther end of the desk and the Cardinal waved Alexander to it. Alexander perched on the edge of the leather seat.

The Rector came swiftly to the point. "As you will know, I have welcomed all you newcomers at morning assembly but I particularly wished to speak to you personally because of your unfortunate circumstances."

Alexander had anticipated that this might be the burden of the interview. The Cardinal went on to explain that Sister Gloria was excellently placed to counsel and comfort him should he feel the need; and that Father Fillery would be ultimately responsible for his pastoral care.

"And whom have you chosen to be your confessor?"

On imparting that he had chosen Father Laskiva, Alexander sensed that the Cardinal seemed less than pleased that Father Fillery had not been given the office. Father Fillery was after all in charge of the Removites.

"There is the matter of your fees. You are only covered for a twelvemonth. Unfortunately Monsalvat is not a charity and cannot subsidise its students. Unless some alternative source is found, you will have to leave at the end of Summer Term next year." The concern on Alexander's face was palpable and the Rector felt constrained to add: "But, rest assured, we shall explore all other possibilities for funding."

Alexander thought it timely to bring up the matter of the Edgars, the kindly couple who had looked after him on board the *Antenor*. He asked whether they had approached the college on that matter and whether he might write to them, and asked for their address. The Edgars had not thought it necessary to give this direct to Alexander.

"I will let you know their address if and when I am apprised of it. I understand Father Laskiva passed the time of day with them at Liverpool but up to now they have not written to the college."

Alexander was devastated. The Cardinal paused awhile in seeming deference to his young charge's evident discomfiture. Then he deigned to close the proceedings with a homily: "Your father has consigned you to us to educate and nurture you. He also intended us to test you. At Monsalvat we have during the history of the school developed certain mores and customs, some imposed by authority, others developed over the years among the boys themselves. Your father was aware of this and has consigned you to us to tax you in the light of these mores and customs. That is the compact between you and your late father." Then he added, ominously: "Be aware that Old Monsalvations habitually do not disclose the full extent of those mores and customs. They are for the new boy to find out and to withstand as necessary." Then, more encouragingly: "Indeed, if you are your father's son I'm sure, Alexander, that you will not be found wanting. Look upon your time here as an opportunity to prepare yourself for a full and productive life and to sit, in the fullness of time, in heaven at your father's right hand."

With that, Alexander found himself dismissed in an ostensibly kindly manner. Once out in the corridor, he looked up once again at the photographs arrayed along the oak panelling. They were not the annual whole-school photographs, for that would have taken up too much room; those photographs were filed in the library. Rather, they were a montage of achievements arrayed in datal order. Alexander was seeking out his father's years when a particular face seemed to jump out at him. It was in a picture of a rowing eight, complete with coxswain, taken at the height of some achievement or other. The subjects were posed in front of the school boat house. In the background was a racing shell and in the foreground was the trophy at hand, above which the crew were holding crossed oars. They were dressed in badged blazers and white duck trousers. The face that had arrested him, that of the coxswain, was unmistakeable. The picture was high up in an array of others and out of reach of an eleven-year-old. Alexander looked around for some means of elevation. There was a short bench adjacent to the door to the Rector's office. Swiftly, silently, he picked it up and moved it along until it was under the picture, then he climbed on it and came face to face with his father's image taken all those years ago. The face was disconcertingly youthful, fresh and clean-shaven, but it was unmistakably his father.

Alexander's thoughts strayed back to his travels with his father in the Far East. How Vudsen Snr. had memorably taken him with him on one of his business trips through mainland China; and how they had become trapped by the outbreak of hostilities in 1942 and had had to retreat to Chungking. From there Vudsen Snr. thought it advisable not to attempt to transit the front line, albeit he and his young son were possessed of neutral documents. The administrational protocols would have been quite unpredictable and the physical risks would have been too great. Instead they had taken the Burma Road, intending to make passage down the Irrawaddy. A few days out of Mandalay they learned of the bombing of Rangoon and had had to return to Mandalay. The pair eventually made their way to Dibrugarh on the Brahmaputra and had taken passage downriver to Calcutta. From there, and with much delay and difficulty, Vudsen Snr. eventually contrived to return himself and his young son to Darien by taking passage in a series of neutrally-flagged vessels. By the time they arrived home Alexander had turned five. They were lucky to achieve this before the concept of total war closed off all possibility of return. Alexander became lost in his memories of this inadvertent odyssey and of how his father had looked after him in such difficult circumstances. Tears welled up in his eyes and began to blur the picture before him. Tentatively, he put out his hand, palm outward, and touched his fingers gently on the glass.

Just then the noise of a footfall alerted him to the fact that he was no longer alone. He turned to find the Cardinal himself at his shoulder. Somehow, silently, the man had emerged from his chambers without Alexander noticing. An inadvertent cry of alarm escaped the boy's lips. He stood transfixed and terrified, fully expecting a scolding from that august being. Instead he felt a strong but gentle hand on his left shoulder and then came the voice, not authoritative and commanding as it had been, but gentle and soothing.

"Remember to put the bench back when you're finished, Alexander." And then, referring to the boat in the background: "That is the number two racing shell. You are a good swimmer, Alexander; that means we can make you one of our water rats." (The jocosely opprobrious term was the Monsalvatian equivalent of the Etonian 'wet bob'.) "You can then cox the same boat your father coxed all those years ago. I'm sure you will be a worthy successor. By the way, Father Fillery is our resident expert at photography. I'll see if he can make you a copy of that picture for you to keep in your locker. Until then you can come and look at it whenever you like. I'll let the Fathers know that you have my permission."

With that, the august being passed on his way, leaving the nonplussed youngster still standing on the bench.

* * *

Alexander thought the Cardinal's earlier reference to his being tested somewhat cryptic and disturbing. The interview had instilled in him a sense of trepidation. Furthermore, he thought the reference to sitting at his father's right hand patronising, although as an eleven-year-old he did not couch it in those terms. More pertinently, he thought it touched on the blasphemous. More pertinently still, he realised that for all practical purposes he had no friends beyond the walls of Monsalvat. Within those walls it seemed he must be content to seek solace with such as William Wepper and among his new-found friends in Remove 'A'.

* * *

Tycho Cotolay Gyles-Skeffington was not much older than Alexander; indeed he was the second youngest boy in the school. From a distance he could be taken for Alexander's brother, if not actual twin. Closer in, the observer would see that his face tended to be more animated and to betray a hint of cheekiness. He was the product of landed gentry disensconced by the vagaries of primogeniture. His father had commendably taken refuge in the consular service and had worked abroad; a fact which accounted for Tycho's fluency in colonial French. He was a passable scholar, although both Barden and Alexander sometimes had to help him out with his maths prep. More noticeably, the boy was a natural comedian. He didn't have to work at it and he never overplayed his hand. He could say more with an askance glance than a literary genius could say with a soliloquy. Barden, laconic and unsmiling, was a natural foil for his wit; indeed, in another dimension the two would have made a credible double act.

* * *

The railway loomed large in the affairs of the college. Much like the blasting in the granite quarries, the distant clatter and whistle of railway workings was a constant background noise to education at Monsalvat, so constant that the new boy would soon become oblivious of it. Heaven forefend that a Monsalvation should stoop to such proletarian pursuits as train-spotting — but in their spare time many, of the younger boys particularly, seemed inclined to drift down to the vicinity of the station nevertheless. There was the constant local passenger traffic and the heavy freight workings from the quarry sidings. At certain times of day, well known to the boys, the impressive 'Day Mails' were to be seen, hurtling dramatically through the station on their way between London and Holyhead harbour.

Dead of night brought a different aspect. Any boy lying fitfully awake in his dormitory bed might hear the Night Mails; hear the pulse of the locomotive and the roar of the rakes of carriages racing along the line that snaked along the foreshore on the flat stretch between the two headland tunnels. The sound of their passing was redolent of sanguine reunions and anguished partings. In the privy solitude that dead of night afforded, not a few silent tears would spot the pillow cases of Monsalvat.

It was the passing of such a Night Mail that caused Alexander to so succumb. An accompanying sob alerted Barden Sender to his flanking bedfellow's distress. Wisely, he declined to make what he judged might turn out to be a clumsy attempt to comfort his form fellow. Instead, he quietly arose and went to alert their pastoral Father Fillery in his adjacent room. In so doing, he was only following Sister Gloria's discreet advice. The good Father made a silent, slippered approach to Alexander's bedside, gathered the boy up and carried him into his room. Barden Sender was bidden to stand by in his dressing gown. He saw the priest set Alexander down into the single armchair in his blankets, saw him anoint the boy's forehead with holy water, heard him whisper a prayer and soothing words of comfort in the boy's ear and saw him gently wipe away the boy's tears with a white napkin. He saw Alexander let fall from his grip the medallion that lay at his throat as his anguish became assuaged somewhat. Again wisely, the priest did not ask or expect the distressed boy to make any responses; he was left to be solely a passive participant in the proceedings. Alexander accepted a few sips of water before being carried back to his bed again in the darkened dormitory. In the dim light that spilled out from the open door of the priest's room, priest and older boy rearranged his blankets and tucked him in. Before retreating, the good Father put a finger to his pursed lips as a signal to Barden Sender to keep mum about the incident. It was a redundant gesture, for thereafter, the astute older boy, acutely aware of his form fellow's circumstances, would never allude to the incident in any shape or form.

CHAPTER FIVE

Coercive Liaisons

Late October, 1949. It was cross-country practice again. In actuality cross-country practice was merely a way of keeping occupied those boys who had not been assigned to one of the games teams on that particular day. Alexander was with a group of his form fellows, forging their way across the varied landscape that lay between the college and the Penmaenbach headland. Eventually they would double back round the check point — usually manned by a solitary and very bored prefect with a stop watch and clipboard — cross the railway line by what was known as the 'country' footbridge and make their way back to the college along the beach and through the tunnel under the railway station platforms.

The pace was leisurely, perhaps too leisurely, the supervision being lax. Alexander, having previously regaled himself on Sparkling Special, found the urge to relieve himself. He made his excuses and broke off from his companions to divert to a convenient clump of the gorse bushes that dotted the sheep pasture through which they were passing. The clump was substantial and he came across the entrance to a kind of tunnel leading into it. Alexander had to bend double as he made his way to the centre. Having penetrated as far as he could, he addressed himself to the act of micturition. Ordinarily, after the manner of most small boys, he would have hoicked up the leg of his gym shorts and let fly, but the thorny gorse bearing down on him left him no headroom and rendered that method impracticable. Instead, he resorted to kneeling down and pressing his knees against a sandy bank while he pulled down the elastic waistband at the front of his shorts. The operation needed some careful managing to ensure that the effluent ran back between his knees without wetting his plimsoles. He was engaged in this delicate management of things when he heard the sound of running footfalls. He judged that there were two pairs of plimsoled feet pounding on the short cropped grass, the one following the other and he could hear the heavy breathing of the breathless runners. Then the pounding stopped as one of the runners seemed to fall heavily to the ground. Alexander heard a treble grunt as the breath was knocked out of the faller. Through the thicket he could glimpse white flashes of games clothing. He had no doubt now that they were fellow Monsalvations. He heard a momentary scuffle as another runner pinned the faller down. More than likely he had been tripped. Then there was silence for a few seconds punctuated by heavy breathing while the two recovered their breath. Evidently there was only the two of them.

Eventually one of them spoke. "Who were you staring at?"

Alexander recognised the voice as that of a Second Former, a handsome enough extrovert fellow whom everybody knew as Tojo. He was one of the few boys at Monsalvat who was not addressed punctiliously by his surname or, in the case of commonly recurring names, his initials. The nickname had followed him from his prep school and was a conjunct abbreviation of 'Tony Jones'.

"I wasn't staring."

Alexander recognised this voice as belonging to another Second Former, one whom everybody knew as Cardi. Unusually for Monsalvat, or indeed any 'English' public school of the time, Alexander was witnessing a convergence of rarities — two boys for whom fragments of their first names had followed them in from their preparatory schools. 'Cardi' was a diminutive of Ricardo. This second boy, Ricardo Pacchatti, was a doe-eyed dark-haired Eurasian, a self-effacing fellow.

As for not staring, Tojo was having none of it: "Don't give me that; every time I look over towards you you're looking at me — and then you look away like you're guilty of something."

"I don't, I don't." Cardi's protestations sounded singularly unconvincing.

Tojo homed in for the kill. "Are you sweet on me? That's it, isn't it, you're sweet on me."

"I'm not, I'm not. Honest, I'm not. I don't know what you're talking about."

"Bollocks! You're sweet on me and we both know it." Despite Cardi's further protestations, Tojo then assumed an acutely mocking falsetto: "Little Cardi's sweet on his Tojo, isn't he? Yes he is. Oh yes he is." And then, more portentously: "What's it worth for me not to tell the other chaps? Eh, what's it worth, my darling little Cardi?"

Alexander was trapped. Initially intrigued, he had let this farce go on for too long to reveal his presence, whether by a diplomatic cough or some other such gambit. He had no option but to stay put and hear it out.

By now Cardi was protesting their lateness and the probability that they would be punished accordingly. Tojo dismissed the prospect as if it were of no consequence in comparison with his catch.

"Then you and I will be caned together. You and I will suffer together. We'll both be martyrs to our new-found love. You'd like that, wouldn't you, Cardi my little sweet." Then Alexander heard the unmistakable sound of a kiss. "There, that's what you want, isn't it, Cardi — a nice big kiss from your handsome Tojo. Then he heard the snapping of elastic.

"Please, Tojo, don't. Don't do that. Yes, yes, alright, I'm sweet on you. I'm sorry, I can't help it. Please don't tell. Say you won't say anything to the other chaps, please, Tojo, please."

"Please, Tojo, please," came back Tojo's mocking falsetto imitation.

Alexander felt for the hapless Cardi. It was Tojo who brought the extraordinary encounter to an end. "Get up and let's get on. We'd better not keep old Mauger waiting any longer. But you and I are going to have to get together, aren't we, Cardi? I'll be letting you know where and when, my nice little new special friend." He finished this off with a cynical laugh. Alexander heard the pair scuffle to their feet and patter off into the distance. Only when he thought it safe did he extricate himself from the gorse patch and pad off after them. All three were late now and there would have to be some explaining to do. They couldn't all plead ricked ankles.

In the event it was Cardi who, obviously by arrangement, proffered the ricked ankle ploy. Tojo's excuse, lame enough, was that he felt he had to assist his form fellow back to base. This left Alexander out on an embarrassingly unsprained limb. Mauger's interrogation of the three tardy runners was in the presence of other boys in the pavilion dressing room. For want of a third ricked ankle, Alexander resorted to an even lamer excuse: something to do with seeing the other two in front of him and not appreciating the passage of time. He regarded himself as being contracted not to lie and this seemed a passable compromise. Mauger was unimpressed and pressed Alexander for a fuller explanation. Alexander elected to remain silent, content apparently to be adjudged guilty of 'dumb insolence'. It was clear to Mauger and the other boys that Alexander was shielding someone. Tojo and Cardi could have no doubt now that it was themselves.

Mauger, realising that he was at an impasse, took another rather surprising tack. "All right then, boy; but if I ask you some general questions will you give me an assurance that you will answer them truthfully?" This was indeed surprisingly erudite phraseology for such a rough fellow as Mauger and the onlookers were intrigued accordingly. Alexander gravely nodded assent.

"Apart from college boys, did you speak to anyone or did anyone try to speak to you while you were on the cross-country course?"

Alexander considered the implications of this before shaking his head slowly and deliberately.

"Did you stop or slow down or make a detour because you were frightened of anyone or anything?"

Again Alexander shook his head slowly and deliberately.

"Very well. I'm going to put you on report for being late in from cross-country without good reason — and for deliberately withholding information."

Alexander and indeed all present knew that being 'on report' usually resulted in an eculeation for the miscreant. The risk of this at least demonstrated that Alexander was a peach who did not peach and he gained credibility among his schoolfellows accordingly. But those present were left wondering — why had Mauger been so circumspect in his quizzing of the errant boy?

* * *

Saturday morning was the time when those 'on report' were called to account. It was presumed among the boys — and not without cause — that the delay was intended to work up the maximum degree of trepidation, the resultant delay in disposal of the matter having the potential to run for up to six days.

At the appointed time and in the appointed place, all those who had fallen foul of the administration in the preceding week were mustered in the appointed dress. The appointed place was the changing room of the old gym. The appointed dress was regulation P.T. kit. Whatever the weather, they were obliged to make their way there in just plimsoles, white socks and gym shorts, the attenuated dress being in obvious anticipation and facilitation of corporal punishment. Fortunate indeed were those who were admonished and sent on their way from the old gym without further penalty, but for most miscreants, admonishment was a forlorn hope. Authority would be present in the persons of Mauger, Father Fillery and the Rector himself.

On this occasion there were five other miscreants besides Alexander. Father Fillery flitted busily about with a clipboard and acted as dispatcher. He mustered the boys in line abreast, noses almost touching the timber partitioning in the short corridor outside the exercise hall. They were under orders not to move and not to break silence. One leaf of the double doors to the exercise hall was lying open. From their constrained position in the corridor none of them could see into the exercise hall but the experienced among them knew what to expect. There were two 'B' Removites in the line-up; the others were Second or Third Formers. As he contemplated the peeling paint on the battered wooden partition a few inches from his nose, Alexander wondered in what order they would be called. He was conscious of his fellow miscreants' rapid heavy breathing and, despite the cold late-October air, he could detect the faint acrid tang of nervous sweat.

The procedure had become routine. On a signal from inside, Father Fillery would usher a boy through the double doors and follow him in, closing the leaf behind him. The other boys would then stand quaking while the noise of conversation punctuated with peremptory commands would issue from the exercise hall. Then they would hear Father Fillery's camera shutter and see the flash of the bulb in the crack around the door. A few moments later this would be followed by the measured zip and dull splat of a cane being brought down on scantily clad flesh. The photography was a before-and-after evidence-gathering measure, ostensibly to protect the school from allegations of gratuitous violence against its charges. After more camera work, some delay and noises off, the door would open and the victim would be sent pattering off at a run. His fellow miscreants, compelled to wait like statues in studied trepidation, were given no opportunity to quiz the face of the emerging victim.

The boys were called in in no seeming particular order and Alexander found himself relegated to last.

"Vudsen."The grating voice and plebeian accent were unmistakably Mauger's. The door closed-to behind Alexander with a sepulchral clatter. He was halted before a trestle table covered with a green baize cloth. On it lay an open ledger, accompanied by a pen in an inkstand, and he took this to be the official punishment book. Father Fillery had positioned himself at one end of the table, to Alexander's left. Before him on the table was a large camera equipped with a flash unit. Mauger stood at the other end of the long table, overlooking two crook-handled rattan rods laid on the table top, the one thicker and longer than the other. Adjacent to these lay an old batsman's glove. Behind the trestle table with the punishment book before him was the Rector himself, seated on a kitchen chair. He fixed Alexander with his piercing black eyes beneath beetling black eyebrows. Away to Alexander's right stood an old battered leather vaulting horse set at a low height. He knew this to be the dreaded *eculeus*, from which the proceedings derived its name. Peter the Painter wasted no time. "Vudsen, you disappoint me. Mauger has given his account of what took place; if you have any issue with it tell me now."

Alexander could only remain silent.

"Very well." The Rector seemed to ruminate for a moment before continuing: "As this is the first time you have stood before me in these circumstances I will be lenient with you. I award you two strokes of the light cane on each count, that is to say, your lateness and your obduracy; that means you will receive a total of four strokes. Carry on."

In a way Alexander felt relieved that he was not to be further interrogated by the Rector. At least he had got away with not having to concoct an untruth. Mauger and Fillery moved in response, the former directing the proceedings.

"Stand over there, face the wall bars and take off your gym shorts."

Alexander was aghast. This was a development of which he had had no warning. He could feel his heart thumping and his cheeks colouring but he could do nothing other than meekly comply. He struggled somewhat in getting the shorts over his plimsoled feet and, not being otherwise directed, he rested the discarded garment on one of the laterals. He was conscious of Father Fillery taking up a position behind him; then a brilliant flash lit up the whole exercise hall and he felt the fleeting warmth of the flash bulb on his bare skin.

"Turn around."

Alexander moved as an automaton to comply. As he did so the set of his countenance was a silent indictment of his tormentors at this concerted assault upon his pudicity. As a reflex, he fixed on some neutral spot, a knot in the floorboards before him, but by way of his peripheral vision he could sense that his tormentors were not affecting to avert their gaze from his body in any way. What of the compact? Did his father really intend to test him to this extent? Was this the way of things at Monsalvat in his father's day? Alexander did not know; nor was now the time for a supplicant to contest such matters. For the moment he was concerned to comply, lest he provoke his tormentors into further excesses.

"Put these on."

With that, Mauger flung another pair of white gym shorts at Alexander's face. This sudden act shocked Alexander but his right hand instinctively shot out to snatch them before they fell away. He now had to wriggle into them in a standing position without any adjacent support. As he went about this, the logic of this bizarre evolution dawned upon him; he could feel that the shorts were intentionally very thin and very tight. They were for such as a nine-year-old and he was an eleven-year-old. The disparity in size was presumably to facilitate the laying on of the strokes. The stretched material would be both semi-transparent to gauge the strokes and so thin as to offer minimal protection. Still under the gaze of his three tormentors, he drew them up with some difficulty. He could feel the single elastic strand of the waistband biting into his midriff, slender enough though that was.

Nobody had warned him about this exchange of garments. None of his contemporaries who had preceded him to the *eculeus* had mentioned it. He could only conclude that it was unique to this occasion and that only he had been singled out for the humiliating process.

Mauger picked up the batsman's glove and drew it slowly and ostentatiously over his right hand. Then he addressed himself to the lighter cane, seeming to savour the feel of it as he flexed it on the air with an ominous zipping noise.

"Stand here." With the tip of the cane downcast, he indicated a place alongside the horse. "Get astride the horse and grasp the forelegs."

At this point Alexander became educated to the fact that a vaulting horse has a head end and a tail end. Otherwise, he remembered what Barden Sender had expounded to his form fellows in the dorm — that the historical *eculeus* had been a Roman instrument of torture; a rack consisting of a three-dimensional pin-jointed X-frame between the upper nodes of which the victim was secured by ankles and wrists and was thus stretched by means of his own body weight. With characteristic sense of occasion the Romans habitually embellished such devices by fashioning two adjacent nodes into the form of horses' heads, from which embellishment the name derived.

Alexander's classical musings thereupon were brought back to the unpleasant present by a bark from Mauger: "Lower down. Grasp the legs lower down."

'This brought Alexander's bare torso into full contact with the cold shiny leather and he gasped at the shock. That morning's prior and reluctant equestrians had left no discernible body heat in the creature. He knew now, although he could no longer see them, why the two 'forelegs' had smoothed bands round them. It was where so many Monsalvations had grasped them with nervously sweaty palms. Alexander could sense Mauger taking up his position and next he felt the cold touch of the cane through the thin cotton gently touching down as Mauger meticulously measured his arc of approach. Alexander instinctively tightened his grip. He felt the cane lift away from his buttocks, heard it flex on the air then heard it zip viciously down. It landed with a dull 'splat' that echoed back from the rafters of the old gym. 'Thus did Alexander take his place in that long line of eternal schoolboys who had been made to endure the more extreme rigours of their estate. When the infliction was over and he was instructed to get off the horse he found his hands gripping the legs so tightly that he had difficulty disengaging them. Little wonder the sweaty grip of cohorts of suffering Monsalvations had made rings round the forelegs. After the infliction Alexander found the earlier process reversed: there had to be a further embarrassing wriggling out of the over-tight shorts, the standing against the wall bars for more photography, then the pulling on of his own discarded shorts, until at last he was given peremptory dismissal.

As his plimsoled feet pattered their way back to the dorm,

Alexander could only reflect stoically that he had no issue with his punishment. He had, after all, been late back from cross-country practice and he had, after all, refused to give a reason or excuse when asked. Furthermore, as many had reassuringly predicted, he had survived the process. In his inner self he now felt more of a Monsalvation. If not the whole school, then certainly the Removes and the Seconds now knew that here was a peach who did not 'peach'. Most of all he was satisfied that he had come through this crisis without letting his father down. It remained now for him to face the fact that the striations across his buttocks would be visible for days if not weeks to come whenever he had to undress for communal bathing, games, swimming or gym. He could only comfort himself in thinking that, with the present regime at Monsalvat, he would scarcely be alone in that.

* * *

In the ensuing weeks Alexander could not but help observe the interaction between Tojo and Cardi, particularly when he saw them at mealtimes in the refectory. Tojo was as extrovert and boastful as ever at table and Alexander could not but help contrast this with the demeanour of Cardi. He went about with eyes downcast and seemed close to tears at times. He seldom smiled or joined in the banter and laughter at table. Alexander was perspicacious enough to sense that Cardi was at once in love and an unhappy boy with it. Alexander could only conclude that this was because Cardi's imagined relationship with his hero had gone all wrong. The relationship was one of master and slave, abuser and abused. Alexander, intrinsically gentle and considerate beyond his years, would have liked to help Cardi but could think of no way in which he could do so.

* * *

There were other liaisons within the confines of Monsalvat which were not in equilibrium. Since the decamping of Heini, Wali's compatriot, in September 1948, Wali had had the old bothy to himself. Accordingly he had taken to entertaining a local lady of some ill-repute. Yseult was a definitive Celt and the classic dark damsel of purple prosody; the vivacious and rebellious daughter of a doyen of the local Catholic Church. Hardly now out of her minority, she had earlier been running wild and out of control. She had taken to consorting with American troops quartered at a camp further along the coast and had born a child by one of them. The child had been fostered out and Yseult consigned to St Bridget's, a refuge for 'fallen women' near Chester. From there she had absconded and had fetched up, destitute and desperate, back where she came from. Fortunately for her, she had fallen in with Wali Waliser. However, once dubbed 'Yank-lover' by the more cavalier locals, she was now at risk of incurring an even more opprobrious appellation. Consequently she was inclined to keep their trysts as secret as possible. Some of the boys knew of her comings and goings on the college estate but were not inclined to noise it abroad. It would have been unwise for Yseult to permanently stay at the old bothy so, with the monetary assistance of Wali, she rented a modest room along in the town. Yseult would ride her bicycle along the main road and, under cover of darkness or diversion, enter the college estate via the country gate where there was no lodge keeper to log her comings and goings. Her assignations with Wali alternated between the rented room and the old bothy.

But it was an unsatisfactory arrangement on two counts. Yseult was dependant upon Wali, both financially and for a bolt-hole. Wali had secured a rise in wages when Heini had decamped but this augment was largely taken up by rent and subsistence for Yseult. Furthermore, although Yseult was intelligent enough, she was intellectually inferior to the patrician Wali. Wali was inclined to remind her of this when at times her wayward vivacity eclipsed the considerable physical attributes with which she otherwise beguiled him.

* * *

As divulged, and nicknames apart, public school-boys are extraordinarily punctilious when it comes to mode of address, only surnames or, occasionally, initials, being acceptable. It was Barden Sender, presumably from his perspective of an older boy, or one entrusted with a proprietorial interest in Alexander, who first addressed that boy by his first name. Hitherto, all of his form fellows had customarily addressed him as 'Vudsen' or, more familiarly, 'Vud'. After a week or two, Tycho Gyles-Skeffington tentatively followed suit. Alexander responded, just as tentatively, so that, eventually, all three found themselves on first name terms. They practised this abject breach of protocol with considerable circumspection, only doing it beyond the presence of their form fellows. For them to have done otherwise would have seemed like excluding them, which was not their intention by any means. This guarded use of forenames seemed to bring into being an unspoken bond between the three stalwarts. Paradoxically, it can come about that an unspoken bond has greater strength than a bond expressly entered into.

Chapter Six

The Dog Walkers

The morning runs along the beach were getting decidedly chillier as the Autumn Term entered November. As they changed in the dorm to go down to breakfast, Tycho 'Farmer' Gyles-Skeffington had a puzzled look on his face. "I say, Sender, every morning when we come up from the beach I see half a dozen or so men hanging round the tunnel exit. Last week, when I came up lame and last, I heard a chinking noise. When I looked round, I saw them handing what looked like silver to Mauger's outstretched hand. What's he up to? What's going on?"

Barden Sender ruminated on this for a second or two before expounding knowingly. "Ah yes, they would be the dog walkers; Mauger provides them with a show and they provide him with his beer money." "But I didn't see any *dogs*," said 'Farmer' incredulously.

"Quite," said Barden, without further qualification.

This didn't satisfy Tycho. "Show? What kind of show?"

"Christ, how naïve you are, Farmer! The show's us... juniors, nice little boarding school boys in wet gym shorts. Why do you think Mauger runs us through the surf in our skimpies? With no tops on? It's not to wake us up or toughen us up, it's to get our knickers nice and wet so they become transparent. That way we give them a show... coming *and* going. That's why he insists on white gym shorts for the morning run. You don't get the same show with blue ones." Tycho was speechless. He contemplated this astounding intelligence while he thought up an appropriate response. Eventually he found his voice. "The dirty old bastard!" It was the best he could do.

"Quite," said Barden. "Those dog walkers come a long way for a show. You'll meet them again in the evenings. On the grill bars."

"On the grill bars?" This was getting worse.

"You know, the railings in the Spinney alongside the public footpath. The dog walkers'll be on the other side. Frankie's men will put you up on the grill bars for a feel. It's ten bob notes in the evening. They give you a cut if you play the game... if you're co-operative."

A 'feel'? On hearing this dubious expression, Tycho's imagination started to run riot and he was beginning to wonder to what sink of iniquity his people had consigned him.

"But... but... can't we complain? To the Fathers?"

At this Barden laughed sardonically. "Err.., that's not advisable. That's not the way of things at Monsalvat. Don't bother complaining, nobody's going to listen to you. They'll say you've made it all up and you'll probably get a caning for being a malicious little liar, and that will put up your price on the grill bars. Frankie's customers pay extra for a feel of a good pattern of weals dontcherknow. Mauger lays 'em on accordingly."

'Farmer' turned away incredulously. Almost inaudibly, he said, "Bloody hell!" to no-one in particular.

One boy had an answer of sorts: "We don't have to stay at their rotten school. Why don't we just leg it down the road?"

Sender was scathing: "Oh yes? And where would you leg it to? With no money and nowhere to go? Cold and hungry? You'd stick out like a sore thumb. They'd just lay hold of you and bring you back. And then you'd be called a beastly funk or some such. There were a couple of chaps who legged it last year. All it got them was a caning. Harassment is all part of the system... It's tradition dontchernow, you can't beat it."

The same boy was not to be deterred. "Why don't we all leg it then? They can't ignore a whole form legging it."

Barden Sender had a dismissive answer to that too. He pointed to the door: "Orf yer go then. The rest of the chaps will be right behind you — I don't think."

Alexander heard all this but kept his counsel. He knew by now that Barden's reference to 'Frankie's men' meant those hefty rugby-playing Third Formers who held smoking parties in the old air raid shelters, who habitually hogged the showers, who muscled their way to the front of the meal queue and to whom even many of their seniors seemed to defer. These were the boys commonly referred to as The Irish Gang. He knew their names by now — Hogan, Rogan, Flynn, Fitzgerald, Regan, Begen and De Leapey. And of course, 'Foul Mouthed Frank' Leport himself. Alexander, as an aspiring Water Rat, was thankful that these reprobates were not represented on the river. It was well known that, alone among the seniors, the Captain of Boats would not brook them. Even the maverick Wepper seemed to feign ignorance of their existence.

Otherwise, the logic of what Barden was saying was beyond him. Fear and quadratic equations seemed strange bedfellows in an education system, mutually exclusive even. But then Alexander did tend to look at thing through the wrong end of the telescope. Compared to the rest of them, Barden Sender was an old hand; Alexander thought that maybe he was having an elaborate joke at their expense. What he could not know was that Barden had not told them the half of it.

Aside from the half of it, Barden's exposition was otherwise not without substance. The situation at Monsalvat reflected the general attitudes obtaining for the times (the difference being that Monsalvat stood to be judged on conditions as they had been — relatively benign for the times — and not as they had become since the advent of Canon Pynxcytte). Complaints by pupils to parents or guardians almost invariably fell on deaf ears, first-hand accounts of ill-treatment or authoritarian impropriety being summarily deemed unfounded or exaggerated. A few apprehensive parents might diffidently represent their misgivings to a headmaster or other principal but such authority figures could easily placate their complainants with platitudinous reassurances and token interventions. Only rarely would any parent reluctantly agree to relocate their offspring and then usually only at the end of their current term.

In the case of Monsalvat a few — a very few — parents *had* listened to their children and *had* put themselves to the trouble of withdrawing them in term time, but they had done so in the knowledge that their action in so doing could be construed as impugning the integrity of ordained dignitaries of established Catholic education; a brave and lonely standpoint in the deferential days of the nineteen-forties

* * *

Later that same week the summons duly came. Not for Alexander; not yet, anyway. In the free time after prep there came an emissary from the Irish Gang. Not one of the gang members themselves; they had plenty of sycophants dancing attendance and only too ready to transmit 'orders'. In this instance it was a fellow named Pooley, himself a Lower Third Former. Glancing furtively left and right to ensure there were no prefects about, Pooley moved in among the juniors in the quad. Pooley clearly — and ominously — knew each new peach by name. He cornered four of them, one at a time, and ordered them to report after supper to one of Leport's lieutenants in the woodland at the townside end of the estate. Mindful of Sender's expositions, the four meekly complied. Pooley's discreet 'advice' was for them to change into games kit before going 'on the bars' and to put their raincoats on over this attenuated dress. Oh, and not to be seen in transit. After supper the rest of the Removites repaired to the dorm knowing that the four would have to be back there in time for Father Fillery's roll call at eight forty-five. The juniors were supposed to be in bed by nine o'clock.

But Father Fillery did not appear to take roll call that evening. Instead one of the prefects came along and saw the boys into their beds. The prefect made no comment on the four empty beds and none of their form fellows felt confident enough to tax him on it. 'Lights out' came and went, and so did the prefect. The boys found themselves alone in the darkened dorm. Nobody spoke. All were wide awake and the silence was palpable. Eventually the door at the end of the dormitory swung open and the four crept in and went to their respective bed spaces.

"How much did you make?" It was Barden Sender who made the inquiry, to none of the four in particular. There was more than a hint of bravura in their various responses.

"We got seven and six each."

"My man's hands weren't half cold."

"So were those bloody railings."

"I had to tell mine not to squeeze so."

"He said he liked my nice smooth skin."

"Beer and tobacco, beer and tobacco... Ugh!"

The noises told the others they were changing into their pyjamas and getting into bed. It was Sender who closed the conversation, such as it had been: "Seven and six... not bad for an evening's work. The rates've gone up a bit since last term." And that was it; there was no more talking as the four settled down for the night. Before he drifted off himself, Alexander thought he heard a stifled sob.

* * *

The next day, to satisfy his curiosity Alexander made a discreet diversion to have a look at the scene of these 'grill bar' sessions. There was a narrow gap in the run of cottages and coach houses along the farther side of the main driveway. He walked through it and found himself in woodland, much neglected and overgrown. Pushing his way through the bushes along what seemed to be well-trodden paths he came upon the townside perimeter of Monsalvat.

The public face of Monsalvat, that which largely marched with the main Chester-Holyhead road, was bounded by spiked iron railings between equidistant brick piers in the run of a dwarf wall. The brickwork was faced with dark flint and thus emulated the Puginesque facade of the main buildings of the college. At the town end of the site, just beyond the main entrance, this boundary fence turned at right angles away from the main road and continued down the hill. Here it ran through an area of woodland known as the Spinney. The Spinney was actually a surviving fragment of the great fox covert that gave Pencadno its name. Also running through the Spinney and outside of the boundary fence was a public footpath. Further down the hill this public path joined up with the private unmetalled track that ran across the sheep pasture between the bridge over the ha-ha and the public road at the railway station frontage.

During the labour-starved war years the Spinney had become much neglected and overgrown, both on the college side and that of the local Council. The Council had also neglected the public footpath, the present condition of which discouraged its use, particularly in wet weather. After dark on certain days it tended to become the exclusive domain of Pencadno's sturdily shod but elusive dog walkers. Some of these even had dogs...

Alexander pushed his way through the thicket until he came face to face with the boundary fence. The whole scene was canopied over by the dripping trees of the Spinney. He found the prospect dank and gloomy and rather sinister. He also noticed that the coping on top of the dwarf wall was wide enough for a youngster such as himself to stand on, providing one held on to the iron uprights. He fell to wondering whether his father had come to this same place. Then his dark reverie was riven by an urge to shun the place and he turned about and made his way through the bushes back to the main driveway. He would tell no-one of his excursion.

* * *

Alexander knew the summons would come his way sooner or later. It was break time again and it was Pooley again. Alexander and Tycho 'Farmer' Gyles-Skeffington were talking together in the quadrangle. There were no other 'A' Removites in the immediate vicinity when Alexander noticed Pooley advancing upon them. He tried to avoid Pooley's eyes but it was no use. Inexorably Pooley approached. The pair looked anxiously round for an escape route but it was far too late for that. He was upon them and his message was curt: "I say, you two, grill bars nine o'clock. Be there — or else... You know the drill."

"Ah yes, Pooley... the drill for the grill." It was Tycho responding with some impromptu bravura schoolboyish inanity. Alexander garnished it with a nervous and unconvincing laugh. Which feeble efforts had no discernible impact whatsoever on the Irish Gang's messenger. Pooley promptly withdrew and left them to contemplate his message. After he had gone Alexander and 'Farmer' looked at each other, each wondering how they could extricate themselves from this iniquitous summons. With considerable misgivings both boys resolved to absent themselves from the appointed place at the appointed time. They knew other peaches had been summoned and would presumably fill the bill for that evening's clandestine 'entertainment', whatever that entailed. The time came and went; nobody actually came looking for them. Maybe they would get away with it. On the other hand both felt they might be storing up trouble for the future.

* * *

As divulged, Barden Sender was older than the rest of the Removites and, having been relegated a form due to previous indisposition, was presumed to be wiser. He was a pleasant and steady enough fellow but at times he did fall prone to taking advantage of his seniority and experience, scant though it was. The conversation in the dormitory had turned round to the 'grill bars' and how to avoid being coerced theretowards. Barden Sender's contribution was cryptic as ever.

"You can always become one of the "*trophimoi*"

"A member of the what?" they chorused.

"The trophimoi. It's Greek." Here Barden spelt out the word for the benefit of his audience. He offered no further information.

"Greek, eh? That doesn't sound very Catholic to me." It was McGuckin making this observation. "Do the Fathers know about this trophimoi thing?"

Sender responded: "It's the Fathers that run it." The dormitory was silenced for long enough by this revelation. At this point Alexander intervened: "It sounds like a secret society to me. Surely it's against the Faith to belong to a secret society, let alone run one?"

Barden made an intentionally audible intake of breath. "I'd keep my trap shut about secret societies if I were you."

Alexander persisted: "I say, Sender, Pooley summoned 'Farmer' and me to the grill bars last night but we didn't go. Do you think they've forgotten that?"

Barden Sender contemplated the inquiry for some time before constructing a response. The response of the all-wise, all-knowing Sender carried within it a note of genuine concern for his two younger form fellows: "Err... no; they won't have forgotten."

Alexander and Tycho were hardly reassured thereby. It was another of their form fellows, Harry Norton, who came in now with: "This trophoi ... So where do we join?" The question was more facetious than exploratory.

By now the bell for vespers had been tolling for some time and the boys were anxious to depart thereto lest they find themselves penalised. The matter would have to rest for the time being. As it was, Barden's parting response was more intriguing than explanatory. "You don't join.., you get summoned."

CHAPTER SEVEN

The Trophimoi

In his infamous essay back in 1946, Third Former William Wesley Wepper made a comparison between boarding boys and day boys. He was concerned to stress that the day boy had the almost daily opportunity to roam beyond the reaches of both school and parental control and to come under the influence of others of other sexes and persuasions, in the streets and at large.

It had manifestly not escaped Wepper's notice that, historically, Monsalvat had hosted a considerable number of day boys. Some of the lay staff, who lived out, were frequently heard to observe that they knew of many local boys who would be eligible to attend. But it had become the Rector's practice of late to restrict pupillage to expatriate boarders. His purported rationale was that this gave the pastoral Fathers greater control over the soul. That this 'policy' militated against the economic interests of the college seemed not to concern him. The resultant situation was that pupillage was undersubscribed, to the extent that Monsalvat was operating significantly below its nominal four hundred capacity. The deficit in fees and therefore income must have been significant and there was a consensus that this deficit must be made up from other, unspecified, sources. It was these other sources that Wepper's essay alluded to, much to the Rector's secret chagrin.

Wepper was a child of his time. Later opinions and revisions of the Church might retrospectively vindicate some of his views, but we must look to the perspectives of the late 1940s. He mused that the ten-year-old or thereabouts becomes aware that what dangles below his abdomen has a subsidiary function as a source of illicit pleasure; a precursor to its primary function as an organ of generation and incidental to its secondary function as a conduit of micturition. Later, that this quizzical appendage seems to acquire a mind of its own. If it is not periodically attended to, it will rise up to meet him at untoward moments; it will haunt his dreams and precipitate rude awakenings. The contemplation of such things, over which he has little or no control, was proscribed in the Catholic canon. And that furthermore, the cloistered boy will become uncomfortably aware that some of his fellows appear to him to be fairer of face, lither of limb and sharper of wit than others; and that he would seek to consort with them or a chosen one of them beyond the bounds of virtuous friendship. And that, within the cloister, that awareness will, in many cases, be reciprocated. Again, such liaisons, over which he has little or no control, were also proscribed in the Catholic canon.

Wepper postulated that once freed of the cloister, the boy — now become the young man — will seek natural solace elsewhere than among his erstwhile schoolfellows, however special some may have been. Here Wepper made his most telling point; that celibate priests must necessarily remain unfulfilled in that regard and would be prone to untoward aberrations accordingly. Little wonder he was denigrated as The Bold Contemner.

Another aspect Wepper's essay addressed, an impliedly related aspect, was the harbouring at Monsalvat of secret societies against a specific tenet of the Church. He made broad allusions to the Irish Gang, that bunch of bully boys, 'upliners' from the stews of Dublin, drafted into the middle school as proxy enforcers of the will of the Fathers. Its members liked to glory in the name The Hell Fire Club, but its default title among the boys remained The Irish Gang. It was an amorphous group rather than a definitive secret society. It lay like a bolus in the craw of the middle school. As its members either graduated to higher forms and moderated their behaviour or, more usually, were summarily expelled from the college for failing to demonstrate the necessary ability for advancement, so newcomers would be brought into the lower forms as apprentice enforcers. Another source of recruits was the co-opting of a selected few from its many 'downliner' sycophants. In deference to the Emerald Isle, it needs to be stressed that not all members of the Irish Gang were necessarily Irish and by no means were all the many Irish boys members of the eponymous gang. Indeed, other 'upliners' were just as likely to be victimised by the Gang as any 'downliner'.

The definitive secret society at Monsalvat was the aforementioned *trophimoi*. This was a secret society that sapped at the very foundations of the college. It clearly breached the bounds of propriety and was the abnegation of a duty of care towards its young charges. The *trophimoi* was not merely connived at but was actively promoted and facilitated by the pastoral Fathers, albeit clandestinely, as befitted a society that was 'secret'. Selected junior boys would be nominated in secret conclave and subsequently inducted at a covert ceremony. They were induced on the promise of certain privileges, but the principle benefit from the perspective of the inductees was freedom from harassment by the Irish Gang. To that extent the relationship between secret societies at Monsalvat was incestuous.

* * *

The *trophimoi* took its name from the adopted sons of the Greek aristocrat and consul Herodes, c.101-177 A.D., a wealthy man responsible for many public works throughout Greece. The word connotes foster sons, of which Herodes had three. All three died in their youth but the one outstanding adoptee was Polydeukion. This boy died at about the age of fifteen, possibly from injury arising from some active pursuit such as hunting or games. Herodes was married, to Regilla, and they had six natural children in addition to the three foster sons. The fosterings seemed to have been more for social rather than economic reasons. According to the available records, Polydeukion in particular was not a child in economic need. He was well connected — to Herodes' maternal kin among others — and of high social standing in his own right. *Post mortem*, he had games instituted in his honour, and was locally rated a hero.

Of the three foster sons, Polydeukion became unique in that he was apotheosised into a demi-god at the obsessive instigation of his adoptive father. This obsession was manifested in a proliferation of votive sculpture. It is conjectured that Herodes' obsession is attributable to pederasty, but there is no direct evidence for this, nor that Herodes was anything other than a normal family man who had philanthropically extended his family merely because he had the means to do so. The intensity of the cult may have sprung from Polydeukion's pursuit of excellence as evidenced by his physique. We might discern his physique from a famous bas relief known as The Apotheosis of Polydeukion in the national museum at Athens. This depicts the youth with all the trappings of deity, principally the serpent, the fig tree, his servant, his horse, his helmet and his magnificent nudity — demigods may be assumed to have no cognisance of pudicity.

Of course, the sculpting was by definition post mortem and may be an idealized representation of the boy's physique.

The lower limbs seem to predominate and are suggestive of feminine proportions; perhaps a swimmer rather than a terrestrial athlete. The figure is a definitive example of *contraposto* (which might translate as *counterpoise*). In the present case the sculptor has achieved *contraposto* by standing the image on uneven ground. This slightly elevates the right foot, putting that knee into a relaxed state and throwing the body weight onto the left leg. This tilts the pelvis to the right and the left shoulder is lowered to compensate. Thus, is imparted to the torso, and indeed the whole, a lifelike sinuousness absent from earlier classical depictions of youth, such as the *kouri*. This natural sinuousness is complemented by the disposition of the arms and hands. The right arm is disposed gracefully out and downwards, ostensibly proffering a fig to the serpent. The left elbow remains tucked into the side in an appealingly juvenile fashion, with the forearm leading outwards and slightly upwards so as to cast the draping toga aside, revealing all but the left shoulder and breast.

* * *

All of which begs the question of how it comes to relate to Monsalvat. The answer is that it was an irregular and unauthorised importation coincident with the advent of Canon Peter Pynxcytte as Rector in the late 1940s. The cult of the *trophimoi* at Monsalvat is incompatible with an institute of Catholic education or indeed a Catholic institution of any kind. To formalise the deference to, if not the actual worshipping of, graven images and certainly those purporting to be demigods, is diametrically opposed to the dogma of Christianity in general and the Catholic church in particular. This is complexed further by the vicarious sensuality inherent in the particular image under consideration.

At Monsalvat, candidates for the *trophimoi* were selected by means of the photography which formed part of the annual medical inspection of the boys. This photography was conducted by Father Fillery (who had therefore become known to the boys as 'Flash Fillery'). Annual medical inspection was conducted in the old gymnasium. The school was put through this inspection on a form by form basis over several days. The boys, paraded in only gym shorts, proceeded from the one to the other. At the photography station each boy had to remove his gym shorts and stand on a turntable before a graduated screen. The turntable was then rotated so that the subject could be photographed anteriorly, in profile and posteriorly. Thus, by means of the images and the graduations on the screen, the physical development of each boy could be gauged by comparing each succeeding annual recording. After professional appraisal the plates would be consigned to each boy's medical file. This procedure was becoming general in schools at the time and would otherwise be unworthy of note, were it not that, at Monsalvat, the plates were later scrutinised in private by the Rector and Father Fillery in order to select particular specimens for induction into the *trophimoi*. That this was an irregularity goes without saying.

The old gymnasium at Monsalvat had previously doubled as a concert hall, before it was superseded in that specific by the new assembly hall built in the 1930s. One end of the exercise hall was elevated to form a stage, with storage space under for gymnastic apparatus etc. One of the roof trusses had doubled as a proscenium arch. At stage level there was a large bay off to one side, effectively making the building L-shaped. This bay had the same function as a theatrical fly tower. It accommodated painted backdrops and theatrical props which, variously, could be drawn out onto the stage as required. Unique among these was an emulation of the aforementioned bas relief. It was a life-sized rectangular frame, its greater axis being the horizontal. It was three-dimensional, the forward elements being fretworked out of plywood and painted appropriately. All that was missing was the demigod himself.

Of those boys who inserted themselves into this frame in substitution for the demigod, those who have spoken retrospectively tell of soothing potions, draughts of warm air, white sound, blinding floodlights, camera flashes and certain physical stimulations intended to take the depictions beyond the intent of the ancient sculptors.

Some of these latter-day depictions succeeded in approaching the perfection of the original bas relief but, despite the most meticulous attention to the pose, most fell short of that. The fluid un-muscled puerile body has its own innate beauty but not all specimens are worthy of the attention of a Praxiteles or a Canova.

There was to be one candidate however whose image would indeed bate the breath of the observer. This boy's flowing juvenile physique would indeed match — and in certain respects exceed — that of the ancient paragon of prepubescent beauty. The Italianate head of Polydeukion would be supplanted with a more nobly fashioned Nordic caput, crowned with wheaten curls tumbling down across the forehead and about the perfect pink convolutes of the ears. High sculpted cheekbones and a rosebud mouth would eclipse the very visage of the pouting demigod. The expression on the face would be enigmatic; the unwritten page of the untutored young.

So effective would be this particular depiction that Canon Pynxcytte would gather it unto himself. He would order Father Fillery to make and enlarge a second copy and to put it in a frame, a frame which he was to hang on the panelling in the darkest corner of his inner chambers. As a further obscuring, the depiction would be framed back to back with another picture of lesser compelling regard, so that the frame would have to be turned in order to view the real reason for its existence. The worthy Rector would hide the frame behind a claret-coloured drape, only to uncover and reverse it to have it look down on him in his more private and contemplative moments.

CHAPTER EIGHT

Love Unrequited

In the Shell there was one Lance Raphael Lapita. At Monsalvat the Shell was interposed between the Thirds and the Fourths. It had not always been so. Over the years it had been moved about to serve the academic aims of the college. In 1949 it functioned as a platform from which the college's budding scientists and artists could be dispersed to their respective streams. Below that level boys were tutored in both disciplines, it being held that premature specialisation would do the boys a disservice. Thus, given the present station of the Shell, Lapita might be categorised as an adolescent; indeed he was fourteen, going on fifteen. He was a handsome enough specimen, both asthenic and athletic with it. Blond-haired and blue-eyed, he had been considered a 'prize peach' in his day. Now older and more assertive, he could be quick to remind another that his name rhymed with 'per capita' and not 'repeater'. He was an exemplary scholar, and he excelled on the Conway River, initially as a cox, then a bow and lately rowing stroke in the coxed fours.

At the beginning of Autumn Term 1949, Lance was occupied in his own devices and didn't take any particular interest in the new 'peaches'. Others confided that they thought the latest crop particularly interesting but Lance was content to leave the field to others for the present. That was to change dramatically when he was in chapel a few days into the new term. It was on the Feast of the Blessed Virgin Mary, a day seared into his memory, that Alexander Fragner Vudsen first impinged upon his consciousness. At the time he had no knowledge of the name or the face. He had heard the voice and had been transfixed thereby; but the voice came down from the dome, disembodied and out of sight, the exquisitely articulated notes floating down like champagne snowflakes to caress the cheeks and intoxicate the senses of the hearers below. Thereafter, for many a day and many a long night Lance had attempted to conjure up in his mind's eye the divine creature down from whom those notes floated. Many a day and many a long night had he schemed for a sight of the creature; but the exigencies of the offices, ceremonies and routines of the day seemed to conspire perversely to prevent any such seraphic mingling of sight and sound. The tensions within him were threatening to tear him apart. At first he began to neglect his studies and disports and to mope about the common rooms, to the dismay of his peers and seniors. Then it occurred to him that his elusive, ethereal prospect would respect him the better were he to resume his pursuit of excellence and garner public acclaim therefor. Therefore he threw himself into his studies and disports with such renewed vigour that his peers and seniors now became concerned for his mental equilibrium. He counted his successes in the number of mentions of his name and the concomitant recitations of his achievements at 'notices', hoping against hope that his elusive prospect would begin to take an interest in this 'most improved scholar' of the day.

He would become insanely jealous of any other scholar who was similarly mentioned and exhibited a pathological resolve to wrest their accolades from them. He scrupulously avoided all Removites lest by some perverse negation of serendipity his impingement upon his unknown prospect should turn out to be a social disaster. He retreated from their presence, on the parterre, on the terrace and in the colonnades, only to spy on them from afar and speculate as to which one might be the object of his desire. Was it too much to hope for the vision to match the voice?

The days went by. The tension remained unresolved. Lance was only too aware that he would have rivals, rivals who even now might be making their play for the creature that had been born only for him. He could not sleep, he could not study, he could not play. His urbanity left him and his indulgent form fellows were beginning to disavow him.

There were several boys to whom that voice might belong. But there was one in particular to whom that voice surely *must* belong. Upon a day and in a place and at a time which became seared into Lance's very being, a creature did indeed pass before his gaze. A boy the vision of which happenstance had hitherto denied him. True, he had not yet matched the voice to the vision but the convergence was an inexorability. But Lance had yet to know the name by which the incarnation of this exquisite convergence of sight and sound was launched upon the world. He didn't even know which Remove this exquisite convergence had been consigned to. He was reduced to leafing feverishly through the published college list 1949-50, trying to find a name mellifluous enough to do justice to the voice and the vision. There were several candidates there but no confirmation to be had. Then he was reduced further to hovering in the vicinity of the Removites like a squalid voyeur, straining his ear to pick up the slightest hint of a name in their comradely badinage. At last he heard one definite 'A' Removite address another as 'Farmer'. On a mission of elimination Lance hied himself back to the college list; there was no Farmer. Frustration again! Then Lance lit upon a Gyles-Skeffington in Remove 'A'. Ah, the vagaries of schoolboy nicknames! Of course, that was it — 'Farmer Giles'...

He could eliminate Remove B; the creature must be in Remove 'A. Back to the list therefore:

Michael Roger Brennan
Philip William Broke
Nigel Scott Catonsworth
Tycho Cotolay Gyles-Skeffington
Neil Francis Frankland
Raimo Haroldsen
Jean-Louis Jouvet
Laurence Marco Loxley
Maurice McGuckin
Harry Norton
Michael Polders-Leigh
Vicente Jaime Rivadavia
Barden Miles Sender
Alexander Fragner Vudsen
Geoffrey Charles Williamson

The creature must be one of these fifteen. Lance speculated endlessly which one it might be, trying to match each name to the face and rating each name as to its mellifluousness and sonority. Then it was birthdates. The creature looked younger than his form fellows. Lance discerned that the latest birthdate was "29/06/38". It was against the name of Vudsen. Could this be the one? Alexander was truly a heroic namc; a name to live up to. It fitted the creature perfectly. Furthermore it was a name that had been read out at notices, along with his own, in the context of academic achievement. But none of this was confirmation. Perhaps the creature was one of the evident 'outlanders'; Jouvet perhaps, or Rivadavia. Those names seemed exotic enough. Surely he could not be a Norton or a McGuckin; the one was too prosaic, the other too angular and proletarian. The only thing Lance was certain of at this time was that he could not be Gyles-Skeffington for 'Farmer' Gyles-Skeffington had been his indicator. The days went by and confirmation eluded him tantalisingly.

At mass he would sometimes find himself paired with a Removite as servers. As if in a protracted process of elimination he would, at an opportune moment, volunteer that he was Lapita of the Shell and would follow this with: "I'm sorry I don't know your name." By this ploy, and by the time of a forthcoming untoward event, he could eliminate no less than three further names. It was a painfully slow process. His frustration raged apace.

Lance knew he had to be careful. Already his obsession had materially altered his behaviour such that his peers had noticed. He had to be sparing in his exploratory movements lest some astute person queried his actions. By craning his neck in assembly and in chapel he could see the back of the creature's neck, see the wheaten locks swirling on the nape and about the dainty pink convolutes that were the creature's ears. How Lance envied the creature's form fellows; to be in such proximity and conversing withal, apparently oblivious of their good fortune. To study with, to sup with, to bathe with, to sleep with the creature — how truly fortunate they must be.

As the term progressed the creature became less elusive. Lance saw him serving Mass for Father Fillery. So gentle and attentive was he, so graceful in his movements in his ringing of the bell and the proffering of the missal. Sight of the creature swinging the censer towards the congregation sent him into transports of delight. Surely the creature swung it only for him? Lance exulted in every swish and fold of the creature's cassock. Never before had he wished to be a cassock. Lance was scheming day and night now as to how he could bring himself into beneficial proximity with the creature. Schemes were conceived, considered and discarded as impracticable with alarming regularity. Lance dreamed up schemes that would work but which could also go disastrously wrong, perhaps bringing puerile ridicule upon him as they did so. Even Lance realised he was in trouble and needed help...

* * *

"Most schoolboy friendships are transitory; the more intense they are the more transitory." These soothing words of wisdom came at Lance through the lattice window of the confessional. But this was a friendship that had yet to start, let alone to blossom. In a frantic effort to relieve his anguish he had surrendered to the bosom of his faltering faith and sought balm for his scorching soul in absolution. Perhaps God might conjure up a scheme for him. If that meant going through God's agents on earth, so be it. Here was Father van Reldt counselling him to join a stamp club or some such on the off-chance that it might bring him into benign proximity with the object of his desire. At least he wasn't condemning Lance out of hand. Van Reldt seemed to have an understanding of his dilemma; perhaps too much of an understanding. Lance distinctly got the impression that van Reldt had been someway down a similar torturous road. But that surely was ever the lot of the celibate priest. Lance was not a priest. His passions did not have to go unrequited.

The priest's gently probing questions moved towards an identification of the object of Lance's desires. He elicited a physical description of the boy and matched it with the reputation of the voice. Disconcertingly the priest mused that he thought he could identify the boy concerned. Lance was concerned; he had never intended to disclose the identity of the boy; it was just that he himself did not know the identity of the boy and he was hoping against hope that the priest would let slip the name. He now regretted going to confession on the matter. The Seal of the Confessional was sacrosanct but he had given himself away and might find himself being brought under surveillance nevertheless. He resolved to be on his guard. One thing that Father van Reldt did let slip was a rather disturbing revelation that the situation of the boy he had in mind was "delicate". He did not enlarge upon this and Lance was left wondering: how delicate? Parents divorcing, perhaps? Bereavement? How could he gauge his gambits without further information? All he knew was that he now felt all the more for his quarry.

Once clear of the confessional Lance resolved to redouble his efforts to get to know the boy. The question was, how? There was of course always the old Monsalvat standby of the napery drawer. Each boy was assigned a 'couvert' at his form table in the refectory and kept it for the duration. Far be it for a Monsalvation to walk abroad with his unique and distinctive uniform bespotted with the fallout from his daily comestibles. Long ago, against such a public embarrassment, authority had decreed that each boy should be supplied with a linen napkin, changed weekly. In pursuance of this, each couvert was equipped with a napery drawer that had the boy's name on it, on an index card slipped into a little brass frame.

As well as providing storage for the table napkin, each drawer served as the repository for incoming mail. Every morning the Bursar, Father Quedda, would pass through the refectory with the incoming mail and he would deposit it in each recipient's napery drawer as necessary. Naturally enough, each boy checked his drawer for incoming mail at each mealtime. Consequently, it was easy enough for boys to leave notes for each other by usurping that particular function of the napery drawer. Of itself such usurpation had not been specifically promulgated as an offence but the practice was open to challenge and scrutiny by any of the pastoral Fathers. Indeed, all incoming mail itself was subject to scrutiny by the pastoral Fathers. For these reasons Lance regarded the napery drawer as too risky for passing notes. Besides, although it might provide a means of communication once a liaison had been established, it was a different matter if one was trying to initiate a liaison. The prospect of being held up to public ridicule by an unappreciative recipient, even as an anonymous correspondent, would be anathema to such a proud and sensitive creature as Lance Raphael Lapita.

Perhaps an oblique approach might work, Lance conjectured. Perhaps a contrived insult or disservice, followed by a feigned apology. Such a gambit would abate Lance's concerns as to inviting ridicule. Perhaps the games field might offer an opportunity for such a gambit. The cricket nets perhaps? As far as Lance knew the boy was not yet recruited as a 'water rat' — he would not meet him on the river. He knew the boy could swim; he had lately passed by the swimming pool and had caught a breathtaking glimpse of his nearly nude body resplendent in ice blue swimming trunks. He was in the water and doing a fast crawl along with some of his form fellows. He seemed as streamlined as a seal. Despite the roiling of the water the exquisite symmetry of the boy's form was unmistakable. Because he was such a competent swimmer it was inevitable that Mauger would soon be steering the boy in the direction of rowing. Perhaps Mauger might do Lance's work for him and he would soon have him as his cox on the river. The boy certainly was small and slight enough — and clearly intelligent enough — to perform the duty.

Reverting to the gambit, the disservice would have to be carefully gauged lest it prove irredeemable. It would bring him inexorably to the attention of the creature; it would then be up to Lance to steer that attention into a benign channel, a channel that could be prolonged, a channel leading to a lasting liaison. However, on reflection Lance decided to eschew all such tactics. He did not wish to garner such a new and special friend by such devious means and he certainly did not relish the prospect of necessarily having to live a lie thereafter. His route towards his seraphic prospect was not to be sullied by duplicity.

The downside of this altruistic self-denial was that it brought him no further to a positive identification. However, as Shakespeare would have Brutus say, *There is a tide in the affairs of men which, taken at the flood, leads on to fortune; omitted, all the voyage of their life is bound in shallows and in miseries.* On September 29th, the Feast of St Raphael, his seraphic namesake, a tide did indeed brim for Lance Raphael Lapita to stem. On this day there occurred a most curious and serendipitous encounter with a serpent...

CHAPTER NINE

The Day of the Serpent

The cross-country course commenced at a muster station in front of the cricket pavilion on the playing fields. From there it led onto the fields and scrubland at the country end of the college estate, exiting via the chase gate. From there it continued northeastward towards the Penmaenbach headland. About a quarter mile short of the headland it rounded a checkpoint manned by a couple of prefects and doubled back towards the college, still on the landward side of the railway line. At an isolated footbridge known as the country bridge, it crossed over the railway line and ran along the beach towards the promenade. Then it went under the station platforms via the pedestrian tunnel and fetched up in the road that served the station forecourt. From here it ran with the uphill track through the pasture land and back onto Monsalvat's great parterre via the bridge over the ha-ha. Finally it proceeded via the *aditus maritimus* and the grand terrace, round behind the glasshouses and back to the muster station on the playing fields. At the start the participants were despatched in waves from the muster station and were tallied back home at the same point, their performances being gauged against elapsed time. Thus each runner accrued an individual time from which could be discerned the overall performance of their respective Quarters. The staggered despatching prevented bunching of the runners and facilitated checking at the far checkpoint and back at the finish line. The late September day was sunny enough with a gentle breeze, but there was a bank of threatening cumulonimbus making up upwind. A group of Shellites and Third Formers was forging ahead. Among them was Lance Lapita. They had just cleared the outer checkpoint when they came up on a quintet of juniors from an earlier despatch. Even at a considerable distance Lance had recognised among them the precious wheaten curls of the boy that filled his dreams. He discreetly dropped back and allowed his peers to overtake the juniors. A few minutes later the two groups had drawn well apart. Seemingly the juniors were tending to dawdle and skylark and were not putting their best efforts into the race. Lance was now running at the same speed as them and was wondering how to play his hand next when fate — or something else — took a hand. He was in gorse scrubland and approaching a cow pasture. There was a stile in the hedge ahead of him and he could see flashes of white sports clothing around it as the quintet of juniors queued to climb over it. The onshore breeze carried their treble tinkles of carefree laughter down to him. Then an urgent cry came down to him on the wind. It was the kind of sound that immediately signals distress. The cry was followed by shouts of alarm. Lance abandoned his easy lope and began to sprint towards the scene.

All five boys were on the far side of the stile. One of their number was seated on the ground, his back against the knees of a companion who had urgently dragged him away from something. The seated boy was the creature, he of the divine form and voice. But his face was as white as a sheet now and he was shrieking in terror. As Lance came over the stile one of the boys pointed to the undergrowth at the foot of the hedge. Lance was just in time to see the tail of a snake disappearing from view. From its markings Lance could see it was a specimen of the venomous adder. It seemed the boys had been larking about and one of them had fallen from the stile, disturbing the basking adder. It had bitten him on the neck and he was now approaching a state of collapse.

Serendipitous or no, Lance realised that the situation with which he was presented could be serious. The location of the bite was critical; the boy could be in danger of asphyxiation from the resultant swelling. Urgent action was needed. The public road was not far away but there was no guarantee of help there. He decided the best course of action was to carry the boy back to the chase gate using a short cut. A dream had come true — he found himself ministering to his very quarry — but the circumstances were very much not of his making. After reassuring and quietening the boy as best he could, he sent off two of the boy's companions to run on ahead and raise the alarm so that an ambulance could meet the casualty at the chase gate. He ordered the other two to stand by him and assist him in getting the casualty over the intervening stiles and hedges. Immediately, he needed them to help get the casualty up on his back.

Thus it came about that Lance, who had spent so much time and energy contemplating this creature from afar, now found himself in as close a proximity as could ever be. He could feel the animal heat of the boy's body on his own thinly clad back. He could feel the bare arms against his neck and see them enfolding across his very breast. His own bare arms were cradling the boy's bare thighs in an exquisite convergence of perfect skins. The boy's chin was resting on his right shoulder and he could feel each stertorous breath and hear each thin moan right next to his ear. Those locks, those exquisite wheaten swirls that for so long had tantalised him from afar, were now tickling his very cheek. The coral pink convolutes of the boy's left ear lolled cool and crisp against his own.

As yet, Lance's burden was light as a feather, but he realised he had a long way to go. Only three years separated him and his burden and, fit as he was, he was undertaking no light task. Lance did not waste his opportunities. He resolved to keep up an encouraging conversation with what was now his patient, in line with First Aid guidelines.

"What's your name?"

"Vudsen."The boy's voice was faint and tremulous; indeed he was now keeping up a continuous tremulous moaning sound. From his necessarily constrained position, Lance could sense tears of fear and pain springing from those intense blue eyes.

"No, no, Vudsen... I mean.., what's your first name?

"Alexander."

"Alexander...That's a fine name, a noble name; a name to live up to."

Alexander was not at the time receptive to such verbal encouragement. His response was pathetic: "I'm frightened."

Lance did his best to reassure the traumatised boy: "No need to be frightened, Alexander. I've got you now. Nobody dies of snake-bite in this country. All you need's an injection and you'll be as right as rain." Lance himself was not reassured. Most snake-bites were to an extremity; this one was to the neck. Speed was of the essence. The sun had clouded over now and spots of rain were on the wind.

"I'm Lance Lapita." Lance would have gone on to invite the boy to address him by his first name but though better of it. The boy might interpret it as indicating that the situation might be more serious than it was; that he might be in danger of death even. Lance decided it would be better to maintain the normal Monsalvation protocols of address as a reassurance of normality. For the present at least...

Lance then decided to take a different tack. When the boy's companions were bringing him to his feet Lance had noticed a gold medallion round his neck. He made an astute guess. "Are you a Child of Mary, Alexander?"

"Yes."

"Then I'm sure Mother Mary is watching over you. Shall we say a prayer, Alexander? To let her know we thank her for taking care of you?" The question seemed incongruous in the circumstances; Mother Mary had palpably failed in her duties on this occasion, but Lance thought it expedient to ignore her derelictions. "Shall we say a Hail Mary"?

"Okay." It was the best Lance could hope for in the circumstances. He took note of the way the boy pronounced his words. Even in adversity there was no trace of anything that might suggest a jarring accent. The boy's articulation was perfect and non-regional, insofar as that can be an objective conclusion. His speaking voice mirrored his singing voice. Lance began the prayer. The poisoned boy made a faltering attempt to follow his words but his tremulous voice petered out after the second line. Lance completed the prayer for him. "Say Amen, Alexander."

But the boy had more urgent and decidedly corporeal matters on his mind. "I'm going to be sick."

Lance was fatalistic; he had little option: "Then be sick, Alexander. I can't stop to put you down now." A few moments later the boy was sick. The warm acrid vomit splashed down the front of Lance's singlet and shorts and bounced off his right knee. That which had been inside the creature was now irritating Lance's skin. For better or for worse it was raining heavily now. Lance could feel the raindrops mercifully diluting the streaks of vomit. He could hardly believe his luck. Not only was the creature, for so long the object of silent worship from afar, being rescued by him, the creature had actually vomited all over him. Lance felt it was a price worth paying. Surely, did he not now hold this exquisite creature forever in thrall? Before long, Lance was just about at the end of his endurance. As he and his helpers approached the chase gate they could see an ambulance waiting just beyond it on the asphalted road and a small group of concerned adults gathered about it. Off to one side was a circle of inquisitive boys. Many wore their raincoats over their games kit against the now persistent drizzle. The chase gate had been opened but the ambulance could not go beyond it because of the unevenness of the terrain. Lance staggered through the gate and was glad to feel the ambulance men taking the weight of his burden. They laid Alexander on a stretcher and wrapped a blanket around him. There was concern lest the venom should cause swelling enough to close his windpipe and gullet or constrict the carotid arteries and interfere with the blood supply to his brain. He was still moaning tremulously, from pain and fear. His face was deathly pale and his skin cold and clammy. He momentarily opened his eyes and met Lance's concerned gaze with a most pathetic glance.

Lance knelt alongside him and put his hand on his shoulder: "They'll look after you now, Alexander, you'll be all right. I promise."

Alexander looked up at him with his intense blue eyes but otherwise didn't respond. Lance himself was now a sorry sight, lathered in sweat, dirt, rain and vomit and exhausted to the point of collapse.

"Well done, you three. Oh, and Norton and Jouvet." These were the boys whom Lance had sent on ahead to raise the alarm. The words were spoken by Father Laskiva, and he said them with a sympathetic smile. "You'd better go and get yourselves cleaned up." He sent them straight to the bath house, detailing Osgodby, one of the prefects, to arrange for their things to be taken there along with clean clothing. Many of the runners who had already arrived back at the check point adjacent to the cricket pavilion had seen the ambulance come off the grand terrace and proceed along to the chase gate. They were naturally curious as to who could be in trouble. Among the several pupils who had drifted down from the cricket pavilion was Foul Mouth Frank Leport. He watched as Alexander was being loaded into the ambulance, then remarked *sotto voce* to his cronies: "Brought up in the jungle and has to come all the way to North Wales to get bitten by a fuckin' snake."

At least it broke the tension somewhat. Those boys within earshot responded with a nervous guffaw. The ambulance pulled away and they could hear its gong sounding as it made its way to the main road and thence to Bangor hospital where, apparently, a supply of snake-bite serum was maintained.

* * *

Lance could hardly contain himself. He had accrued something of a heroic status — and he had been in intimate physical, emotional and spiritual contact with the creature who had been dominating his every waking moment for most of the autumn term. The following morning a brief account of the incident was given at 'notices' by the Rector himself and the names of those boys who had assisted in the emergency were read out. His own name of course was the most prominent and a round of applause was garnered. Later, back among his peers, Lance would protest that he only did what any Monsalvation would do for another in the circumstances. Alexander himself was still in hospital and the Rector reassured the boys that he was recovering satisfactorily. What he thought best not to reveal however was that Alexander had been transferred to Liverpool Royal Infirmary as a matter of some urgency. The account was followed, understandably enough, by an advisory regarding the presence of adders in the surrounding countryside.

But more was to come of the incident. Two days later Lance was paged during physics summoning him to the Rector's chambers between periods. Ever the eternal schoolboy, he was left wondering what could be the cause of such a summons. He had been summoned there several times before and for not entirely felicitous reasons. Once more did he leave the familiar surroundings of the colonnade to enter into the dark panelled corridors of the presbytery. The door to the Rector's suite was ajar; Lance leaned forward and rapped on it with what he gauged to be suitably deferential timidity. Summoned inside, he found himself in the presence of the Rector and Father Fillery. He was motioned towards a chair. This clearly was a matter of some import, and Father Fillery was the one to elucidate.

It seems Alexander was asking for Lance to visit him in hospital. Lance was both relieved and inwardly elated. The boy wanted to thank Lance for plucking him from a dangerous situation. He also wanted to apologise for being sick all over him. This caused the Rector and the priest a modicum of amusement and they expressed their sympathy to Lance for the inadvertent indignity. They seemed inclined to indulge the boy, but there were conditions. Lance knew there would always be conditions. Furthermore, he remembered Father van Reldt's allusion to the boy's 'delicate situation' in the confessional earlier in the term.

Lance had no idea that the boy was an orphan, orphaned moreover in recent and drastic circumstances. Alexander's circumstances were not generally known among the pupils. The information had only been entrusted to his form fellows and they, commendably, had kept their counsel. The purpose of the present summons was to apprise Lance also, so that he might conduct himself appropriately at Alexander's sick bed and not commit an inadvertent *faux pas*.

The information devastated Lance. He was visibly shocked and distressed, disproportionately so in the estimation of the two churchmen. Of course, he was caught off-guard and had had no chance to steel himself against the tragic revelation.

At the same time he realised he was vulnerable and that his manifest distress might jeopardise the priests' naïve facilitation of his anticipated friendship with the creature of his desire. He apologised for his sudden indisposition but the priests seemed sympathetic enough.

The upshot was that he was given leave to visit Alexander in hospital in Liverpool the very next day. Unbelievably, the visit was to be unsupervised and furthermore they advanced him the train fare and expenses on the spot. It was a relieved and elated Lance Raphael Lapita who found himself walking back along the colonnade with leave to go and the money in his pocket. His route back to his next period took him across the west end of the chapel nave via the transit ports. Here he made a special effort in elaborately genuflecting to the high altar, in contrast to the usual perfunctory obeisance accorded by most Monsalvations as they went about their daily occasions.

Lance made no secret of his good fortune although he was careful not to vaunt it as such. His form fellows merely congratulated him on having secured a day out in the big wide world away from the cloistered confines of Monsalvat. In the intervening hours Lance agonised over what would be appropriate dress for the occasion. Authority had accorded him a vacation from school uniform. He needed to impress his chosen boy but without overt ostentation. Of his several suits he decided upon a subdued clerical grey, with a white shirt and his favourite red silk necktie. Although the weather had flattened out since the incident he took a raincoat to protect his raiment from the vicissitudes of third-class public transport. Thus arrayed he made his way down to the station to catch an early 'local'. He would change at Llandudno Junction for a faster service to Liverpool Central via Chester and Birkenhead.

Walking up the hill from Central Station, Lance stopped at a barrow in London Road to buy a bunch of grapes for the young patient. Liverpool Royal Infirmary in Pembroke Place was a severe soot-encrusted Victorian brick-built edifice with long corridors smelling of carbolic. There were large open wards glazed in white tiles, rather redolent of a public convenience Lance thought. He was directed to the tropical ward where Alexander was languishing. Although the adder was a native species it seems Alexander's reaction to its bite had accrued complications which, it was thought, necessitated more experienced clinical care than was available at Bangor.

Having arrived at the tropical ward, Lance made himself known to the ward sister and gave her the name of the patient. Her response was cordial: "Oh, that's our little star patient." It was evident the boy had magic to work and had worked it to good effect with the staff at the infirmary.

The ward sister conducted him to the boy's bedside. "Alexander, you have a visitor." Then to Lance: "Only ten minutes, mind, he's still very weak." As she withdrew Lance wondered if this was a euphemism for something worse.

As he had walked the length of the ward the object of his great exercise had come into view. He had seen the tumble of wheaten locks against a bank of pillows. Now, at the boy's bedside, the moment of truth was upon him.

The noble young head lolled against the pillows. A pair of piercing blue eyes looked up at the visitor. The boy's face, so often seeming sculpted in flawless white marble, was now suffused somewhat and there was a large inflamed area on his neck where the serpent had bitten him. He made a faint attempt to raise his head from his pillows but was unable to complete it; it was clear he was indeed very weak. The boy's pyjama jacket was unbuttoned and Lance could clearly see the golden medallion lolling at his throat. He was minded to lift it off and fondle it but decided to, as it were, bank this asset for later.

Lance took a chair and positioned it right up against the bed on the patient's right side. He sat down and leaned in towards the boy, who brought his right arm from under the covers and extended his hand towards Lance. The movement seemed to take some effort. Lance clasped the proffered hand in his own right hand, palm to palm, and the little fingers curled round between his palm and thumb. The boy's hand, much smaller than his own, felt warm and moist.

Now the boy spoke and his voice was soft as velvet: "I knew you'd come."

Lance was devastated. What prompted the boy to make such an assumption? He decided to let him continue nevertheless.

"When you rescued me you called me by my first name. Are you still going to do that?"

Public schoolboys are punctilious as to mode of address. Surnames are *de rigueur.* The protocols are only breached in very extenuating circumstances — such as between brothers in private. Lance naturally held that such circumstances obtained.

"But of course I am... Alexander. And you must call me by my first name. Do you remember what it is?"

"No... You never told me." Lance promptly made good the omission. For the first time he heard his quarry enunciate his own name.

"Lance..." and then: "You looked after me when I was in distress. I'll never forget that." Lance's heart skipped a beat and he feared for his equanimity. This was going better than he could ever have anticipated.

"Of course I looked after you. What else could I do? I couldn't just leave you there." Lance thought it politic to qualify that statement: "Just as I would have looked after any of the chaps. One does the civil thing. You'd do the same." After ostensibly detaching himself with such a disarming qualification he homed in again with a daring re-qualification: "Mind you, I did think you were rather special though." He realised he was out on a limb and he waited anxiously for some kind of reaction. Alexander smiled the more; the smile was trusting and innocent. Lance felt the grip on his right hand tighten a little. It was now or never. He leaned forward and gently touched his lips on the little curled fingers. He felt as if his head would burst. He realised he could be dangerously over-extended and struggled to dissemble his emotions."There. I've done it. I suppose you'll now think me a sentimental old fool." It was a line he remembered from somewhere. As soon as he'd said it he wished he hadn't. He thought it timely to put out some bait. "Alexander... I want to talk to you about something. It's just that I have a brother. His name is Mark and he's about your age. When's your birthday, Alexander?" As if the date was not already seared into Lance's innermost being!

"June the twenty-ninth. I'll be twelve."

"Then he's a month younger than you. He can't come to Monsalvat; he had polio when he was nine." (Actually it was Duchenne Muscular Dystrophy; but this was no time to burden his prospect with medical detail.)

"Oh, Lance, I'm so sorry."

So far so good, thought Lance. He carried on: "He's a right royal rip, though. Full of mischief and fun, despite his disability. You'd love to meet him. I can see you and him getting along like a house on fire. He looks a bit like you — only a bit, mind; he's not as handsome as you." This was brave stuff. "We all spoil him, he's got a dog, a cat and toys galore — but he really needs someone his own age to keep him cheerful." Lance thought it politic to qualify his words again: "Oh and don't think you'd just be another pet for him. You'd still be Alexander and only ever Alexander. In your own right. Let's put it this way; you'd still be a full member of the household — even after your first fight."

Alexander laughed now; weakly, but a positive, reassuring laugh nevertheless. "What about after our second fight? Or our tenth?" He was wondering where all this was leading.

Lance was dismissive: "Mark and I have fights galore. He's still my brother though and I love him very much. Don't ever tell him I said that though."Alexander chuckled conspiratorially. "Oh and you'll also meet my cousins. Three girls, that is — and very pretty girls at that. Just think.., you'll probably have three girls fighting over you."

"Oh, Lance, your people seem fun. When can I meet them?"

Lance inwardly congratulated himself. More by good luck than good judgement he had so steered the conversation that Alexander was as good as under his family's roof. But there was another hurdle to be overcome. Lance visibly pondered Alexander's question before delivering the inevitable loaded reply: "That would depend on the Fathers. They're very wary about friendships between boys of different ages." He then continued as if a sudden wheeze of an idea had hit him: "I'll tell you what, what say I write to my people telling them about you? About your particular... err... situation? I'll suggest they write to the Rector asking if they can have you over the Christmas holidays. Not for me, you understand, as a companion for Mark. That's bound to work. Would you like that?

"Oh and by the way, we've got a big house in its own grounds; with a cook and a housekeeper and outside staff. We've got horses and ponies and I've already told you about the dog and cat. There's excellent fishing to be had — trout on the fly — and we can follow the hounds if you like. You can have your own room if you want, with a big double bed all to yourself. Oh, and we've got a ghost. Ghosts are just the thing for Christmas. You could rent them out if only they were amenable. Ours is friendly enough..."

"Stop, stop! Alright you've convinced me. What time's the train?" Alexander was clearly thrilled at the idea of spending Christmas with Mark and Lance and his cousins. But there was unfinished business yet. Alexander's demeanour returned to diffidence.

"Lance?"

"Yes, Alexander?"

"Father Laskiva told me I was sick all over you."

Lance laughed reassuringly. "Well, Alexander... if it were up to me I would spare your feelings by denying all knowledge of it — but I can hardly gainsay the word of a man of the cloth, can I? Don't you remember what happened? We were saying a Hail Mary together but you tailed off and I had to finish it for you. I asked you to say Amen and what did you say to me in return?"

"I don't know, what did I say?"

Lance smiled. "Instead of amen you said, 'I'm going to be sick.'"

Alexander smiled back and gave a semblance of a giggle. Then the giggle gathered momentum.

Lance seized the opportunity for a little harmless irreverence. Mimicking the sepulchral tones of the Rector as from the pulpit, he intoned the tail end of The Lord's Prayer:- "... for Thine is the kingdom, the power and the glory, forever and ever..." Alexander came in right on cue and both boys intoned the response in perfect unison: "I'm going to be sick." They were laughing now. Other patients in the adjacent beds were smiling indulgently.

Alexander continued the theme. "I'll never be able to keep a straight face again in chapel when the amens come along. If I'm taken to task for laughing I'll have to blame you."

The boys looked into each other's eyes and laughed long and uncontrollably until the duty nurse left her desk and came over to see what all the fuss was about. She took one look at the change in Alexander's demeanour since Lance had been with him and pronounced her verdict: "Why I do declare! He's quite perked up. We'll have this boy back at school before next weekend for sure."

Lance had enfolded the boys' handshake with his own left hand. She had never actually seen boys of that age holding hands before. But then she rarely came across patients as special as Alexander. She left them to it for the moment but indicated that visiting time would soon be over for this special patient. Lance had to work fast.

"Would you mind awfully if I looked at your medallion?"

"Of course not." Alexander made no effort to proffer the object, however. Heart pounding, Lance leaned in and plucked it off the younger boy's bare breast. Lance could feel the precious animal heat in it as he held it between thumb and forefinger. He could tell by the weight that it actually was gold alloy, probably eighteen carat. He turned it between his fingers. On the face was the standard *Agnus Dei* device of a lamb and a cross with banner. Lance held it and intoned the concomitant prayer under his breath so that only Alexander could hear:

'Agnus Dei, qui tollis peccata mundi, miserere nobis. Agnus Dei, qui tollis peccata mundi, miserere nobis. Agnus Dei, qui tollis peccata mundi, dona nobis pacem.' Then he turned it over and saw an inscription on the reverse: *'To Alexander with love, Maman and Papa, May 1949.'* He noticed the continental spelling but also realised he was on very unsure ground. He placed it gently back down again onto the boy's bare breast so that the inscription was against the flawless juvenile skin.

As he did so Lance became conscious of the still-inflamed blemish on Alexander's neck where the snake had bitten him. Insofar as he was versed in such matters, he could not help thinking that the blemish looked for all the world like a love bite. A thought came to him unheralded — would that he were an adder... but then he banished the repulsive and sacrilegious thought and inwardly castigated an aberrant psyche for having proffered it. He guiltily returned himself to propriety and the matter of moment.

"That must be very precious to you, Alexander. Maybe I shouldn't have touched it; I'm so sorry, Alexander, please forgive me." Lance's tone was imploring. Alexander became concerned.

"It's all right, Lance. There's nothing to forgive, I did say you could touch it." Then he added assertively, "It was blessed specially for me by the Bishop of Shanghai." Lance could only make a wan smile in deferential response. He felt he had been fortuitously extricated from a delicate situation.

It was time for precious goodbyes. Just then Lance remembered his grapes. "Oh, Alexander, I brought these for you." Then, seeing an already generous bowl of Tunis grapes on the bedside locker: "Not very original, I fear... All I could think of. Err... you seem to have a surfeit."

Alexander smiled. "Yes, Lance, Sister Gloria brought them in for me. Please don't think I'm being ungrateful but you can see I'm now rather down by the head with the bloody things. Perhaps you won't mind if I share them with the other patients." The gratuitous adjective and the boy's phraseology confounded Lance. He took the opportunity to return the boy's boldness: "'Rather down by the head'? What the bloody hell does that mean?"

Alexander enlightened him. "Oh, that's seagoing talk... down by the head.., down by the stern..." Here Alexander lapsed into a feigned pomposity: "...it means one's vessel is out of longitudinal trim. Hey, I must have picked that up on the *Antenor.*"

Lance shook his head in mock despair: "Along with a few choice adjectives, I note. Alexander, you're a closed book to me." They both laughed again.

Lance had established that for all his apparent religiosity the boy had a mischievous streak and was not on occasion above using terminology otherwise proscribed for Monsalvations. Upon such attributes and derelictions he felt he could build.

Bowing his head, Lance lifted his left hand off the enduring handshake and touched his lips once more against Alexander's curled fingers. His lips tingled as they impinged against the precious flesh. This time Lance felt no compunction in taking this liberty or necessity to justify this manifest display of affection. As if on a signal each released the grip on the other's hand and Alexander's forearm fell back on the sheets. Lance could now see tears beginning to well up in those piercing blue eyes at the parting. He leaned forward and whispered insistently:

"No tears, Alexander. Only happiness from now on. Remember... it's what your people would have wanted for you. Think ahead. Think of Christmas and leave it to me..."

Lance seized this poignant moment to introduce a matter of some delicacy and of no small importance to himself. To an eleven-year-old, even in early October, Christmas is a long time away. Lance saw an advantage.

"Alexander, if you like, you and I can meet again back at college. Perhaps once or twice a week. Would you like that?"

"Of course. But what about the Fathers? You say they're wary about friendships in college if we're different ages."

Lance had to be careful; he did not want to appear to be leading Alexander into breaking the rules. He would have to do his best to reassure the boy that the matter was of little moral or disciplinary consequence.

"Well, Alexander, I certainly wouldn't want to be seen to be leading a Child of Mary astray. Although I suppose I would be doing that... but only a little bit. And only in the eyes of the Fathers. They're inclined to be over-protective. As I see it, so long as no harm comes to either of us — and I can't see that it could — the Fathers needn't know. We would just be talking and planning ahead for the holidays. Would you like that?"

"But of course." Lance pressed the matter home without waiting for Alexander to respond further:

"I know a place... a secret place. Where we won't be disturbed. Can I tell you about it?"

"But of course," said Alexander again. He looked intrigued now and exhibited no hint of reluctance. It could not have been better. Lance began to discourse on the old peach house with its secluded peach yard, historically long proof against schoolboy 'scrumping' incursions. The long back wall with its double door and wicket gate. How to play the prominences in the wall, where the old bothy and the boiler house and the ivy outcrops obligingly stuck out, the better to conceal one's approach or departure. How to test the wicket gate by leaning against it; if it yielded it was safe to enter. Lance explained that he was in possession of a key that fitted the wicket gate. He omitted to say how he had come into possession of it. All-in-all it was all very schoolboyish and satisfyingly conspiratorial. Alexander was thrilled. He recalled Will Wepper and the *poste restante* arrangement. Perhaps Monsalvat wasn't going to be such a chore after all. Lance would have preferred to defer further advice but it was a now or never situation. Alexander would be discharged from hospital in a day or two and Lance knew he wouldn't have another unsupervised opportunity like the present one. He decided to set the conditions for their clandestine meetings in the peach house.

There were two curricular opportunities for the boys to meet. One was during evening prep. Both boys were exemplary scholars who could be relied upon to finish their work and get permission to leave early. But Lance was adamant that academic progress must be maintained; at the slightest falling off in performance, as evidenced at the monthly placement 'notices', the meetings would have to be discontinued. Form fellows came first; if there was an opportunity to help a form fellow with a problem, that must take precedence. Lance wasn't going to come between Alexander and his form fellows. He stressed that on those grounds not to turn up at the peach house was just as satisfactory; the one would know that the other was fulfilling the conditions.

The other opportunity was on games afternoons when there was some unsupervised time between the games period and supper. As a junior, Alexander was assigned a games day different from that assigned to Lance as a middle scholar. He would necessarily be passing the glasshouses on his way back from the games field and this provided an excellent opportunity for him to slip into the peach house on his way to the bath house. Similarly, Lance could arrange to be absent from prep on some plausible pretext.

And so it was agreed between the boys. The time had come for parting. Lance reached out and clasped Alexander's right hand as before. Once again he bowed his head and gently caressed Alexander's knuckles with his lips before letting the boy's forearm fall back onto the sheets. Then he got up to leave. As he walked the length of the ward he glanced back several times. While he remained in sight, Alexander never took his eyes off him.

* * *

As he walked back down the hill towards Central Station, Lance basked in an intense inner warmth. It remained now for him to write the necessary letters. From a hundred miles distant he felt confident he could manipulate his parents and the Fathers to suit his own devices.

Lance was not free of a lingering doubt however. He had just seen Alexander on his sick bed. He wondered, would the boy's demeanour towards him change when he was back at college and back to being a fit, running, gambolling, laughing, active fellow larking about with his form mates? Lance resolved to eschew such negative thoughts.

* * *

Lance decided to take the ferry rather than ride the train under the river. He alighted at James Street, took the elevator to street level and walked down to the Pier Head and the great floating stage; that same installation that had facilitated Alexander's auspicious journey towards him some ten weeks before. At the foot of the sloping flying bridge he crossed the timbered decking and boarded the Woodside ferry. Once on board Lance took the opportunity to use the toilet. This led him to the after end of the vessel's maindeck. When he emerged the vessel was springing off her berth and Lance found himself looking down into the roiling waters of the wake. His mind was in similar turmoil. He was beset by the miser's dilemma — how to both use and preserve the precious gold that the day had laid in his lap. He of all people knew that love, especially the love between boys of such disparate ages, was a fragile and capricious thing. Just then, the low boom of a powerful steamer's whistle rived his reverie. He looked up. As the vessel angled out into the open waters of the Mersey river, a brave panorama of ships was opening up — other ferries, tugs, tenders, cross-channel packets and ocean liners, all in line astern along the length of the great landing stage. Lance ascended to the flyingdeck to get an all-round view of the great river and its varied traffic.

At the far end of the stage lay the liner that was blowing her whistles. There were ten thousand farewells in that mournful sound booming out over the water and being reflected from the waterfront buildings. It was a place of departures and a departing liner is ever the reluctant chariot of a myriad final severings, past, present and future.

One thing was still puzzling him. Why had authority, in the form of the Rector and Father Fillery, so readily facilitated his unescorted visit to a junior? Then the liner blew again and in that dolorous chord the resolution of his mental turmoil came upon him with all the force of a tidal wave. His head swam and he had to cling on to the handrail to stop himself from falling to the deck. He could feel his heart pounding as if it would burst his breast and he feared it would throb to destruction. He threw his head back and gulped in great volumes of the salty air in the hope that this would return him to some degree of equilibrium. It did not. This was it! He must now live what was left of his life on a different plane. The die was cast. The signs were too obvious to ignore — the plaintive summons by the boy himself, the disconcerting forbearance of authority, the serendipitous serpent. Surely The Immanent Will had decreed; The Spinner of the Years had spoken. Here was the virginal boy, caressed by the mother, unsullied by the touch of the temptress; to be fixed forever in time, before the ingenuous perfections of childhood fell away and venality made its insidious incursions. Here too was the putative author of the boy's apotheosis — and by that same token the author of his own destruction. Each must be the nemesis of the other. Despite dark and fog, the one had found the other, as the fleeting bark and the static berg had found each other on the vasty waters of Life. It was upon him... The Convergence of the Twain.

CHAPTER TEN

In the Peach House

Lance had kept a key to the peach house ever since his last meeting there with Wepper. It had been several terms now and the passion which had once waxed so torrid between them had waned to a glowing ember. Cupid had sent his later darts off at a tangent and Wepper had transferred his affections to Rhiannon. Lance could not keep the key with his personal effects; every so often, or whenever they felt they had reason, the Fathers would descend upon a dormitory and search through every boy's personal effects. Every dormitory was open to such circumspect scrutiny but the middle forms were particularly targeted in that regard. Instead he kept the key cached about the property in some secret location, a location which he changed periodically just in case.

The peach house was a convenient place for clandestine meetings. It was but a short diversion from the well trodden path between the habitations and the sports field. Lance computed that meetings were possible on at least a weekly basis by dint of concentrating slack time between points of surveillance. The peach house was a private place. The glazed building was in some state of disrepair but it was still reasonably weather proof and it looked out on the enclosed peach yard, which itself was an enclosure bounded by high lime-washed walls. There were wicket gates in the walls but these had always been kept padlocked to deter 'scrumpers' and the place was thus secure from sudden invasion or prying eyes. Lance knew the staff work routines and when they would be off duty and out of the way. Wali Waliser, the remaining resident of the old bothy, was seemingly complicit in any case.

Lance could have had a copy of the key made and given it to Alexander — there were local locksmiths who would do the job — but he thought that inadvisable. He preferred to remain in control of the secret venue. Besides, the younger boy might not be as careful as he in guarding a key from loss or discovery. Wednesday afternoon was the ideal time for meetings. Wednesdays were games afternoons when a junior could drift desultorily in from rugby, cricket or cross-country without time pressing. There was no prep on Wednesdays and supper in the refectory would not be until six o'clock at the earliest.

As soon as Lance got back from visiting Alexander in the hospital, he wrote to his parents as promised. Homing in via the usual mundane stuff, he broached the delicate subject of Alexander. Starting from the traumatic circumstances of their first meeting, he laid the circumstances of the orphaned boy's situation before his parents in the most sympathetic light in the hope that they would rise to the bait. He was careful to mention his brother Mark, disabled and the same age as Alexander, stressing the prospect of mutual companionship.

He was not disappointed. A few days later found him frantically tearing open a letter from his parents. What he read set him walking on air. Here was his father telling him that he had written direct to the Rector offering to have Alexander as a house guest over the forthcoming Christmas holidays. Lance struggled to retain his composure. Inside he was ecstatically cock-a-hoop at the prospect of having manoeuvred that exquisite creature under the familial roof. Alexander! — all to himself or nearly so. Of course he would have to share him with Mark — and his cousins — but that would be a small price to pay. The two Monsalvations would dine together, bathe together, play together, go walking on the fells together. True, they wouldn't sleep together; in that he would again probably have to defer to Mark, but Lance felt he could live with that.

It remained now for the Rector to respond positively. Lance could not discount the possibility that there might be rival claims for Alexander's companionship. As far as he could ascertain, most of Alexander's contemporaries were, in Monsalvatian parlance, 'outlanders' — non-domiciled pupils the majority of whom would be consigned to the homes of guardians or to recreational camps during the long holidays, it being impracticable for them to travel to their far distant homes. Most but not all; there were a few who might have a better social lien on the boy than himself. The key factor was age. Lance considered himself fortunate that he could field a brother the same age as Alexander and a disabled brother at that. Surely in the event of conflicting claims the Rector must award him the sympathy vote?

The crucial Wednesday afternoon came at last. Alexander and he had had no further communication since their meeting at Alexander's hospital bed. Would the boy remember? Would he forget the venue? The time perhaps? Would some caprice of authority or school routine detain him? At the agreed hour Lance hied himself to the peach house and, making sure the coast was clear, turned the key in the lock and let himself in. In the absence of peach trees, none of which had survived wartime neglect, the peach house was used as a contingency store and there was a deal of garden furniture about. It was usually only taken out for college sports day. Lance set about meticulously arranging some of it so as to accommodate a twosome.

Both the peach house and the peach yard had seen better

days. The glazing of the long lean-to structure had not been cleaned or repaired since the six gardeners' boys had gone off to war in 1939. They had been replaced post-war by the two German ex-prisoners of war, Heini and Wali, but their duties had necessarily ranged elsewhere, functioning as they had as kitchen porters, groundsmen and general handymen about the complex. The peach yard, a much elongated rectangle, had been given over to soft fruit bushes and raspberry canes and these had been allowed to run riot, growing to some six feet and beginning to occult the light to the peach house itself. The riotous growth and the dirty windows, along with the old 'anti-scrumping' precautions of locked wickets and broken glass cemented into the wall copings, all conspired to make the long lean-to a secluded and secret trysting place for any who had a key. Lance thought he knew precisely who else had keys; William Wepper for one, and he was satisfied that the secrecy of his trysts would not be breached.

* * *

The furniture arranging done to his satisfaction, he made himself comfortable on a chaise longue, lit one of his perfumed Balkan Sobranies, counterfeited urbanity as best he might with a heart pounding within, contemplated the designated wicket gate... and waited.

Distant treble pipes told of the passage of Alexander's contemporaries beyond the long wall. Lance looked at his watch. The precious minutes were ticking away. Lance was by nature something of a pessimist and Burns' poem kept recurring in his fevered mind: *"The best laid schemes of mice and men gang aft aglay and leave us nought but grief and pain for promised joy..."* Was his lot going to be grief and pain yet again?

From Alexander's perspective the door in the long wall was

largely masked from oblique view by growths of wild ivy on either side of it. One could slide along the wall for some distance checking to see that no-one else was about. If others should turn the corners it would be an easy deception to continue on one's way as if in innocence of the door. The door itself was a heavy enough deal construction with rusted hinge straps and key escutcheon. Frame and door were well weathered in the sea airs of Pencadno and were at least a decade in deficit of a lick of paint. There was no knob on the door, just a rusted black iron bow handle located over the keyhole.

Alexander followed Lance's instructions meticulously. He had delayed his passage on the way back from the sports field so that for the moment there was no-one in sight. Once past the first growth of ivy he veered off the path to his right and flattened himself against the wall by leading with his right shoulder, turning his head the while to check whether any others were coming into view round the ivy growths. He reached the door; it was hung on the side of his approach. At some risk to his cricket whites he leant against it with his back. It yielded. Adroitly he did a body swing round the leaf so that he fetched up facing the door on the inside of it. The key was in the lock as Lance had promised it would be. Swiftly, silently, he pushed the door to and turned the key. Only then did he turn and look about him in the peach house. Already the perfumed scent of Lance's Balkan Sobranie cigarettes was reaching his nostrils. Everything was falling excellently into place. To his left was the end of a bank of staging bearing white lilies in large pots. To his right a stack of garden furniture towered over him. Before him was the glazed facade of the peach house with a broad shelf running along the glazing. Between the shelf and himself was a paved pathway disappearing right and left and presumably running the length of the structure. Beyond the glazing, in the peach yard, was a veritable forest of overgrown soft fruit canes as tall as a man. Alexander stepped forward from the door and turned right round the stack of furniture. The sight that met him was redolent of some well-connected person taking his ease on a Mediterranean patio.

Lance had opportunely appropriated some of the garden furniture and had laid it out on a paved area about a central table in a hospitable pattern. He himself was draped languidly atop the chaise longue and was beaming at Alexander with what he hoped was a reassuring smile. On the table top lay his gold cigarette lighter and a large cut glass ashtray supporting his elegantly long and charged meerschaum cigarette holder. The whole scene was redolent of a Rattigan play.

As for Lance, he now found himself confronted by a veritable little demigod resplendent in cricket whites.

Lance Raphael Lapita, feigning nonchalance, parked his cigarette in the adjacent ashtray and stood up to face Alexander Fragner Vudsen. He found himself fixed by the most intense piercing blue eyes he had ever seen. The eyes were set in the most alert and boyishly handsome visage he had ever clapped eyes on. The visage fronted a head noble enough to command the attention of a Canova. The head topped a frame redolent of the Polydeukion of Herodes or the boy of Kritios, notwithstanding the respective nudities would be masked in the present situation by the cricket whites. The Twain had Converged.

Immediately Lance was seized with misgiving. The creature before him was patently not the injured, frightened, vulnerable child of the cross-country course or the weakened waif in the hospital bed. Here was a natural boy at the top of his game. He was quite restored to his normal, virile, confident self, agile of movement and easy of address. The protocols had shifted, and not in Lance's favour. Lance cast his arms akimbo in a welcoming, inviting gesture. He was hoping that this might culminate in an embrace; but as the creature advanced in response, he hastily shifted to handshake mode. Thus it was that he greeted Alexander; as one might socially greet a fellow of no particular personal consequence rather than the light of one's very existence. The boy's hand in his was still soft and moist and dependently small nevertheless. And had he not arrived as summoned? Lance decided to brazen it out and motioned Alexander to the chair he had tactically placed alongside the chaise longue. Lance was nervously effusive.

"Welcome, Sir Alexander, welcome to the peach house. I see you have serendipitously tumbled through the Sire de Maletroit's door."

Alexander looked puzzled. Lance set about regaling him with the tale of the eponymous door and the predicament of the Sire's uninvited guest.

"And what happened to him?"

"Oh, he got married. But not to the lady to whom he was betrothed." At which the two independently decided not to pursue the increasingly diverging analogy any further. Matters of moment obtruded.

"Where's your cricket bag?"

"Oh, I got one of the chaps to take it up for me. It's all right, he thinks I'm going on to the tuck shop."

"Then you'd better take him back something to keep him sweet. A bottle of Sparkling Special or some such. Got any dosh on you?" Alexander shook his head. Lance chucked him a florin and the boy snatched it in mid-air, along with the intention. Lance had managed to shift the protocols just a little. Alexander had been playing for his Quarter and Lance asked him how the game had gone. It was abject small talk and Lance was impatient to progress his friendship with the boy. It was reassuring that Alexander was clearly intrigued that a senior of Lance's standing should take such an interest in him. Lance thought it time to up the ante.

"I've heard from my parents about Christmas. If you'll have us we'll be happy to have you."

He waited tentatively for the reaction; it was instantaneous. Alexander sprang up from his chair and came and knelt alongside the chaise longue, his excited face upturned towards Lance.

"Oh, that's great news! Oh thank you. Lance; thank you a thousand times!"

This was more like it. Lance looked down into those intense blue eyes. Then he put out his left arm to enfold the boy's shoulders. "Perhaps you might like to share a celebratory puff of a half-decent cigarette." Here Lance proffered the butt end of his meerschaum. Alexander did not recoil from this overture; instead he put his lips to the holder and took an inexpert puff that set him coughing. Lance was suitably solicitous of the boy's welfare. He shifted his hold and patted and rubbed Alexander's back.

"That's enough for now. I don't want to be responsible for setting your head swimming — or for you being sick again," he added with mock apprehension. At this, the recovering Alexander laughed. Lance took a chance and, inclining his head, lowered his left cheek onto the boy's tumble of wheaten locks. Again Alexander did not recoil from this further overture. Instead Lance felt the boy's right arm reach up round his back as if to enfold it. He could feel the little fingers warm and moist through the material of his shirt.

For a few precious seconds the two remained locked in this embrace. Was this just schoolboyish mateyness on the younger boy's part? No matter; it was more than enough for the present. Then they parted and Alexander returned to his chair. Lance was happy with the day's work. Had he not secured a chaste kiss on the end of the cigarette holder? A scented kiss, a kiss fit to be bless't of Eros and Morpheus (would that his exotic tobacco been laced with opiates)? He felt he was in control once more and it merely remained now to terminate the meeting without letting down the tension too much.

"We're not out of the wood yet, Alexander. Don't forget, the Rector still has to agree to your going. But I don't think that will be a problem. Right now, remember you've got to loop in to the tuck shop and pick up that Sparkling Special, you'd better get moving. Saturday?"

"Saturday," Alexander replied, then he added cryptically — and rather uncertainly: "I might have a surprise for you."

Lance was intrigued but time was pressing now. "Oh? I can hardly wait." Alexander would have to be content with that throwaway response for the present.

Lance got up and walked to the wicket gate. He gingerly opened it and looked left and right to make sure the coast was clear before beckoning Alexander forward and waving him through. He closed the gate behind the boy and returned to the arranged furniture. His heart was going like a kettle drum. It occurred to him he didn't exactly know what he required of Alexander. Of course he wanted his proximity; his company. But what else? His regard and respect, of course — and ultimately his love. But what kind of love? How was this love to be manifested? Those answers were not immediately available to him. And what was Alexander's surprise going to be? Tensions had been set which would have to go unresolved until their next tryst.

* * *

Part of the length of the peach house had at some time been fitted with three tiers of wooden staging over the ground where the peach trees had stood. This tiered area was on the other side of the wicket gate to where Lance had arranged the garden furniture. The staging was for plants in containers to be positioned on it so that they could be presented to the sunlight without casting their fellows into shadow. The tiers were under-utilised however due to staff shortages, most of the staging being left empty. Thus it was on the Saturday that Lance found himself seated among an array of white lilies on the highest tier against the lime-washed back-wall; and this at the behest of Alexander. A cluster of urns containing tall mature lilies obscured his view of the furnitured area on the other side of the wicket.

The wicket gate had given, as on the preceding Wednesday. Once again the youthful demigod had appeared before Lance Lapita. But on this occasion, cricket flannels had given way to more attenuated attire. Alexander stood before Lance in singlet and gym shorts. White ankle socks and plimsoles completed this brief ensemble. This was the standard rig for athletics on the sports field. Lance was treated to the sight of a great deal more of Alexander than on the previous occasion. He could see the *Agnus Dei* glistening on his breast. He also sensed that the boy was somewhat less at ease than on the previous occasion. Perhaps, Lance thought, it was the coolness of the weather and the brevity of the boy's dress.

Alexander had promised him 'a surprise' of some sort and Lance was naturally curious as to what the boy would do. What the boy did actually do was ask Lance to leave his chaise longue and take himself to the tiered area and there to take a seat on the highest tier. Lance languidly complied, naturally taking his ashtray and elegant gold lighter with him. From his position against the lime-washed back wall, Lance could look down on the wide walkway which ran the length of the peach house. Having seen Lance thus seated to his satisfaction, the boy retreated back to the arrangement of furniture and out of sight. From here he called out to Lance: "Close your eyes. Are you eyes closed?" Lance assured him that they were. "Put your hands over your eyes then."

Lance was intrigued now and getting impatient somewhat; their minutes here were limited and precious. What on earth was the boy up to? Away to his right, beyond a bank of containered plants, he could hear noises off; the unmistakeable fall of a plimsole, the snap of elastic...

Lance next heard what sounded like the faint patter of bare feet on the stone flags of the walkway. He certainly could hear the boy breathing deep and fast through his mouth, an unmistakably juvenile sound.

"You can open your eyes now."

"Alexander!" It was an incredulous exclamation from Lance.

The sight that met his gaze set Lance in a panic. There was the boy, proceeding from right to left before his eyes along the walkway. His arms were raised above his head and his gait was slow and deliberate, with a lifting of the knees in a prancing kind of goose step. He was looking straight ahead and he had a kind of uncertain half-smile on his face. When he had proceeded a few yards beyond the point where Lance was sitting he turned about and retraced his steps, perambulating in the same arcane manner. He was putting on a display. The performance was coquettish and provocative. And he was quite naked.

Struck momentarily lost for words, Lance pointed in the direction from whence the boy had emerged and he was eventually able to splutter: "Go and put your things on... this minute!" He sounded like an affronted nursemaid. The boy stopped in mid-prance and turned to face Lance. The artificial expression on his face crumpled, to be replaced by one of extreme concern and distress. What the boy said next pierced him to the very heart.

"But.., you're one of them.., aren't you? You know... they come for us at night... they make us do things..."

It took some seconds before the import of what the boy was

saying impinged on Lance. He responded: "Oh, Alexander... For God's sake, what are you saying? No, I'm not one of them. I'm in the Shell, you idiot. They're below me. Now go and put your things on. Right now."

But the naked boy stood transfixed. He suddenly realised he had overplayed his hand — and grossly at that. He promptly hid his face in his hands and burst into tears: "Oh Lance, I'm sorry, I'm so sorry, I'm so, so sorry..." The words tailed off into an unintelligible flood, obfuscated by sobs.

Lance stood up and took off his blazer. He stepped down from the high staging and sat down on the bottom tier. He held out his blazer towards the naked boy. His exhortations assumed a softer, more conciliatory, tone.

"Alexander, come here, come to me."

The boy moved towards him and Lance enveloped his naked form in the blazer and wrapped it round him. The older boy's blazer reached quite to Alexander's knees and his nakedness was no more. Their faces were inches apart now. With what he later thought was great presence of mind, Lance seized the moment to gamble with the affections of his prize.

"So it's my protection you want rather than my friendship." The words hit home; although as soon as he said them Lance regretted his punt. Pertinent though they were, they completed the destruction of the wretched creature before him. The boy saw all his hopes, all his aspirations for the future, falling away. He was struck speechless now but his half-hidden face told the story and he now sobbed uncontrollably. Genuinely contrite now, Lance pulled the boy towards him and held the face against his right shoulder. He buried his fingers in the precious wheaten locks. He leaned his cheek against the boy's head and spoke softly and soothingly.

"Oh Alexander, I shouldn't have said that. It was unforgivable. Here you are, a frightened little boy looking for help and here am I, concerned for my blessed dignity. Forget what I said, I didn't mean it; not in the way it came out anyway. You want my protection — you've got it. You want my friendship — you've got that as well. In fact, Alexander, I'll out with it and say you've got my love — my unconditional love." Lance himself was in tears of sympathy now.

The boys stayed in close communion for some time until the younger one became more composed. He lifted his face from Lance's shoulder and looked up with tear-filled eyes. Lance reached into his blazer pocket and pulled out a clean white handkerchief. With it he gently wiped away the boy's tears, muttering soothing platitudes as he did so.

"I'll tell you what, Alexander... Let's say this meeting never happened. Let's forget all about it and you can come here again on Wednesday just as if nothing had happened. Go and put your things on now. Be quick, it's time we were both elsewhere."

The boy went away still enveloped in Lance's blazer. Lance remained seated on the bottom tier of the staging while the boy put his games kit back on. And his *Agnus Dei*; it had not escaped Lance's notice that the boy had removed it before doing his preposterous naked prancing.

Lance retrieved his ashtray from the top tier of staging and re-lit his half-smoked Sobranie. The wreathing smoke helped him dissemble his emotions and compose his thoughts. His battle was not one for Alexander's soul; he regarded that as inviolate. Lance himself was ambivalent as to faith. He still clung on to the ways in which he had been schooled but he lately had the example of William Wepper to impart a healthy scepticism — or to lead him astray, depending upon one's point of view.

Nor was Lance's battle one for Alexander's body (not that he did not worship every fibre of the boy's being). True, happenstance had delivered Alexander into his power more than his own calculating design ever could have — but not in any way that Lance could have envisaged or indeed would have liked.

Lance no longer knew — if indeed he had ever known — what he wanted of Alexander. The fly was now inexorably in the web but the spider remained nonplussed. Of course he wanted the boy's love. But what form that love could or would take, he knew not. He was acutely aware that Alexander was a Child of Mary and, despite this latest dramatic lapse, must be respected as such. Furthermore, he could not imagine Alexander, however beholden, allowing another to take improprietous liberties with his person. But there again, the boy had actually offered his person. As it was, Lance had, in this moment of sudden crisis, not been found morally wanting. Clearly he had been seen to abjure eroticism— but he could not otherwise say in what direction their friendship might have wandered in the fullness of time. The hurrying bark had swerved from that particular berg, but the night was yet long and dark and the ocean still treacherous. There was now a certainty about their relationship of which, paradoxically, he was uncertain.

By the time the boy reappeared Lance had recovered his composure somewhat. The proprieties having been restored, Alexander relinquished Lance's blazer to its owner. Then he spoke.

"Lance, I must ask you a question."

"Ask away."

"A very important question."

Lance stiffened in apprehension; he had a shrewd idea of what was to come. "Go ahead; I'm ready."

"Lance, what is it that you want of me?"

There was a pause; each fixed the other with his eyes. "Not what the world might think".

"What is it that the world might think?"

Lance shifted his posture and looked ill at ease. "Alexander,

I can understand your misgivings. Forgive me but these are delicate matters for one of your tender years. The world would think that the lusts of the flesh are not to be denied. That it is imperative they are indulged. It does not have to be so; and it is not so between you and I. If that were truly the case, Alexander, then be assured, I would seek satisfaction elsewhere. When I see you before me I see Polydeukion. One does not — one cannot — seek fleshly satisfaction from the image of a god — nor yet a demigod, for that's what Polydeukion was. That would be sufficient; but there is more...

"You are a Child of Mary among other things. Your faith will be reinforced here. It will also be tested... but I am certain it shall not be found wanting." Lance continued, now with a discernible catch in his voice; in moments of stress he was inclined towards rather archaic phraseology: "Since you came to Monsalvat you have become a beacon unto me, a blinding beacon, unquenchable by any adversity. I quail before your image and your intellect and am minded to look to my own faith and my own worldly integrity. I have to measure up to, and reflect, what I see in you. You are become the very spur that drives me in pursuit of excellence. Ever since I've been aware of you I've striven to work harder, to look to my inadequacies, to achieve more, to measure up to your expectations of me. When you see me at the podium collecting another prize, when my name is read out approvingly at 'notices', it is you that I am reflecting. I do not do it for the world, Alexander, the world's approbation is merely incidental; I do it because of you. No, I do not seek fleshly satisfaction from your body. Yes, they say the lusts of the flesh are not to be denied but if that were so, they can be consigned elsewhere. When I see you, I abjure any such thoughts. It is your purity, your inherent chasteness, that is not to be denied."

After delivering this tense but necessary exposition, Lance was visibly trembling and tears were stinging his eyes. Archaic phraseology notwithstanding, he had spoken beyond his years. As to whether Alexander understood every detail of this unburdening can only be conjectured. He sat contemplating the spectacle of the distraught Lance for some time. Then he moved forward to put his left hand on Lance's shoulder. With his right hand he drew Lance's kerchief from the breast pocket of the blazer. With it he wiped the tears from Lance's cheeks with a concern and tenderness that was palpable.

But despite his discomfiture Lance Raphael Lapita still had an ace to play: "At our next meeting it is *I* who shall have a surprise for *you*. Oh... and we'll both be keeping our clothes on." Alexander managed to raise the ghost of a wan smile at this badinage.

Not another word was said. As before, Lance checked the wicket gate for passers-by; there were none. As he held it open for the scantily-clad boy to pass through, he chocked it off with his foot, leaving his hands free. As the boy passed before him he reached out and briefly cradled the boy's face between his hands. He leaned forward and planted a gentle kiss on the boy's forehead. He was now closer to Alexander in all respects than he could ever have hoped to be. He waved him through and closed the wicket and this most anguished of trysts was over.

* * *

Lance felt much exercised on the strange turn of events in the peach house. Alexander had cast himself down before him. In Lance's experience it was normally a gambit that he employed himself, in that it was himself who did the casting down. But, glory of glories!, Alexander had done that part of the job for him. Was this not evidence of some overarching 'Immanent Will'? Be that as it may, Lance now felt it incumbent upon him to rehabilitate Alexander.

He set to casting about for some means to accomplish this. He repaired to the college library for inspiration. After several false starts his eye lit upon music teacher Parry-Jones's prized collection of opera scores and libretti. Oversize and ornately bound, they occupied a special shelf outside of the glazed bookcases. Knightly virtue beckoned. Lance would imbue his fallen companion accordingly. He had a choice of knights. There was Tannhauser — but he was already a penitent knight who ended up dead. There was Parsifal — but Parsifal's path had been from folly to redeemer-extraordinary — and folly could not be Alexander's starting point. Lance eventually lit upon Parsifal's son, Lohengrin. Yes, Elsa's champion would surely fit the bill. Lance leafed through the libretto, looking for inspiration. Towards the end he came upon the denouement in the shape of Lohengrin's revelatory aria *In Fernem Land.* There was an English translation. Lance, an accomplished plagiariser, set to work on it.

* * *

Wednesday again. Lance had arrived first and had set out the mise-en-place of his 'surprise' for Alexander — a large glass vial primed with dark red communion wine and the stub of a candle. He had also brought an opulent leather container shaped like a small oval hat-box; and a set of patterned white linen napkins. The box had a sleeving lid, which was held captive by a looped carrying handle. By the time Alexander arrived in the peach house he had laid these out on the potting bench and had lit the candle. The potting bench ran the full length of the peach house under its front windows, except where two sets of glazed double doors into the peach yard interrupted its run.

Alexander surveyed this brief panoply. He was appalled. "Lance you've pinched the communion wine. Isn't that the blood of Christ?"

"Then it will do for us." Then, to assuage the younger boy's concerns: "Actually, it strictly isn't until it's in the chalice and been blessed by the priest."

Lance then turned to the leather case. Alexander could see that it bore the discreet legend *Lalique, Paris'* embossed on it in gold leaf; not that this meant anything to him. Lance unlatched the lid and slid it up the arms of the carry handle. This brought into view the upper part of an ornamental vessel. He reached inside and withdrew the vessel, then placed it on the potting bench. It was no ordinary vessel. Alexander's eyes opened wide in apprehensive amazement.

"Lance, what on earth's that?"

"That..." said Lance with some sense of considerable occasion "...is the Great Grail of Monsalvat-Pencadno." He paused to let this sink in, then: "You won't have seen it before. It usually only comes out at Eastertide and on special occasions. It's been here since the chapel was rebuilt back in 1880. Today is a special occasion for us so I've 'liberated' it from the sacristy for the occasion."

If Alexander was earlier appalled, he was now struck aghast. "Lance, you'll have us hung drawn and quartered!" Lance did not respond other than with a knowing smile and a further gesture towards the great artefact. Alexander duly contemplated this 'Great Grail of Monsalvat-Pencadno'. It was an imposing object of the jeweller's art, so finely fettled as to instil awe and respect into the most cultured and sophisticated of viewers, let alone a naïve young schoolboy.

Consider two perfect parabolic bowls of flawless and polished crimson carnelian of the most exquisite diaphaneity; the smaller inverted to form the base of the larger. Consider the two bowls seized together by an ornamental frame of pure gold, principally forming a vertical stem between the two vessels. Consider a decorative orb halfway up the stem. Consider an opposed pair of elegant serpentine handles, linking the two bowls. Consider the quadrupedal gold seizing around and over the lower vessel to be inset with an array of finely cut diamonds and rubies. Consider the whole set on a shallow plinth of polished ebony; the upper bowl some six inches in diameter and the whole some nine inches in height. Presumably the upper vessel in its simple unadorned symmetry was in replication of the Holy Grail itself, that simple cruse used at the Last Supper and at the foot of the Cross. This simple vessel was now mounted and embellished by the jewellers' art. The wan sunlight glanced off the facets of the stone insets and illuminated the translucent claret-coloured carnelian, suffusing it with a warm glow.

"When I say I liberated it I did so courtesy of the sacristan."

Alexander knew by now that the sacristan of the chapel was William Wepper and that, paradoxically, he was notoriously known as The Bold Contemner; he who never genuflected nor took Holy Communion. Otherwise, this was the first intimation he had that Lance and William Wepper were acquainted beyond the normal occasions of schoolfellows.

"It's all right to touch it. It's not consecrated or anything. Not until it's used for the Good Friday Mass. Just for heaven's sake don't drop it or knock it over or anything."

Alexander reached out and gingerly brushed his knuckles over the upper vessel. It responded by ringing almost imperceptibly. Alexander withdrew his hand.

"Sooner you than me. I'll not be touching it."

"Oh yes you will, Alexander. You and I will be drinking from it. Then it will be put back into the aumbry and no-one will be any the wiser."

It was at this point that Lance thought fit to embark upon the rehabilitative peroration he had composed for his young companion. He had rehearsed the heart of his speech and felt himself word perfect. First he needed to set the scene. Alexander saw him assume an air of pious solemnity. First he cleared the round top of the wrought iron garden table of its burden of ashtrays, lighters and cigarette packets. Then he draped it with a trio of the napkins. Lifting the Grail from the potting bench he carefully set it down on the draped table top. He then positioned Alexander opposite him so that the two were facing each other over the Grail.

"Alexander, I have something to impart to you. Something that will set at nought the things that happened the last time we met here." Alexander looked away, visibly pained at the unwelcome reminder. Lance felt for him. "I have a healing invocation. Look me in the eye, Alexander." Reluctantly, the boy looked up and fixed him with his piercing blue eyes. Lance launched into his prepared peroration in suitably silver tones:

"On this fair hill, which steps profane must not invest,
Stands the fortress of Monsalvat;
Within its walls, a gleaming temple,
Whose like for splendor is unknowable without.

Therein resides the holiest of treasures,
A vessel bless't with mystic strength
Carried down by an angelic host.
And tended pure by priests and boys.

Each year a dove is sent from heaven,
To ever reaffirm its wondrous powers;
The vessel is the Grail, and bless't pure faith,
Is drawn from it by its votaries.

The chosen ones who serve the Grail
It arms with all its supernatural might;
'gainst them all vile deceit is vain,
'fore them, the very dark of death must yield.

And one consigned thereto from distant lands,
To learn to use its strength for virtuous cause,
Cannot but then retain its holy power;
When standing unrevealéd as its knight.

So rare a thing the vessel's benediction,
So rare, it must be veiled from doubting eyes:
No eyes presume to quiz the secret knighthood,
For if the knight is named, he must depart."

Here the address shifted to the first singular — and would touch upon the delicate familial. Lance, for all his poise, was inwardly apprehensive. He paused to reach out and cradle the boy's left cheek with his right hand:

"In secret tryst I solve the secret question,
'Tis you were called among us by the Grail;
Your valiant father wore its diadem;
His knight you are, and Lohengrin your name."

The rehabilitation was complete. Lance gently withdrew his hand. Alexander stood silent and looking suitably impressed.

His eventual response was something less than impressive. "I seem to have acquired another name..."

Lance was not to be deterred: "Your secret name. Your knightly name. Known only to you and I. No other must know it." Alexander nodded solemnly.

Lance then produced a razor blade and held it in the candle flame to sterilise it. "Bare your forearm and give it to me. Look away.

He held the boy's forearm over the Grail, pinched the skin twixt thumb and forefinger and nicked it with the blade. Alexander winced and made a face. Lance squeezed a drop of blood from the incision until it swelled enough to drop into the vessel.

"Now me."

Coached by Lance, Alexander performed the same service for the older boy, efficiently enough. The droplets mingled in the wide bottom of the shallow vessel. Lance then took the wine cruet, removed the stopper and poured the wine onto the blood droplets until the vessel was about a third full.

"Now we each take three draughts. You first. You have to say the words first. Take the Grail by the handles and lift it to your lips. Say the words after me and take a sip."

Alexander reached out with both hands and grasped the handles. As he took the weight he exclaimed, "It's so heavy!"

"Yes, Alexander, that's because the frame's solid gold."

Alexander lifted the cruse to his lips, his wide blue eyes fixed on Lance's as he intoned a rehearsed invocation at Lance's prompting: "With this cup I thee bond once."

He took a solemn draught, making a bit of a face as the unaccustomed heady bouquet filled his nostrils and impacted on his senses. At a nod from Lance he placed the Grail back on the table. Lance then purposefully grasped the handles and lifted it to his lips so as to drink from the opposite side. He repeated the invocation and took a draught before placing it down before Alexander once again and nodding for him to proceed.

The second invocation ran: "With this cup I thee bond twice."

And so the ceremony proceeded. The last invocation took the form: "With this cup I thee bond thrice, while our two lives endure and beyond."

It fell to Lance to take the last draught and drain the vessel. He then took up the linen napkin and carefully wiped the vessel so that no trace of its use could be discerned.

Alexander looked on as Lance returned the Grail to its

container and closed and latched the lid. Then he spoke. "Have you done this before, Lance?"

"Yes I have."

"Then you must be another's blood-brother. How can that be? I cannot share you with another."

Lance moved to reassure the child. "Alexander, blood-brothers are like ordinary brothers — they grow up. As you are now so I once was. As I am now so he once was and so you will become. After I have graduated you will be free to initiate another blood-brother. Thus it is that the blood-brotherhood of Monsalvat will continue indefinitely."

Alexander was not to be put off: "Then I must be another's half-blood-brother. May I know who he is?"

"I am not obliged to vouchsafe that to you... as you shall not be obliged to vouchsafe my identity to any future blood-brother of yours when I am gone. Be content that there just might be another here in college who would take a superior interest in your wellbeing."

This pretentious taradiddle seemed to assuage the younger boy's doubts as to the intensity of Lance's regard for him. Lance's explanation seemed to imply that his elder blood-brother had graduated from the college and could therefore constitute no threat or bring no benefit to the arrangement just entered into.

The tension of the ceremony now over, Alexander returned to the realities of life at Monsalvat apropos the Great Grail and the wine cruet on the bench.

"You'd better get those things back to the chapel soon or there'll be hell to pay."

Lance made a face in mock horror at Alexander's use of the word 'hell' in the presence of the Grail, putting his finger to his lips in apparent disapproval.

"Alex.... ander! Language!" he exclaimed. And then: "Besides, don't you think heaven might exact the greater price?"

At this they both got the giggles and ended up falling about with helpless laughter, no doubt aided by the heady communion wine. Eventually Lance recovered enough to gather up the ceremonial accoutrements. Their lily-scented tryst was over and the two new blood-brothers made their discreet and separate exits from the peach house, their lives altered inexorably.

* * *

On the following Saturday something happened which, if not quite eclipsing the high drama of the preceding two assignations, introduced a darker note in the burgeoning relationship between the two boys. Once more the well-oiled hasp yielded and Alexander did his now familiar deft body swing round the door leaf, closing the wicket behind him all in one swift movement. There again was the reassuring aroma of Balkan Sobranie. There again was Lance, distributed along the chaise longue as to the manner born. Yet again did Lance stand to greet and embrace his younger friend. Soon their third tryst was tripping gaily along on small talk when Alexander noticed something on the potting bench opposite to where they were sitting. This time it was no Grail.

"What's that?"

'That' was a coil of gantline that Lance had purloined from the boat house weeks earlier. Comparatively heavy stuff, used for towing the whaler and suchlike. The whipped tail of the rope had been pulled out from the coil and it snaked along the bench for some distance before falling to the flags of the walkway several yards away.

Alexander was mischievous: "Have you taken to smoking old rope now?"

Lance laughed dutifully before ostensibly diverting his

attention to that which had elicited Alexander's curiosity. "Come, I'll show you."

Once again, Lance cleared the table top of smoking paraphernalia. He then picked up the tail end of the gantline and brought it over to the table top. With a practised hand he flaked out the gantline so that it tripled back along its length on the table top. Gripping the triple span in his left hand, with his right he then threw the tail end round it again and again; nine times in all. He then passed the tail end through the upper loop thus formed and pulled on the lower loop to seize the stub of the tail end in place. He then slid the knot thus formed to adjust the size of the lower loop before dangling the result before Alexander's eyes. There revealed to him with all its grisly implications was a classic hangman's noose. Lance noticed his companion's incredulity and breezed ahead with an explanation of sorts.

"Well you never know when you might need one. Mind you, if you're hanging yourself from a low beam you'd be better off with a running bowline. This one's really for breaking people's necks with a long drop." Alexander looked decidedly perturbed now. Lance looked down at him and began to reflect his companion's perturbation. He realised that he was the one who had overplayed his hand in the peach house now. If he was in jest he had gone too far. He had been flippant; careless, thoughtless, crass even. Had not Alexander had enough of death without having its grisly accoutrements set before him? Lance felt obliged to extricate himself from his predicament without making too much of a drama about it:

"Perhaps I shouldn't be showing you this, Alexander. It was crass of me. Please forgive me. I just though it an interesting knot. There's plenty of others I can show you." And then, unnecessarily and against his better judgement: "Just treat it as a joke."

He let the fashioned noose fall to the flags and reached out to gather Alexander towards him. The younger boy's response was to back away and laugh nervously. The tension was not quite relieved. Explanation notwithstanding, he still thought Lance's demonstration quite macabre. He became aware that his knowledge of his new-found blood-brother formed only a part of a whole; and, for him, that whole was unfathomable.

As for Lance, his contemplation of Alexander was essentially as an ethereal, a transitory, creature on a pedestal. A creature that must be seized in time — crystallised before venality inevitably claimed him. As for abject carnal lust (that juvenile predilection that so exercised the minds of the pastoral Fathers), insofar as Lance ever contemplated that uncontemplatable, such must never be consummated; for such consummation could only bring about an erosion of the respect for perfection and a diminishing of the exquisite tension that resided in their relationship. No, Alexander must only ever be the unclimbed peak, distant and tempting, the unsolved equation, ever intriguing and never wrangled, the impregnable fortress, always ready to spring a sally upon any who would invest it. But in that commendable philosophy inhered a latent tragedy for both protagonists.

* * *

In the dormitory that evening, a curious Tycho Gyles-Skeffington discreetly watched Alexander, in satisfaction of his own curiosity, managing to fashion a passable hangman's noose on the end of a spare shoelace. Belatedly becoming aware of Tycho's attention, Alexander instantly undid the knot as Lance had shown him by pulling the sliding arm of the lower loop upwards through the nine coils. The convolutes fell clear, albeit leaving a brand new shoelace kinked somewhat.

"Who taught you that?"

"Lance... Lance Lapita," was Alexander's unguarded reply.

Tycho was aware that the asymmetric friendship founded in an encounter with a serpent had developed somewhat. He now distinctly got the impression that there was more to that friendship than met the eye.

Indeed there was. Lance equated the virginal Alexander with perfection — and perfection with unapproachability. But Lance desired to approach. The requiting of his esoteric desire demanded imperfection in Alexander. In selecting Alexander's *nom de guerre* Lance had contemplated his options. Tannhäuser, as we have seen, was quite ineligible. Galahad was virginal in perpetuity, therefore perfect and therefore unapproachable. Parsifal had sired Lohengrin and therefore could not be virginal, could not be perfection, could not be Alexander. Lohengrin on the other hand was in legend merely unconsummated for the time being; his virginity was suitably transitory. Hence Lohengrin's estate was coincident with that of Alexander.

But it did not end there. Imperfection would have to be corporeally visited upon Lance's new knight — but Lance's philosophy prevented him from being the agency of such an imperfecting. Neither must any such imperfecting inhere in the knightly candidate himself. That was why Lance had reconstructed him with the aid of the Great Grail. No, that agency must be some other; external, random and capricious. At the Roman Catholic College of St Michael Monsalvat Lance would not have to look far for his agency.

CHAPTER ELEVEN

Deliverances and Doves

Saturday November 5th 1949. It was Alexander's first Guy Fawkes Day in Britain. He was used to occasional fireworks in the Far East but not to such a concentration of pyrotechnics as the commemoration of the Gunpowder Plot accrued in the United Kingdom. Monsalvat usually laid on a good show for boys, staff and indeed many of the townspeople; among other things the idea of this was to steer the boys away from the mischief that the occasion habitually caused. For several weeks the gardeners had been building a bonfire on the sports field near the chase gate and well away from the college buildings. The town's traders were under a standing request not to sell fireworks to Monsalvations but, as usual, this did not stop the more enterprising boys from getting their hands on quantities of firecrackers and rip-raps in anticipation of the big night. Such things as sparklers, Bengal matches and non-percussive cascades and fountains were actively encouraged however and, on the night, these would be freely handed out on the field from a central compound. The lay science master would be in overall charge of the main display which was laid out in a roped off enclosure. Head gardener Handel Trefor would work under his direction with Wali Waliser assisting.

The big day was a Saturday and the weather was amenable. Scant regard was paid to academic matters in the antemeridian and supper was a hurried affair before the boys began drifting over to the sports field for their disports and diversions. The last grey fingers of late autumn daylight had long since retreated from the mountain backdrop. Long before the bonfire was lit the college buildings and distant bosk echoed back the reports and flashes of firecrackers and the crackle of rip-raps. There was an exciting whiff of cordite on the chilly night air. Matters were running true to form if not true to plan.

The tuck shop was open later than usual and there had been a lively queue at the Bursar's office for withdrawals of savings and advances of pocket money. Alexander joined his form fellows in making their way over to the bonfire. On the way they walked past the long back wall of the peach house. Wali was evidently busy with the arrangements for the evening. There was a light on in the old bothy and the double doors of the peach house stood wide open. Alexander knew this was to facilitate the breaking out of garden furniture for privileged spectators. He knew this was routine for the occasion but he felt uneasy at seeing their secret trysting place apparently standing open to casual incursion. He wondered if Lance had the same misgivings; he would certainly be passing the same way. Hardly anybody else noticed and certainly nobody else cared. On the morrow the place would be secured as normal, the furniture put back in storage.

Scarcely an hour found them all standing round the raging bonfire at a respectful distance. All eyes went skyward as a particularly spectacular rocket arched over the spectators. Alexander felt a gentle tap on his shoulder. He turned to see Lance's face directed upwards and illumined by the glow from the rocket. Without looking down he passed onward. Their eyes never met. Nobody saw. Mutual love was satisfied for the moment.

The great bonfire roared, the 'Guy' was duly incinerated, chestnuts and potatoes were roasted and eaten, bottles of Sparkling Special were upturned and drained, shoes were muddied, eyebrows singed, fingers scorched and a good time was had by all. Elsewhere, in the covering darkness, several crates of Buckle Brand ale were smuggled onto the college estate via the bridge over the ha-ha. They were taken diagonally across the great parterre and into the redundant wartime air raid shelters hidden in the bosk on the far side of the old gym. Monsalvat's Irish Gang intended to round off the evening's proceedings with one of their inimitable 'cabaret nights'. The intention boded ill for the juniors...

* * *

The first Alexander knew of his predicament was when a gag was forced into his mouth. The blankets and sheets were roughly pulled off him and strong hands seized his pyjama'd limbs. He was turned face down, his arms were pinioned and he was frog-marched out of the dorm, down the stairs, along the corridor, out onto the south-eastern arm of the colonnade, across the carriageway and into the bosk alongside the old gym. He was not alone in his impotent panic; Tycho Gyles-Skeffington was to be his fellow victim. Frozen in fear, Alexander thought he would die, indeed wished he might die. Gagged with his own underwear, he could only make pathetic whimpering noises as they took him down to where the descent into the shelters yawned before him as the very gates of the Pit. As they carried him through he could sense a cloying smell of exhaled alcohol and the acrid reek of cigarette smoke. A raucous cheer went up as the two Removites were carried between a gauntlet of carousing Third Formers. Somewhere a camera flash bulb went off, recording the scene. As they were carried along the shelter the two victims found themselves looking down on a brace of canvas exercise mats placed end to end, evidently commandeered for the occasion from the adjacent gymnasium. The frogmarch ended in a curtained-off length of the shelter. Here the same rough hands eagerly stripped the pyjamas from the writhing bodies of the two juniors and they were set down on their bare feet, presumably to await some sort of summons. It was then that through the curtain they heard a voice calling out. It had a message and was purposefully more strident than those of the carousing array:

"Frankie, Frankie... the fire alarms are going off."

The shouted message carried through the noise of the general mêlée. There was much cursing, muffled and not so muffled. There was a scramble for the exits. One of their tormentors turned to the two juniors and motioned to the discarded garments around their feet: "Put them back on and make yourselves scarce. Go on, get the fuckin' hell out of here."

In a few seconds the two boys found themselves alone in the shelter. It behove them now — as it did the Irish Gang and their fellow-travellers — to get to their emergency muster stations before their absence was noticed. They did that. On the great parterre the two were castigated by an officious prefect for not putting on their dressing gowns. That they were also barefoot was hidden from authority by their peers crowding round them. It was a false alarm. Alexander assumed that Lance must be the instrument of his — and Tycho's — deliverance.

* * *

Friday November 25th 1949. Leport and his lieutenants were not to be so thwarted. Three weeks later another 'cabaret night' was arranged. They were always scheduled in secret. Whereas Guy Fawkes Night might have been predictable, Friday November the twenty-fifth was not. The same two boys were surprised again in their beds. The Irish Gang's *forts à bras* went to their dastardly work with a will and practised skill. The same dragging, the same gagging, the same frogmarch out into the frosty night over the same ground and down the steps of the shelters. The same raucous crowd of booze-fuelled Third Formers, arrayed on either hand down the narrow chamber of the shelter. There was the same popping of flash bulbs, the same ignominious stripping in the curtained-off chamber. At a shouted summons Alexander was propelled naked through the curtain, Tycho close behind him. The show was about to begin. The flash bulbs popped again. Foul Mouthed Frank himself was very much the master of ceremonies.

The ritual degradation began with a relatively mild imposition.

"Right, you, Vudsen, give us a fuckin' song."

"Aye, give us a song!" echoed the array. The imposition reflected the boy's prowess at singing the offices from the dome. Ominously, it told him that the Irish Gang knew him by name. It did not do to displease the Irish Gang — and in ignoring Pooley's summons both boys had so done. The two juniors knew that the Gang's ultimate sanction lay a few yards' frogmarch away.

Alexander gauged it was time for 'the song'. The song that Wepper had cautioned him to learn back in August. Naked and terrified though he was, he stood his ground, stared straight ahead and commenced to sing. His tormentors expected him to quail and fail as so many, to their cost, had failed before him. He didn't fail. Understandably his voice quavered and faltered but he forged ahead nevertheless:

"Hail, glorious Saint Patrick, dear saint of our Isle,
On us thy poor children bestow a sweet smile;
And now thou art high in thy mansions above..."

"Not that song. Not that one, you little bastard!" It was Leport who was interrupting him.

Alexander continued nevertheless:

"On Erin's green valleys look down in thy love..."

"I said not that song! Are you fuckin' deaf or something? Shut the fuck up!" Leport's voice rose to an uncharacteristic falsetto. His lieutenants began to suspect that there was more than just capricious aversion bearing upon their leader. As for Alexander, he merely closed his eyes and continued without pause:

"On Erin's green valleys, on Erin's green valleys,
On Erin's green valleys look down in thy love."

Leport was livid now. Drink contributed to the disassembling of his composure. He reached down into the crate at his side and withdrew a full bottle of Buckle Brand ale. Before anyone could stop him he hurled it at Alexander. An arm reached out to catch it but merely deflected it. The heel of the bottle struck the singing boy in the mouth. Shocked, he fell back against Tycho, who caught him under the arms and stopped him from sinking to the mat. Blood flowed freely from the corner of his mouth where the impact of the flying bottle had split lip against tooth. An incredulous gasp went up from the arrayed spectators. Things had gone very wrong. This was not part of the show. To put a mark on the face of a victim, such that it would be so publicly visible, was simply not done. Leport knew he had gone beyond the bounds of even his cavalier cavortings. He railed hysterically: "Get him out of here... get him out of my sight!"

That was it; the show was over. Whatever the intended proceedings were to be, they did not include abject battery of juniors. Leport's lieutenants were embarrassed by this excess.

In response to his frantic implorations, rough hands hauled the naked boy from Tycho's embrace and bundled him towards the exit. Tycho sidled apprehensively after him, surprised to find himself unimpeded by the Gang members. The two boys found themselves on the shelter steps under the stars in the chill night air. The door banged shut behind them; only to open a second later to allow their hastily bundled up pyjamas to fly through and hit Tycho in the back. Alexander and he grabbed the garments and fled further into the bosk, putting some distance between themselves and the air raid shelters. As soon as they thought it safe they untangled the bundle of garments and struggled back into them. Freezing and barefoot, the two boys gingerly picked their way out of the bosk and across the carriageway towards the colonnade. At Tycho's suggestion they made for the dimmed lights of the bath house. On the way they met Barden Sender and another boy, Catonsworth, who had come to look for them. On assessing the situation the two searchers turned about and went back to the dorm for slippers, dressing gowns and towels. Meanwhile, in the bath house Tycho took off his pyjama top, folded it, ran it under a tap and used it to apply a cold compress to Alexander's bleeding lip. The two searchers returned with the apparel. Leport's erstwhile victims washed the dirt from their feet and they were escorted back to the dorm. Both were shivering, Alexander the more so, from a combination of cold and shock.

Back in the air raid shelter Leport himself was fuming inwardly. His lieutenants were disconcerted to hear him muttering under his breath: "Damn you, Wepper, damn you, damn you, damn you..."

For him the language was disconcertingly temperate. He reserved his round rolling oaths and gratuitous obscenities for the trivial matters of the day. What had just happened was a much more serious matter and struck to the base of his very soul — that entity which he had for so long denied. His lieutenants knew that Wepper used to be an 'upliner'. They distinctly gained the impression that he knew more about Leport than Leport himself cared to know about.

* * *

Tuesday November 29th 1949, 10.00 a.m. "If I'm confronted with a bill for seven guineas for dental work I think I'm entitled to an explanation." So said Canon Peter Pynxcytte, Rector of Monsalvat. The man on the spot was Father Quedda, the Bursar. The occasion was the daily general convocation.

Father Quedda floundered. "I presume he got into a fight of some sort. It was Father Laskiva who took him to the dentist; I assumed he'd got all the necessary details."

All eyes swung down to the foot of the table. The named priest was somewhat wiser now in the politics of Monsalvat. His response was defensive: "It was Father Fillery who referred the boy to me. I assumed he had already elicited the details of the incident. I did not consider it incumbent upon me to go over old ground with the boy. I was merely the chauffeur."

The Rector was not to be put off: "But you must have spoken with him on the way. What did he have to say for himself?"

"Nothing."

"Nothing? You drove him all the way to Llandudno and back and did not converse with him at all?"

"Err... no Rector. He was injured in the mouth. He couldn't speak. At least not without considerable discomfort. I did not press him accordingly."

The matter was put back to Father Fillery. He testified that he only proceeded on the basis of what Godred, the duty male nurse, had entered in the medical log on the night of the incident; a document concerned with medical, rather than investigative, detail.

The Rector remained adamant. "I need to know if the college was responsible for the incurrence of this expense. If another of our boys was responsible for the injury, be it by negligence or design, I need to know that boy's name. I need to know the names of any witnesses. Kindly investigate, Laskiva, and let me have your report in the morning."

Father Laskiva knew the Rector was asking for the impossible. Boys do not tell, whatever might be the parity of the situation. More astute now, the priest suspected the Rector's motives; that he was gratuitously rnanoeuvring Alexander towards an eculeation for some concomitant transgression, such as dumb insolence. He felt protective towards the boy but found himself in a moral dilemma. He could not, in conscience, concoct an untruth.

His dilemma was resolved later that very day. It transpired that while the convocation was taking place one of the Third Formers — clearly one of the Irish Gang's many sycophants and probably acting under duress — had reported that a cricket ball in an aberrant trajectory had bounced up to land amongst a group of juniors and had injured one of them in the mouth. Detail was conspicuous by its absence but the account was perfunctorily accepted and the Rector's reluctant decision was that the college would absorb the expense. Father Laskiva thought the whole affair smacked of legerdemain but decided to keep his counsel...

* * *

The year was drawing to a close and the college became increasingly preoccupied with preparations for Christmas. On their next assignation in the peach house, Alexander was somewhat disturbed to note that two bales of straw had appeared just inside the wicket gate. Lance reassured him.

"Don't worry. These things are delivered in working hours and Wali sees them into the peach house. By the time we get here everybody's knocked off. We won't be disturbed."

Lance explained that the straw bales were for the construction of Christmas cribs "and to fill your manger".

"My manger?" asked Alexander incredulously.

"Yes, your manger. Yours and your fellow songsters up in the dome. Come, I'll show you."

Lance took him along the peach house to a point well beyond the staging that bore the pots of white lilies. They came to where a rough hewn timber frame was stored. It consisted of a rectangular openwork container slung between two robust X-shaped end pieces. It had rope carry handles at each corner. Alexander could see that it did indeed resemble a manger, although a little impracticable in terms of size.

A few days later Parry-Jones the music master did indeed divert the five songsters from the upper gallery of the dome. The five altos from the lower gallery of the dome were also drafted in for the occasion. The ten found themselves assembled in the chevet, that rectangular space circumscribing the drum of the dome and the chancel plateau. They were to be rehearsed in the ancient processional carol *Vom Himmel hoch, o Englein kommt.* Since it was the second year of the teaching of German at Monsalvat it had been decided that the carol would be sung in its original language. Carol sheets were handed round and after the practice the boys were instructed to learn the words by heart in the interval between rehearsal and the event itself.

The next evolution was a rehearsal of the full choir, including the monks of Basingwerk, in the assembly hall. There was a problem in that those choristers from the Thirds and above had not been taught German. The postulated solution was to sing the carol as an antiphon, giving the narrational lines to the ten songsters who had been receiving instruction in German since their arrival at the school. This left the rest of the choir with a line of sonorous 12th-century nonsense words and a couple of 'hallelujahs'. It would be a mere bagatelle to instruct them to pronounce these in the German manner; indeed, that could be done on the song sheet.

The final evolution was to rehearse the procession itself. For this purpose the ten boys from the dome were directed to the colonnade where they were assembled just below the steps leading up to the south transit port adjacent to the great west door. Sure enough, there was the manger, brought from the peach house, but now it was filled with straw, the straw cradling a candle lantern symbolising the Christ-child. There also was Sister Henrietta and two more of the nuns. They were there to fit up the boys with beatifying long white gowns. There was much flourishing of tape measures and fussing about with pins and marking chalk over the taking up or the letting down of hems. It seemed that boys inconveniently grew and were replaced by others of differing stature and the same rigmarole had to be gone through anew each twelvemonth. Once the boys were all angelically gowned, albeit provisionally held together by pins and tack stitches, it was Mr Parry-Jones who took over the show, assembling the newly created seraphs around the manger.

Parry-Jones stationed a boy at each corner. Alexander found himself leading at the left hand side, which meant he had to grasp the rope carry handle with his right hand. The spare boy of the five was directed to lead, carrying a minor processional cross. Of the five altos, older and taller than the Removite sopranos, one was to bring up the rear with the censer and the other four were placed on the wings with tall processional candles in brass sconces.

Before proceeding into the chapel, the four manger carriers practised marching up and down the colonnade, leading with alternate feet so as to keep the manger steady. They then had to rehearse carrying it up the short flight of steps leading up to the transit port without disensconcing the symbolic candle and possibly setting light to the straw. When all that was done to Parry-Jones's satisfaction he re-assembled the ten choristers and marched them up the steps and into the chapel. Here they had to do an obtuse-angled turn into the centre aisle before proceeding along the nave and up the two shallow steps onto the chancel plateau, to arrest before the high altar.

Cadence was all-important. Parry-Jones stood to one side and beat time and the boys stepped out with a slow and stately processional march. Markers were determined along the processional route so that the carol would be completed just after the halt on the chancel plateau. The rest of the choir were not present for this particular evolution; it was agreed that as long as the ten boys in white were setting the pace it could safely be left to the rest of the choir to shuffle along after them in no particular order. As to musical accompaniment, Blackhurst, a prefect and organ scholar, was at the console for the rehearsal and would be there for the event itself. This left Parry-Jones free to supervise the procession. These rehearsals all seemed to go satisfactorily. But Monsalvat's music master had other rehearsals to conduct.

* * *

"I'm fucked if I'm going to stand there and be kissed by De Leapey."

"I'd say there's a good chance of both."

This had the rest of the Remove 'A' dorm falling about laughing at the first speaker's discomfiture. That first speaker was Barden Sender; the respondent was Tycho Gyles-Skeffington. It was not that such young boys habitually disregarded the proprieties, it was just that the occasion presented the opportunity for some bravura precocity. Despite their apparent urbanity each knew he was speaking beyond his years. Some of the bolder boys occasionally resorted to obscenities, but, significantly, hardly any to profanities. The spectre of eternal damnation still hovered.

The event which triggered the present outburst arose from the forthcoming production of *The Adventures of Robin Hood* as part of the end of term entertainments. The seniors, which for this purpose meant the Fourths, Fifths and Sixths, would be doing Shakespeare's *Henry V* which conveniently tallied with the current exam syllabus. The Thirds and below had been auditioned for the *Robin Hood* production. For reasons of height if nothing else, only two Removites had made it onto the final casting list. Barden had drawn the short straw and found himself playing a winsome Maid Marion to De Leapey's robust Robin. Tycho was cast in the role of the diminutive Much.

Barden railed on: "Ol' Crotchets only told me about it at the dress rehearsal." Old Crotchets was the nickname of Parry-Jones, music master and director of both performances. "He did that deliberately; he knows damn well it's too late now to rehearse someone else for the part."

Tycho feigned sympathy for Barden's predicament: "I'll see what I can do to save you from a fate worse than death."

This drew yet more laughter from the array.

* * *

Came the day of the performances. *Robin Hood* was to occupy the first part of the evening's entertainments. The assembly hall had filled with Monsalvat's boys, a few of their parents, the pastoral Fathers and senior teaching staff members. An array of invited local dignitaries graced the front row.

The final scene was imminent: hitherto the wicked Sheriff of Nottingham had been appropriately vanquished and King

Richard had been restored to his throne. *The Adventures of Robin Hood* was reaching its romantic climax. Now there were troths to be plighted and the air of expectancy was palpable. This time however the scene change seemed delayed somewhat...

In an adjacent washroom a strange encounter was taking place. Barden, now pulchritudinously resplendent in very fetching wig and white satin gown, stood facing De Leapey who was clad in a Lincoln green tunic and matching tights and was suitably accoutred with horn and dagger. Between them was a small trestle table. On the table top stood a jug of water, two glasses and a bottle of TCP antiseptic. Looking on and consumed with impatience was 'old Crotchets' himself. Voluptuaries notwithstanding, it was clear there was little love lost between the two players. Each watched balefully as the other tilted a glass of dilute TCP into his mouth, gargled for a full and timed ten seconds and then expectorated the liquid into an adjacent wash hand basin. This procedure had to be repeated two more times before each antagonist considered himself satisfied with the other's oral hygiene. The whole procedure was redolent of a duel, with Parry-Jones acting as umpire: "Can we get on with it now?" he fulminated.

* * *

Eventually the curtains parted to reveal a brightly lit sylvan scene. The merry men were arrayed on either hand, appreciatively watching as Maid Marion and Robin engaged in lyrical dialogue centre stage. The audience were suitably enthralled. Except, that is, for some insidious tittering. It seemed that Tycho, in the role of Much, had caught the attention of much of the audience. Standing stage left rear, he was rolling his head, pulling faces and rolling his eyes in response to the more tender points of the dialogue. The tittering became louder. The fatal kiss was imminent.

Without warning, Maid Marion turned from her Robin and exited stage left. The action stood pregnantly paused. A moment later a satin clad arm reached out from a convenient break in the backdrop and cuffed Tycho on the back of the head. The upward swipe of the admonishing hand dislodged his feathered cap and it fell at his feet. The audience gasped incredulously. The next thing they saw was Tycho's inimitable looking of pantomime daggers at, presumably, his retreating admonisher. It was this, more than anything, that threw the audience into paroxysms of barely suppressed laughter. Another moment saw Maid Marion re-emerge stage left to resume the dialogue as if nothing had happened. The audience greeted the lady's reappearance with a cheer.

But it was all over for De Leapey's Robin. After a few faltering re-starts he clapped his hand over his mouth and turned away from the audience, convulsing with involuntary laughter. Other members of the cast became similarly afflicted. Eventually the only straight faces on stage were those of Tycho and Barden. Romance had degenerated into high farce. It was clear the final triumphant chorus would have to be abandoned. All Parry-Jones could now do was to signal frantically for the final curtain. To his further chagrin, when the somewhat abashed cast came forward to make their customary bows and take their plaudits, it was Tycho and Barden who were accorded the loudest cheers.

The fatal kiss had been averted. But that could not be an end of the matter. The two Removites had outrageously upstaged one of Foul Mouthed Frank's lieutenants. It was in the nature of things at Monsalvat, at the junior end at least, that Foul Mouthed Frank staged the jokes and the rest laughed to order. It did not do for others to usurp that prerogative. There would have to be consequences.

* * *

Thursday, December 22nd 1949 was the day of the carol service. It would start with a hearty breakfast, some free time and then the traditional carol service, followed by festive fare in the refectory. On the morrow there would be a boisterous dispersal to homes and guardians. In the days before the event, boys and staff had been set to constructing cribs at strategic points around the college. Decorations had been put up in the refectory and dormitories and Christmas trees got in, erected and decorated. At the kitchens, hampers arrived daily from Ireland, their contents a welcome augment of the meagre rations of post-war Britain. All-in-all, it was going to be an excellent Christmas at Monsalvat. Individually, the boys set to writing Christmas cards to relatives, favoured members of staff and, rarely, other boys. Alexander favoured Wali, Godred and Geddington and Father Laskiva in that particular. Of course he would have liked to favour Lance also but caution counselled circumspection short of that point. Certainly he had no-one to write to beyond the walls of Monsalvat. According to the Rector, the Edgars, the couple who had looked after him on board the *Antenor,* had not fulfilled their promise to write to the college.

* * *

In the free time before the carol service, Alexander found himself being paged to the Rector's chambers by another of the Cardinal's Men. His heart missed a beat. This surely must be it, the decision had been made; whether he was to stay miserably in house or to spend Christmas with Lance and his family in the wilds of west Cumberland. Ever the optimist, he did not steel himself for disappointment. He hurried to the presbytery without more ado. Once again he found himself before the great oak panelled door. Once again was it ajar and once again did he knock and once again was he summoncd by that great imperious voice.

He entered, leaving the door ajar. Once again there was the seeming endless ocean of purple carpet to be traversed before he found himself looking across the great ornamented desk at the august arbiter of all their fortunes. Alongside the desk stood Father Laskiva. Both faces beamed down at him; he felt relieved and optimistic. Then the Rector began to address him in measured tones:

"The application of Lapita's parents for you to stay with their family over the Christmas holidays has been carefully considered in pastoral conclave. I am able to tell you that a decision has been made. It has been made in your own best interests. Lapita himself has already been informed of the decision."

Alexander felt much concerned now. The Rector was addressing him in a most formal manner, seeming to prepare him for some bad news. Surely he must not have to steel himself for yet another cruel disappointment? But the Rector seemed to be having a game with him.

"I am able to tell you that the application has been approved. You may go to the Lapitas for Christmas with our blessing." Alexander felt his heart turn into a bouquet of roses and float up through the panelled ceiling and into the clouds beyond. He had to struggle not to let too much emotion show. He showed due elation nevertheless and Father Laskiva saw his eyes grow large and shine like beacons. In order to mask an improprietous excess of elation he responded in rather an unorthodox manner. He executed a long, low and elegant bow to the Rector. The two surprised clerics presumed it was some custom he had picked up in the East.

Alexander straightened up with his eyes closed; he spoke almost inaudibly: "Thank you Father."

He looked as if he might continue but fortuitously the Rector cut him short with a timely homily. To Alexander's surprise he found himself being addressed by his first name.

"At holiday time I pray for the health and happiness of all my boys, Alexander, but for you I shall keep a special place in my heart. Were it possible I would strive to shoulder some portion of the sadness that lies on your brave little heart. But we know that this is never possible. Grief is a lonely furrow and, when the Lord in his infinite wisdom burdens us with it, we must plough it alone. But otherwise, Alexander you are never alone. You are in our hearts and prayers every day. I can only counsel, Alexander, that in your darkest moments you must remember that you are your mother's treasured son and your father's representative on this earth. People will expect you to carry forward the good works and strengths of character that they imparted to you. I am sure you will not be found wanting. Go now and enjoy your Christmas holidays with the Lapitas. I know they will do their very best to make it as happy as it could be for a boy who has been burdened beyond his years. But enough of melancholy. Have a very merry Christmas, Alexander, and let's look forward to a happy and successful New Year for you at Monsalvat." Father Laskiva felt emboldened enough to add to his superior's felicitations: "Yes, Alexander; a very merry Christmas to you and a happy New Year. Go with God."

Alexander took this to mean that the interview was over and, more than somewhat relieved, he turned about and made for the door. At the door he turned about and bowed once more before exiting. The two clerics were intrigued.

Back among his own, the change in Alexander's demeanour was enough to let them know the good news. He now felt able to disclose the details. Of course the assumption was that his good fortune stemmed solely from the day of the serpent and he did nothing to disabuse his form fellows of that. Assignations in the peach house and blood-brotherhood must reside forever in the shadows. They in their turn were uninhibitedly happy for him and crowded round to smite his shoulders approvingly and to shake his hand on the matter. It was a rare scene for supposedly reserved 'English' schoolboys but Alexander seemed to have that effect upon people.

* * *

The chapel was packed. Some parents and guardians had come to collect their offspring and the pews at the west end of the nave had been augmented with stacking chairs to accommodate them. The boys would take their normal seats in the pews. Song sheets had been printed and distributed. A large Christmas tree stood inside the great west door opposite a most elaborate crib and two more trees were positioned on the chancel plateau, framing the high altar. A profusion of flowers and luxuriant green foliage and many candles in colourful lanterns made the chapel a most welcoming place.

The choral procession was assembled in the colonnade and was brought up the steps and through the south transit port to stand just inside the great west door. The great double doors had been closed; entry now could only be made via the transit ports. The candle flame in the manger, symbolic of the Christ-child, was lit with due deference and a prayer. In the transept the Rector ascended to the pulpit and, as per tradition, bade the congregation rise to their feet. Parry-Jones stood at the foot of the nave to give the signal to Blackhurst in the organ loft. An expectant hush quieted the congregation. Parry-Jones's baton came down and Blackhurst executed the introductory bars. The point of no return had been reached. The ten boys in white stepped out in formation and commenced the opening line: *"Von Himmel hoch, o Englein kommt":*

And Colly selected that moment to circle down from the

dome, fly along the nave and, with a flurry of wings, alight on Alexander's head. A few seconds later and she transferred herself to his right shoulder. The beat of her wings had alerted the congregation and many heads turned. It was too late to do anything about it, presuming anybody knew what to do. As for the visiting parents, they assumed it was all part of the show. When the dove landed the procession had yet to execute the obtuse-angled turn into the centre aisle. On the apex of the seating opposite stood Wepper. His eyes met with Alexander's. In his anonymity he smiled and winked. As to the carol, the rest of the choir responded on cue:

"Eia, eia, susani susani su su su"

Clear as a bell, avian adventures notwithstanding, the ten boys in white rendered the third line:

"Kommt singt und klingt, kommt pfeift und trombt"

Equally undismayed, the rest of the choir, now backed up by the congregation, made the response:

"Hallee-lujah, Hallee-luja"

All the while Colly sat quiescent on Alexander's right shoulder. The snow-white dove eclipsed the whiteness of the bleached gowns worn by the ten songsters. Impotent authority decided to do nothing and hope for the best.

The best prevailed. The procession proceeded, the unexpected, uninvited dove complementing the angelic figures in white. The ten completed the verse:

"Von Jesus singt und Maria."

Blackhurst at the organ console followed with the conjunction which gave the five sopranos the timing for the opening of the second verse:

"Kommt ohne Instrumente nit
Eia, eia, susani susani su su su
Bringt Lauten, Harfen, Geigen mit
Hallee-lujah, Hallee-luja
Von Jesus singt und Maria."

By this time the procession had drawn level with the pews of the Shellites and Third Formers. Lance, taking advantage of the displacement of bodies arising from the presence of parents and guests, had taken a place next to the aisle at the end of his pew. The procession inexorably brought the two friends into a fleeting proximity. Alexander was conscious of Lance's discreet smile to his left, a gentle smile only for him. Mindful of his present very public duties — not to mention the disconcertment of having a dove on his shoulder — Alexander could only respond with a fleeting glance to his left when his eyes briefly met those of Lance. All too soon the moment was past and the sopranos were into the penultimate verse:

"Lasst Hören euer Stimmen vie
Eia, eia, susani susani su su su
Mit Orgel und mit Saitenspiel
Hallee-lujah, Hallee-lujah
Von Jesus singt und Maria."

Then came the rather tricky negotiation of the two shallow steps leading onto the chancel plateau. The procession came to rest before the high altar. The four boys carrying the manger could now gently rock it back and forth as they opened the final verse:

"Singt Fried den Menschen weit und breit
Eia, eia, susani susani su su su
Gott Preis und Ehr in Ewigkeit
Hallee-lujah, Hallee-lujah
Von Jesus singt und Maria."

Their processional duties now complete, the manger was gently set down before the altar and, as rehearsed, the ten boys ceremoniously filed off to right and left. Once out of sight of the congregation they hurried round the chevet to where the iron staircase started for the dome, discarding their white gowns on the run as they did so.

Not so Alexander. Colly stayed in situ on his right shoulder all the while as he warily ascended to his place in the upper gallery of the dome. She had remained on her best behaviour throughout the procession. Now she gave a gentle nuzzle of her beak against Alexander's ear before hopping off his shoulder and onto the handrail. She then waddled round the gallery on the handrail to a point opposite the five sopranos and there she remained until the end of the carol service. Authority would later decide that such entertaining avian diversions in the chapel of Monsalvat ought not to be countenanced...

CHAPTER TWELVE

The Curse of the Lapitas

Christmas Eve 1949: Lance basked now in the warmest glow of contentment that could ever wash over a human being. He had cast his hook, played his catch expertly and had landed it eminently satisfactorily. On this auspicious eve the most perfect being ever fashioned by the Hand of God lay sleeping under his roof. Or rather his parents' roof, but he thought that of little consequence. It was sufficient. It was his parents who had suggested that Mark should move into the guest room with its large double bed so that Alexander could sleep with him. Both Alexander and Mark were agreeable and so it came about. Lance loved his younger brother and was in no way jealous of him in this particular. He felt that Mark with all his health problems was entitled to any and all the benisons that came his way. Alexander was a benison *par excellence*.

Lance had been under intolerable strain during the preparations for the holiday, trying to appear nonchalant and matter-of-fact when all the time he had been walking on air. He could not betray his euphoria to his contemporaries and certainly not to the Fathers, lest they suspect there was more to their relationship than met the eye. As far as the Rector was concerned, Alexander was being put up over the Christmas holidays as a mutually beneficial arrangement apropos Mark. Without Mark it is extremely doubtful whether the Rector would have allowed it, given the age difference between Alexander and Lance.

It was Alexander's first Christmas away from the Far East. The old house was decked out in all the panoplies of the season complete with Christmas tree, decorations and a veritable jumble of presents awaiting their joyful recipients. When the boys had arrived, Lance's three female cousins were already in residence as guests for the holidays. On the requisite introductions being made it was clear that the trio was enraptured by the boy Lance had brought with him. The Lapitas had made a special effort for their young male guest. Gently and at an opportune moment, Lance's father let it be known to Alexander that he was there in his own right and not merely as a companion for Mark, and that he was to consider himself to be at home in all respects.

The boys had been met at Carlisle's Citadel station by Lance's parents. From there they had been driven the dozen or so miles to the family seat, *The Purpress,* in the Gurney Nutting drophead Wraith. The choice of transport was at Lance's insistence. There was also a Riley 1.5 saloon in the garage but Lance did not consider that a fitting conveyance for such an auspicious occasion. The Wraith was pre-war but was still going strong. Alexander rode in style with Lance in the rear seats as befitted an honoured house guest. The Wraith had ample room in the boot for the boys' luggage. This included hatboxes, for straw cadies did not travel well unpacked. Lance had his trunk with him with personal effects 'all up' as per Monsalvat's regulations for holiday vacations. Alexander was allowed to leave with only his valise and hat box. They allowed him to leave his steamer trunk and contents at the college because Monsalvat was the only discernible home he had in the United Kingdom.

Immediately upon arrival there was much fussing of dogs

and other animals. Toby, the Jack Russell, clearly had not forgotten his young master and responded with a hysterical display of barking and tail wagging. Meanwhile Sukie the cat had, uncharacteristically for her species, condescended to an immediate and lasting friendship with Alexander by way of loud purring and a prolonged winding about his ankles.

After the turmoil of reception and introductions and a memorable and expansive dinner, it was agreed that an early night was advisable for the new arrivals and they were despatched to their rooms upstairs accordingly.

The boys found themselves alone together at last and Lance took his chance. He held out his arms towards the younger boy. "Come," he said gently. Alexander went to him and was gathered in to the older boy's breast, Lance's right hand against his cheek. Lance sighed with an infinite contentment and breathed: "Oh Alexander... God knows, Alexander, I love you so much. We've got to go back to that dreadful place but for now I have you safe under our roof and I can look after you as you should be looked after."

Alexander looked up into Lance's eyes: "I love you too, Lance. I wish this could go on for ever and ever..."

Lance spilled out his plans for the holiday. "Tomorrow we'll wrap up warm and go walking in the woods with Toby and you can throw sticks for him. He likes that game. You can push Mark in the wheelchair. Don't worry, I'll give a hand on the hills," he added with a smile. Next day we're to go shopping in Carlisle and in the evening we'll attend mother's choir concert. On Christmas Eve we'll go carol singing with a lantern and everything. There'll be mince pies and mulled wine going at some places. Then it's midnight Mass and home to bed. You can get up when you like, but it'll be Christmas Day and we can open our presents. Then we'll have a slap-up Christmas Dinner. Oh, Alexander, we'll make sure our house is the bestest place for you to be for Christmas — and for ever!" Each face reflected the joyful anticipation of the other.

Alexander was intrigued by the name of the family seat. Lance's response to his curiosity was tantalising: "Listen to my father at Christmas dinner — he's bound to come out with the old anecdote."

Alexander would just have to wait for enlightenment in that particular.

* * *

And so the old clock on the landing ticked; the warm old house gently creaked; and Lance luxuriated in his wide and warm bed knowing that next door the beautiful boy lay with Mark. He lay looking at the intricate mouldings on the bedroom ceiling as he idly pictured the two angelic heads asleep on the pillows. As we have observed, Lance loved his younger brother unreservedly and was in no way jealous of him in this particular. For Lance, bringing Alexander home was sufficient. It is said that familiarity brings contempt — but Lance was finding that his familiarity with Alexander only elevated him to a sublime and boundless plateau of contentment.

Lance, alone in the bathroom shared by the boys, contemplated Alexander's toilet things laid out along the glazed shelving. There was the ample sponge, the genuine article — a rarity in post-war Britain. Alexander must have brought it from the Far East. It was an implement necessarily familiar with every interstice of the boy's body. Lance felt compelled to advance his hand towards it but at the last moment averted contact. Such contact would constitute an unforgivable carnal betrayal of his treasured guest. Then there was the nail brush; and the toothbrush. In reaching past the latter Lance allowed himself an inadvertent brush of the back of his hand against it. Lance saw it was a Rexall product, a brand with which he was not familiar. He again assumed Alexander must have brought it with him from the Far East. And he saw the part empty tube of toothpaste in the glass, squeezed by the precious hand. Alexander was using Kolynos, whereas Lance was currently using Pepsodent. He resolved to change to Kolynos at the next opportunity. Lance felt himself somewhat ashamed of these secret curiosities; curiosities that were satiated for the moment.

But in the silences of the night other forces move in dark and insidious ways. The temptations of the flesh are not lightly to be denied and Lance was on the cusp of succumbing. It was then that he made a conscious effort to eschew eroticism in his dreams and instead embark upon some knightly pursuit of purity while Alexander was under his roof. But Lance was fourteen, going on fifteen — he knew he could not abstain for ever or he would explode. Nevertheless, he resolved to pray for deliverance from fleshly lusts until the start of the new term delivered his house of its precious burden. Thus in such sublime denial and deference did Lance love Alexander.

* * *

On the journey up from Monsalvat the boys had travelled First Class. Lance was insistent on that; after all, his parents were rich enough and nothing but first class would do for his younger consort. Lance was adamant that nothing would be spared to give Alexander a memorable and quality holiday.

On the journey up and once free of the cloistered confines of Monsalvat, Lance had no inhibitions about showing off his young consort to all and sundry. Alexander was his exclusive trophy. Male or female, young or old, all should know of his more than proprietous relationship with the golden boy. And Alexander, in all his innocence, responded accordingly, seeming to have eyes only for his hero, much to the intrigued entertainment of their fellow passengers. It was clear to the perspicacious that these were more than just schoolboy pals.

Once the train had cleared Preston the boys found they had the compartment to themselves. Lance kicked his shoes off and sprawled on the cushions, facing the corridor with his back to the compartment window. Only his left foot still rested on the floor. In total disregard of the empty banquette opposite and quite unbidden, Alexander sat down with his back against Lance's extended right leg. He too kicked himself shoeless and, as if it were the most ordinary thing in the world, he turned towards the corridor, lifted his stockinged feet onto the cushions and leaned back so that his head came to rest against Lance's starched shirt front.

"Oh, Lance! I can feel your heart beating. It's going nineteen to the dozen."

"Close your eyes, Alexander. You can go to sleep and slow it down. It's been a long day so far and we've still the best part of an hour to go." Alexander cast his magazine aside and immediately complied as if it had been his own idea. A few minutes later and Lance's breast became a willing pillow for an engaging little sleepyhead. Now Lance took perverse pleasure in seeing people passing by in the corridor looking in and momentarily wondering what the relationship was between the two boys. That they were public school boys, and affluent ones at that, was very evident. In appearances they were not brothers. Cousins, perhaps. But lovers? Such a possibility was hardly likely to occur to the blinkered onlookers of 1949. And yet...

The ticket inspector came in with his punch and asked to see their tickets. Lance had retained the tickets for both of them and now he made a proprietorial show, pregnant with deliberation, of producing them for inspection. He reached for his wallet, taking care not to disturb the noble head slumbering on his breast. He could sense the official scrutinising the pair and wondering what to make of them. The man was apparently so intrigued that he felt compelled to ask a question:

"Is he all right?" The train was gathering speed and there was such a thing as train sickness.

Lance glanced down at the tumble of curls in response before smiling back at the inspector. "Yes, of course. It's just that he's a little tired. It was an early start."

The inspector returned Lance's bland smile with one of uncertainty, then retreated, and Lance enthused in the knowledge that the man had in some measure been made aware of the specialness of their relationship.

The next incursion was that of the dining car attendant handing out tickets for lunch. Yet again Lance took a certain pleasure in the man's discomfiture and satisfied himself that yet another lesser person was now aware of their great love. Lance's demeanour and behaviour was outrageous for the time but he took defiant satisfaction in the thought that the world was not yet ready for such public displays of affection between boys of their respective ages. He regarded himself and Alexander as pioneers in that particular. Lunch however was impracticable. There simply wasn't enough time between Preston and Carlisle to give it justice.

* * *

Earlier, as they waited for the connection at Crewe, Lance enjoyed himself immensely on seeing the impact he and Alexander had on their fellow travellers and railway staff. Handsome himself, he made a veritable play of showing off his beautiful younger companion to anyone who so much as glanced their way. The people in the streets of Britain were a drab and down-at-heel lot in 1949 and the two public school boys made a notable exception to the norm. Out of their clerical grey overcoats they were a picture of patrician smartness and urbanity with their straw cadies at a jaunty angle, neatly pressed dark grey flannels, white shirts, mauve neckties and smart blazers. On their breasts could be seen the sombre escutcheon of their college. It bore a depiction of the Great Grail of Monsalvat-Pencadno and was embellished with the mottoes *"Quis Ut Deus"* and *"Secura Nidificat"*. It was evident that they were from an establishment of some gravitas and that they were conducting themselves in the certain and secure knowledge of that fact. There was also a hint of conspiratorial intrigue between them as they went about buying magazines at the bookstall and taking railway coffee in the platform buffet. Not only that; Alexander was a natural charmer. Small though he was, he veritably filled a room with his vivacious presence and he had a ready smile for anyone who looked his way. And there were many. Not a few of their fellow travellers seemed to glance not just once but several times in their direction. Whether in admiration or in exception, Lance cared not. He was just happy that they glanced. Many smiled indulgently; just a few smiled knowingly. Middle-aged matrons and sad-faced businessmen attempted to strike up conversations with the pair, and palpably for divergent reasons. It seemed to Lance that the mundane and dysfunctional existences of these lesser creatures were momentarily abated in the presence of such paragons of youth and the cultivated human condition as the two collegians of Monsalvat. Enjoy our passing, his demeanour seemed to imply, for we may not pass this way again. There was also an unstated air of confidence that they had the ability, given equal matches, to duff up any oiks who might feel forward enough to take issue with their patrician presence. As it was, none came their way.

* * *

At *The Purpress* and out of earshot of the children, Lance's parents considered the possibility of fostering Alexander with a view to eventual adoption. That they were instantly captivated by the orphaned boy from Manchuria would be a monumental understatement. But they had to consider matters in the longer term. There was the matter of Mark, Lance's younger brother. He had been afflicted with Duchenne Muscular Dystrophy and was in delicate, indeed declining, health. He had not been robust enough to accompany his brother to Monsalvat and had to be educated locally. Lately there had been ever longer periods when he had to remain at home and a local tutor had been got in to continue his education. In their inner hearts his parents knew it would all be of no avail. It was optimistic to expect that Mark would survive to attain his majority.

On a more optimistic note there was the matter of Lance's three cousins. The two younger ones were of an age with Alexander and could match him in vivacity and social attributes. In the fullness of time either would make an ideal match for the handsome boy from Manchuria. His advent in the house of Lapita augured well for the future.

* * *

There were several guests for Christmas dinner, to the extent that all the places at the great dining table were taken. Before the ladies and the children left, Lance's father did indeed hold forth on the matter of the name of the estate. It was at the prompting of one of the gentleman guests — clearly a prearranged gambit. Lance smiled knowingly at Alexander; he knew the gambit of old and waited for the inevitable exposition. It seemed *The Purpress* was a truncation of 'purpresture'. Anyone versed in land law might think that opprobrious. And so it originally was, the property having been the subject of an adverse lawsuit, it being deemed parasitic on the estate with which it was surrounded. However, it seems the plaintiff was embarrassingly nonsuited when the defendant eloped with his daughter (and heiress!). On accession in the fullness of time, the erstwhile defendant facetiously retained the opprobrious appellation in order to memorialise the contretemps. As *purpresture* did not trip lightly off the tongues of the local inhabitants, they promptly abbreviated it. It was the acknowledged prerogative of Lance's father to regale his guests with the anecdote on suitable occasions.

But Lapita senior had not told the whole story. It was a story of which Lance himself had yet to be apprised. A story which touched, among other things, on his parents' hopes apropos Alexander. They had to take due cognisance of what had become facetiously known in the salons of other places and times as 'The Curse of the Lapitas'. In order to abate this so-called 'curse' the nineteenth century patriarch of that mercantile family — historically not an overly fecund tribe — had purposefully scattered his offspring to the four corners of the world in the hope that they would then marry outside the small Catholic enclave of the minor Baltic port from which they originated. This familial scatterance was on the best medical advice of the day. It was a genetic exercise intended to ameliorate an increasingly disconcerting problem of inbreeding. Succinctly, the Lapitas needed to outbreed and Lance's grandfather, initially consigned to a London adjunct of the family business, succeeded in that particular by marrying a minor offshoot of the British aristocracy. It was his son, Lance's father, who had thereby inherited *The Purpress* together with the encompassing estate of land. It was to this estate that the two Monsalvations had travelled to celebrate Christmas 1949.

The future did indeed augur well. However, that the course of true love might be more complex than logic might devise, was made evident when Lance found himself caught in an unguarded moment. At a soiree, at which Alexander was being discussed in his absence, Susannah, the eldest of Lance's three female cousins, said something which immediately threw Lance on the defensive.

"You really love him, don't you, Lance?"

It was quite unexpected, statement of the obvious though it was. It triggered alarm bells in Lance's brain; he felt he was on shaky ground. As ever, he feigned languid urbanity and turned his response into a defensive interrogatory, delivered with a knowing smile:

"I'm sure we all find him eminently lovable, wouldn't you agree?"

It elicited but another smile in response and the moment of tension receded. But Lance thought he detected a knowing inflection in Susannah's smile. Be that as it may, it had been a bold exchange for the late 1940s. Perhaps each hoped that the imminent 1950s would be more accommodating in such delicate matters.

Only one incident marred the idyllic interlude at *The Purpress,* a most curious incident. As divulged, Lance's mother was a member of a local choir. That choir gave an annual Christmas concert and on the occasion of Alexander's visit the programme included excerpts from Handel's Messiah — hardly part of the Catholic canon, but the Lapitas' tastes were catholic enough in that regard. And it was natural enough for the rest of the family to attend as privileged members of the audience. All went well until the advent of Chorus 26, *"All we like sheep".* A few bars into the piece saw Alexander leave his seat and make for the nearest exit with what seemed to be indecent haste. Lapita Senior would attempt to make light of it: "Great Heavens! Is your mother's singing that bad?" Lance was in an inner seat and could not readily extricate himself to go after the youngster. His cousin Susannah was better placed. She left the building and instinctively made for where the Gurney Nutting Wraith was parked. Sure enough, there was Alexander seated on the running board, his kerchief in discreet use. Susannah had been well briefed; it did not do to facilely inquire of the boy what might have triggered this reaction. She sat down alongside him and gently put her arm about him to shelter him from the bitter winter night and the winter of his reverie. Fortuitously, the concert was nearing its end and when the rest of the family arrived back at the vehicle Alexander seemed well enough in Susannah's solicitous company. There seemed no occasion for even Lance to broach the subject and it was allowed to rest.

It was only weeks later, when the two boys were back at college, that the occasion for Alexander's distress became known to Lance. He was passing the music room when he became aware of some inconsequential tinkling on the piano keys. Some boy practising, he thought. Then he heard the same three descending notes that had seemed to trigger Alexander's distress at Christmas time; but this time the notes were rendered *sforzando* and were immediately followed by what seemed to be some exercise in march time — but not any exercise that Lance could ascribe to *Czerny*. Then the plangent notes of this seeming exercise began to gather strange arpeggios, clearly not of the western hemisphere. Intrigued now, Lance felt compelled to glance in through the open door. His heart skipped a beat — it was Alexander at the keyboard. Throwing caution to the winds he entered, confident that he could always conjure up a plausible pretext if challenged. As it was, there was no sign of music master Parry-Jones. Lance advanced to the piano stool, to stand in pulsating proximity to the very boy who ruled his being. By now, Alexander had brought the piece to a triumphant climax.

"What the devil was that you were playing?"

Alexander stared ahead, as if caught in some clandestine

act. "That..." he replied, in palpably controlled tones "...was the national anthem of Manchukuo."

By now, Lance had gleaned enough of Alexander's history to know that Manchukuo was lately the Japanese-aligned State under which Alexander and his sister had been born and raised. Apparently, the anthem had been one of his first accomplished piano pieces.

* * *

On the matter of the fostering of Alexander, at *The Purpress* a decision was made that Lance's father would consult the family solicitor after the Christmas holidays with a view to making due inquiries and setting the requisite arrangements in train. Logic told the Lapitas that they were on first acquaintance and that they might be precipitate and imprudent and premature, but instinctive love and the sheer lovableness of the boy from Manchuria was swaying them otherwise. In their hearts they knew that an ineluctable rightness prevailed. As for the 'family curse', it was assumed that, in the Cumberland branch at least, it had become so genetically diluted as to be considered eradicated.

Lance's parents did not make him privy to the decision. Nevertheless, he knew he had set in train a significant sequence of events; a drama even, one that only he could move towards an inexorable climax. In Alexander he had secured a healthy replacement for the doomed Mark. But Lance perceived a dilemma regarding his young friend. Not for him must the sultry sulks of adolescence displace the beguiling smiles of childhood's innocence. Not for him must the perfect symmetry of childhood's peak be eclipsed by the ensuing descent into the mediocrity of maturity and the venality of adult life. Somehow, Lance must find a way out of that dilemma.

Chapter Thirteen

Unfinished Business

Monday, January 9th, 1950; the day of Saint Adrian of Canterbury. It was a new year and the start of a new term: Tycho and Barden had arrived back at Pencadno on the same train. As soon as their train drew abreast of the linear panorama of the college they noticed what seemed to be steeplejacks working on the lantern of the chapel dome. The boys were curious as to what they were doing and, imbued with some misgiving, they resolved to ascend into the dome to satisfy their curiosity as soon as time permitted on what would be a very busy arrival day.

By the time Lance and Alexander arrived on a later train, the short winter day had ended and the steeplejacks were long gone. Tycho and Barden purposely didn't mention what they had seen, nor their intended inspection of the dome. They left the refectory as soon as was prudent and repaired to the chapel. They climbed the iron staircase to inspect the lower and upper galleries. There were no religious offices scheduled for arrival day; the building was in darkness save for the sanctuary lamp. Barden had equipped himself with a flashlight. The boys walked round the lower gallery. Opposite the entrance door they came across an open metal canister balanced on the handrail and some crystals scattered along the circular walkway. Tycho went to take hold of the can but Barden reached over and knocked his hand away with scant ceremony: "Don't touch it... it's poisonous." He didn't know that, but he guessed. He shone his torch onto the canister and sure enough it was blazoned with a skull and crossbones hazard warning sign and it had on it uncompromising textual advisories as to the nature of its late contents — hydrogen cyanide crystals. Perturbed now, each boy looked at the other in unspoken anxiety. Quickly they made their way back to the ladder and ascended to the upper gallery. From this higher position Barden was able to shine his torch into the drum of the lantern. Through the part-open ventilation louvres they could see wire netting which had not been in place before. It had obviously been the work of the steeplejacks. Cautiously they started to make their way round the narrow gallery, Tycho in the lead. He stopped and knelt down so suddenly that Barden almost tumbled over him.

Tycho called over his shoulder: "It's Colly."

Barden looked over Tycho's shoulder and shone his torch. He could see the snow-white fantail dove apparently in repose on the walkway, her head under her wing. Tycho softly called her name. Then he put a hand out and gently stroked the feathered back. The bird made no response.

"Oh, Barden... She's dead."

Then both exclaimed at the same time: "Alexander...!" Both had the same thought but it was Barden who articulated it: "He mustn't find out. We'll have to hide her somehow..."

The two set to urgently planning the secret disposal of the treasured bird. It seemed Tycho had an old shoe box in his wardrobe which he could empty of things and use to encase the dead bird. Within the half hour the two were back in the upper gallery with the shoe box. They had taken pains to avoid their form fellows. Tycho had lined the box with cotton wool from the debris of one of the Christmas cribs. Now he gently cradled the dead bird in his cupped hands and lowered her into the box. Then he reached into his blazer pocket and pulled out an oval one-hundred-day indulgence card backed with red velvet. This he placed in the box with Colly. Barden also relinquished the same indulgences to the repose of the dove. These symbols of their religiosity had been in their respective possessions for most of the previous term. They were not lightly relinquished.

The boys decided that they should take the box to Wali at the old bothy with a view to arranging a discreet burial. The evening was quite advanced now and 'lights out' would not be far off. At the old bothy Wall was sympathetic but as to the practicality of burial he counselled otherwise.

"By the time we dig deep enough to thwart the foxes and badgers it'll be midnight. In any case, Colly was a creature of the air, not of the earth. Let us return her to the air."

He was proposing cremation. He had plenty of straw and paper to burn from the dismantling of the numerous cribs around the college and he sought, as it might be said, to kill two birds with one stone. He advised that Colly should be cremated in the boiler furnace of the old peach house. This was where he occasionally burned trash when the weather precluded an outside bonfire. The boys were diffident about his proposal in view of the Catholic proscription upon cremation, but Wali reassured them that this would not apply to dumb animals. "After all," he reasoned, "we eat most of them."

Thus did the three walk round to the boiler house, Tycho cradling the precious casket. Wali locked the outside door of the boiler house to make sure they would not be disturbed. He then walked through the communicating door into the peach house and returned a moment later with three white funerary lilies. He handed one to each of the boys and retained one himself. At the furnace front Wali took the box from Tycho and positioned it some distance in, on the fire bars. He then reached in and gently placed his own lily on the lid and motioned the boys to do the same. As they did so they could feel the updraft on the backs of their hands and see it rippling the lily petals and shivering the cobwebs between the fire bars. The wind had got up and it moaned in the uptake. The flue concentrated the noises of the night and through it they could hear the pulsating exhaust of a locomotive as it hauled a rattling ballast train out of the quarry sidings.

The two boys watched as Wali expertly built a fire round the box with the tinder dry straw, some sticks and some old newspaper. He augmented this nesting with more substantial kindling and lined it with coals. Then he struck a match, touched it on the straw and closed the furnace door. Soon the furnace crackled and roared and the stokehole louvres gave off an orange glow that suffused the whitewashed walls of the boiler house.

"Shouldn't we say something... as long as it's not blasphemous?" It was Tycho making the tremulous inquiry.

Recognising their need, Wali rose to the occasion. He knelt down before the furnace door and the boys knelt either side of him. The boys' bare knees touched down on the gritty floor but they seemed not to care at the discomfort. Wali hesitantly put together some suitable words of comfort for them, doing his very best to display a sincerity he did not really feel:

"O *Lord, we return to your good fresh air where it belongs, this your most beautiful creation, Colly, late companion of our great friend Alexander and a creature of the air struck down by man's cruel and thoughtless action. Please receive her spirit in the hope that we shall all meet again in the hereafter Amen.* Wali's invocation was quickly cobbled together on the spur of the moment but it would suffice. Tycho had difficulty in adding his 'amen'. Tears were in the eyes of both boys now. Wall reached out either side and gathered the boys to him. They remained locked in this triple embrace for a full minute, all three kneeling before the roaring furnace. Then Wali rose and unlocked the outside door. The boys rose and dusted the grit off their bare knees. All three repaired outside and stood for a while looking up at the smoke and sparks from the boiler house chimney streaking away into the night on a stiff offshore breeze. Truly the treasured dove was being returned to the air from which it had been so wantonly taken. After a respectful minute and mindful of the curfew, Wali closed the melancholy proceedings by urging the two boys back to their dormitory.

Back in their dormitory, the two boys necessarily shared in their form fellows' bravura tales of the Christmas holidays before junior 'lights out'. Each felt that appropriate obsequies and offices had been performed for Alexander's late avian friend.

What Wali did not tell the boys was that he had been instrumental in the death of the dove, albeit inadvertently. Bringsam, the assistant caretaker, had approached him for advice on fumigating a compartment, presumably on the premise that as a merchant seaman Wali would know about fumigating compartments to rid them of rats. As a consequence, it was Wali who found himself tasked with making a trip to a local yacht chandler for canisters of hydrogen cyanide crystals. Bringsam had not specified which compartment or compartments he intended to fumigate; Wali assumed it was the old air raid shelters which had in the past sporadically harboured colonies of field mice. He had been present at the back of the chapel during the Christmas processional when Colly had landed on Alexander's shoulder. Had he known that Bringsam was under orders to fumigate the dome, orders which had issued from general convocation, presumably to put down any birds inadvertently trapped inside by the newly installed netting, he would surely have done his best to ensure that the dove was not among them. As for Alexander, he naturally assumed the dove had flown away about its own devices — and nobody was about to disabuse him of that.

* * *

When the two boys left the peach house after the cremation ceremony they had not gone unobserved. Yseult, Wali's paramour, had been watching for some time from the adjacent shadows, her nose decidedly out of joint. Left out in the cold — literally — while Wali attended to the sensitivities of, according to her, silly schoolboys, she spiritedly took Wali to task on the matter as soon as she had him to herself. Wali told her to shut up.

* * *

Saturday, January 14th, 1950. It was late afternoon and it was very evident that something was 'up' at the bath house. An inordinate number of boys were hanging about and talking nervously among themselves. A group of Removites who had come over for routine ablutions began to assess the situation. Many of these younger ones seemed loath to go in and they hung about the doorway. Some of the bolder ones ventured into the interior to satisfy their curiosity.

It seemed the Irish Gang were making an example of someone who had offended them in some way; and they had selected the junior section of the bath house in which to do it. They had a reason for this; the senior part would routinely be visited by prefects and the Irish Gang did not want to embarrass them in their policing duties. The junior section itself was supposed to be patrolled by the duty prefect but for some reason best known to themselves those incumbents seemed routinely inclined to dereliction of duty. The sight that met the Removites was gross to say the least. A Third Former whom they knew as Bass had been stripped naked and tied down hand and foot on the duckboards in one of the shower bays. He was tied down in such a manner that his heels had been passed over his head, thus bending him double and elevating his buttocks. They'd used old sash cord to tie him down. He was moaning in pain at the restraints on his wrists and ankles, and imploring any within earshot to release him and ease his discomfort. The watchers, however, knew better than to interfere with the Irish Gang's 'arrangements'. After having their fill of the victim's discomfiture, and realising that they themselves were not at present risk, they proceeded on their respective ways to the shower bays, washroom or water closets. There was no-one from the Irish Gang immediately on hand to enforce the sanction against Bass; there was no need for them to be.

Among the transient clutch of watchers a diminutive figure thrust his way to the fore. It was Alexander Fragner Vudsen. He had a towel over his shoulder and a sponge bag in his left hand. He was also carrying something in his right hand, something concealed by the towel. It was a Sabatier knife with an eight-inch blade, which he had purloined from the kitchen. Presumably he had earlier come across Bass's predicament and had gone and equipped himself accordingly. He now knelt alongside Bass and began to cut the cords that secured him to the duck boards. There arose from the concerned watchers a subdued hiss of advice for him to desist; this was Third Form business and no concern of any junior. The watchers were concerned for his wellbeing. They had reason to be. One of the Irish Gang's sycophants, who had been hanging about, had already seen what was happening and had gone in search of a gang member. As luck would have it, it was Flynn who was in the vicinity. Alexander had freed all but a wrist when an angry shout assailed him: "Hey you, you little bastard..." On seeing the knife, Flynn modified his mode of address: "Give me that knife, Vudsen, or it'll be the worse for you."

Alexander ignored him and cut the final bond. Bass rolled to one side and lay there all of a heap, trying to reinvigorate his cramped limbs. Flynn advanced upon Alexander, blocking his escape route from the shower bay. The watchers stood transfixed, wondering what would happen next. Alexander sprang to his feet and assumed a crouching stance. Flynn fixed him with a leering grin; this pretentious Removite was going to be easy meat. Alexander spread his arms akimbo then he threw the knife from his right hand and caught it in his left in what was clearly a practised manoeuvre.

Flynn hesitated now. "Oh, clever little cunt, aintcha."

Alexander passed the knife back to his right hand in like manner; Flynn had been warned... Conscious of the watching crowd, he nevertheless decided it was time to move in. In response the knife positively zipped up in a gutting fashion. Flynn flinched away but was not quite quick enough. The tip of the knife nicked the tip of his nose. The watchers gasped in amazement; never before had a member of the Irish Gang been so outfaced and in such a manner. Flynn danced furious attendance on the crouching boy but the watchers knew he was only feinting now.

In Alexander's right hand the knife bobbed and weaved like the head of a menacing snake, deterring any attempt to grab the arm. Alexander's eyes purposefully did not meet Flynn's angry stare, rather he was looking at no fixed point. He was using his peripheral vision to record any hostile move from any quarter, at the same timc taking every move of Flynn's person into view and anticipating his every attempt to disarm him. Flynn would have aimed a kick but the prospect of having a foot impaled dissuaded him.

The gap in the entrance to the bay was small enough but Flynn prudently stepped back as Alexander sidled past him. Once out of the reach of his antagonist Alexander simply turned his back on him and walked calmly away, knife held down by his side.

He felt no remorse. He had not equipped himself with a knife with the intention of cutting anyone up. His sole purpose and intention had been to free the unfortunate Bass from further hurt and ignominy.

As for Flynn, Alexander had simply sought free passage from the place and Flynn had attempted to deny him that — at some cost to himself. In the eyes of the onlookers Alexander was a resolute boy but a foolish one in having thus antagonised the Irish Gang.

The nick on Flynn's nose now had him bleeding like the similitudinous stuck pig. Trying to save face, he called after Alexander: "You're in real trouble now, boy — big time". The fact that he was now having to hold a handkerchief to his nose to stem the bleeding did little for his dignity; indeed he sounded like one afflicted with a severe cold. There were unsuppressed giggles from the onlookers now. This was rare entertainment. Off to one side, willing hands were helping Bass to his feet and offering him towels to cover his nakedness. Like others before him, Flynn was discovering that one did not trifle with a boy partly brought up in Tsingtao.

As to retribution, Alexander did not feel much exercised. Had not some unseen hand already delivered him from the clutches of the Irish Gang on no less than two occasions?

In the refectory that evening there were knowing nudges when the hapless Flynn walked in with a conspicuous dressing on his nose. The table of the Irish Gang was uncharacteristically subdued throughout the meal. Knowing nudges notwithstanding, there was an uneasy feeling among the boys that Alexander was 'unfinished business' in the view of Foul Mouthed Frank and his cronies. Those junior to the Irish Gang speculated among themselves as to what trick Alexander might pull off next. The Irish Gang for their part felt obliged to find out. Neither party knew that Alexander had no more shots in his locker.

* * *

In Alexander's form was a boy known as 'the big Swede'— Raimo Haroldsen, a stocky, big-boned, blue-eyed, fair-haired fellow. The appellation had been Mauger's and like many such gratuitous teachers' jests the appellation had stuck. Haroldsen was actually of Danish extraction but nobody thought to make the distinction. As for Haroldsen himself, insofar as he was aware of the appellation, he never made an issue of it. Haroldsen was not your average new 'peach'. Those in the know conjectured that he had been selected to serve as an apprentice bully. The reasoning was that the Irish Gang were moving up the school and were subject to much lateral attrition for reasons of academic inadequacy. New recruits were always under consideration. If this were the case, the mystical selectors had misunderstood this ungainly peach. Haroldsen might be something of a bruiser — but he was no bully.

Thus it was proved some days after the incident with the knife. Mauger was holding forth for the benefit of a semi-circle of 'A' Removites. The venue was the old gym. For reasons of urgent maintenance the forms' gym period had been transferred there from the newer facility uphill of the grand terrace. Space in the old gym was cramped because of the piles of stored furniture but there was room enough for Mauger's purposes. "Your foreigner... your dirty foreigner... will fight dirty. He will use a knife. Your English gentleman, on the other hand, will always use his fists." The boys received this wisdom with appropriate diffidence;

but none would deny that Mauger's words seemed directed at Alexander because of his exploit with the knife in the bath house. Clearly word of the incident had got out to 'authority'. And by now all his form fellows knew — and knew that Mauger knew — that Alexander wasn't strictly an English boy. Next to Mauger, to reinforce the burden of his pugilistic peroration, was a large wicker basket full of dusty old boxing gloves. A boxing ring had been rigged up in the centre of the gym.

"So today, boys, we're going to learn how to fight like English gentlemen; and box under the Queensberry rules." Here he digressed on the subject of the exemplary contribution of John Sholto Douglas, Marquess of Queensberry, to the sport of prize fighting. The upshot of all this was that eight of the boys were paired off and equipped with boxing gloves. Mauger had a clipboard with all their names on and professed to have matched each pair of boys evenly. Each pair was called into the ring in turn and set to, to decide which of the pair was the better boxer. Barden Sender was entrusted with Mauger's stop watch and set as timekeeper. Mauger himself stood in the ring as referee and coach.

There was little method in Mauger's coaching. Most of the matches ended inconclusively, each boy being somewhat reluctant to gratuitously batter his form mate lest some unsupervised retribution might later ensue. Some of the boys had some idea of the sport, others less so.

Alexander had not been included in this first evolution; he stood by with others to watch the bouts. Eventually the gloves were passed on and Alexander, according to Mauger's clipboard, found himself matched against Raimo Haroldsen. It was clearly a mismatch, the slight Alexander being up against a much bigger and heavier opponent. A boy moreover who had boxed for his prep school. Some of the boys actually pointed this out but Mauger gave them no audience. He was clearly intent on teaching Alexander a salutary lesson as to how true Englishmen settled their disputes. It was Sender and Gyles-Skeffington who elected themselves the duty of tying the gloves on Alexander's wrists. They both commiserated with him and presumed to offer advice. Instead he walked away and seemed to find something of interest in a bank of fire buckets ranged on hooks against the wall. These buckets were a legacy of wartime air raid precautions, the old gym being a timber lined structure particularly susceptible to fire hazard. Some contained water, others sand for quenching incendiary bombs. Mauger homed in for the kill.

"Come on, Vudsen, you won't find any inspiration in a fire bucket. Let's have you in the ring." Alexander pointedly hesitated before turning round with downcast face. He held his hands under his chin, one glove faced against the other, as he walked reluctantly towards the field of battle. Haroldsen himself had complained that he was mismatched. Alexander was the youngest boy in the school — and looked it. Indeed, of all the 'A Removites, only Sender would have been anything like an even match for the big Swede, Sender being a year older and that much bigger than the rest of his form fellows.

Mauger seemed to take particular relish in the ensuing bout. Haroldsen, on the other hand, was clearly reluctant to demonstrate his considerable skills against so slight an opponent. After a while this incensed Mauger, who threatened to have Haroldsen placed on report for 'not putting his back into it'. As for Alexander, he consistently backed away and adopted a passive defensive technique which, in the history of boxing, would later famously become known as the 'rope-a-dope'; that is to say, he fell back against the ropes with his chin on his chest and with his gloved hands protecting his head and face, his elbows tucked in so that his crooked arms protected his upper body. Even so, the technique of itself was not enough to prevent some damage and after some time into the second round the spectators could see that Alexander's bare torso was showing signs of leather burn. Between rounds Mauger berated the pair for not getting 'stuck in', as he put it.

In the third round Haroldsen moved in, under duress, for the kill. Alexander on the other hand fell to constantly hanging on to his opponent in desperation. An exasperated Mauger found himself constantly calling "Break". But something untoward was happening in the ring. At each breakaway Alexander had been bringing his left hand upwards and across Haroldsen's face in a kind of screw punch that grazed his opponent's left eye socket. After several such breaks Haroldsen's eye became puffed and inflamed. In the interval Mauger examined it and considered it of little consequence.

Against all the established rules for amateur boxing the bout went into an unprecedented fourth round. Four clinches and breaks later, Haroldsen's eye exploded in a welter of blood. His blood spattered his opponent, himself, the ring in general and not a few of the spectators. Mauger had no option but to stop the bout. The first aid kit was broken out and Haroldsen was soon on his way under escort to the bell tower for urgent medical attention. Alexander went over to Sender and Gyles-Skeffington to have his gloves removed but Mauger called him back. There were no other boys in earshot now. Mauger grabbed Alexander's wrists and examined the gloves. Both gloves seemed discoloured. Mauger felt the contact surfaces; they were decidedly damp — and not from any blood. They were also gritty. Before the bout, when Mauger was calling him over to the ring, Alexander had been dunking his gloves in the water of one fire bucket and rubbing them in the sand of another. Both gloves were lethally abrasive. Clearly one didn't trifle with a boy partly brought up in Tsingtao.

Mauger muttered something under his breath so that none but Alexander should hear: "You crafty little bastard." It was a lapse of propriety unprecedented even by Mauger's plebeian standards.

As for Haroldsen, to his credit he never made an issue of his humbling encounter with the boy from Manchuria.

* * *

Over the ensuing weeks, gently, sympathetically, at opportune moments, Rhiannon coaxed from Alexander some details of his late family and their life in China. Eventually he was persuaded to talk about his little sister, Sabine. It seems Sabine was eight years old when she died with her parents on the flight out of Manchuria. It was clear that Alexander had loved his little sister dearly and now missed her dreadfully.

Eighteen-year-olds do not normally 'adopt' eleven-year-olds — but this was not a normal situation. Alexander was going to be ejected from Monsalvat at the end of the present term for want of school fees. It was tacitly agreed between Wepper and Rhiannon that Alexander could come and live with them, and that when Wepper attained his majority the couple would apply to adopt Alexander into their proposed family. If this conflicted with the pastoral Fathers' waning lien on Alexander, then so be it. The status of Rhiannon's father would lend legitimacy to such an arrangement. Furthermore, the Adoption of Children Act 1949 would have come into force by then, negating the impediment that Alexander was not a United Kingdom citizen. For the time being Alexander could spend time with the pair. The couple decided he was not to be made privy to their further intention in case their plans went awry. As for Wepper's and Rhiannon's privacy and time to themselves as a loving couple, they reasoned that they would have plenty of time to themselves when Alexander was in school or occupied elsewhere on some other school evolution. It would be a feasible, albeit highly unusual, arrangement. Out of term time, if he were not away in Cumberland with the Lapitas, he would be invited to stay with Rhiannon's parents in their substantial house in Pencadno town. All this was on the assumption that no prior or better claim would have been made on the boy.

A warm late March Saturday found the three of them taking their leisure in the rare old Victorian resort of Llandudno once again. It had taken Wepper some ingenuity to 'spring' Alexander from the paranoid cloisters of Monsalvat and to spirit him down to the station in anybody's company but that of a detested Bold Contemner; but it had been managed. An hour or so later found Rhiannon and the boy seated on a sun trap park bench contemplating the ocean and working up an appetite for lunch. Wepper had drifted off on some trifling diversion in the vicinity.

Picking the moment carefully and with much misgiving, Rhiannon took a chance and spoke with Alexander on a delicate matter: "Alexander, Will and I are looking ahead. You know we're planning to get married as soon as Will leaves for Paris. My father knows Will has a brilliant future and he won't stand in our way. He knows Will hasn't had an easy time up to now and he thinks it's about time that some happiness came into his life — our lives. He'll give us every support. The thing is, Alexander... the thing is... we want to start a family pretty soon." Alexander looked intrigued and fixed her with his piercing blue eyes. "You know that means there's an even chance we'll have a daughter, a girl. We've talked about this and I want to ask you a question. If it *is* a girl, Alexander, we'd like... only with your permission, you understand.., we would like.., we would like to call her... Sabine. There! I've said it."

Rhiannon looked down into his face and waited apprehensively for the reaction. The eyes blinked and misted with tears and became downcast and the boy's lower lip trembled ominously. Rhiannon's arm shot out in a comforting gesture and her next words spilled out urgently, effusively.

"Oh now I've upset you. I'm so, so, sorry, Alexander. Please forgive me. Let's forget the idea; I knew it was insensitive of us."

The eyes were cast upwards again. Rhiannon's other hand reached forward with her kerchief and dabbed at the tears. "No... it's all right, Rhiannon. No, really it is. That would be nice. I'll be able to look after her and..." At this point Alexander changed to being positively enthusiastic: "...when she's eight years old I'll be big and strong and able to protect her."

At these words Rhiannon's anguish fell away and she was relieved and ecstatic: "I must tell Will right away."

But that was not all. Alexander reached up and gave her an oh-so-very gentle peck on the cheek. Sufficient to say that the proceedings were concluded, predictably, in joyful, tearful hugs.

These were interrupted by a discreet cough and the approach of Wepper from behind the bench. "Can I take it we have concord?" he asked. He was apprehensive and put on a broad and somewhat unconvincing smile.

He need not have worried; Alexander shifted to a jesting mood. "You've been watching us all the time... from a safe distance... you coward".

A relieved Wepper spread his arms so as to encompass the other two and, reaching down and meeting Rhiannon's upturned face, he kissed his fiancée on the lips. From there he turned and planted an avuncular kiss on Alexander's forehead.

"There you are then. Sealed with a kiss.., a triple kiss". And with that the three of them repaired to one of the better hotels for what amounted to a celebratory lunch.

But that was not all. A few short years span the gap between boyhood innocence and adolescent angst. From a discreet distance a pair of hungry eyes had been fixed on these sublime proceedings. By dint of some nifty dodging, Lance Lapita had followed the trio to Llandudno, unseen on the same train. His cover, were he to be challenged, was to be that he was visiting the local book shops. But there was no book shop to be had in Happy Valley. And Alexander's blood-brother did not like what he was seeing. Rhiannon had come between him and his elder blood-brother. Now it looked as if she was going to come between him and his younger blood-brother as well. It was too much. The sight of the incongruous but happy trio locked in a familial embrace on a park bench sent Lance Raphael Lapita spinning into the depths of despair. He now felt guilty and furtive in the realisation that he was consumed with jealousy. Surely, somewhere in the scheme of things there had to be a resolution of his anguish...

CHAPTER FOURTEEN

Cabaret Night

Barden Sender awoke with a start. He didn't know what had awakened him but he knew better than to show any evidence of his waking. He lay still under the blankets, his young heart pounding, listening for any menacing footfalls approaching his bedspace. After a few moments of acute anxiety he realised there were no interlopers in the dormitory. He sat up and looked about him in the darkness. He called out in a loud whisper: "Anyone awake around here?"

At the same time he reached over to his dresser drawer and grabbed a torch. He flashed the torch beam around, keeping it low so as not to disturb those who might still be asleep. He played the beam over the two end bedspaces next to his own; the bedclothes in disarray told their own story. Tonight's abductees had been Alexander and Tycho. Again. Their abductors had moved swiftly and silently enough not to immediately awaken Barden.

Most of the other boys had drifted off again after the initial disturbance but some were still wide awake, wide-eyed and apprehensive. Barden gently reassured them in tones that feigned experience; he was after all a year older than they.

"It's all right, they won't be coming back. At least not

tonight anyway. I'll go and see to Tycho and Alexander. And then, feigning reassurance: "Go back to sleep." He got out of bed and put his dressing gown on over his pyjamas and slipped on a pair of plimsoles. Satisfied that his younger form fellows' apprehensions were quieted, he left the dormitory and went down the stairs and into the lower corridor, taking his torch with him. There was no other light except the starlight coming in through the tall windows. Apprehensively he crept through the doors into the south-east arm of the colonnade and then down onto the grand terrace opposite the old gym. At this point the noise of distant carousing met his ears.

Crossing the grand terrace, he made his way into the woodland and crept cautiously towards the old wartime air raid shelters hidden amongst the trees. Here he stood and listened by one of the air vents. If the anti-gas flaps were open it was possible to hear what was going on below. He stood and listened, and waited.., and waited...

* * *

Down in the shelters none of the gang members or their sycophants could disagree that the night's abductees had given satisfaction and that the acts they had been forced to perform upon each other had been both entertaining and satisfactorily recorded on photographic plate. But Leport now feigned displeasure with the 'floor show'. There were scores to be settled and this was the opportune moment. The leering Flynn was prominent and vociferous among the onlookers. The erstwhile knife-wielding junior was about to get his comeuppance.

Leport pointed to Alexander: "Come here, you pious little prick, you sanctimonious little sod." Alliterations were a feature of his verbal abuse. His voice betrayed a drunken slur.

As Alexander came within his reach he grabbed the *Agnus*

Dei round the boy's neck and snatched at it viciously. The clasp gave and it came away in his hand. Hc made a show of reading the inscription on the reverse; it fuelled his invective. "Well damn and blast your poxy mother's soul to eternal hell fire. She ain't gonna save you tonight, laddie. Is she, boys?"

This raised an appreciative cheer from the array. Mercifully, Alexander was too traumatised to take in what his tormentor-in-chief was saying. It was an unequal match, the big, beefy rugby-playing Dubliner Third Former holding forth from his chair and the youngest and slightest boy in the school quaking naked before him. Leport roared forth: "Yerragh! Away with this bauble..." With a much less than Cromwellian gesture he flung the medallion away from him, down the length of the shelter. It landed in some dark corner and slipped unnoticed through the duckboards.

Worse was to come. Much worse. Foul Mouthed Frank's gaze coursed down the length of Alexander's naked form and arrested on a particular physical attribute. He pointed gleefully and exclaimed: "Well, well, well... Look 'ee here... They've slipped a little Jew-boy in among us."

Tycho had not the faintest idea what Foul Mouthed Frank was talking about and Alexander could summon neither the wit nor the time to protest any non-Jewishness, not that it would have done any good.

"We don't allow Jew-boys at Monsalvat, do we boys?"

The array roared its agreement. Leport waxed forth: "Now's our chance to give a Jew-boy a *real* Christian baptism. Give little kosher-cock here the royal flush."

With that, the worst fears of the two abductees became realised. A drunken roar of unforgiving approval echoed along the shelter. Anxious to curry more favour, four of Leport's Third Form sycophants came forward and seized hold of Alexander. With practised ease they turned him face down, pinioned his arms and legs, and proceeded to frogmarch him out of the shelters and over to the Irish Gang's ultimate bullying chamber.

The ultimate bullying chamber was the squalid latrine block adjacent to the old gym. It contained five water closets and it was from these that the revolting ordeal took its name. Since the letting out of the greenhouses to local contractors, the latrines had become relegated to the use of the likes of carters and labourers coming onto the estate to deliver goods and collect produce. Otherwise, since the obsolescence of the old gym, the college had little use for the facility. It was seldom visited by plumber or janitor, so it would be in its usual state of disorder. That was the way the Irish Gang liked it. It was the threat of the 'royal flush', unstated but implicit, that made the two boys comply with the outrageous demands made upon them during the 'floor show'.

A line of leering gang members and sycophants followed the frogmarching party out of the shelter and over to the latrine, a distance of a few yards. In the shadows, the crouching Barden could hear Alexander's treble shrieks above the gruff tumult. He was pleading pathetically and ineffectually: "Please no... Please no..." As they carried him over he was repeating the phrase continually.

Back in the shelter, Tycho, still kneeling on the mat, had desperately tried to give his companion's reflexive pleas some substance: "But you can't do that... We did what you said... We did what you said..." And then: "*He* did what you said... It's not fair. Don't take him, don't, don't, please don't." And then, perhaps less earnestly, less stridently, more to himself than to the array, a moderation for which he would in the ensuing days castigate himself mercilessly: "Take me... take me..."

As it was, nobody took any notice. Above ground, Barden Sender put his hands over his ears to shut out the pathetic, fruitless pleadings of the struggling boy and the merciless clamour of the onlookers spilling out of the shelter. It was too much for him. Unseen, he turned and fled back onto the grand terrace, along the colonnade and up to the north transit port of the chapel. He burst through the double doors and ran up the nave towards the high altar. Only the red sanctuary light guided his progress. He flung himself on his knees at the altar rail and looked up towards the great crucifix that was suspended over the chancel. He launched into a 'Hail Mary' but did not complete it. He remembered it was still Saint Cazimir's day, the patron saint of all youth — for mercy's sake — and appealed to him. Finally, in his desperation composition failed him and he railed up inarticulately at the great Christ Crucified and any saint whose image might be within earshot: "Do something... please, please... do something." And then: "Why don't you do something? Stop them, please... please stop them..."

Christ Crucified gazed impassively down on the distraught boy.

'The words "take me... take me..." seared his conscience. Those words had come up through the air vent. Barden knew the voice that had spoken those words had been Tycho's. If Tycho was a fool to say that, by God he was a brave fool, braver than Barden knew he himself could ever be. Or perhaps Tycho knew that his implorations would go unheeded by the drink-fuelled mob triumphantly frogmarching Alexander over to the latrine block.

Sister Gloria had entrusted Alexander to Barden's care, a care which he had exercised discreetly enough. Hitherto, this had been a light enough burden; the other boys were considerate enough and Alexander himself was popular and respected among them. But now, here in the darkness of the night, Barden found himself impotent to exercise his care. The bullies would have their way with his charge and there was nothing he could do to stop them. Casting his eyes upwards towards the supposedly compassionate faces looking down at him, he bit his knuckles and tears of frustration coursed down his cheeks. It was near midnight. Perhaps these divine luminaries did not work nights. St Cazimir himself would be knocking off. To whom else could he turn? He knew that none of the Fathers would be available. He knew they always made themselves scarce on 'cabaret nights'. There was Father Laskiva but he was away for the weekend. He knew the prefects would not intervene in matters involving the Irish Gang. There was Wepper. But he was one and they were many. And had he not lately taken to living out at Rhiannon's parents' house, far away from this night's infamy? The impotence of the saints had delayed Barden too long. By the time he could rouse anyone to help it would be all over.

Barden had already taken on risk enough himself. Being found out of bed and bounds after 'lights out' without good reason would get any boy a caning. Furthermore he was running the risk of falling foul of the Irish Gang himself. If they came across him, they would be more than happy to rope him in for their execrable evolutions.

The desperate Barden left the chapel by the way he had entered and made his way to the south-east arm of the colonnade leading to the dormitory block. All was quiet now; the Irish Gang would be back in their dorm, celebrating another successful 'cabaret night'. Alerted by some movement ahead of him he flashed his torch along the colonnade. The beam revealed two boys of about his own age making a laborious progress towards him. One seemed to be helping the other who was walking with head bowed. Both were quite naked. Both were streaked with water, dirty water, the one more so than the other. There was no doubt who they were. They seemed to have no direction other than to distance themselves from the place of their torment. The light airs of the night carried a foul and disgusting stink to Barden Sender's nostrils. He recoiled in horror.

"Oh my Christ, oh my Christ, oh my Christ! What have they done?" And then: "Stay there, don't come any further." He realised some resolute action was needed; he addressed Tycho: "Take him to the night station. I'll go on ahead and warn Geddington." He turned to run on his errand and then, looking back, in a lame attempt at reassurance: "We'll soon have you cleaned up."

Mercifully, Geddington was on-station when Barden Sender arrived. Geddington was nothing if not methodical. It could be that he'd dealt with similar incidents before. Acting on the information hurriedly gabbled out by Barden, he prepared the ground for the arrival of the Irish Gang's latest victims. Mops, buckets, bowls, jugs, stools, glasses, brushes, combs, facecloths, rubber gloves, disinfectant liquid, shampoos, all had been hurriedly assembled by the time the distressed pair arrived at the door of the night station. They were directed straight into the showers in the sanatorium. Geddington asked Barden to mop the floor over which they had made their approach, still dripping water of dubious origin. He made Alexander sit on a stool under a shower jet. Gently, efficiently, he saw to it that the boy's body was washed clean and he worked a medicated shampoo several times into the despoiled wheaten locks and brushed and combed and combed and brushed, until he was well satisfied all was sanitised and sweet again. He cleaned out the boy's ears and made him gargle with TCP antiseptic solution as a precaution against ingested infections. Tycho, who had become sullied himself as a result of lugging his distressed companion over to the night station, was left to clean himself up under an adjacent shower.

Geddington checked both boys for signs of injury. Both had inflammations on arms and legs that would become bruises, as a result of their rough handling. Those on Alexander were consistent with him having been frogmarched while struggling violently. More outrageously, Geddington found what appeared to be cigarette burns on Alexander's genitals. He gently cleaned and dressed these injuries with burn dressings and fitted a suspensory bandage. As he performed these tasks he asked Tycho who was responsible for this outrage. Tycho looked away, shaking his head compulsively. Geddington had a good idea why.

His next question was gently probing and pertinent. "Tycho, did they make you do this?" Without waiting for a response he continued: "No, there's no need to answer that. It's all right... I know the way these... these bullies... go about things."

Tycho was not comforted.

Geddington's chief concern was Alexander. The boy was trembling uncontrollably. Geddington had him seated on a stool swathed in towels and he would not or could not speak. If his condition did not improve Geddington thought he might have to call an ambulance.

Tycho's concern for his companion in adversity was touchingly palpable. He crouched alongside Alexander, his arm about him, coaxing him with the glass of medicated gargle and whispering words of encouragement in his ear. The watching Geddington was struck with remorse. He knew only too well that he had been in considered dereliction of his duties in not patrolling the dormitories on 'cabaret night'. He had his price and he was too cheap. Looking at the touching scene before him he resolved that never again would he be induced to neglect his duties so.

Alexander was in no fit state to go back to his dormitory. Geddington decided to take the initiative and put Alexander into one of the hospital beds, and went into the ward to prepare it. On coming back into the bathing area he saw that Tycho was still alongside his companion.

Tycho looked up. "He's still trembling, sir."

Geddington was not normally addressed so deferentially. "Yes, I see. He ought not to be left on his own. Perhaps it would be best if you slept with him. Would you mind?"

"No. Of course not."

Geddington picked up the towel-clad Alexander and carried him into the ward. Tycho followed. Geddington had taken the towels away and was standing ready to fold the bedclothes over the prostrate Alexander; he motioned for Tycho to get in alongside him.

Tycho hesitated. "I'm naked, sir," he said plaintively.

Geddington was devastated by this simple pronouncement. The boy sounded so pathetic. In his supposedly efficient haste to deal with his principal patient, he had quite failed to notice what was so blindingly obvious about Alexander's companion in adversity. His voice was soft and his words solicitous: "Oh... Of course. I'll get you something."

He raided the adjacent laundry room for a spare pair of gym shorts and, the proprieties thus satisfied, Tycho climbed in beside Alexander, who lay on his side facing away from Tycho. Geddington saw Tycho put his arm across his still trembling companion and take hold of Alexander's right hand. Alexander's eyes were closed but Geddington saw his fingers and thumb gently close round the proffered hand. Dear God! Diminished though they were, it seemed the worst excesses and divisive designs of their tormentors could not sunder the bond between the two stalwarts.

Geddington drew the bedclothes up and over the pair and withdrew, leaving a night light on and a bell handy in case Tycho needed to summon him in the night.

Geddington returned to the night station, sat down at his desk and commenced writing up the medical log with the details of the incident. It was the first time he had logged an incident of this nature. He wrote with difficulty, for his hand trembled and he was continually dabbing his eyes with his kerchief. His tears were those of contrition. And of anger; anger that his anger could not be righteous.

* * *

One member of the Irish Gang did return to the Remove A dormitory later that night. An unseen hand cast some underwear and two crumpled suits of pyjamas into the dormitory laundry basket.

CHAPTER FIFTEEN

Retribution

As coincidence would have it, the weekly 'general congress' was scheduled for the Monday morning after Saturday's 'cabaret night'. At the meeting the Rector was holding forth in his inimitable manner. He had the medical log before him and had just perused its latest content with his quizzing glass.

"Geddington is not playing the game. Incidents of this nature should be dealt with otherwise." He deigned not to specify that other.

Father Laskiva thought discretion the better part of valour and decided not to press the Rector on that omission. Instead he ventured diffidently: "I feel that on occasions, Rector, there are things amiss with our patrol and reporting regimes." Laskiva did not feel inclined to be more specific than that. "May I suggest we convert to a clock-and-key regime? The cost would not be prohibitive and it would ensure that the dormitories are effectively patrolled at regular intervals. In the present case both Geddington and Father Fillery seemed to have been absent at critical times."

The Rector was not in receptive mood. "You are well aware, Father Laskiva, that we do have an effective fire and security patrolling regime for the dormitories and indeed all the school buildings throughout the night. Furthermore, we cannot expect each pastoral Father to remain in his quarters all of the time. Once the boys are settled down each Father is free to go about his rightful occasions elsewhere. And boys are devious creatures; if they are determined to circumvent the protections we put in place then at some time or other they are going to succeed. That has always been the way of it."

But Father Laskiva tremulously persisted: "Surely we can find out from the boys themselves who was responsible?"

The Rector was dismissive: "They won't tell. They never do." Then to Father Quedda: "Better see what we can do to tighten up on the patrolling regime."

And that seemed to be an end of the matter — for the moment...

* * *

Later that day Father Fillery was in the chapel taking confession, ostensibly in anticipation of the Eucharist the following morning. In the chevet, the rectangular area circumscribing the dome, and just beyond the south transept doors, the five confessional closets stood against the wall. They were a veritable wealth of dark varnished gothic panelling. The wall was common to the chevet and the hypotenusal ambulatory of the presbytery garth. Normally, each of the pastoral Fathers had his own confessional. The exception was when the Rector took confession himself. In which case he would use the same station as Father Fillery. He rarely did, the only 'regulars' being Wali Waliser and — before his decamping in September 1948 — Heinrich Daser. It was an urgent need for confession on Heini's part that had brought the two Germans to the gates of Monsalvat on a frosty night in December 1945. As for his compatriot, many thought Wali an unlikely penitent; he seemed to attend confession on a contingency basis and never followed it up with the Eucharist. It seemed an enduring anomaly.

In each compartment priest and penitent were separated by a subdividing partition equipped with a latticed window above a narrow shelf and a kneeler on the penitent's side. The latticed window was hinged and could be opened from the priest's side if necessary. Each compartment had three doors, two for the penitent, the third for the Father confessor. Priests entered from the ambulatory, penitents from the chapel. On the chapel side there was an auxiliary pew adjacent to each door where the waiting penitents could sit or kneel and pray if they were so inclined. Once a penitent had entered the confessional and closed the door behind him, the Father confessor would secure it by throwing a latch. Throwing the latch threw up a red disc which told other aspiring penitents that the compartment was occupied. The process worked something like an airlock in that, when the penitent had received absolution he could exit via the second door which would discharge him into the ambulatory. This procedure kept those thus absolved away from the contaminations inherent in the penitents still waiting. The priest would then unlatch the door on the chapel side and the red disk would go down, signalling the next penitent to come forward. A little handbell was provided by which an aspiring penitent could signal his presence if necessary.

For some reason best known to himself, Father Fillery arrived later than his colleagues. Eventually his were the only penitents left in the adjacent pew. The other Fathers had left the chapel. But in the shadows of the north side aisle another aspiring penitent was waiting. This penitent eschewed the solace of the pews. Instead, he was pacing silently up and down on rubber shod shoes, exhibiting an impatience unbecoming to the occasion. At last, the penultimate penitent became closeted. The pew had emptied. After a lapse of several minutes the red disk duly went down and Foul Mouthed Frank Leport walked the short length of the empty pew and entered the confessional.

But there had been yet other eyes in the further and darker interstices of the chapel. Unseen and similarly rubber-shod. The chapel was otherwise empty now. All the other boys would be at prep. William Wesley Wepper, The Bold Contemner of Monsalvat, rang the little handbell and waited. He could hear a low murmuring of voices emanating from Father Fillery's cubicle but it was too indistinct for him to make any sense of it. In any case he knew what his business was to be and felt no need to eavesdrop. In the prevailing silence he could however hear the lattice window being opened and then closed. He then heard the far door into the ambulatory opening and then closing as Leport exited into the ambulatory. Wepper became concerned lest Father Fillery should also leave his cubicle. He rang the bell again. The red disk went down in response. He advanced to the door and entered the dark cubicle. As the Bold Contemner of Monsalvat he had long absented himself from the confessionals but he knew the procedure from his younger days. He knelt at the lattice window and began the age old ritual.

"Bless me, Father, for I have sinned. It has been three years since my last confession. My sins are legion and reprehensible. So reprehensible that I cannot possibly intone them. Instead I have listed them in a document which I beg leave to render to you. Please open the lattice, Father, and I will pass it to you. If you do not grant me this indulgence I must turn away again and go wretched and unabsolved and unable to take Holy Communion."

This was an unprecedented departure from procedure. There was a distinct pause while Father Fillery considered this strange request. Wepper made no attempt to disguise his voice; there was no point. Everybody knew everybody else at Monsalvat. Father Fillery was suspicious. Why Wepper, why now and why him? That last was pertinent; Father Zackary would normally be the priest-confessor for the Sixth Form.

"Is that you, Wepper?" Normally the protocols forbade identification of the penitent but this was not normal.

"Yes, Father."

"This is not some kind of joke, is it? Are you truly contrite?

"Yes, Father, I am truly contrite."

Father Fillery could not believe his ears. If Wepper was a genuine penitent then his was surely the catch of the century. He was still cautious however and declined to exhibit any enthusiasm until he had confirmation. True, a three-year deficit of absolution might well justify a written deposition — and Wepper's record of derelictions in the interim had been prodigious.

"Very well then, you had better pass me your document. I trust it will not be too tedious."

Wepper heard him move and saw the latticed window ease in its frame as the priest withdrew the bolt on his side. Wepper had no document. Without waiting for the window to open, he sprang up from his knees, jerked it wide open, reached through and grabbed the priest by his garments with one hand and thrust the heel of his other hand under the priest's chin. By pulling the priest towards him he had him jammed in the window aperture, forehead against the top of the frame and head pitched backward at a painful angle. Wepper let go of the priest's garments and hooked the hand thus freed round the back of the priest's neck, pulling him towards him. The wooden partitions along the row of confessionals shivered with the shock. A crucifix over the window fell to the floor. Fillery feared for his neck. Wepper had him eyeball to eyeball — and the window aperture was too small for Fillery to bring his arms up to do anything about it.

Wepper launched into an obscene harangue, a harangue with a purpose: "Gimme the film cassette, you fuckin' cunt, I mean now, you bastard, you heard me, the fuckin' film cassette, just give me the film cassette or I'll break your fuckin' neck, you slimy Irish twat, come on move, I'm not seein'' it, faster, faster where is it?" And he continued in similar vein.

The hapless priest could only respond with a curious screeching noise through clenched teeth. He couldn't open his mouth and Wepper wasn't about to accord him an audience. Fillery swiftly got the message. Wepper saw his hand go down to fumble in one of his pockets. The hand came up again with difficulty, clutching a camera film cassette which he managed to let fall onto the window shelf. Wepper released his grip on the man and grabbed the cassette. He ran out into the ambulatory where there was some daylight from the leaded windows onto the garth. He gripped the tail of the film and ripped it out of the cassette. He held it up to the nearest window, exposing it to the light and thus ruining any images it might have contained. He then turned and flung open the priest's door of the confessional. Fillery was slumped against the opposite partition, dishevelled and in some state of distress. He looked up at the big Sixth Former with fear in his eyes, wondering what further violence he might inflict.

Wepper leaned forward and draped the exposed film round the priest's neck. "There you are, you fuckin' lousy twat, your poxy crowd'll get no joy from *that* cabaret night. Now what about some of your Catholic abso-fuckin'-lution? On second thoughts, you can ram it up your poxy jacksie."

And with that, Wepper withdrew, unrepentant and unabsolved. His choice vocabulary left the chapel in need of reconsecrating but only Fillery was witness to its vocal desecration and in view of the circumstances he would be loath to pursue the point.

Wepper had destroyed the film Leport had just rendered in exchange for money. He could have retained the film cassette intact but that would have rendered him a definitive blackmailer, of which role he wanted no part. Fillery would know better than to complain about being manhandled and Wepper had performed a signal salvage service for Tycho and Alexander.

* * *

The Bold Contemner had another retributive call to make that day. He picked a time when the Irish Gang would all be together in the Third Form dormitory. Foul Mouthed Frank welcomed him in characteristic style.

"Well fuck me if it isn't our Bold Contemner! To what do we owe the honour of your presence? Don't tell me you've been stickin' your dick in the ciborium again."

That last was a scurrilous allusion to Wepper's duties as sacristan. Foul Mouthed Frank was seated on his bed, cigarette in one hand, beer bottle in the other. Most of his lieutenants were draped languidly over the adjacent beds, similarly equipped and in several degrees of sartorial ease. They laughed like drains at his irreverent chaffing.

Wepper responded diffidently enough: "It's the Vudsen boy. He's lost a medallion he was wearing. It has some value. If any of you've seen it I would be obliged if you'll let me know."

"Yerraaagh!"It was Foul Mouthed Frank again. "Tis right you are..." Then on an impulse he added "...me bold contemner."

This was a cue for a song; in fact a parody of an Irish rebel song. His lieutenants took it up with gusto, taking full advantage of its antiphons:

'Tis right you are,
(Tis right you are,)
'Tis right you are,

('Tis right you are,)
'Tis right you are, me bold contemner
Right you are.

Just then Fitzgerald wandered in. "What's all the fuckin' row about then?"

"It's Wepper here. He wants to know if any of us've seen Vudsen's medallion."

"Oh, that precious little songbird and his blasted bauble! Last time I saw it, it was airborne; considerably airborne. In a trajectory. Probably on the Wirral by now. I doubt anyone'll see it again."

The rest of them guffawed. Wepper seemed unfazed. They were many, but he was big. He responded with a quizzical question: "What direction's the Wirral from here then?"

It was Fitzgerald again who obliged: "I think you'll find it somewhere in that direction." He waved airily towards the sash window at the end of his bed.

Without more ado Wepper moved in and picked him up by crotch and collar. Fitzgerald found himself lifted high above Wepper's head and being turned around like the rotor of a helicopter. A couple of hanging lampshades were sent reeling. Shouts of alarm and protest went up from his cronies. Some made as if to move in but Wepper was too quick for them. At this point he prefaced his intentions by paraphrasing, variously, the Roman orator Cicero, Job Chapter 4 Verse 8 and Galations Chapter 6 Verse 7, neither necessarily knowingly nor in that order, *videlicet:* "As ye sow, so shall ye fucking well reap."

As he delivered himself of that augmented homily he also delivered himself of Fitzgerald by heaving him at the aforesaid window. The glass and glazing bars yielded on impact and Fitzgerald found himself pitched headlong out of a first floor window.

"Fuckin' 'ell." And other expressions of disapprobation similarly phrased. "You daft twat, you've probably killed him." Several of them rushed out and down to the gardens below to retrieve their erstwhile garrulous compatriot.

Actually, Wepper knew there was a large bush below the window which would probably give the flying Irishman a sporting chance of an unbroken neck. He addressed the remaining gang members: "When he's found the medallion, on the Wirral or wherever, perhaps he'll be kind enough to deliver it at my study. Before prep tomorrow. Otherwise, I'll be back." As he strode out he turned and delivered a parting shot to a decidedly alarmed Foul Mouthed Frank himself: "And get that fucking window fixed, Leport. Christ knows you've enough money in your shitty kitty."

Outside he passed Fitzgerald being assisted in between two of his cronies. The bush had indeed saved his neck but it had otherwise not been kind to the flying Irishman. Unfortunately for him, it was a pyracantha in full thorn. His garments were torn to shreds and he was bleeding from multiple lacerations.

* * *

Later that evening, Wepper, who was working late, heard a timid knock on his study door. The door was ajar; Wepper looked up from his studies; it was De Leapey. Wepper addressed him in a mode appropriate to their respective stations: "And what do you want, you horrible little Donnybrook get?"

De Leapey was dangling something in front of him, as if it were a defensive talisman. "I've come to return this." It was Alexander's medallion .

Wepper reached out and took the precious object from De Leapey's hand. "And did Foul Mouthed Frank send you with this?"

"No. I've come of me own accord. I saw where it might have

ended up so I went looking for it in the shelter." He shuffled uneasily before continuing: "What we did with it didn't seem right. Frankie doesn't know I'm here. He'll fuckin' kill me if he finds out."

Wepper was unconcerned at De Leapey's domestic problems: "Such commendable concern for a medallion! Pity you didn't have some concern for the boy who was wearing it."

This had De Leapey shuffling again. "Perhaps we were a bit drunk" he ventured; then, realising his vulnerability he hastened to qualify that statement: "I'm not sayin' that's an excuse... maybe a reason though."

Wepper's response to that was puzzling for the contrite Irishman: "I know what's pulling Leport's strings.., and it ain't booze." De Leapey didn't press for enlightenment. The burden of the meeting seemed discharged and Wepper was suitably dismissive: "Well, you've done your good deed for the decade, you can piss off now. Oh, and you're still a fucking horrible little get."

Actually, as a hefty rugby scrum half, De Leapey wasn't all that little for his age, but he was not inclined to dispute the point with the towering and powerful Wepper. Instead he appeared to concur. "Aye, that's about right." And with that he shuffled diffidently away. He and Wepper seemed to have come to an understanding of sorts.

* * *

Wepper mused on the surprising fact that De Leapey had turned out to be a chink in Foul Mouthed Frank's armour. Wepper was only too aware that none of the present protagonists in the evolving story of Monsalvat was the complete master of his fate. Not Leport, not himself — and least of all Pynxcytte.

* * *

After De Leapey had left, Wepper examined the medallion. It was all there, the clasp was intact; just one link, an intentional failsafe, had been pulled out. The next day Wepper took it to a local jeweller. He gingerly spilled it out onto the counter from an envelope, telling him that it had been retrieved from a sewer. The jeweller picked it up with a pair of tweezers and examined it through his magnifying eye-glass. He could not fail to notice the intimate familial inscription on the reverse. He glanced up at Wepper who felt constrained to deny ownership. "Err... it's not mine. It belongs to someone else..."

The jeweller kept his counsel. He dutifully disinfected medallion and chain in alcohol and re-polished it with jewellers' rouge. He replaced the stretched link but at Wepper's insistence left the old link hanging, so that no part of the original would be missing. He returned it to Wepper in a crisp fresh envelope. When Wepper got it back to the college he wrote a message on the cover. He wrote it in violet ink and addressed it to Alexander.

Later that evening a young hand opened Alexander's napery drawer in the darkened refectory and slipped in the envelope. Later still, a younger hand opened the same drawer and took the envelope out.

* * *

Later that week Monsalvat's very Welsh music master requested an audience of that day's general convocation. He was ushered in, seemingly in a state of some agitation.

The Rector addressed him perfunctorily: "Yes, Mr Parry-Jones, what is it?"

"It's Alexander... err... Vudsen, that is. I can't get him to sing.

I give him the cue and he just shakes his head and looks down and won't sing a note."

The Rector was unfazed. "Why don't you threaten him with an imposition or detention or something? You have the authority."

"No, he won't sing because he can't sing. Besides, I've never done that and I'm not going to start now. Boys... my boys... sing because they want to sing. Not because somebody is lighting a fire under them."

This proprietoriness did not please Pynxcytte. 'They're not *your* boys, Mr Parry-Jones; they're *our* boys."

Such pertinence did not deter Parry-Jones, who responded with a steely determination in his North Welsh lilt: "Oh really, Rector. Your boys? Perhaps you should take better care of them then. *Secura nidificat* indeed! Somehow we seem to have silenced the best songbird in the nest."

"That will do, Mr Parry-Jones." Pynxcytte was somewhat taken aback that a hired hand should risk his stipend with such abandon. Things seemed to be getting out of hand with this Vudsen boy. He thought it politic to continue in a more conciliatory tone: "All we can do is return this..." The ghost of a smile passed across his face "...this fledgling.., to lessons and give him some time. He has become somewhat unsettled of late."

This last seemed to incense further the forthright Mr Parry-Jones. "As far as I can see the boy is in a permanent state of unsettlement. He came to us a wholesome, well-balanced, intelligent boy with much promise. In just a few short months we've managed to turn him into a furtive, nervous wreck."

"Is there anything more, Mr Parry-Jones?" asked the Rector, rather pointedly.

The music master thought for a moment then replied resignedly: "No, Rector."

"Then we bid you good morning."

And with that Parry-Jones left the room. The convocation expected the Rector of Monsalvat to comment on this latest untoward development but he elected to remain silent and the meeting deployed to other business. Worse was to come...

* * *

"You disappoint me, Vudsen. When it comes to a career I can only recommend the law for you. It's the one profession wherein remuneration is in inverse proportion to intellectual velocity."

This rebuke was accompanied by the consigning of an exercise book to a trajectory between physics master Calthrop and the boy so castigated. When the boy made no effort to catch or otherwise avoid the flying object, Mr Calthrop realised that something more urgent than scholarly tardiness ought to be commanding his attention. Mr Calthrop had previously noticed that the normally alert and responsive boy had become inattentive and sluggish of late; was exhibiting a faraway look and had developed staring, bulging eyes. His complexion had lost some of its fairness and he looked pasty and pale.

The flying book bounced off Alexander's desk top and ended up on the floor. The boy meanwhile sat with his eyes closed, seemingly oblivious of Calthrop's unaccustomed castigation.

At this point it was Tycho who thought fit to intervene. Querulously putting his hand up, he imparted the news: "He hasn't been to the toilet for a week." The class greeted this intelligence with astonishment and one or two suppressed sniggers.

"Silence!" Calthrop took commendable command. "We need to get this boy to the san. You, Gyles-Skeffington and you... er... Norton, remain here. McGuckin, run to the bell tower and alert Godred to attend here most urgently with the wheelchair. The rest of you, take your books with you and transfer to the prep room. Wait for me there. Meanwhile, you, Sender, will be in charge. Off you go."

Later that morning Alexander was examined in the sanatorium by Doctor Tulloch. On undressing the boy he expressed considerable concern at the fading bruises on his arms and legs. Doctor Tulloch opined that they were consistent with the boy having been frogmarched. The matter was subsequently put to the Rector but he assured the doctor that he was aware of the contusions and that the matter had been dealt with. Otherwise, in the sanatorium the good doctor passed a practised hand over Alexander's taut and distended abdomen and immediately recommended hospitalisation.

The upshot was that Alexander found himself in hospital once again, this time under treatment for an impacted colon. Once again it was the peripatetic Father Laskiva who was tasked with visiting him. On his second visit the priest was disconcerted to learn that Alexander's condition had worsened and that he seemed to have contracted an infection. When he arrived at the boy's bedside he became seriously concerned. Alexander was running a high temperature. He was babbling incoherently and plucking at the sheets in an ominous manner. The priest knew the signs of old and thought he could sense the Angel of Death dallying over the boy's bed. Impulsively he put his hand under the sheets to feel the boy's feet. They were reassuringly warm. The priest leaned back in the visitor's chair and heaved a sigh of relief. He prayed for thc boy but otherwise made no issue of it with the nursing staff, believing the impression lay within himself.

Within a day or so Alexander's fever had responded to medication. On his next visit Father Laskiva was relieved to find him duly purged and x-rayed and pronounced returned to regular health. Rest and a bland diet completed the work. His complexion lost its sallow look and he became alert and bright of eye once again. He remained disturbingly uncommunicative and introspective, however. True, the remedial treatment had been an ordeal for the boy and he was still physically weak from the purgings and enemas but it did not warrant this development.

A visit from Lance, arranged with the permission of the Fathers, did little to lift the boy's spirits. Alexander lay on the pillows and remained passive and uncharacteristically unanimated. He seemed faintly pleased to talk with Lance about things that had happened during the Christmas holidays but didn't seem much interested in future matters. Lance came away disappointed and disturbed and confided as much to Father Laskiva.

It was only when the priest made another visit that the reason for the boy's introspection became evident. The priest mentioned God in passing, as priests are wont to do. Alexander's immediate response shocked him to the core. "What God?"

The boy's voice was flat and his tone betrayed cynicism. Coming from such a young and trusting boy, the response was incongruous in the extreme.

Father Laskiva initially was speechless; but then he recovered and purposefully decided not to respond in kind. The bedside of a sick child is not the place or time to enter into a theological discussion. Resolution of Alexander's state of mind would have to wait. Sufficient for the present that he said a prayer for his young charge's peace of mind and continuing recovery. Significantly, the boy declined to join in the prayer or to endorse it with a reassuring 'amen'. Despairingly, Father Laskiva took Alexander's left hand and clasped it between his own hands; somehow it surprised him to feel how small and dainty a young boy's hand could be. He became quite overcome. Alexander look puzzled; the priest felt it necessary to say something. All he could find to say was, "Oh, Alexander, your hand is so small". The boy fixed him steadily from his pillows with his piercing blue eyes. He was otherwise expressionless.

The hospital was ready to discharge its young patient. Easter was imminent and Father Laskiva had to be mindful of the intensifying burden of priestly duties accordingly. He said a gentle goodbye to his young charge and promised to return on Maundy Thursday to bring him back to college. Only then could the battle for Alexander's soul commence...

CHAPTER SIXTEEN

Dark Nights of the Soul

Maundy Thursday, 1950. The Easter break at Monsalvat was due to commence on the ensuing Saturday and it was considered expedient, given the approval of the doctors, that Alexander should be discharged prior to the break. And so it came about that Father Laskiva was given the duty of collecting him from Llandudno hospital.

During the short journey back from the hospital, neither priest nor boy spoke. Father Laskiva had seated Alexander in the rear seat of the Humber as if to isolate him. By the time they arrived back at college, lunch would be over and the refectory would be closed. Father Laskiva decided to break the ice, so to speak, and treat Alexander to an impromptu late lunch. Rather than turn into the college town gate he carried on into the town, turned right off the main street and drove down the hill towards the railway station. He parked the car on the station frontage and the pair walked through the tunnel under the station to the little beachfront café.

After a snack eaten largely in silence, they lingered over an ice cream. Father Laskiva had a coffee, Alexander a bottle of Sparkling Special with a straw. The place had emptied of the Easter day-trippers, the bill was paid, the young girl who waited at table had retired to the rear and they had the place to themselves. Father Laskiva took the opportunity of returning to the subject of Alexander's wavering faith. He commenced with an opening salvo.

"Alexander, there is much evil in the world. That is nothing new, it has always been so. And, as you have seen, some of that evil can occur even within the walls of Monsalvat. But evil is offset by much good. Much more good than evil. Otherwise the world would not work for us. We must strive to do good. The battle is unceasing. And our striving is better done within a framework. The Catholic faith is such a framework. Your striving will be all the more effective for it. There is a good fight to be fought — and I think it is time you were returned to the fray."

Alexander agreed that good must be striven for; but he gave short shrift to the framework argument. Shortly into the ensuing conversation he was holding forth. "Are all those whose lives have passed before the advent of Christ condemned to limbo? Those who built Stonehenge, for instance? Those whom you call heathens? Are they lost to salvation? 'Tis a strange logic to come from such an understanding being. Could you explain it to me please, Father."

Father Laskiva became more perturbed now. Here was a priest and a little boy conversing over an ice cream but the conversation had taken a strange and un-childlike turn. He found himself consumed with anguish for the very soul of the poor, strange, beautiful, vulnerable and confused creature he had before him. The creature had the form and visage of a seraph but the devil's words seemed to be issuing from its mouth. Father Laskiva had been schooled in all the arguments but, coming from such a palpably innocent and child-like source, Alexander's utterances were enough to plant the worm of doubt into the mind of a saint. The priest found himself compelled to look to his own sustaining faith. The matter was not to be resolved there and then. The little beachfront café was an incongruous setting for an impending Dark Night of the Soul. In the far distance a faint rumble of thunder could be heard, seemingly portentous. By now the priest could distinguish thunder from Pencadno's background noise of sporadic blasting in the granite quarries high in the mountainside.

The words Alexander was using were not the words of a typical English schoolboy. But Father Laskiva was the boy's confessor. He undoubtedly knew more of Alexander's history than anyone else at Monsalvat. He knew the boy before him was not a typical English schoolboy. Indeed, he was not English at all and, in truth, the only bit of English *terra firma* he had ever walked upon was a short length of pavement between the college limousine and one of the flying-bridges at Liverpool landing stage. The English border was some forty miles to the east of where they were. Alexander was stateless. His had been an old Hanseatic family. His father hailed from Lübeck, his mother from Switzerland. Furthermore, he was not of this hemisphere in more ways than one. He had witnessed things that were mercifully beyond the experience of the average English schoolboy. He had grown up in Manchuria during the Japanese occupation and had seen man's inhumanity to man at first hand. Elsewhere in the East he had seen the bloated corpses, many tied hand and foot in murderous genocide, swirling in the muddy river currents of Asia; had seen — and smelled them — bursting odoriferously against the stem bars of the steamers he rode.

Of those innumerable bloated corpses, Alexander was now asking him to explain what happened to the concomitant souls. Those souls, insofar as they were acknowledged to exist at all, were not Catholic, he urged; indeed, they were not Christian at all. Alexander had paced the temples and pagodas of the East. Those souls belonged to a multiplicity of faiths. Were they all consigned to some limbo at the whim and caprice of this priest's God just because they were born in other latitudes than Christendom? Was there not some monumental injustice in that?

Father Laskiva had no ready answer, at least none that would serve a young boy. He decided to turn the question aside and get to the crux of the matter; the incident which had damaged the boy's trust in the Monsalvatian concept of *secura nidificat* and the greater concept of its underlying faith.

"What happened to you that night was unspeakably horrid. But people do unspeakable things to other people every day, Alexander. All over the world. I don't have a ready answer. We must assume it's part of some great design of which we can know nothing in this world."

At this supposed reassurance Alexander's eyes became downcast and his voice took on a steely tone. "Then I'd rather not be a part of that design. If that's the kind of design you priests preach then I'd rather not be a part of it." There was a hint of distress in his voice now. "No matter it was my father's faith, I'd rather not be part of it."

Father Laskiva was appalled. He reached out and grasped the boy's forearm. "Alexander! What are you saying? Oh my child, my poor, poor, child, what have they done to you? What have they done to you that you would deny God *and* your own father — your own poor, dead father? You came to us as your father's son; now you're talking like the son of nobody."

There was a long silence. The priest spoke first. He decided to take a different tack: "All right, let's calm down; let's see if we can get to the bottom of this. You no doubt know there's a senior everybody knows as The Bold Contemner. Was it he who put you up to this?"

Alexander denied this vehemently. "No, no. Don't try to blame The Bold Contemner. I met him just two times at the beginning of last half and he never did or said anything to persuade me from my faith. I assumed he was a Catholic, same as me. I only knew him as William Wepper. I never knew he was called The Bold Contemner until Barden — Sender, that is — told us about it in the dorm later in the term." He fell silent for a while, lost in thought, then he suddenly asked: "You know of Pascal's Wager?"

Father Laskiva felt free now to gently chide Alexander and be dismissive. "Yes, Alexander, I am a divinity graduate; we did things like Pascal's Wager." He regarded the boy expectantly.

Alexander was not to be deterred. "In the Far East we have people like the Buddhists and the Taoists and the Shintoists and suchlike. They don't set out to do deliberate harm to people like you Christians seem to do here." Father Laskiva was disturbed by the boy's use of the disassociating pronoun but let him continue unchecked. "In whose God is one to believe? Pascal seems to exclude about two thirds of the world population, would you not agree? Are they all going to a Christian hell, Father? In any case, why believe when that very belief must surely demean you in the eyes of your chosen God?"

"Perhaps you could enlarge upon that," said the priest, somewhat more cautiously now.

Alexander duly obliged with an example closer to home than the priest felt comfortable with. "The chief bully at Monsalvat surrounds himself with henchmen but he also finds himself surrounded by toadies — sycophants."

Not for the first time was the priest impressed by the range of the boy's vocabulary. Alexander didn't name this bully but Father Laskiva knew well enough he was talking about the one known among the boys as Foul Mouthed Frank, the instigator of 'cabaret night' among other things.

Alexander continued: "They know he despises them, but they fawn on him and do what pleases him in case he might turn on them and hurt them too. In your philosophy God is no better than such a bully and you would have us be his toadies. Surely a just God — one who was not a bully — would think more of someone who didn't believe in him but who nevertheless did good or at least did no harm — because it was the civil thing to do — rather than some toady who only worshipped him and did things that pleased him because of fear of what that God might otherwise do to him. Is your God a jealous God... an unjust God?"

Divinity or no, Father Laskiva was both impressed and stymied. Of course he was familiar with the arguments, but he never expected to hear them emanating from one so young. And to hear Almighty God likened so eruditely to Foul Mouthed Frank Leport...

Having delivered himself of his monumental interrogatory, Alexander returned to his bottle of Sparkling Special. He sucked on the straw, casting his eyes expectantly upwards towards the priest. He had spoken with serenity but his expression remained glum. Under the table he crossed his ankles and swung his legs, rapping the heels of his shoes repeatedly against the crossbar of the chair, acting like a child half his age and betraying thus an inner tension. He knew he was taking liberties with Father Laskiva. Any of the other priests would give him short shrift, content to believe that a punished boy is going to be a devout boy eventually; or if not that, at least a salutary example to his peers. Alexander took the priest's silence to be acquiescence.

"Then The Bold Contemner is right." Priest and boy stared at each other over the table for what seemed a long minute. Then Alexander continued unrelentingly: "I've heard it said that man created God in his own image..."

At this, Father Laskiva sighed; it was going to be a long night, he thought resignedly. Up to now he had managed to retain his composure. But now he had to ask himself: how did he himself fare in the scenario Alexander had painted? Was he one of Alexander's sycophantic believers, chary of some sanction in an afterlife? Could the Almighty embrace such a fleshly sentiment as jealousy? It was absurd of course — but he had no ready riposte for an eleven-year-old boy.

But semantic hypotheses were to be the least of his worries on this portentous day. Darker thoughts assailed him now, thoughts long since suppressed, thoughts which had lain undisturbed in the innermost interstices of his mind since his own schooldays and his days in the seminary. He began to see the creature before him in a different light; a light which his upbringing and training had been unconsciously occulting ever since he had clapped eyes on Alexander. He became uncomfortably aware that the creature before him exuded all those epicene attributes that attached to young boys. And this particular boy was at this moment as perfect a specimen as the human condition could render. From this point on there could only be detractions, those inevitable deteriorations of both mind and body that came with the onset of maturity. Indeed, the creature before him might turn out to be a latter day Gilles de Rais! The priest extinguished the thought as the outrageous absurdity it was. Nevertheless, he was left contemplating the piercing sapphire eyes, the immaturely handsome visage, the carefree tumble of wheaten locks, the flawless honeyed skin, the delicate frame, the little hands, the dulcet voice, the maddening dimples, the sinuous way he moved. The priest's turbulent mind began throwing up other aspects of human relationships and confounded faith. He contemplated his own mature and already-failing flesh and felt repelled by it. He could feel his inclinations beginning to move from pastoral concern to incipient envy. And from thence towards certain desires ...

His unconscious mind took this moment to remind the priest that his family name had originally been spelled with a 'c' where the 'k' now stood. Why had some recent ancestor felt compelled to make the change? Was there something in the Laskiva blood line that merited such a distancing? The prospect of an unwarranted guilt loomed large now. In that little beach front café he now found himself alone and adrift on an ever darkling sea off a dangerous and unlighted coast without the stars of his faith to guide him or the power of prayer to buoy him up. He had seen others go thence and not return; would he go the same way? In his erstwhile complacent scheme of things, the priest had never expected to find himself consigned to a boys' school. Notwithstanding he had been a boy himself he was now finding boys to be strange, beguiling and disturbing creatures. Not that Father Laskiva had ever, would ever, harm any of his young charges; he was an honourable man — but he found himself reeling without a compass now on uncharted waters.

For the first time since childhood Father Laskiva found himself experiencing personal guilt. He now felt defiled and unworthy in the presence of this creature. In his mind's eye the innocent scene of priest and young boy enjoying an ice cream in a beachfront café took on a more sinister cast. Father Laskiva found himself looking about him furtively, wondering if other eyes might be passing judgment on him. Mercifully there were no other eyes present. He tried to reassure himself that the scenario he was painting was subjective to himself alone, but that did not assuage a mordant sense of guilt.

Then another thought pierced his heart like an icy stalactite. Had those words of the devil emanated from an instrument of the devil? Was this exquisite creature such an instrument, sent of its own volition to beguile him away from his own faith and towards the jeopardising of his own soul? Was he the one who was being tested here? The creature could be an instrument of God, set across his path to shake his complacency — or an instrument of the devil, likewise. As must the devil then so must

God be aware of those long-suppressed thoughts of his. He felt biblically naked and ashamed. Doubt and fear and shame were bearing down upon him in equal proportion. This day, which had begun in complacent certainty, had become a day of crisis. Beads of sweat sprung from his brow and he became visibly agitated. His young adversary became concerned: "Are you all right, Father?"

"Yes.., yes... boy, yes." The words came staccato and with more than a hint of petulance. It was the first time the priest had addressed him thus. Alexander was perturbed.

Father Laskiva responded to these disturbing thoughts with the only feasible countervailing force he could think of. He must pray. Pray for the deliverance of Alexander from doubt. Pray that Alexander himself was not an instrument of the devil. Pray that he himself should be delivered from the temptation of evil thought. Yes, the priest knew that he had never, would never, do harm to any of his charges. He could not say however that his thoughts would not do harm to his own soul. Truly that last must be the greatest burden of his implorations to his Maker?

The priest decided to take yet another tack with his troublesome charge. He knew Alexander was unaware that his school fees would soon run out and that he would have to leave Monsalvat unless something turned up.

"Alexander, do you understand that if you persist in denial of your faith you will have to leave Monsalvat?"

The boy's response was pertinently oblique: "That would make no difference to the bullies, Father; they would just carry on bullying the others."

Father Laskiva despaired; of the boy — and of Monsalvat.

From his lowly position in the college hierarchy he knew he could find no words of comfort that would pass muster with such a perspicacious boy.

But Alexander had not finished. "And what of the Bold

Contemner? What a nick-name! Why hasn't *he* been expelled?" Again, from his lowly position in the college hierarchy the priest knew he could find no explanation that would pass muster with such a perspicacious boy. Alexander had wrong-footed him again.

The priest could only fall back on Sister Gloria's rationale; that the Rector of Monsalvat forbore the transgressions of The Bold Contemner in the hope that Monsalvat could publicly redeem his soul before he graduated; and that such a public redemption would be a timely and a salutary exemplar for the rest of the boys. Alexander's response was to point out that the Rector had the option of extending to him the same indulgence. The priest could only weakly respond that "Monsalvat could not sustain more than one such exemplar at any one time". To which the boy riposted to the effect that, as the Bold Contemner was on the point of graduation, their respective tenures would largely be discontemporaneous. Alexander had wrong-footed the priest yet again. Neither priest nor boy could know that the real reason for the Rector's supposed forbearance lay within a locked attaché case in a London safe deposit.

Wary of his young charge now, the priest set out to be rid of him. For the time being at least. With his countervailing logic in disarray he needed to reconsider his approach and re-group his mental forces. In the ridding he did his best to sound matter-of-fact: "Leave me now, Alexander. Take your things from the car, it's not locked. You can go straight back to your dormitory. Sister Gloria has made up your bed for tonight. After the Easter break I'm afraid you'll have some catching up to do." He avoided mentioning the possibility of Holy Communion before breakfast; that must be a matter for the boy's conscience. Father Laskiva held out little hope. If only the clock could be put back...

The heel of the bottle of Sparlding Special bubbled dry on the end of Alexander's straw. As he got up to leave the table

Father Laskiva made one last desperate play for the boy's conscience. Against his better judgement he would throw an extreme example at his youthful adversary. He began by going over old ground.

"What they did to you that night was unspeakable, Alexander... but we must keep it in perspective. People do bad things to other people every day, all over the world. As we know, you've seen some of that for yourself in the Far East. Such inhumanities do not furnish a reason for denying one's faith." Then the *coup de grace:* "For instance you cannot compare the Passion of Our Lord with the tribulations of a bullied schoolboy. Indeed, to attempt to do so would amount to blasphemy."

"So you say, Father... but which of the two would be the more terrified?"

Alexander had succinctly destroyed the priest's ultimate exemplar with a comparison, a relative that proceeded to an absolute truth. Father Laskiva could conjure up no feasible rejoinder. He was reduced to looking blankly at his adroit juvenile adversary.

"If you need me, Alexander you'll find me in the chapel." Then, looking away: "I must pray for you, my child."

The boy made no reply. Without more ado he got up from the table, passed through the door, out of sight and out of earshot, to take the short walk up the hill to the college. Father Laskiva was left contemplating a straw in an empty lemonade bottle; the trappings of childhood. In that contemplation fell upon him a better understanding of a child's perspective and he inwardly castigated himself for having been so blindly indifferent to the tribulations of childhood's estate.

" ...and for myself," he added, under his breath. It was indeed going to be a long night.

* * *

But Alexander had other plans afoot for the rest of that day. It was a games afternoon when normally — insofar as anything was normal now — Lance and he would surreptitiously make their respective ways to the peach house. Lance would surely have found out that his blood-brother was coming out of hospital and Alexander felt he would surely be there.

And so it was. On their respective ways to the peach house two young hearts palpitated in expectation. At last, the two blood-brothers found themselves in each other's presence. Absence had indeed made hearts grow fonder and Lance's embrace was exceptionally prolonged and passionate. After which the two compared notes. Except that Alexander made no mention of his loss of faith. He was sensing that Lance had something up his sleeve. That sense was intensified when Lance asked him to take off his shirt.

Alexander thought the request strange but he trusted Lance implicitly. He moved to comply. Perhaps Lance simply wanted to see more of him... He cast his shirt onto one of the chairs and stood before Lance in singlet and shorts.

"Turn around."

Intrigued now, Alexander made a play of spinning round several times and ending up facing away from Lance. He waited, expectantly. He could sense Lance moving in behind him.

Now Lance spoke slowly and deliberately: "I've got something to... to return to you. You might guess what it is. It's an object. I have passed it through methylated spirits and shaken it with jeweller's rouge to purge it of the hands that have profaned it. You must have guessed by now what it is."

Alexander caught a glint of something in his peripheral vision. He cast his eyes upwards. At long last he could see his precious *Agnus Dei* dangling on its golden chain. Lance brought it in under the boy's chin. Alexander felt the cold of the metal against his bare skin as Lance fumbled to secure the clasp behind his neck. That task completed, Lance sealed the ceremony by leaning in and planting a chaste kiss on Alexander's right cheek.

"I know what this means to you; I'm only so sorry that it had to be my unworthy hands fastening the clasp. I'm so conscious that there must have been.., other hands, in other days..." Lance's voice tailed off with the ghost of a sob.

For a moment Alexander did not move. He was still standing with his back towards Lance and, incidentally, facing towards the door by which he had entered. Suddenly, without a word, he ran towards the door, struggled frantically with the handle, threw it open and took off as fast as his legs could carry him. Lance was concerned; he had not expected this reaction.

"Alexander, your shirt..."

But the boy cared not for the discarded garment. Lance could see that Alexander was not running towards the college, instead he was running in the direction of the chase gate. Lance would have called after him but he realised he must be discreet; there might be other people about. He guessed that Alexander was running down to the beach.

Alexander knew not what he was running towards or what he was running from. He only knew that he must run; run in the hope that somehow he would arrive somewhere where his present anguish might be assuaged. Instinctively he ran downhill and towards that arm of the ocean that had born him to Monsalvat. Almost without knowing, he crossed the railway line by the country footbridge, about a half mile north-east of the railway station. The setting of the sun found him seated on a shingle scarp with the land at his back. Now he abjured that land for the balm of the open sea. He fixed his eyes on the horizon, for somewhere out there lay the track of the *Antenor* stretching back... back.., into the long happy days of the past, days of love and certainty; days now irretrievable. Would that he could rewind that westbound passage and somehow translate himself back to those halcyon times within the bosom of his family. How they would caress him and how he would hug his little sister!

Dusk was being hastened by beetling storm clouds gathering above the boy's head. Of them he was heedless. Let the storm rage; perhaps the lightning would strike and his anguish would be over for all time. And his dilemma. Let the lighting blast him back to a past where he could believe in the faith of his fathers and find succour therein. It seemed a fair bargain. He just hoped it would be quick.

Lance hid the boy's discarded shirt under his blazer, then he locked the wicket gate at the peach house and hurried to the great parterre to look for any of Alexander's form fellows. As it was a games afternoon, there was no prep. He was in luck. There were small groups of them hovering around the benches. He recognised Tycho and, at some risk of discovery or challenge, he furtively beckoned the younger boy over to him. After a hurried and surreptitious consultation, during which Lance necessarily kept most of his cards close to his chest, it was agreed that they should wait until supper. If Alexander had not appeared by then, Tycho would organise a search party. It was never mooted that Father Fillery or anyone else in authority would be informed.

By the time supper was over and the boys were coming out of the refectory, the early evening sky had taken on a menacing blackness and distant flashes of lightning lit the sky. Out of sight of authority a small group of 'A' Removites donned their dark blue raincoats, armed themselves with torches, and sallied forth from their dormitory. They made their way across the sports field, climbed over the chase gate and headed for the country footbridge about half a mile to the north-east of the railway station. Some were concerned now at the lightning activity and there was much urgent discussion about the supposed propensities of lightning. The footbridge loomed up ahead.

It was a metal lattice affair with a timbered decking and they knew they would either have to cross it or risk running across the railway line. The consensus was that they should run over the bridge in twos, it being believed that the animal heat of any greater number might attract a lightning strike.

It was quite dark by the time they got to the bridge but sheets of lightning were showing up every last detail brighter than day. As they passed over the bridge the lightning flashes revealed a diminutive figure far out on the sands, seated on a shingle scarp. They knew it was Alexander.

Out on the shingle scarp the scantily clad boy contemplated his wretched condition, oblivious of the chilling wind and careless of the dangers of the storm. He was gazing wistfully towards the horizon. He was clutching the medallion and holding it to his lips. The coldness of the metal seemed to change to a burning fire, searing into his flesh. This was the very medallion — the *Agnus Dei* — which had been blessed by the Metropolitan of Shanghai and which his dear mother had placed around his neck at the moment of their parting. Her very hands had fastened the clasp and mother and son had prayed together for Godspeed on their respective journeys and in the hope of a happy reunion in a distant land, a reunion that could now never be. The amulet was the symbol of all that he had now rejected. Now it was his turn to regret. And to reconsider. His sufferings and degradations at the hands of his fellow Monsalvations, gross as they were, might not after all be comparable with the historic agony of his Redeemer. The argument he had put to Father Laskiva about a child's unique capacity to experience terror was irrefutable, but that argument stood to be subsumed in the greater contemplation of a superhistoric event. He contemplated that he might have committed an act of arrant arrogance in presuming to compare it. Father Laskiva could be right. Under the touch of the talisman round his neck Alexander found his very soul assailed by an incipient mordant remorse. Quite incidentally, he found that by dint of stretching the chain to its fullest extent he could put the medallion in his mouth. He sat there sucking on it vacuously, as a baby might suck on a comforter. Perhaps, he thought, when they found him burnt to a crisp by a lightning strike they would find the medallion burned into his tongue.

By the time the search party had walked the narrow scrubland alongside the railway line and come level with the figure, the storm had intensified. The wind had got up and the lightning was grounding in lurid red columns. The distant rumblings had changed to deafening cracks and earth-shaking reverberations. The party fetched up in a tunnel of overhanging bushes, crouching low and fearful of venturing further, for there was no shelter now between themselves and the distant figure. They tried calling out his name but the wind took their voices away. The lightning bolts intensified, seeming to strike each side of the figure on the scarp. There was no doubt now that Alexander was in real danger.

It was Raimo Haroldsen who took the initiative. He broke away from the others, holding his right arm out with the palm aspected backwards in an arresting gesture, and called out to them to stay where they were.

Haroldsen stepped from the cover of the bushes and started to run across the sands. The others watched him with mounting anxiety. Haroldsen was terrified now and had no inhibition in calling aloud upon God to preserve him. But still he carried resolutely on towards the figure on the shingle scarp. As he ran he kept his head down in a futile protective posture, conscious of the menace that could strike any second from the great dark bowl above him.

Alexander must have heard the approaching footsteps grinding over the shingle but he didn't turn round. Haroldsen fetched up behind the scantily clad figure. He grabbed him under the armpits and lifted him to his feet. He could feel Alexander's skin deathly cold to his hands. He turned to go back to the safety of the bushes, dragging Alexander unceremoniously behind him. Alexander was stiff with cold and 'the big Swede' was slowed down considerably.

Alexander spoke for the first and last time that night: "Leave me. Run. Save yourself."

But Haroldsen did not relinquish Alexander's hand. Alexander could hear the terrified Haroldsen calling hysterically upon God the Father, God the Son, the Holy Ghost, the Blessed Virgin Mary and any saint he could think of to save them both from death by lightning strike. He implored Alexander to join him in this but Alexander himself clearly was past caring and remained silent. Then a deafening crack of thunder was followed by a most eerie and sonorous booming noise. The shock wave had set the bells of Monsalvat's carillon ringing, sending a sombre metallic chord out into the night. It sounded for all the world like a final funeral orison for the two insignificant figures running across the open sands.

There was rain on the wind now. By the time the pair reached the comparative safety of the bushes it had become a deluge. Haroldsen quickly unbuttoned his raincoat and flung it around Alexander's bare shoulders, then he came round to face Alexander and buttoned him into the coat.

Alexander now had to consider that Haroldsen, a mere form fellow and an erstwhile adversary, albeit a reluctant one, was not beholden to him in any way. Remembering Father Laskiva's words, he had to consider that Haroldsen's brave and selfless action did indeed more than serve to offset the evil that stalked Monsalvat. Furthermore, on the way back from that shingle scarp, Haroldsen had graphically demonstrated that he would not have so acted had he not been fortified by a faith. Alexander's pragmatic logic told him that his deliverance from danger was due to that faith; and that faith could only be the very same faith of his father. It was a working hypothesis if nothing else. In the absence of that faith he would still be out on that shingle scarp. It might have been at this point that Alexander came to acknowledge that a Greater Hand was indeed directing matters that night; and was directing them via the agency of the faith upon which Monsalvat had been founded. True or false, his deliverance from real and mortal danger was indubitably attributable to that faith.

More such good was to ensue, good that was the logical corollary of what had gone before. The bedraggled party headed straight for the dimmed lights of the bath house. There would still be enough hot water in the system to serve their purposes. Caring hands stripped the wet clothes from Alexander and held him under a hot shower. Those same hands restored the blood to his skin with vigorous towelling. Other willing hands brought slippers, pyjamas and dressing gown and, thus accoutred, he was half carried back to the dormitory. A mug of hot cocoa was thrust into his hands. Minutes later the boys had him tucked up in bed. Kind hands threw on an extra blanket; others smoothed it out over the prostrate form. Exhausted, he fell into a deep sleep. Father Fillery was not at his post; for the moment authority was blissfully oblivious of the boys' adventure. It would be left to Sister Gloria to take exception to the piles of wet clothing and shoes that would affront her gaze in the morning. Urgent stories would have to be made up and tallied, based on being caught out between buildings in a sudden downpour. She might not be convinced, but they knew she would make good for her boys. She always did.

* * *

Against his better judgement Father Laskiva retired for the night. But for once the sleep of the just evaded him. He found himself troubled with dreams and the dreams became nightmares. He found himself transported to some gothic subterranean labyrinth which parodied the architecture of Monsalvat. Wherever he turned his head Alexander would appear to him in its darker and further alcoves, his angelic head perched atop a body clad in a flowing white sheet, a body with a snow-white dove on the shoulder. The priest would strive towards the apparition but the apparition would then transmute into a cadaver in a winding sheet, the head now a grinning skull, the dove a fire-eyed raptor. Repelled now, the priest would flee, but found himself weighed down with leaden limbs. A foetid wind blew through the chambers and catacombs. When the nightmare grudgingly granted him mobility he ran to find an exit but his efforts were futile. There seemed no way out.

Then the nightmare scene shifted; capriciously, illogically, as nightmares are wont to do. Delivered from the suffocating catacombs, the priest now found himself on a barren rocky landscape, a landscape lit only by the lurid glow of distant volcanoes and fiery stars. He was hand in hand with Alexander and the pair of them were running from ever encircling fumaroles and fissures with no sign of relief. An earthquake rocked the ground beneath their feet and distant reports boomed deep down in the torrid earth like the slamming of some great subterranean door. There was some high ground in the vicinity and the priest instinctively made for it, dragging the boy after him. But then a great fissure rived the rock beneath them and Alexander was pitched into it. The priest found himself lying prone on the edge of the fissure, looking down into it at the boy's upturned face and hanging on to him with one hand. In the depths of the fissure the glow of raging fires could be seen. Alexander was imploring the priest to save him but their hands parted and Alexander fell away into the abyss, down... down.., towards the fires of hell. The earth rocked, the fissure closed up and Father Laskiva found himself trapped by his arm up to his shoulder. The fissure might open again or it might stay closed for aeons. There was no pain but he was conscious of the lateral pressure of millions of tons keeping it closed and him trapped...

The priest awoke lathered in sweat. The bedclothes in disarray bore witness to his nightmare excursions. Instinctively he reached out and grabbed his chaplet on the bedside table and clutched it to his breast with shaking hands. Outside a great lightning storm was raging. The priest lived in a world of certainties. He strove to be interpretive of the nightmares inflicted upon him, presumably at the will of God. But the two scenarios seemed contradictory. He had at least been given a salutary lesson in the nature of true terror. He now had something to weigh against his perception of Christ's passion; a passion that He knew would end in serene certainty whereas the terror of a child in the hands of those whose intention was to inflict terror had, in the moment, no limit and no ending. The Almighty seemed to be castigating his disciple yet postulating no answers.

Further sleep was out of the question. He knelt at the bedside in urgent prayer but found no solace. He got up and dressed and made his way from the presbytery to the chapel. The ambulatory sheltered him from the downpour and he entered via the south transept door. At the door he tried to light a votive candle, but his shaking hands fumbled the attempt and the match fell to the floor. He persevered, succeeding at second attempt. He carried the candle into the transept, the flame guttering eerily in the draughts got up by the storm winds without. The troubled man thought himself unfit to mount the chancel plateau as would otherwise be his right as an ordained priest. Instead he knelt on the step at the altar rail as a common supplicant and, rosary in hand, launched into a marathon of prayer. Every so often the flashes of lightning beyond the clerestory windows lit up the interior of the chapel as the brightest of days and rendered as nought the sanctuary light and the guttering flame of his own votive candle teetering on the altar rail.

The storm that raged without was matched by the storm that raged within. The power of prayer was seeming to offer no solution or consolation. Eventually the storm without gave way to hours of silent darkness but the storm within would not so abate.

At long last a golden dawn illumined the windows of the clerestory. The storm without was gone and the peace of Good Friday had taken its place. Good Friday was the annual Day of the Sign of Peace when personal slights and transgressions within the community of Monsalvat stood to be publicly expiated. But that peace had yet to reach the heart of the priest kneeling at the altar rail. The silence of the chapel was still being broken by the frantic clicking of his rosary and his now-incoherent murmurings of holy invocations. In the chill of the long night unstemmed tears of anguish had dried cold and salt on the priest's cheeks. Prayer had not expelled the worm of doubt the image and wranglings of a young boy had planted in his mind. He was still unsure whether this creature which had so beguiled him was an instrument of God sent to test him or an instrument of the devil sent to ensnare him. Furthermore, he still did not know whether he was being inveigled into succumbing to long suppressed fleshly lusts. His pastoral relationship with Alexander remained beset by fatal pitfalls.

After an inordinate number of times round the rosary, Father Laskiva sensed a presence at his elbow. Surprised, he desperately tried to feign equanimity. Until he saw who it was.

"Alexander! You're up and dressed. It's not yet six o'clock. 'What ails you, boy?"

"I couldn't sleep, Father. You said you'd be here. I need to ask you something."

"Yes, Alexander, what is it?" Then more in hope than expectation: "You wish to make confession perhaps?"

"Later perhaps, Father. For now, I just wanted to ask you..."

Father Laskiva was alert and expectant now. The tiredness of his vigil became banished by a surge of adrenalin. His heart started to pound and his palms became moist. Still on his knees, he turned awkwardly on the step so that he half faced Alexander. As he did so his eye caught a glint of something. The missing *Agnus Dei* had reappeared round the boy's neck.

"... I just wanted to ask you what prayer would be suitable to... to..."

"Yes, Alexander?... Yes?... Yes?" There was no pretence at equanimity now. Could this unbeliever actually be asking for a prayer?

Alexander's quest for a suitable phrase resolved at last: "... to celebrate my return to the faith of my father." Father Laskiva's head quivered from side to side in ecstatic incredulity. His mouth fell open as if to speak but only an inarticulate gasping came forth. In an instant he felt himself delivered from the demons of that longest of nights. The power of prayer had prevailed. The beautiful creature before him was manifestly not an instrument of the devil. Neither could that creature be the temptress in disguise. Both child and priest had been sorely tested throughout this darkest of nights and in the end had not been found wanting. Father Laskiva could not have known of the dramas that had been played out in the peach house and on the dangerous foreshore but he instinctively knew that the boy had been delivered from a dark trinity of doubt, depression and remorse, and that the instrument of that deliverance must have been the mysterious return of the blessed medallion to a noble young breast.

The priest, in turn, now felt himself delivered of his own doubts — and from the most acerbic guilt. All the complexities that had tormented him throughout his long and lonely vigil fell away and were replaced by a divine serenity. He cast his eyes upwards and towards the great crucifix over the high altar. Then closing his eyes and raising his arms as if in crucifixion, he answered the boy's question, declaiming hysterically up into the great dome so that the words came echoing back down. It was clear his ordeal had drained him of all intelligible counsel.

"Any prayer you like, Alexander... any prayer you like."

The pastoral Fathers and their acolytes coming in for early morning Mass found Alexander on his knees at the altar rail, perfectly composed and quietly praying. They found Father Laskiva prostrated on the marble flags alongside him, his forehead resting on his forearm, his eyes on the praying boy. He was sobbing ecstatically.

CHAPTER SEVENTEEN

The Great Purgation

The storm had freshened the air and Good Friday morning waxed bright and clear. The fasting boys of Monsalvat thronged the chapel under the watchful eyes of the Fathers. Good Friday was traditionally the day of the annual Sign of Peace, that unburdening of guilt and undoing of disservices the form of which was unique to Monsalvat. The service was to be conducted by the Rector himself. In milder spring weather, such as today, many of the younger boys wore their shorts and went without their blazers on these occasions, the arbiter in such matters being Sister Gloria. One such was Alexander Vudsen, resplendent in white shirt, mauve House necktie, smart grey shorts and knee socks springing from well polished black shoes that rapped on the marble flags. There was upon him no trace of the traumas of the previous night. In the chapel, all was going according to plan until the time to take the Sacrament came about.

The pastoral Fathers stationed themselves in the transept so as to supervise and marshal the traffic. All the boys had fasted and nearly all — the exceptions being notable — had prepared themselves for Holy Communion. But first the Rector announced the obligatory pause to allow for those that wished to extend the Sign of Peace to make their mark. The Fathers were finding their duties light; so far only two of the boys had extended the Sign of Peace, absolving two others from some transgression or other. The procedure for this was fixed and formal. Advance notification was not considered necessary nor was it politic publicly to disclose the trespass being absolved. It was understood that the trespass was palpable and that it was impolitic to reject the offer made by the absolving party. The result was a public pact binding on the parties and against which it was unthinkable to retrogress. The parties proceeded to the altar rail to take the sacrament hand in hand in public reconciliation.

Thinking the ceremonial slot to be over, some began leaving their pews to take Holy Communion independently. Feeling themselves unexercised by such proceedings, Hogan, Rogan, Flynn, Fitzgerald, Regan, Began and De Leapey (not necessarily in that order) had taken up their usual station in one of the central pews to the right of the aisle with Foul Mouthed Frank Leport himself on the inner end. He and his lieutenants were engaging themselves, as was their wont, in cynical conclave, unfazed by any priestly presence. Of course, none had taken the preliminary confession as none had any intention of taking the Sacrament. As we have seen, for them, confession was merely a cynical ploy that furthered the machinations of their Irish Gang.

As the communicants began to drift past his pew Leport became aware of a diminutive figure in white shirt and grey shorts standing expectantly at his left elbow. He turned to see Alexander Vudsen who, unusually, had come up the aisle from the rear of the chapel rather than from the Removites' pews at the front. Leport was astounded to see the boy's right hand extended towards him, palm upwards, in obvious anticipation of a response. Unbelievably, in view of what had taken place a fortnight ago, Alexander was extending the Sign of Peace to the leader of the Irish Gang. Along the length of the pew the faces of

Leport's lieutenants turned towards the spectacle in incredulous amazement. Those intending communicants already in the aisle froze in their tracks. Amazement threatened to decay into cynical amusement when his lieutenants heard Foul Mouthed Frank hissing *sotto voce:* "Piss off, you pious little prick".

This exhortation gave rise to suppressed sniggers from all along the pew and from the Irish Gang's sycophants within earshot. Apparently oblivious of the rebuff, Alexander remained standing with his right hand extended towards Leport. It looked as if some kind of stalemate was going to ensue. That is, until Leport became aware that Father Laskiva had come up the aisle from the rear of the chapel and was standing looking on to the scene that was being played out. It was clear from the expression on his face that Father Laskiva was as taken aback as anyone at Alexander's gesture. Clearly he had not put the boy up to it.

Father Laskiva was the one priest not yet in the pocket of the Irish Gang. Leport thought it politic therefore to comply with the summons. He affected a resigned expression and, after an irreverential pause, extended his left hand towards that of Alexander. Many a smirk was being suppressed now; this was going to be rare entertainment. Leport had recovered all of his swagger and he fully intended to 'play it for laughs'. He rose from his seat and stepped into the aisle. The two boys' hands made contact, the ham fist of the elder closing around the dainty little hand of the younger. By now those in the forward pews had sensed the unfolding drama and could not resist turning to face the advancing pair. All eyes were on them as Foul Mouthed Frank Leport started on the longest journey of his life.

As they advanced towards the altar rail the watching eyes saw the incongruous pair involuntarily exchange glances. Leport looked down into those piercing bright eyes that he had done his worst to dim. Leport was suddenly reminded that they were the eyes of the boy who had sung the plaintive song in the air raid shelter on the aborted cabaret night; the song that had had such an effect upon him, the leader of the Irish Gang.

The watchers saw Leport falter in his step and look upwards into the dome. Then they saw him turn deathly pale. As the pair reached the transept they saw Leport stop abruptly. This action brought the younger boy round so that he now faced Leport. The pair were still a few feet short of the altar rail. The atmosphere was electric now. Even those kneeling at the altar rail turned to look at the stalled pair. As for the Rector, that august presence stood speechless and rooted to the spot on the steps of the altar, wondering like everybody else what would happen next.

They saw Leport drop to his knees then sink back onto his haunches. The movement was one of collapse rather than any attempt at religious supplication. Constrained by the hand hold, this brought Alexander to his knees also. Then they saw Leport gazing into the serene and beautiful countenance of his erstwhile victim. Those that could, saw his own visage assume a look of intense anguish. The onlooking Fathers recognized it as the kind of look they might see on those present at the death of a loved one. None could know the torments that seemed to have come upon him. Perhaps some instant revelation of past, present and future was hovering now and assailing his conscience. Then they saw his head become bowed and his body pitch slowly forward, down, down... and down, until his anguished brow came to rest against Alexander's bare knees.

Those in the farther pews were standing now, craning to see the strange and unnerving drama that was playing out before them. Their view had become largely obstructed by those intending communicants who were behind the two on their progress towards the altar rail. These had come to a halt and a sea of faces now looked down on the kneeling pair. Father

Laskiva had come to the fore and was wondering what he should do next to resolve this unprecedented situation.

Alexander was looking down onto the back of Leport's head now. For a significant while nothing happened. Then they saw Alexander move his free left arm and, ever so gently, bring his hand down onto Leport's head. On feeling the gentle touch, Leport responded with a noise and his broad shoulders shook perceptibly. The noise was a sob, a sound that seemed to well up from the very depths of his soul. In the pregnant silence all in the chapel could not but help hear it. It reverberated around the building and up into the dome. The sob spoke of that most dark and excoriating of all human emotions; it spoke of remorse.

Many a slow second passed in total silence. Nobody moved. The Rector himself remained dumbstruck on the chancel plateau. It was left to Father Laskiva to relieve the tension. Swiftly recruiting the prefect Osgodby to his aid he moved to break up the frozen tableau. He and Osgodby took position either side of Leport, hooked him under the armpits and gently lifted him to his feet. He relinquished his hold on the younger boy's hand. His head remained hanging down like that of a drunken man. As for Alexander, still on his haunches, he was looking up into the face of Father Laskiva, seemingly for guidance. No guidance was forthcoming. Gently the priest and the prefect conducted the distraught Leport towards the south transept door where they sat him down on one of the confessional benches. This took him out of sight of most of the boys now.

In the transept Alexander remained on his haunches on the marble flags, looking up into the uncomprehending faces that surrounded him. It was left to a kindly Sixth Former to reach down and hook him to his feet. In the absence of any guidance he started to walk back down the centre aisle.

He was looking straight ahead. Back in the pew of the now-decapitated Irish Gang, seven pairs of eyes were apprehensively monitoring his approach. When he reached a point some three pews short of where they were seated, they saw him glance to his left and sweep his piercing blue eyes along their ranks. Still he came on. They had no inkling of his intentions but this was no time to take chances. In a blind panic De Leapey, who occupied the seat next to that vacated by Leport, elbowed the ribs of Began, the boy on his right, before standing up and turning away from the advancing child. Began elbowed the ribs of the boy on *his* right and so it went on down the line. In their standing up the Irish Gang were going down like a row of dominoes. The situation approached high farce and not a few barely suppressed guffaws could be heard from the adjacent pews. Hogan, the boy on the end, was the last to rise. He could do no other than lead the abashed line out of the far end of the pew, into the south aisle and forward towards the transept. At this point a triumphant prefect on point duty took the greatest of pleasure in directing them towards the altar rail. In a state of unpreparedness they may have been, but all seven of Foul Mouthed Frank's lieutenants found themselves now inexorably committed to the sacrament.

At this so very public casting down of tormentors and machinators, a feeling of divine euphoria swept over the congregation. Those below that malignant bolus which had for so many terms stuck in the craw of Monsalvat were relieved of their burden of intimidation and fear. For this was the very instant that signalled the end of 'cabaret night' and 'the grill bars'. Those above that bolus were at last relieved of their chronic derelictions; derelictions which had for so long troubled their consciences and which had so bedevilled the discipline and serenity of life at Monsalvat.

Almost to a man, the boys of Monsalvat spilled into the aisles and surged towards the altar rail in quest of the Blessed Sacrament. Any that might seem laggardly or undecided were chivvied along by their form fellows. The supplicating crowd was so unprecedented that the Rector, re-animated now by the urgency of the moment, had to send Father Fillery scurrying to the sacristy to bring up more wafers and wine.

But that was not all on that momentous morning. The gathering tumult was suddenly overridden by a great, prolonged chord from the chapel organ. The questing throng in the aisle was momentarily stopped in its tracks. The chord was the precursor to a triumphant theme, expressed pregnantly at first, then swelling to a great sforzando. This further intervention to an already unfolding drama was not Catholic music; it was not Church music; indeed it was not sacred music of any denomination. It was exultant and definitively secular. The pastoral Fathers might have had cause to object, had they not been run off their feet bringing up wafers and wine to the altar rail.

The author of the intervention was Parry-Jones, in the organ loft. He had been looking down on the drama below; had seen the extraordinary routing of the college bully-boys by his cherished 'prize songbird'. It was too much for him. Throwing caution to the winds, and with tears in his eyes, he had launched into the ultimate valedictory of his concert repertoire. It was an inspired and virtuoso performance, for his flying fingers and feet had to emulate orchestral as well as organ parts. The boys knew the work from his concert performances and were enthused all the more. The staccato strokes of the great finale reverberated throughout the chapel, bringing the burgeoning euphoria to its zenith. It was fitting, for no droning liturgical dirge would have fitted the occasion. Thus on Good Friday 1950, at the Roman Catholic College of St Michael Monsalvat, was the Eucharist celebrated to the orisons of Saint-Saens' symphonic *tour de force*.

In the exultant and exculpatory throng, a final drama was being played out. Second Formers Ricardo Pacchatti and

Anthony Jones could be seen advancing towards the altar rail, hand in hand. The latter's head was downcast in contrition. Tojo had accepted the Sign of Peace from Cardi.

Almost to a man... For there were three boys who did not take the sacrament on that cathartic Good Friday, the day that was to become known as The Day of the Great Purgation. Foul Mouthed Frank never made it to the altar rail, Alexander had returned to his pew and The Bold Contemner had never left his.

* * *

It must be said that The Great Purgation did not relieve all the undercurrents of tension at Monsalvat. That momentous event stymied the aspirations of one particular sybaritic member of the Shell. He now found himself re-encompassed by a dilemma from which he had considered himself extricated. For him, surely the Spinner of the Years would yet speak and the Immanent Will yet manifest itself?

It must also be said that the Rector and the rest of the pastoral Fathers had not felt themselves swept up in the general euphoria that had gripped their charges. Alexander's work at Monsalvat was not yet complete.

CHAPTER EIGHTEEN

Times and Tides

Fresh from what would forever after be known as The Great Purgation, the fasting boys of Monsalvat repaired to the refectory and fell upon breakfast with gusto. The general feeling of deliverance and unburdening was palpable and the talk was animated. The Fathers felt disinclined to suppress the increasingly unruly excitement of their charges. Unusually, they set no readings of the gospels from the lectern. Only the abashed members of the Irish Gang were subdued on that morning. Their leader was nowhere to be seen and there was much speculation as to his whereabouts. Then it became known that a sum of money was missing and two and two was duly put together. It was assumed that Foul Mouthed Frank Leport had decamped back to his native Ireland. Everyone assumed the Rector would be writing to his people accordingly and that no further action was necessary on the part of the college. As if in confirmation, Leport's effects were summarily bundled up and put into store, ostensibly awaiting disposal instructions from the family.

* * *

In the ensuing weeks the academic performance of the juniors improved noticeably. The prefects were now more circumspect in their supervisory duties and pastoral obligations, especially towards the juniors, secure in the knowledge that their efforts were no longer going to be thwarted. Godred and Geddington, who alternated as first aid nurses and night patrolmen, fulfilled their policing duties without the derelictions that had previously assisted the Irish Gang in its depredations. Intimidations and bribes no longer prevailed to insidiously circumvent good order and discipline.

In general, morale at Monsalvat was returned to that which had prevailed prior to the advent of Peter Pynxcytte and his current cohort of pastoral Fathers.

For several weeks after Wepper's retributive excursion, Father Fillery bore a scar across his forehead like the mark of Cain. Bowker, the assistant caretaker, was nonplussed as to how a lattice could be fractured and a crucifix be dislodged from its fastening over the aperture in Father Fillery's confessional. He repaired the lattice and re-fastened the crucifix as bidden nevertheless. They had to get a glazier in to fix the window in the Lower Third's dormitory. The lower sash frame had to be completely rebuilt. There was no inquiry into the cause of the damage; at least no inquiry that resulted in a public pronouncement. As for The Bold Contemner, his status had escalated from being an ostensibly moral threat to the school to that of a physical danger to the school's authoritative incumbents. Clearly something had to be done about him.

It may be assumed that his position at the college was discussed in pastoral conclave, for later on a secret proposition was put to him. He had taken the examination for the Sorbonne and, on the basis of his past performances, a reasonable projection was made that he had been successful. The secret proposition was that he should leave Monsalvat as soon as was practicable rather than wait for the end of Summer Term. It was made known to his guardian that a temporary berth could be found for him at a college in Paris that was affiliated to the university. Monsalvat would withstand the expense of the concomitant tuition fees and also the accommodation and subsistence of both Wepper and his fiancée, Rhiannon. The proposition was put, on the again secret understanding that certain unilateral intentions regarding an attaché case in a London safe deposit were to be reconsidered. Those intentions were indeed reconsidered, to the apparent mutual advantage of the parties — and of a third party. The proposition was accepted. It was arranged that Wepper would leave for Paris some four weeks after Easter 1950. Rhiannon was to follow him a few weeks later. That the proposition was put at all clearly evidenced that all was not yet well with the regime at Monsalvat.

As for the revivified Alexander, he went from strength to strength. There was not a boy in the school, junior or senior, who did not now know that one did not trifle with a boy partly brought up in Tsingtao. He forged ahead academically, winning commendations for essays and other academic achievements. He swam for his Quarter and swept the board for his age group; treading on the competitive heels of the seniors even, the achievement bringing him a medal which was publicly awarded to much acclaim.

He was also fielded as a 'Water Rat' and thus began his induction into the art and mystery of being a cox. Initially this meant riding with the Captain of Boats on the Conway River in the umpiring pinnace as an observer while the fours and eights went out on practice runs.

Unlike in adult competition a school cox did not attract a weight penalty. Because school only competed against school, it was therefore a competitive imperative for each school to search out the lightest boys available commensurate with the requisite presence, initiative, and ability to take direction. In the boat they would come under the immediate direction of the stroke. Otherwise they would be under the direction of the Captain of Boats supervising from the umpiring pinnace. At Monsalvat, Alexander was the lightest as well as the youngest boy in the school. He had never aspired to the largely feigned — and fragile — urbanity of his form fellows but the Captain of Boats was confident he could bring on a presence in him. His intelligence was never in doubt. He was a quick study and within a few weeks he was considered competent enough to cox the college fours and eights. Becoming a Water Rat took him out of Mauger's clutches to a great extent. True, the 'dog walkers' were still being afforded their morning's entertainment, courtesy of Mauger; but with the vanquishing of the Irish Gang their erstwhile iniquitous evening disports at the 'grill bars' were gone for good.

Thus did it come about that Alexander and Lance, rowing as stroke, would spend considerable time facing each other in joint endeavour on the river, Lance co-ordinating the motive power and Alexander conning the boat. Becoming a cox also took Alexander into a different social dimension. The Water Rats had a less rigid hierarchy and greater camaraderie. This was particularly apparent on the now frequent journeys by charabanc between the college and the boat house on the Conway River.

* * *

It must not be thought that The Great Purgation had instantly rendered the boys of Monsalvat paragons of all the virtues, not even the author of that significant event himself. Alexander was a child of his time, a product of his history and not immune to the influence of his peers. The eternal propensities of schoolboys are not easily circumvented. It transpired that Second Former Anthony 'Tojo' Jones was — among other things

— also a Water Rat of comparatively long standing. On one memorable charabanc journey, Tojo, whom we have seen was unusually perspicacious when it came to friendships between schoolfellows, sought to impose upon Alexander in company by remarking that he and Lance, as cox and stroke respectively, could now spend their time on the river looking up the leg of each other's shorts. In the wake of The Great Purgation this scurrilous observation was little other than abject bravura on Tojo's part. That bravura was well matched. There being no prefects within earshot, Alexander, to everyone's scandalised surprise, had no compunction in dismissively telling Tojo to get fucked — an exhortation eminently available to a boy who had shovelled coal with the best — and worst — of them on the stokehold plates of the *Antenor*. The so-publicly-rebuffed Tojo was thus set to minding his own business, having been reminded once again that one did not trifle with a boy partly brought up in Tsingtao. It can of course be relied upon that Alexander made a mental note of his improprietous riposte in anticipation of his next Confession.

It must also be born in mind that he had little or no compunction in deceiving the Fathers by engaging in his clandestine trysts with Lance; or indeed failing to confess those trysts. Albeit by reason of their derelictions the Fathers might be thought eminently deceivable, Alexander had no knowledge of such derelictions and could accrue no defence thereby.

* * *

In many ways the weeks that followed The Great Purgation were both prosaic and idyllic; prosaic in that they reflected the normal work of a well-run school, idyllic in that peace reigned at long last throughout the corridors, chambers and outfields of Monsalvat. But, as has been said, all was not yet right with

Monsalvat. As with Wepper, some in authority now found Alexander's presence in the school an embarrassment. Clearly there was more work to be done. The final push was to be triggered by a capricious convergence of events.

* * *

Wepper's impending departure from Monsalvat became generally known, although the intrigues attendant upon it necessarily remained secret. It was a week after Easter that Wali Waliser handed a sealed envelope to William Wepper. It was annotated on the face with the following legend: *"To be handed to William Wepper on June Twenty-ninth 1950"*. The annotation was in violet ink.

The reason Wali handed the cover to Wepper so long before the due date in the first place was because he now knew that Wepper would be leaving Monsalvat before the due date, and in the second place both Wali and Wepper knew that date to be Alexander's birthday. For those reasons Wali had felt decidedly uneasy about this particular *poste restante* item.

Back in the privacy of his study Wepper carefully opened the envelope. He scanned the contents with increasing disquiet. It was a single sheet of premium foolscap, with the following lines similarly penned in violet ink:

> *Weepe with me all you that read*
> *This little storie:*
> *And know, for whom a teare you shed,*
> *Death's self is sorry.*
> *'Twas a child that did so thrive*
> *In grace and feature,*
> *That heaven and nature seemed to strive*
> *Which owned the creature.*

Yeares he numbered scarce eleven
When fates turned cruell
He gave us but few months of heaven,
Monsalvat's jewell;
And did sing so dulce and bold
Old songs so duely,
As, sooth, the Fates thought him of old,
He trilled so truely.
So, by error, to his fate they did consent;
But viewing him since, (alas too late),
They now repent.
And would seek (to give new birth)
In bathes to steep him;
But, being so much too good for earth,
Heaven vows to keep him.

If Wali had been uneasy at the external annotation, Wepper was alarmed at the contents. This verse spoke to him from beyond the grave. Indeed, from beyond two graves; graves as yet undug. In his mind's eye he could see the glint of spades turning the sods. Fortuitously, a conspiracy of circumstances had delivered the message ahead of its intended time. Urgent action was necessary — but he had to proceed with caution.

* * *

Coincidentally events seemed to be crowding in and Lance was reminded of the document the drunken Heini had entrusted to him just before he had decamped in September 1948 and which he had cached in his personal *poste restante* in the revetment of the ha-ha. He felt it now timely to retrieve it.

It wouldn't do for him to be seen scrabbling about in the ha-ha with a nail on a stick, so Lance picked a time when most boys would be at prep. Having checked that the great parterre was clear of stray pupils, he descended into the ha-ha in the bosk at the country end, hard by the old gym, and walked along it under the carriage bridge so there would be no danger of him being seen from the colonnade or the presbytery windows. When he reached the bosk at the townside end he entered into a kind of tunnel formed by the overhanging bushes. It was a place not unknown to other Monsalvations; there could be few interstices of the estate that were not open to exploration by curious juniors — or indeed used as trysting places for a convivial cigarette or other illicit congress. Fortunately, the particular field drain outfall was still concealed by the ivy hanging down over the retaining wall of the ha-ha. Lance parted the ivy and carefully put his stick into the outfall. Sure enough he could feel it make contact with the coffee jar he had put there all those months ago. By dint of manoeuvring the stick so that the nail impinged on the far side of the jar he was able to hook it and drag it towards him, disturbing the peace of a few spiders as he did so. He was then able to grab the jar and, after wiping off the cobwebs on a convenient tussock, he tried to unscrew the lid; it was seized solid. The envelope inside could be seen tantalizingly. He didn't want to break the glass; he might be heard and besides he wouldn't want to leave any broken glass in ambush for another's unwary foot. He had no alternative but to hide the bulky jar under his jersey. As it was, he retraced his steps and managed to dodge back into his study without running into his study mate, any prefects or any of the Fathers.

By dint of wrapping the jar in a cloth and rapping it with a poker over the waste basket, he was finally able to get his hands on the envelope once again. There it was again, the now-absent Heini's spidery handwriting on the face. It was in German — and archaic gothic German at that: *"im Falle meines Todes geöffnet zu werden"*, which Lance took to mean "to be opened in the event of my death". Heini had entrusted the package to Lance on the understanding he would pass it to Wepper. Lance could not do so at the time because Wepper was in London taking an examination.

But Heini had not specified whether the passing was to be done before or after his contemplated demise. And because he had absconded, how was Lance — or indeed anyone — to know whether Heini was alive or dead? On the evidence of the stolen staff car Heini was very much alive and, by reason of the car having been abandoned at Llandudno Junction, clearly anxious to permanently distance himself from Pencadno. In his perverse logic Lance decided at the time that there was no longer any point in troubling Wepper with the matter. Any threat to Heini resided at Pencadno and probably emanated from his compatriot, Wali. Surely, Heini's absconding had rendered his testimony a dead letter?

As a dead letter, Lance had felt justified in opening it and he had done this as soon as he learned of Heini's absconding. He found himself confronted with a sea of closely packed gothic script that veritably swam before his eyes. As might be expected, it was all in German — Heini had never developed the language skills of his erudite compatriot. As soon as schedules allowed, Lance had repaired to a secluded corner of the college library and, under pretext of extra studies, had begun laboriously and surreptitiously to translate it. This had taken several days, particularly as he had to be on constant watch for the inquisitive incursions of invigilating Fathers. Having eventually got the gist of Heini's supposedly redundant message, Lance perceived that he might have a use for it. Its contents were indeed momentous stuff, stuff that would have dismayed a less unique and focused boy than Lance Raphael Lapita. At the time, September 1948, he had stuffed the note and his own English transcription of it back in the original envelope and had then put the envelope in the coffee jar and secreted it in the drain outfall in the revetment of the ha-ha.

Right now, Summer Term 1950, back in his dormitory, Lance took out the retrieved envelope and, by dint of canting his wardrobe backwards, secreted it out of sight under that piece of furniture. He was taking a risk — the Fathers' intermittent searches could be that circumspect — but he had a feeling it was short days now. Wepper was on the point of leaving. Lance decided it was politic to render the document to Wepper after all. He approached Wali at the old bothy with a view to arranging a meeting. Naturally Wali was not made privy to the subject of the meeting. However, Wali had a message for Lance; as to meetings, it seems Wepper had pre-empted him.

At the appointed time Lance, as he was by now well accustomed to doing, walked along in the shadow of the long back wall of the peach house and, after looking ahead and behind to check there were no witnesses about, he dodged round the buttresses and an ivy outcrop and leant against the wicket gate. As expected, it yielded to the gentle pressure of his shoulder. As he entered the peach house and secured the wicket gate behind him, the aroma of Balkan Sobranie cigarettes told him that he who had summoned him had made himself at home in characteristic fashion. Sure enough, there was The Bold Contemner draped languidly over the chaise longue and wreathed in clouds of smoke. He waved Lance to one of the garden chairs which he had placed in close proximity. On the potting shelf rested a packet of the precious cigarettes laid open invitingly, together with a gold lighter. Lance reached into an adjacent plant pot and withdrew his elegant long meerschaum cigarette holder, that same which he had flaunted before Alexander at their first meeting... that same which later had gathered the precious first kiss from the boy's lips. Lighting up with an appropriate flourish, he settled back in his chair and blew a smoke ring. Wepper was the first to open the conversation; the pace was desultory.

"Hello... blood-brother."

Lance felt compelled to respond in like vein: "Hello... blood-brother."

"It's been a long time," said Wepper.

"Yes indeed..., a long time. Why are we here? Why now?"

Wepper took a leisurely draught on his cigarette and contemplated the figure of Lance through the slowly rising smoke cloud before responding. Eventually he reached into the inside pocket of his blazer, withdrew a sheet of paper, unfolded it and flashed it before Lance's eyes. The younger boy paled perceptibly. Significantly, Wepper did not relinquish his hold upon it.

Feigning nonchalance, Lance leaned forward in his chair and made a pretence of digesting the words on the page. Unprompted, he ventured: "That could have been written by anybody."

"In violet ink?" expostulated Wepper. "I doubt there was a bottle of violet ink in the whole of North Wales until I brought one up from London — and decanted the half of it to you. No, Lance, your attempt to disguise your handwriting doesn't fool me."

In the interim Wepper, by referencing an index of first lines, had identified the penned lines as a transcription of a poem by Ben Jonson. But Jonson's lines had been tinkered about with, such that the subject of the poem (Salomon Pavey, an historical boy actor, dead in his thirteenth year) had been usurped by another — and in the circumstances that other could only identify as Alexander. On the due date the lines inferred *post humus*. They were either a sick joke or a threat. Knowing Lance as he did, Wepper assumed the latter.

The two sat eyeing each other for a while, and then Wepper continued: "We're here about my blood half-brother. I know you will have made him your blood-brother. With the Great Grail of Monsalvat-Pencadno you asked me to spring from the sacristy last term; the same august vessel we used so long ago when you were a winsome little Removite and I was as you are now. That makes Alexander my blood half-brother, would you not agree?"

He paused to let this sink in, then: "Where are you taking him, Lance?" Wepper's question was rhetorical rather than geographical. On encountering Lance's purposeful silence, he continued: "Would you have him extinguished in his present perfection? I know that in your scheme of things he's a Polydeukion to your Herodes." He paused, and then added as a seeming afterthought: "Or — could it be that you see him as a Tristan to your Isolde?"

Lance flinched and blanched perceptibly. Wepper knew he had hit the spot. Whereas both boys were cognisant of the cult of the *trophimoi,* Wepper also knew that music master Parry-Jones would have instructed his Shell pupils in European operatic history. The dramatic double fatality alluded to could not be circumvented. In the context, the death of the one connoted the suicide of the other. And in the absence of operatic happenstance, that death would have to be brought about by an act of deliberation. In other words, an act of homicide. Wepper became much troubled; he now knew with even greater certainty that he had both blood-brothers to salve — and neither to betray.

He continued addressing Lance, in a state now of some uncertainty. He shifted to a lower gear.

"Would you do with him as we have done together? Would you sully a Child of Mary? An innocent? For my own part I purposefully eschew all contact with Alexander in term time. If I didn't, I would be seen as an adverse influence. Yes, I'm not a believer but I'm wiser now than to be a proselytiser of non-belief. I won't have it said that I would ever come between him and the faith of his parents." Wepper then leaned forward and added vehemently: "Lance — for Christ's sake — it's all he's got left."

Lance felt compelled to respond: "I know that. And I have never — would never — knowingly come between him and his faith. I love Alexander for what he is, not for what I would make him; or for what you think I would make him. As for sullying..."

Here Wepper held up his hand. "There's no need to answer that. I apologise for making the insinuation. I know you haven't had your way with Alexander in that fashion. But something tells me his image does haunt your lone nightly reveries nevertheless — and that in the light of day you strive to sublimate your fleshly lusts." He closed that sentence forcibly, mockingly, before shifting back to a higher gear, giving vent to his fears: "Your dilemma, Lance, is that Alexander came to us in perfection — and was therefore unapproachable in the venal sense. For you to approach him you needed him to be rendered imperfect — but in your esoteric scheme of things it couldn't be you who'd do the rendering. So you got the Irish Gang to do the dirty work for you. Alexander became defiled — and it was none of your doing. Your plan had worked. He was approachable, propositionable, just like any other Monsalvat peach. But then he went on to execute The Great Purgation. On his own he spiritually revivified Monsalvat. In so doing he rendered himself unapproachable again; perfect again. That frustrated your plan. So now you seek unity in death."

Lance cringed under Wepper's succinct and excoriating analysis of his dilemma. Wepper continued: "Being Lance Lapita, you cannot sublimate; instead you must destroy. Destroy him and then yourself." With that he shook his head slowly. "Lance, I cannot let these things happen. Understand that I must intercede."

At this point it was Lance that did the interceding. He

affected to downplay the depth and darkness of his relationship with Alexander.

"Ah, you sound like Wali Waliser. He does me a great disservice too when he warns me not to harm Alexander. He's just as protective of him as you. But neither of you understand the nature of our relationship. I'm no plucker of peaches. For a start he's not quite the innocent seraph you would like to believe. Don't forget, he used to ride his bike around Mukden during the Japanese Mandate. He even hobnobbed – albeit innocently – with the Kenpetai. And he's ridden the rivers of Asia in turbulent times. He's seen things no nicely brought up little English schoolboy should see. Now he's going on twelve and can be a handy little bastard... as some have found to their cost. Alexander is nobody's fool."

"Nobody's fool but God's," mused Wepper ruefully. Then, more vehemently: "Christ, Lance, he's young enough to still be in prep school." And then: "Bloody hell, Lance, your people had him for Christmas. There was no need for blood-brotherhood ceremonies — he's practically your little brother already. Play your cards right and he's yours. Yours... to look after, to cherish, to guide, to protect... What more do you want? You two can grow up together... Share the same house, the same table, the same bathroom." And then, mock-incredulously: "The same school even. If you eventually grow apart..." Here, predictably, Lance made a face. Wepper blundered on: "...well, people do. Even grown-ups. Especially grown-ups." Wepper realised he had overplayed his hand in articulating the sticking point in Lance and Alexander's relationship. He shifted to a more sombre note. "He can be the younger brother that... we both know... tragically... Mark cannot fulfil. We both know Mark's remaining years are numbered in single figures. Alexander would be a worthy successor in your family's scheme of things." Then with renewed vigour: "You've got everything you could possibly wish for with Alexander. Why take things to such extremes? Why destroy perfection? Why wreck your own family for decades to come with your potty and dangerous philosophy? Leave him be. Let him grow up. Let yourself grow up. Tell me you'll stop this nonsense now — or I'll be forced to intervene."

Lance maintained his silence.

"You were drawn to him as a moth to a candle. Why couldn't you have left him alone? To get on with his education; with his life; with his contemporaries? He didn't need you, Lance; you imposed yourself upon him; albeit you had the aid of an adder. Sufficient you have him as your blood-brother. Now withdraw I say; leave him to it. As your blood-brother I'm asking you to relinquish him."

Lance was dismissive. "What, in this place? Leave him to the tender mercies of Pynxcytte, Fillery and their like? To the Irish Gang? Or their successors? He's better off with me, for all my faults. What would they make of him? He would emerge from this place a calloused casualty, like so many of the rest. Look at the likes of Quedda and van Reldt and their ilk. Porcine bastards, oozing corruption. Were they 'peaches' in their day? It's hard to believe. If they were, maybe it would have been better for them also to have been seized in time, crystallised in the innocence and beauty of their youth, rather than left to degenerate into what they are today. Would not the world be a better place? Would not the memories of their youthful selves be a better legacy than the infliction of their present machinations?"

Wepper interceded: "Who is to survive in your philosophy to appreciate your youthful paragons? You'd have us all dead before we could procreate!" He paused to let Lance digest this ineluctable logic. Then: "Sounds like you've already consigned Alexander to history. He's vanquished the Irish Gang, scattered them in remorseful disarray. And I've a shrewd idea he'll get around to vanquishing Pynxcytte and his cronies, but at what cost I don't know. Whatever is to happen, at least he's equipped to survive in this world. You want to take him out of it."

Lance was vehement. "Survive as what? He cannot be allowed to survive. The sacred vessel — the Ming vase — the Grecian urn — surely is to be dashed down from its pedestal and into a thousand irreparable pieces..." and here his voice descended to biting sarcasm "...not to survive as a fucking piss-pot. One way or the other, Alexander must never emerge from these cloisters. If I am to be his nemesis — and his saviour — then so be it."

Lance then launched into a long exposition of his philosophy on fate and beauty...In that philosophy all things of beauty contain the seeds of their own destruction. They are to be seized at the peak of their attractiveness; plucked as the rose while in full bloom. Where their attributes are transient, like those of the rose in bloom, they must be crystallised at their peak; scattered across the bed as the rose petals by the alleviating hand of kindness and not be left to decay. Furthermore, they must be sequestrated to the will and whim of the beholder and are not to be bequeathed to others. It was the duty of all savants such as he to return beauty to the pit from whence it comes and in the meantime to portend that return by orchestrating destructive encounters. Such encounters could only enhance the beauty inherent in the object, the creature, of his desire. This was the turbulent philosophy that had driven his affair with Alexander. In some elegiac future both boys would return to the same womb, a place of oblivious warmth where they would reside for ever in each other's arms, united in death beyond the day and night of the physical world. In this nebulous hereafter Alexander would understand and forgive Lance, understand the demons which drove him to do the things he did, understand that his love of Alexander and the worship of his being had all along been intense and genuine, despite that it had been destructive and ultimately fatal.

Lance then launched into some more lines of poetry. Wepper readily recognised it as Wordsworth's *Intimations of Immortality from Recollections of Early Childhood*:

> "*Our birth is but a sleep and a forgetting:*
> *The Soul that rises with us, our life's Star,*
> *Hath had elsewhere its setting,*
> *And cometh from afar:*
> *Not in entire forgetfulness,*
> *And not in utter nakedness,*
> *But trailing clouds of glory do we come*
> *From God, who is our home:*
> *Heaven lies about us in our infancy!*
> *Shades of the prison-house begin to close*
> *Upon the growing Boy,*
> *But he beholds the light, and whence it flows,*
> *He sees it in his joy;*
> *The Youth, who daily farther from the east*
> *Must travel, still is Nature's priest,*
> *And by the vision splendid*
> *Is on his way attended;*
> *At length the Man perceives it die away,*
> *And fade into the light of common day.*"

"*Shades of the prison-house...* It is my duty to deliver Alexander from those shades. The light of common day shall not come down upon him with its barren, baleful glare. Venality shall not have him. He... our mutual love... must terminate in this place, at this time. If I am to fall with him so be it. It is in the very stars."

Wepper was unimpressed with this dangerous philosophising: "Then I must arrest the stars in their very courses. You should have read that poem in its entirety. Wordsworth gives us hope towards the finish."

"Ah yes. A morsel. A crumb." Lance shook his head. "Time shall not pluck a withered flower. I cannot allow it."

In a last-ditch effort to dissuade Lance from his disastrous course Wepper launched into a finely balanced argument: "You have a dilemma, Lance. You and I and Alexander are blood-brothers. You and I are also members of the *trophimoi* and I'm sure that Alexander will be initiated in the near future if he hasn't already been. The *trophimoi* has the same tenets as you — but without invoking infanticide. Which would you say has the greater claim on your loyalties? Which should dictate your subsequent actions? 'The *trophimoi?* Or the Blood-Brotherhood bond?"

Lance considered his response: "I would say it's no contest. The *trophimoi* was instigated by the Fathers for their own devices. The Blood-Brotherhood was instigated by us for our devices. Our devices are not necessarily impure whereas the Fathers' devices are not necessarily pure."

This last was a sophistical understatement; the Fathers' devices were decidedly impure.

Lance continued: "There's a fine distinction. However, in Alexander's case the Blood-Brotherhood bond cannot be other than pure. Furthermore, Blood-Brotherhood is voluntary whereas induction into the trophimoi is under duress; candidates get summoned. I would say that, insofar as morals can be invoked, the Blood-Brotherhood transcends and supersedes the *trophimoi* on both counts. It's the Blood-Brotherhood bond that will dictate my future actions."

Wepper countered: "Morals, you say? I didn't invoke morals. I would say that both the *trophimoi* and the Blood-Brotherhood bond are the negation of morals. Otherwise — finely reasoned, my friend. But my humanistic considerations must have regard to the seriousness of the consequences. You imply there are no moral consequences for Alexander and yourself because you are both earmarked for early destruction. But you fail to take into account that I'm also under the Blood-Brotherhood bond and I have every intention of surviving. Furthermore, I must have consideration for those whom you'd leave behind, even if *you* don't. And for those whom Alexander would leave behind — because I'm certain that sooner or later someone from the Far East will come looking for him. On these grounds the least bad solution is that transient impurity trumps the permanence of infanticide. The *trophimoi* must prevail. Alexander — and you — must live."

"You argue a fine point, Will, but you embrace the flaw that inheres in it. You're arguing for immorality. But as I said, it's decreed in the very stars — and the stars brook no immorality..."

"Ah yes, Lance, those bloody stars again. There's no argument I can put up versus the stars. That's why I must, to reflect your own expression, arrest the stars in their very courses."

On an impulse Wepper sprang off the chaise longue and knelt alongside his erstwhile paramour. Placing a proprietorial hand on Lance's right breast he implored: "Let him go, Lance, let him be a natural boy, let him grow up. As I let you grow up."

"I can't. Can't you see that I can't? Our mutual destiny doesn't go beyond this place; he and I end here, at Monsalvat; we are fated. It's decreed in the very stars."

Wepper said it once more: "Then I must arrest the stars in their very courses."

"You cannot Will, you're powerless in the matter. The Immanent Will has decreed, The Spinner of the Years has spoken."

"You're speaking like a bloody gipsy now."

But Lance was undeterred: "It was all revealed to me the day I visited him in hospital in Liverpool. I took the ferry back to Birkenhead. At the landing stage there was a liner just departing for America. I was at a place of departures and in a departing liner resides a myriad final severings. I watched and it all came to me. The coincidences were too great to ignore — the serendipitous serpent, the unsupervised visit, the departing vessel. Alexander is the virginal boy, caressed by the mother, unsullied by the touch of the temptress; to be fixed in time before the perfections of childhood fall away. I am destined to be the author of the boy's apotheosis. He will indeed be a Tristan to my Isolde. Each must be the vindicator of the other." Lance now seemed to refer to the 1912 disaster: "Despite dark and fog, despite an inherent aversion, the one found the other, the fleeting bark and the floating berg, on the vasty waters of Life. Alexander and I constitute... The Convergence of the Twain once more. Centuries from now, when you and all around you are long forgotten and beyond recall, antiquaries might resurrect us and wise men will see and admire us as the paragon of a great love."

Wepper was all the more unimpressed now: "That would make you a Herodes to his Polydeukion. Tell me, Lance, why is it that whenever I hear you philosophising, the expression 'half baked' springs so readily to mind? Think where you're going with this. Think about your people. Your father, your mother, your brother. What's Mark going to do when you've gone on this... this great adventure?" Wepper was railing now. "Think of your dog; the pussycat; anything outside of these god-blasted walls. Get your pedal extremities back on terra firma, for Jesus Christ's sake, or you'll end up being consigned to the looney bin... and I'll be the consignor — if that's what it takes to save Alexander."

"You would betray your blood-brother?"

"I don't have to betray you, Lance; you'll betray yourself. It's in the very stars."

Lance stood up now and consigned his unspent cigarette to the ashtray. "You must do as you think fit. I must do as I'm destined to do."

Lance would have concluded the meeting there and then but Wepper thought it timely to release a bombshell: "It's clear to me now that you've been intercepting my messages to Alexander. Wali wouldn't of himself betray me in that manner. What's the hold you have over Wali?"

But Lance did not blanch any further at this accusation. His confidence was not shaken. He sat down again and then delivered a monumental *coup de grace,* first with a feint then with a flourish: "You must ask Heini."

Wepper was irritated at this evasion. Both boys knew Heini had absconded in September 1948 — along with one of the college staff cars. Wepper's response was understandably petulant: "I can't ask Heini; Heini's long gone — as well you know."

"Quite. And a few days before he absconded he gave me this — to give to you."

Now it was Lance's turn to reach into the inside pocket of his blazer and to withdraw a document of his own. Unlike Wepper a few minutes ago, he proffered it to his adversary without reservation. Wepper took it from his hand; it was in the envelope Lance had lately retrieved from his personal poste restante in the revetment of the ha-ha. Before leaving his dormitory Lance had abstracted his English transcription from the envelope and put it back under his wardrobe. Consequently, Wepper would have to rely upon Lance for a ready verbal translation of the original now in his hand. Wepper's linguistic disadvantage gave Lance that extra frisson of power.

Wepper contemplated the handwritten legend on the cover for a moment: *"Im Falk meines Todes geöffnet zu werden".* Wepper knew German enough to deduce that the contents of the cover might be a last will and testament. It wasn't; it was more testimony than testament. Wepper took the document out of the envelope and unfolded it. Heini's closely packed spidery hand-writing swam before his eyes as it had swum before Lance's. Alexander could have translated it with ease but Wepper realised he would have to rely on Lance.

"I take it you've translated this?"

"I have indeed," said Lance confidently.

"And...?"

"If you'll just hand it back I'll give you the translation."

Realising his disadvantage, Wepper meekly complied. Now it was Lance's turn to release a bombshell; and what a bombshell!

"Well, it's not Heini writing about Heini, as you might think. It's Heini writing about Wali." Lance paused to let this sink in. "Heini had been afraid of Wali long before the day they both fetched up at Monsalvat. On that day, Wali was in murderous pursuit of Heini. And with good reason. Of course, you and I long ago guessed that Waliser wasn't his real name. He had no ancestral connection with Wales. But neither was he a real merchant seaman. His presence on board the Cap Frio was nothing more than opportunistic. In another time and in another place Wali had another reputation and another name. And a nick-name. Look in Heini's testament, you'll see it there — The Beast of Natzweiler. Our solicitous friend Wali is an SS man. Meet Hauptsturmführer Dieter Gressler, fugitive war criminal. He was in charge of medical experiments at Natzweiler — among other things..."

Wepper was speechless. Lance went on: "A group of them legged it just before the camp was liberated. They bribed their way to Vigo and got aboard the Cap Frio. The Cap Frio had been interned there for the duration of the war. According to Heini, Gressler and his accomplices murdered the stewards just before the ship made a break for Buenos Aires. They stuffed their bodies into the boiler furnaces and stole their identities. Heini was a lowly Unterscharführer – an NCO – and an unwilling accomplice in the proceedings. Anyway, that's how Gressler came by the name Waliser. They were desperate... desperate and ruthless. And after all they must have had plenty of practice..."

Lance had Wepper's undivided attention now.

"Why did Heini give that document to *you?*"

This put Lance on the defensive somewhat, but he had a ready response: "He gave it to me under seal to give to you, still under seal. Then he took off. But you were away in London at the time, taking that exam. You came back next day but he obviously wasn't dead. The dead don't steal cars. Whatever was in the envelope, the theft of the car rendered it a dead letter. The putative addressee fell out of the equation. As a dead letter I saw no harm in opening it."

Wepper could have taken issue with Lance's reasoning on that, but something else sprang forward from the back of his mind. It was his turn to pale before Lance's gaze.

"Will, are you all right? What's the matter?"

Wepper found his voice: "The stolen car was found abandoned in the station car park at Llandudno Junction. With almost a full tank of petrol. Christ, you can practically walk back to Pencadno in an hour or so. Heini didn't get very far. Not by car anyway. Hardly worth stealing it then, wouldn't you agree?"

"I didn't know that."

"Christ, don't you read the papers? Oh of course, only we Sixth Formers are allowed to be exposed to the corrupting influence of the popular Press." He paused awhile, then looked penetratingly at Lance and said: "Are you thinking what I'm thinking? Remember Wali's late night 'burns'? When it rains a lot and he can't have a bonfire?" At this point Wepper affected to glance meaningfully over his shoulder. "He uses the old peach house boiler furnace to burn garden refuse. And maybe other things... After all, he had all the tools for the job on site here; sacks, wheelbarrows, paraffin, kindling, coal, a choice of ripsaws, hosepipe, a wash house with a faucet and a floor drain...

It's clear now that Heini was a threat to him. He was a garrulous drunk and he knew too much for Wali's comfort. Ask yourself, why would Heini want to abscond? Why would he jeopardise his job, his work permit and his immigration status by stealing a car and going absent? It doesn't make sense. The only thing that makes sense is that he was dead scared of Wali. This document — his testimony — tells us why he was scared of Wali, scared of what Wali might do to him.., was capable of. Well I don't think he got round to absconding." Wepper then revealed what was on his mind: "Maybe it was Wali, not Heini, who drove the car to Llandudno Junction — and then walked back to Monsalvat."

Lance was inclined to scoff. "At that time of night? Too risky. Ten to one the police would pick him up on the A55. Failing that, someone would be bound to see him. If he walked along the railway track he'd have to go through the Penmaenbach tunnel. And there are platelayers about then. The signalmen or the platelayers would see him. The only other way is by the sheep trails over the tops — and that would take him hours."

"Lance, he could have walked back round the headland. Along the beach. In the dark. Then across the railway tracks, over the fields to the chase gate and back to the old bothy. Unless he had the most inordinate bad luck, he could do all that without being seen by anyone. It could be that the abandoned car was a ruse and Heini had never left Monsalvat."

"What are you saying, Will? Are you saying that Heini could still be here? At Monsalvat? But... dead?"

"Dead and gone up the chimney Well... Look at it this way, Lance; as you said, Wali must have had plenty of practice..."

It was Lance who was incredulous now. "I think you're the one who's in the realms of fantasy now, Will. There's been people who've tried to walk round the headland. If their relatives are 'lucky' their bodies wash up a few days later."

"But it's entirely possible, Lance. Parties from here have done it. In daylight, of course. And with a local escort. Given calm weather it's possible to walk round the headland at low water on an equinoctial spring tide."

"Well..., you know the date Heini is supposed to have decamped. It was the night before you got back from London. Back end of September, as I recall. All you need to know now is the weather and the state of the tide in the small hours of the morning. I think you'll find you're in the realms of fantasy."

We'll see, Lance... We'll see."

Time now pressed and the pair made their separate ways from the peach house. Each had retained their incriminating document. Lance had retained Heini's; the document that took his testimony as a good Catholic beyond the Seal of the Confessional. And Wepper had retained Lance's menacing verses about Alexander.

* * *

Wepper was left musing. Could it really be that Heini had never left Monsalvat; was still on the premises in some form or other? As residue in the furnace ash pit? The idea was preposterous, not to say horrific. Nevertheless, the worm of doubt had been planted and during the next few days it worked its way insidiously through Wepper's mind. Wepper knew that the local library kept tide tables — but public libraries were out of bounds to Monsalvations lest they be swayed from the True Faith by the heresies residing therein. But he had Rhiannon. He would ask Rhiannon to do the research for him.

* * *

"But what's all this about, why do you need the tide tables for these particular dates?"

Wepper did not feel confident enough to apprise even his fiancée of the dark thoughts that troubled his mind. He spun her some story about a retrospective school marine biology exercise, something to do with the life cycle of the lugworm.

"Who but a bunch of silly schoolboys could be interested in the life cycle of the lugworm?"

Wepper took to transferring the blame. "Silly biology masters, more like."

Rhiannon duly made the inquiry but her report back was not helpful. It transpired the library did keep tide tables but only for immediate and future reference. They retained no records reaching back to the September of 1948. But the librarian did give Rhiannon some possibly useful information. It seemed that the pier master at the ballast sidings kept a historical record of tide and weather information in much the same form as a ship's deck log.

The ballast pier was served by a narrow-gauge railway operated by the quarrying company and which crossed the main line by an overbridge to the west of Pencadno station. Wepper felt confident enough to approach the quarry officials; the granite workings were the object of standard field trips for the pupils of Monsalvat and the college and the quarries had a good relationship. What he would need would be some plausible pretext upon which to base his inquiry. It was either that or write to Bidston observatory. Wepper knew from previous field trips thereto that Bidston kept tidal information for the whole world. That seemed overkill. Wepper decided to try his luck at the ballast sidings; after all, they were just down the road, so to speak, and he was a very senior pupil. It was just that the life cycle of the lugworm seemed a little implausible ...

The passage of scarcely an hour found Wepper in a gaslit office lined with shelves full of identical journals. The pier master's clerk seemed helpful enough. On being given the effective date he took down one of the journals and leafed through it. Wepper looked at the open logbook and was able to check, albeit upside down, that the clerk had the right date. Of course, as a matter of curiosity the clerk asked the obvious question. Wepper felt compelled to be more inventive than the lugworm.

"It's to do with the life cycle of the... err... spinifex worm." The clerk's brow knitted. "I must say I've never heard of the spinifex worm."

Neither had Wepper until he heard himself saying it. Things were beginning to border on the farcical.

To Wepper's relief the clerk returned his gaze to the logbook and continued: "It says here we had the *Alacrity* alongside at the time. Weather was calm with light airs but for some reason she sprang off and anchored out at 21.00 hours without completing loading." He then referred to another panel of the page. "Ah yes, I can see why she needed to get off sharpish. She was running onto Maximum Low Water Equinoctial Springs at 02.00 hours." And then: "Oh, are you all right?"

Wepper had turned quite pale.

* * *

The very next day found Lance and Wepper in the peach house once more, at the latter's urgent summons. Both of them looked along the building to where a door in the peeling lime-washed wall gave access to the boiler room. And they shuddered. For these blood-brothers the old trysting place would never feel the same again.

Wepper opened with: "I've no evidence but I've a shrewd suspicion that Wali's been playing a double game... that he's been in Pynxcytte's pocket all this time. Maybe Pynxcytte's known about our meetings all along. And your meetings with Alexander." Lance paled visibly. Wepper went on: "Yes, I've seen Wali go forward to Confession about once a month over the years — and it's always been with Pynxcytte. I've a shrewd idea why; it wouldn't do for our illustrious Rector to be seen consorting otherwise with such a lowly fellow as Wali, would it? Sure as hell, somebody would notice the one going to the other and be bound to think it odd, if not suspicious. The Confessional now... that would be a different matter. Yes... Pynxcytte could get away with that. I've seen Wali take Holy Communion too — but that's just another blind if you ask me. I don't think he gives much of a fuck for the Catholic faith."

Then Wepper asked Lance a very pertinent question: "In order to blackmail Wali you must have taxed him about Heini's testimony. That must have been a considerable risk; a little English schoolboy trying to browbeat an historic mass murderer! I take it you took appropriate precautions?"

"Of course. Credit me with a little intelligence. I told him I'd appointed a 'sleeper' who would raise the alarm if anything untoward happened to me... and that they'd know where to look." At this Wepper gave out with an ironic guffaw. "Well damn and blast my bloody soul! Wali's been performing the same service for me for the past three years. Just in case Pynxcytte decided I'd become too much of an embarrassment."

Lance was triumphant at this. "So that's why the Bold Contemner of Monsalvat has managed to lead a charmed life — you've been blackmailing Pynxcytte all these years."

"Wrong, Lance. I may be a thief but I'm no blackmailer. The sum total of my sins is that I stole an attaché case and had it put in a safe deposit. It was locked when I stole it and it remains locked to this day. I never had the key. The only blackmailer of Pynxcytte is Pynxcytte's conscience."

Lance produced Heini's testimony and handed it to Wepper. For his part, Wepper retained Lance's incriminating verses; two fatally incriminating documents in such close proximity. Why had Heini, good Catholic though he might be, felt compelled to render his devastating testimony beyond the Seal of the Confessional?

Wepper asked a pertinent question: "You have a written translation?"

"Yes — but it's in my own handwriting. It'll have no evidential value. Just the febrile imaginings of a silly schoolboy. The one you've got there... that's the McCoy."

True enough. Neither boy knew it but this would be the last time the peach house would serve as their trysting place. The business of their meeting could be taken no further. The time had come for these blood-brothers to part. Wepper was on the point of leaving Monsalvat for the last time anyway and now neither knew what the morrow might bring. Instinctively they drew together; in that place, for so long so secret and special for three boys but now rendered awful by what might have taken place there, Will and Lance embraced in fond remembrance of passions long subsided. Then they drew apart and Lance turned and walked towards the wicket gate. He threw the lock, opened the wicket and cast one last lingering look at Wepper before passing through and closing it.

Wepper stood looking at the closed door for fully a minute before quietly reiterating and rephrasing his earlier injunction: "Now I must arrest the stars in their very courses."

* * *

Later that day Wepper repaired to the chapel and an urgent appointment with Father Laskiva. In the security of the confessional the priest pored over the sheet of paper that Wepper had passed through the lattice. It was Lance's plagiarised poem; Heini's document remained securely in the inside pocket of Wepper's blazer. After having given the priest time to digest its contents Wepper, ever the manipulator, was careful to point out that Alexander's birthday roughly coincided with the end of term — when his fees ran out and he would have to leave Monsalvat anyway and fall back on supplicating the immigration authorities for leave to remain in the country. This reinforced the menace inherent in the document. One way or another, the mysterious writer was going to lose him.

"And how did you come by this?" Wepper demurred at the question, as was his right under the rules of the Confessional. Those rules delivered him of his dilemma. He must act to protect Alexander but he would not betray his blood-brother. He was, however, content for Lance to take his chances with authority; and for the purposes of his dilemma Father Laskiva represented that authority. And it was clear to Father Laskiva that his supplicant could not — or would not — vouchsafe anything more about the document and that the matter now rested with himself.

The priest duly fulfilled Wepper's purpose: "I must find the dedicator of these verses and have him removed from our midst."

Excellent, thought Wepper. The resolution of his dilemma was falling into place. He was thinking on his feet — or rather his knees — now: "You must do as you think fit, Father. Before I go..."

"Yes, what is it?"

"I understand that Alexander's missing medallion has turned up."

On the other side of the lattice Father Laskiva struggled to dissemble his emotions at the broaching of this delicate subject: "Yes indeed. I saw it round his neck on the morning of the Great Purgation." (The priest now had no compunction in using that seemingly pretentious expression.)

Wepper feigned surprise: "Only *that* morning? But I put it in his napery drawer in the refectory at least a week before.

I checked the napery drawer later that day and the medallion was no longer there. Yet Mauger told me he hadn't seen it on Alexander — and Mauger sees him stripped for gym at least twice a week. I suggest you ask Alexander who it was returned it. Chances are that whoever dedicated those lines to Alexander will be the same person who intercepted the return of the medallion. After all, why intercept an anonymous donation only to remain anonymous oneself?"

By such ineluctable logic did Wepper aspire to swerve the stars from their courses. He felt himself delivered of his moral dilemma; the matter was in the priest's hands now. But while the logic might be manifest, the resultant was not. While Wepper knew that "nobody's fool but God's" would not concoct a sinful untruth in response to the direct question, he did not foresee that the same heavenly fool would not be able to bring himself to betray his blood-brother either. Nor could he foresee that Laskiva, blinkered and irresolute as ever, would subsequently feel compelled to put the matter to his immediate higher authority; an authority that would have no compunction in holding his heavenly fool 'mute of malice'...

CHAPTER NINETEEN

The Eculeation

As on all previous occasions, Alexander was following Lance's instructions meticulously. He had delayed his passage on the way back from the sports field so that for the moment there were no other boys or staff in sight. At the first growth of ivy he had veered off the path to his right and flattened himself against the long high wall between the buttresses, leading with his right shoulder and turning his head the while to check that no others were coming into view beyond the ivy growths. As before, he reached the door; as before he leant against it with his back. As ever, it yielded. He did his usual adroit body swing round the door leaf so that he fetched up facing the door on the inside of it. As ever, the key was in the lock as Lance had promised it would be. With practised confidence, swiftly, silently, he pushed the door to and turned the key. Except that on this occasion the otherwise unmistakeable scent of Lance's cigarettes had not reached his nostrils. This should have alerted him to danger but by this time it was too late. Only then did he turn to look about him in the peach house. There looking down on him were Father Laskiva and the Rector himself.

* * *

Eculeations normally took place on Saturday mornings but this one was urgent in the eyes of authority. Alexander had been ordered to parade in regulation gym attire; white cotton shorts and plimsoles. Nothing else. This time there was to be no delay, no placing 'on report' or waiting in trepidation until the Saturday morning defaulters' parade.

Half an hour later saw Alexander in the old gym. He was naked. The discomfort of the icy chill of the shiny black leather of the vaulting horse, the dreaded *eculeus,* against the bare skin of his chest and abdomen, his inner thighs and his intimate appendages, had become surpassed by more acute sensations. His fingers were encircling the 'forelegs' of that dumbest of dumb creatures in a sweaty iron grip painful enough to counter the torment he was experiencing as the cane zipped down, again and again across his bare buttocks; a torment as the laying on of a red-hot poker; a cumulative pain as the strokes began to converge, weal upon weal. Through this torment he could hear the gentle questing voice of Father Laskiva.

"With whom were you meant to meet there? Just tell us the name, Alexander... just say the name. Just say the name and it will all be over."

As on the previous occasion when he had found himself in too close a communion with the same piece of gymnastic apparatus, the Rector had indeed deemed Alexander 'mute of malice'. Of course, he was never going to betray his blood-brother, whatever they might do to him.

The proceedings had started with the Rector himself leading the interrogation: "I shall ask you one more time. Give me the name of the boy who returned the medallion to you." And: "We need to know for your safety and wellbeing, spiritual and temporal."

This corollary meant little to the boy from Manchuria. As the Rector spoke, the object of his ire was a diminutive figure cowering against the wall bars, clad only in the aforesaid gym shorts and plimsoles. As the Rector spoke, that figure became bathed in a ray of sunlight that unexpectedly shone in through the dusty panes of one of the windows. In desperate realisation that he was challenging ultimate authority, Alexander despairingly adopted an attitude of considered defiance. In answer to the repeated interrogatories his voice was steady enough, if barely audible:

"I'm sorry, Father, I cannot tell you."

Alexander could have easily made up some plausible story as to how the medallion had come back to him. His conspiratorial arrival at the peach house was another matter. Either his assignation with Lance had become compromised or someone had set a trap for him.

In addition to the Rector, Father Laskiva and Mauger, present also in the old gym was Father Fillery with his camera. The contusion on his forehead resulting from Wepper's retributive excursion had faded by now, so that none was conscious of it but himself.

In his enforced obduracy Alexander had taken matters beyond the point of no return. The Rector feigned displeasure accordingly: "So... you would defy me. Let me remind you, Alexander Fragner Vudsen, that I am your ultimate confessor on the surface of God's Earth. No interstice of your being shall be closed to me." At the boy's continuing silence his voice shifted perceptibly to a softer, lower, menacing timbre. "Very well, you leave me with no alternative." And then: "Carry on, Mauger".

In response to some prearranged procedure Mauger now took over the conduct of the proceedings. Evidently, that prearranged procedure involved studied humiliation.

"Drop those gym shorts to your ankles and step back out of them."

Father Laskiva was appalled. He thought this stricture was

unprecedented. Alexander knew differently. Even so, the boy hesitated and looked to the priest, possibly for some ameliorating intervention. None was forthcoming. it was the first time that the priest had been summoned to witness an eculeation. It was a procedure which he had hitherto considered to be commendably regulatory and limiting. Now, on closer acquaintance, he was finding the experience distinctly disturbing. The trappings and the protocols seemed highly contrived, bizarre even.

Mauger's voice rapped out like a whiplash: "Quickly now, boy."

Resignedly, Alexander moved to obey. His father had made no mention of eculeations. Perhaps the omission was intentional. All Alexander knew was that he must not flinch or fail; must not break the compact with his late father, whatever adversities might be visited upon him according to the mores and customs of Monsalvat, its priests and its pupils. As it was, if this divesting exercise was meant to humiliate Alexander it was a failure. This was his second eculeation and he knew what to expect. And was he not a boy who had swum uninhibitedly nude with local village boys — and in some small danger of crocodiles — in half the rivers of Asia? Little did they know it but the would-be humiliators stood to be humiliated.

Alexander bent forward and pulled the shorts down until they dropped free to his ankles. As he went to lift his feet out of them they snagged on the rubber of the plimsoles and he inadvertently brought the discarded shorts up on his right heel. Reaching behind, he took hold of them and freed them with his right hand. As he did this he dislodged the plimsole and it fell to the floor with a soft thud. He straightened up and stood looking slightly to his right, fixing nobody with his gaze. The garment now hung from its waistband on the fingertips of his right hand, as if on a clothes peg. Keeping his elbow close in to his side he extended his forearm out to his right and languidly turned his hand over, letting the garment fall to the floor. It was a gesture charged with hauteur and contempt; whether deliberate or not Father Laskiva could not tell. Alexander then lifted his left foot and, reaching behind again, discarded the left plimsole. Nobody had told him to do this and nobody challenged him on it. In what seemed to be a choreographed tableau, he had rendered himself ultimately naked, seemingly as an indictment of his intending tormentors. The only adornment they could now see on his person was the *Agnus Dei* on his breast, glinting in the ray of sunlight that bathed his form.

The boy seemed to be undergoing an apotheosis before their eyes. His countenance assumed a beatific serenity and his nakedness transmuted into a noble nudity unburdened by any hint of pudicity. The perfection of his unadorned presence took on the symbolising of the triumph of youth and the eclipse of age. Those who had sought to humiliate him found themselves gazing on a golden god and feeling humbled. Their august presences, presuming to speak from knowledge, experience and achievement, were rendered little other than a bunch of dubious reprobates with a camera. And they knew it.

As for Father Laskiva, it was the first time he had seen Alexander naked. He would avert his gaze in deference to the boy's feelings but found his eyes drawn inexorably to the image before him. In the priest's eyes The Hand of God had indeed sculpted a most exquisitely contoured creature. Every last detail was proportional and perfect; the tumble of locks, the immaturely handsome visage with its captivating dimples, the lissom limbs, the pink nipples, the taut abdomen, the unencumbered navel, the dainty little appendages. The boy was the very reincarnation of Polydeukion. Not that Father Laskiva knew anything of Polydeukion at this stage; his education in that regard had yet to be completed. For the moment he stood transfixed along with the other adults. It was Pynxcytte who affected to rive their guilty reverie with a peremptory exhortation.

"That *Agnus Dei* round your neck... remove it."

Alexander hesitated. The Rector elaborated: "It is unfitting for one who is in defiance of holy authority to have any pretence to the protection it affords." Father Laskiva thought this a bit much. He saw Alexander reach behind and begin to fumble with the catch. Seeing the boy's difficulty, the priest felt compelled to walk over to the nude little god to undo it for him. He was so close now... so close... The priest's fingertips inadvertently touched on the exquisite hairless skin. His hands shook. He awkwardly shuffled his feet so as to aspect his face away from the watching trio. It was to no avail. Pynxcytte and Fillery exchanged knowing smirks. After what seemed an age, the clasp yielded and he was able to pluck the golden talisman from the boy's neck. He dropped it into the palm of his hand and felt a frisson of illicit pleasure: the animal warmth of the boy's body was still in the weight of the precious metal. In the absence of any direction from the Rector, he placed the medallion in the pocket of his cassock and turned away, to walk back towards the mats and the horse.

It was the Rector again: "Carry on, Mauger."

But Mauger was nothing if not a stickler for protocol. Seeing a material departure from normal procedure he made a pertinent observation: "But he isn't wearing anything, Rector."

"Carry on," Pynxcytte repeated, but this time more forcefully. Alexander cast his mind back to the bizarre protocols of his previous eculeation. It seemed that this time there was to be no proffering of a pair of over-tight gym shorts to give the proceedings some semblance of propriety.

Apparently reassured on that aberration, Mauger affected his usual practised ostentations. He doffed his tracksuit top to reveal his scrawny, hairy torso under a tight singlet. Then he picked up the obligatory batsman's glove and slowly and deliberately pulled it onto his right hand. Moving to the trestle table he picked up one of the three canes that lay along it. Almost lovingly, he drew it through the curled fingers of his left hand. Then he flexed it on the air and executed a simulated stroke. The rod whistled and zipped menacingly. Then he used it as a pointer.

"Stand here, boy."

He indicated a position alongside the horse with the down-pointed tip of the cane. The boy advanced across the dusty old floorboards to the canvas mat upon which the horse was stationed. He had a grace of movement redolent of an infant Christ going to a premature crucifixion. He was in extreme adversity yet there was not one in that chamber who would not have changed places with him; not one who would not have relinquished his own flawed, calloused being, mind and body and the burden of his years, were he able to trade it for this elegant epitome of a new beginning. That the boy was demonstrating a sacrificial loyalty to his supposed accomplice added to their discomfiture. Would they have been capable of such a rare and noble gesture? In such circumstances?

More immediately, Father Laskiva was appalled that the boy's perfect symmetry was to be disfigured by the cruel canes laid out on the green baize cloth. There were three of them, laid out in order of length and thickness. The greatest was a stunted malacca well furnished with growth nodules at close and regular intervals along its length, the better to mortify the flesh. As it was, Mauger had selected the lightest of the three, presumably thought commensurate with the boy's age and juniority.

Under Mauger's direction the naked boy straddled the horse and prostrated himself along the top. They saw him visibly wince and gasp at the shock of bare skin touching down on the cold, shiny leather. The horse had been rigged to pitch the boy's buttocks at optimum height for the purpose of inflicting corporal punishment. Mauger took his stance, legs apart, and gently touched the cane down on the bare skin.

Pynxcytte intervened once more at this point, his tone of voice flat and peremptory: "Say the name, boy. Who were you to meet? Who was it who returned your medallion to you?"

But Alexander remained silent. A nod from Pynxcytte signalled Mauger to proceed. Mauger lifted the cane, flexed it on the air and brought it down with a practised expertise. It landed with a dull 'splat' squarely across the boy's buttocks. The watchers saw him give an involuntary quivering intake of breath followed by a long exhale through pursed lips. They could sense him inwardly gauging the extent of his ordeal and his ability to withstand it — so far, so good it seemed.

An impatient Pynxcytte spoke again: "Say the name, boy."

It was at this point that Father Laskiva felt desperate enough to intervene. He moved in and knelt at the head of the horse and put his hands over the dainty little hands of the boy.

"Alexander, just say the name. Say the name and it will be all over."

Alexander remained silent. The priest found himself looking into the opalescent eyes of a trapped animal. He remained kneeling and facing Alexander, but he could only watch what was happening with increasing rage and frustration...

The naked boy on the horse had endured seven strokes now. His stubborn fortitude was evidenced by the perspiration dulling his skin, misting the cold black leather and acridly reaching the nostrils of the onlookers. Under his own enveloping hands Father Laskiva could feel the dainty little hands moving; the fingernails biting into the hardwood legs of the horse. Alexander was breathing quaveringly through his mouth now.

Pynxcytte exhibited more impatience: "We're getting nowhere. Use the malacca."

In response, Mauger turned and reached for the heavy gauge noduled rod. Laskiva was appalled. In his mind's eye now he was picturing the hapless, friendless, naked O'Neill boy being mercilessly whipped on Reginald Gough's 'pig bench' on that remote Shropshire farm some six years ago. A righteous rage welled up in the priest's breast and at long last he spoke out.

"Surely you're not going to mar the lad's fair flesh with that monstrosity?"

His outburst elicited no response. Mauger shifted his position slightly and flexed the rod on the pregnant air above the boy's buttocks; it whooped ominously. Fillery's camera flashed. Unrelentingly, Mauger brought it down diagonally across the existing striations. Father Laskiva, looking over the boy's shoulder, saw the impact quiver the taut young flesh. It was enough.

The boy went deathly pale and his eyes rolled up alarmingly so that only the whites were visible. Father Laskiva felt the little hands go limp under his own and he saw the braced arms relax reflexively.

Someone called out: "Catch him..."

The boy's unconscious body hung momentarily lopsided on the horse, his fall arrested only by the clamminess of his skin. Then the adhesion broke and he started to slide from the horse. Mauger sprang forward to grab him but it was the kneeling Father Laskiva who reached up and broke the boy's fall. He felt the bare skin cold and moist against his palms. Gently the priest lowered the limp, flopping body to the canvas mat. The action brought him into a kneeling position alongside the boy's head. Alexander was face down into the canvas padding and in some danger of asphyxiation. Gently the priest lifted the boy's head and turned it on one side so that the face was towards him.

Mauger was the first to speak. "Ethyl chloride?" he said; more of a statement than an interrogatory.

"Yes. Ethyl chloride," agreed Pynxcytte.

The First Aid box was resorted to, a glass spray vial of clear liquid was abstracted and Mauger warmed it in his hand and shook it. Then he knelt and directed the cooling spray over the ugly pattern of weals that now disfigured the boy's buttocks.

Pynxcytte continued: "Now you've got your pictures. Fillery, go and round up two prefects and escort Lance Lapita to the bell tower. I'll be writing to his people in the morning."

Father Laskiva looked up from his ministering to Alexander. "You knew?" he asked incredulously. "All this time… you knew? And you put him through this? For nothing?" And then: "Dear God… what kind of people are you?"

Pynxcytte was unmoved. "We've known for months, man. Nothing happens at Monsalvat that I don't know about," he replied dryly.

Instinctively Father Laskiva knew that the Seal of the Confessional had been breached.

Pynxcytte turned back to Mauger: "Wrap him in the blanket and take him along to the sanatorium. He'll need icepacks on those weals as soon as possible."

In response to the soothing effect of the anaesthetic spray the boy moaned and stirred. Father Laskiva gently lowered his hand onto Alexander's head and soothingly caressed the flaxen curls. The boy's eyelids flickered briefly and opened to reveal the intense blueness of his eyes — not even this present adversity could dull those. The eyes closed again and stayed so and the boy spoke, his lips working against the canvas. Father Laskiva had to bend close to catch his words:

"Is it over, Father?"

"Yes, Alexander, it's over now. Don't try to move."

"Did I fail my father?" Alexander asked plaintively. At this, Father Laskiva choked and visibly struggled to control his voice before attempting his response.

"No, Alexander, you did not fail your father." He then repeated the assurance with a change in emphasis. Looking up accusingly towards where the Rector and Father Fillery were standing, the kneeling priest uttered: "No Alexander, *you* did not fail your father." There was now a cold fury in his tone which intensified as he continued. He looked directly at Pynxcytte now: "I've heard it said of you, Pynxcytte..." (this was the first time that Father Laskiva had addressed the Rector in such cavalier terms) "... that you are inclined to do good by stealth. I have to say I've seen a deal of stealth today and precious little good. This child thinks he must live up to a compact with his late father. That he is being tested according to..." and here his voice assumed a biting sarcasm "...the mores and customs of Monsalvat; and that he must not be found wanting. For this reason, and only for this reason, he has endured the pain and indignities that this House has inflicted upon him. Inflicted by way of the acts — aye and the omissions — of authority. Your authority. It is only this... this... purported compact... that has kept him from running away; running to the sanctuary of the Edgars." The priest's voice now rose to an hysterical pitch. "In Holy Truth it is a compact which his father would never have imposed upon him. His father consigned him to our care in his knowledge of Monsalvat as he knew it. *Secura nidificat* as it indeed then was. Not as it has now become — a nest of vipers."

This last was veritably spat out. Then he turned his gaze back upon the trembling little body by his side, upon the cruel striations disfiguring its integument and he continued in a quieter voice: "This child in our care has been betrayed and abused. And I, God forgive me, have stood idly by. In my naïvety and gullibility..." and his voice rose to an anguished screech "...I have joined the betrayers and abusers." His head dropped and the onlookers saw the broad back of thc priest shudder with silent convulsive sobs.

Pynxcytte seemed unmoved. He addressed his subordinate in mock conciliatory tones: "You really must control yourself,

Father Laskiva — I wouldn't wish to have to send you back to the diocese."

The erstwhile meek and compliant priest was having none of that. From his kneeling posture alongside Alexander's head, he rounded upon Pynxcytte with invigorated authority.

"It is not I who should control himself. Mark this, Pynxcytte, and mark it well. This boy... this pupil of this school..., of which you are the headmaster and custodian... has undeniably been punished beyond his endurance. And surely you, as a headmaster, must know the implications of that. If you presume to exert your authority against me I might be inclined to take matters beyond these walls."

The others stood transfixed but in the face of such emotive and unprecedented opposition Pynxcytte wisely kept his counsel and merely motioned Mauger to proceed.

But Father Laskiva had not finished. "From now on — albeit much too late — I shall take charge of this boy and I shall be responsible for his welfare. It is clear that no-one else in this school can be trusted." Then turning to Mauger: "Get him to the sanatorium right now. I shall go on ahead."

Mauger sensed that the power positions at Monsalvat had irrevocably shifted. Without demur he came forward with a blanket and he and the priest gently rolled the prostrate boy into its comforting folds. Mauger gathered him up in his arms. But just as Mauger was whisking the boy from the gymnasium, Pynxcytte stopped the PT instructor in his tracks. Father Laskiva paused at the exit door and looked back to see Pynxcytte draw the blanket aside so as to look into the trembling boy's face. He spoke, and for the first time that day his voice was soft and soothing: "Today, Alexander, you have been very foolish — something which I might, with the passage of time, be inclined to forget." Laskiva thought this patronising. But then the Rector added: "You have also been very brave — and that is something which I shall never forget."

With that, he waved Mauger away with his precious burden. Father Laskiva was left wondering about this strange man and his strange ways.

Word had earlier got out that Alexander had been ordered to parade at the old gym in regulation gym strip. Some had seen him pass in the colonnade. Such an advanced state of undress allowed for no doubt that he was in for an eculeation. This was usually an occasion for some nervous sniggering on the part of the more cynical of the boys. On this occasion there were no sniggers. Since the Great Purgation every move and event touching upon the boy from Manchuria had become of interest to every boy, senior and junior. Ever since the routing of the Irish Gang there had been an expectation of a final confrontation between him and the authority that had seemed to connive at its existence.

Later, when the eculeation could be assumed to have taken place, some of the seniors drifted down from the dormitories and gathered in hushed groups along the colonnade. They saw Father Laskiva stride purposefully past on his way to the sanatorium, his face a picture of contained fury. Then Mauger, following, had to pass them with his precious burden. Where necessary some moved desultorily aside to facilitate his passage. It was obvious that such considerations were for the benefit of his burden and not for him. He stared straight ahead as he passed within a few feet of them and could sense the cold scrutiny of hostile eyes. All they could see of Alexander was a pair of dainty bare feet protruding from the enveloping blanket. Why did the boy have to be carried? Why was he so silent? The silence was palpable, broken only by the sound of Mauger's footsteps echoing along the colonnade. Then, heedless of the consequences, one of the boys called after him:

"Damn your rotten soul, Mauger... you... fucking... lousy... cunt."

The studied detestation in the measured delivery of the concatenated obscenities was palpable. Each arrested word echoed down the colonnade as a staccato indictment. Mauger felt the back of his neck prickle in response to the gaze of hostile eyes. He hurried on without turning or making any acknowledgment of this gross and unprecedented insult. He could readily identify the boy who called out but was not inclined to seek retribution. He was coming to the uncomfortable conclusion that Monsalvat was on the verge of open rebellion.

And what of Wepper? Where was he in Alexander's hour of need? As on 'cabaret night', as Barden Sender had been only too aware, he was again sojourning in the arms of Rhiannon at the ap Gruffydd homestead; and momentous events would come to pass before he would become aware of the grave disservice he had unthinkingly perpetrated against his cherished half blood-brother.

Forewarned by Father Laskiva, Godred was hurriedly preparing ice bags in the sanatorium when Mauger carried Alexander up the stairs. He waved Mauger through to the ward. Here the naked boy was turned out of the blanket to lie face down across a draw sheet on one of the hospital beds. Godred gently applied the icepacks and Alexander winced. Then they could see his trembling, taut body visibly relaxing as the icepacks began to sooth away the burning pain. Present also was Wali Waliser whom Godred had pressed into service to break out and crack the block ice. Godred and Wali each seized two hospital blankets. Tossing Mauger's blanket aside, seeming contemptuously, they gently covered Alexander's nakedness, packing the blankets around him and leaving just his buttocks exposed under the icepacks.

Wali approached the boy's head with a sliver of ice. He spoke and his voice was soft and gentle: "Put this in your mouth, Alexander, it will help. In a little while we'll take off the icepacks and get you a nice drink. Then you can sleep. I promise you, you will not be disturbed." He said this in German. Then, turning away, he said to no-one in particular: "The price is too high. This child has suffered enough." He said this in English. Those hearing it wondered what he meant and what he might do.

The uncomprehending Mauger now chose this moment to manifest his disapproval of the proceedings in which he had just officiated. Mindful of the import of Father Laskiva's outburst in the old gym, he realised he had been co-opted into a dubious evolution that could have serious consequences. He saw himself between the Scylla of job security and the Charybdis of legal sanction (although he would not have phrased it so). He found himself hoping that Fillery would have the good sense to destroy the pictures he had taken.

He voiced his new-found discomfiture: "I've 'ad enough of this. From now on 'is bloody nibs can do 'is own eculeations."

With that, he stamped out of the sanatorium and went about his own devices.

* * *

Mauger was not the only one to undergo a Damascene Conversion that morning. Another hour found Wali Waliser sitting contemplating a sealed foolscap envelope on a tabletop in Yseult's rented room along in the town. Yseult was not present. Wali was dressed to go out. He had poured himself yet another drink from a three-quarters empty bottle of whisky and sipped at it as he stared at the rather dramatic hand-written legend on the cover:

> "To be opened immediately and without fail by the
> designated custodian hereof in the event of the death,
> disappearance, absconding or expulsion of William Wesley

*Wepper pupil at the Roman Catholic College of St Michael
Monsalvat at Pencadno in North Wales or otherwise upon
his eventual graduation from that same whichever event shall
be the earlier"*

It was written in violet ink, ink that had long been dry. After another drink for old times' sake he put the envelope in his raincoat pocket, walked down the stairs to the street and left Pencadno, never to return.

CHAPTER TWENTY

In the Bell Tower

Among other things, the lilies in the chapel had not been refreshed and at the kitchens the swill bins had not been hauled out for the contractors to exchange. Wali Waliser was being uncharacteristically remiss in his duties. Father Quedda hastened to the old bothy to find out why. There was no Wali. All the drawers and cupboards hung open and his street clothes were gone. Such petty cash as he was allowed to keep had gone also. There was little doubt that he had left Monsalvat with no intention of returning. Father Quedda checked for any parting notes but found none. As an ex-enemy prisoner of war, Wali had been given a right of abode in the United Kingdom and a transferable work permit. He was free to go whither he wished — but in the present circumstances the Bursar would have appreciated some form of notice. The amount of cash involved was unquantifiable and negligible and would not furnish cause for police action. Father Quedda made a discreet excursion to Wali's girl-friend, Yseult, at the modest room she shared with Wali along in the town. Neither party was there and it was clear from the state of that place that Wali's decamping had been a precipitate decision, possibly fuelled by drink. It remained for Father Quedda to report to Canon Pynxcytte accordingly and to urgently arrange with the local labour exchange for a replacement.

Word quickly spread among the boys that the college's assistant gardener had gone missing. His apparent absconding put the more senior of them in mind of the similar absconding of Heinrich Daser in September 1948. Except that on this occasion the absconder had not helped himself to one of the college staff cars.

* * *

The time had finally arrived when William Wesley Wepper, Monsalvat's Bold Contemner, had to say his goodbyes and take his leave of Monsalvat forever. For all his characteristic urbanity he was experiencing all the emotions that flood in with the ending of schooldays, that breakpoint in life when the dependency of the juvenile has to be relinquished and the trappings of maturity have to be assumed. It is a time much looked forward to for years on end but on the hour itself, whilst anticipating the unknown with much excitement and some trepidation, the subject must inevitably cast a longing look behind at the pains and pleasures of schooldays, achievements, friends and occasions, those dynamic years which have forged the man the world has yet to meet. It was a time of handshakes and well-wishing, some more sincere than others. Even Canon Peter Pynxcytte and his six priestly appointees harboured some grudging respect for their departing contemner and manipulator. He had proved himself to be a worthy adversary, a brilliant scholar and a survivor *par excellence*. More pertinently, he was leaving behind him a secret contractual legacy that was going to bind Pynxcytte for at least another six years.

But, as Robert Burns annually reminds us, the best laid schemes of mice and men 'gang aft aglay'. The decamping of Monsalvat's assistant gardener might well have knocked Wepper's clandestine arrangements into a cocked hat. It was arranged that Wepper was to make a late evening departure, taking the slow 'local' from Pencadno to Crewe and from thence the overnight 'sleeper' to Euston. In order to facilitate this and to save disturbing his dormitory, it was arranged that he should move into the bell tower accommodation some twenty-four hours before departure.

Thus it was that he found himself in close proximity to the quarantined Lance Lapita. As a result — ostensibly — of evidence elicited at Alexander's eculeation, Lance was now confined there, pending arrangements to have him withdrawn by his parents. A problem had arisen with this. His parents were touring Ireland in the Riley 1.5 and were incommunicado. Their intention was to land at Holyhead coincident with end of term and to pick up Lance as they passed through on their way to the English border. Thus, the Fathers of Monsalvat were having to host Lance Lapita for several days more than they would wish.

Lance was under orders not to leave the bell tower without permission and escort, and Godred and Geddington were charged with enforcing this sanction as they worked their respective shifts. In the bell tower accommodations, however, vestibules, corridors and bathrooms were common compartments and it was inevitable that Lance and Wepper would come across each other during their intended brief stay. Thus, it came about that Lance heard a knock on the door of the room he had been assigned to. William Wepper had come to say the most critical of his goodbyes.

"Come in."

Wepper found Lance sitting despondently in an armchair surrounded by books and letters.

"I suppose your people will be coming for you on Thursday." The statement was a rhetorical interrogatory; the day was a

Tuesday and end-of-term was on Thursday. "I'm off tonight on the late local to Crewe. I'll be joining the sleeper from Preston." It was with some trepidation that Wepper then moved on to the major burden of their meeting. "I suppose you've heard that Wali has gone missing." He waited until Lance nodded assent. "I went looking for him at the old bothy but I ran across Yseult instead. She's very upset. She thinks Wali has gone to surrender to the authorities. She didn't say as much but she as good as implied it was as a fugitive war criminal."

"Why on earth would he want to do that? Why now?"

"Conscience perhaps. Or it could be he wants to save Alexander from any further tender ministrations of Pynxcytte and his cronies." Here Wepper pre-empted Lance's interjection: "Yes, I know... The blood of thousands on his hands and he balks at the tribulations of one little 'English' schoolboy this late in his career. Perhaps he sees Alexander as his potential salvor, whether of his soul or his neck I don't know. I know Alexander was special to him — and not just because they spoke the same language. Christ knows, he's special to us; and after what's happened here this term I think he's special to a lot of people. You and I know he's special to Pynxcytte and his cronies as well — for all the wrong reasons. I've checkmated them bastards until he matriculates from this place. But it's not all hunky-dory, Lance; Yseult is blaming Alexander for Wali's decamping. And Wali is Yseult's meal ticket. It's a matter to be settled between the two of them. Right now, I want to talk to you about Alexander and yourself."

Wepper went on to remonstrate with some emotion: "Lance, you must relinquish him. And you must tell him that you relinquish him. I know it will break your heart as well but it's him we must protect from further anguish. Make it right with him, you can do it, you're good at speeches. I've been talking with Laskiva. We think it would be a good idea for the two of you to have a final meeting. Oh, it would be under the supervision of the Fathers of course. It's so he'll know that it's all over between the two of you. There's no need for him to know the full story — the way you've misled and betrayed him. His heart will be broken enough as it is. Can we trust you to finally do right by him and send him on his way so's he'll think it's for the best?"

Lance looked up uncomprehendingly; the strain on his face was palpable.

Wepper became more acerbic now: "The trouble with you, Lance, is you want to sojourn for evermore in the Gardens of Daphne... plucking peaches. Face facts, man. Boys grow up. You're growing up. I've grown up. You must let Alexander grow up.

"Will, he's my blood-brother."

"I know. And you're *my* blood-brother. Remember that day in the peach house when you were in the Remove and I was in the Third? That makes me his blood half-brother. For his sake break the bond. The circumstances are unique. Lance, let him grow up; let him form friendships with his peers."

Lance made no immediate reply. Wepper continued: "Lance, what's it to be? Selfishness or altruism?"

This last triggered a bitter response: "Altruism is it? What you really want is for me to relinquish him to you and Rhiannon. That's not altruism, Will."

Wepper grimaced with frustration. "Oh, Lance, he isn't a trophy to be fought over between rivals." There was another pause before Wepper continued: "Okay, let's strike a bargain. Let all three of us let him go. I know I can get Rhiannon on side. Let him go forward without the baggage of all our affections if that's the better course."

Wepper paused a while before continuing: "He has a future here. I've arranged it with Pynxcytte. Pynxcytte is now responsible for his safety and welfare — and his school fees right up to graduation, whenever that will be. Let him accede to what is his right. Christ knows, he's suffered enough. Will you do it, Lance?"

Lance's attitude shifted again at this revelation. "So, you've secured his future like you secured yours. That's going to be another six years. Six more years of Pynxcytte and his cronies. Your arrangement didn't stop the bastard from giving Alexander a beating severe enough to put him in the sanatorium. And six more years of the Irish Gang — or their successors. For the sake of one boy you're going to inflict that on the rest of the school. The hell-hole that is Monsalvat is going to be protracted for another six years. Six more years of new peaches lying in terror at night, crying themselves to sleep, being put on the grill bars... All that was supposed to end with your graduation. And you... you're no altruist, Will; you're the hypocrite *par excellence*. Are you content with that?"

"Of course I'm not fucking well content. But aren't you forgetting? Alexander has cleaned up this Augean stable for... well, let's say the foreseeable future. The Irish Gang are vanquished. By the time Pynxcytte moves to rebuild his empire it will be all over for his crowd. They'll be too busy securing their bolt-holes. Pynxcytte knows the axe falls when Alexander graduates."

"Ah, but Alexander isn't like you, Will. Alexander's a believer. He can't be told from whence his immunity comes. If he ever gets to know, he'll pull the plug on Pynxcytte — and his own future, whatever the sacrifice. It was up to you to clean up Monsalvat; you could have done it years ago. It was only your own selfish interest that kept this hell-hole going. All right, you would have been sacked for lack of fees but you're a smart fellow; you would have survived outside. You say you don't know the contents of your precious 'attaché case in a safe deposit' but you know only too well the power it gives you over Pynxcytte and his cronies. You may hide behind a technicality but you still have the morals of a blackmailer. Alexander isn't... won't be... can't be... any of that. You could spring the trap now and clear the bastards out once and for all. I don't know who'd take over... Laskiva, I suppose. We know he's not one of them; although Christ knows, he's been fuck-all use otherwise." But Lance was digressing; he returned to the matter of the moment: "By your own precepts Alexander will survive, whether inside or outside of Monsalvat. In any case, it's a fair bet there'll be people from the Far East — friends of his people — looking for him as we speak. As soon as they've got their own affairs sorted out they could end up paying his fees; even adopting him."

Wepper was dismissive. "Yes — but they ain't alongside yet, are they? Okay, so Pynxcytte's crowd get a reprieve for six years; while Alexander's around they're not going to rampage as sadistic voyeurs and peddlers of dubious pictures as they were doing before his Great Purgation. And now you're off the scene he'll give them no more excuses to beat him. The poor little sod went through that on your account."

Lance visibly recoiled at the sting of this truth. "I know... I know. But, Will, you're still leaving the wolves in charge of the fold. Look, we both know I'm a lost cause but I still know right from wrong... and what you're doing is fucking well wrong." Lance intoned this last phrase with vehemence.

"You should care," riposted Wepper facetiously. "And mind yer language, Lance. You're the one who's supposed to be the good Catholic here." The mild — and insincere — rebuke seemed to pause the conversation, both boys seeming lost in thought.

Eventually Wepper broke the silence. "Anyway, fuck all this philosophising; it's too late to change anything now. What about Alexander? Will you say a lasting goodbye to him — blood-brother? Speak up and I'll fix it with Laskiva. Time's getting short."

Lance rose to his feet as if to make a momentous announcement. When it came it was more of a sigh: "All right, I'll do it for Alexander — and for you... Blood-brother."

In relief the blood-brothers now embraced, eyes closed. But there was one more item on Wepper's agenda. As the boys drew apart he patted his inside blazer pocket. Both knew he was referring to the incriminating documents he held there; the testimony of Heinrich Daser and Lance's menacing verses regarding Alexander.

"Wali's been a good friend to me these past three years. He looked after me when I was younger... when this college had become a very hostile place for me. When it was just me against the rest. And remember, he's helped our friendship... our... love. He didn't judge us, Lance. Instead he gave us a key to the peach house... our trysting place. And..." he added significantly "... the trysting place of you and Alexander." He patted his pocket again. "Your document could hang Wali — although I'm sure there's enough evidence elsewhere to hang him ten thousand times. Lance, what shall we do with it? For old time's sake, Lance, let's spare him this makeweight. After all, maybe Heini's still alive somewhere and this is a load of old bollocks. What say we burn it?"

"It's with you, Will, you must do as you think fit." Then, as if anticipating Wepper's further question, he added: "As far as I'm concerned I'll say I handed it to you still under seal — I'll maintain I have no knowledge of its contents."

"Ah but the seal's broken. As is the seal on your verses. Will you trust me to burn them together — blood-brother?"

Lance nodded his acquiescence. Wepper reached into his blazer for Heini's testimony.

"And the translation?"

Lance rummaged in a half-packed valise on the floor and produced the requisite document. He handed it to Wepper.

Wepper briefly flourished Lance's verses then pocketed all three documents with an air of finality.

Then for some curious reason Lance asked a patently redundant question: "Where will you burn them then?"

True, there were no fireplaces in the bell tower accommodations; it was centrally heated by a steam line from the bath house. Wepper looked at him as if he were daft. He inclined his head in the general direction of the greenhouses. "The peach house stove furnace; where else? But we're not out of the wood yet, Lance."

"What do you mean?"

"Wali is one of the custodians of the code to the safe deposit box — where the attaché case is. I'm hoping he's destroyed it; the code, that is. 'Cause if he's still got it on his person and he does turn himself in to the authorities — it could bring the whole show down."

Lance contemplated the ramifications of such a contingency. "There's not a lot we can do about that, Will."

"No, Lance; not a lot. We'll just have to wait and see what happens." He paused then: "Whatever happens, at least I know I can trust you to do right by Alexander. I have your word as my blood-brother?"

"Yes, Will, as your blood-brother you have my word."

"Well, Lance; we've already said our goodbyes in another place. For old times' sake, eh, Lance? Remember the peach house..."

"Ah... the peach house..."

The door closed berween them, leaving each alone with his thoughts.

* * *

Wepper approached the long back wall of the peach house with some trepidation. The dark of evening was upon the outbuildings of Monsalvat now. A dim light shone in the window of the old bothy. Yseult was there, still keening for her absent lover. Wepper was content to leave her to her anguished reverie. He turned the key in the lock in the wicket gate and let himself into the peach house. A wind had got up from the sea and was rattling some of the loose panes in the weathered glazing bars. He stepped along the walkway and through the door into the stove house. The rusted furnace door groaned on its hinges as Wepper drew it back to reveal the dusty maw of the grate inside, redolent of long dead fires. He contemplated what untoward things might have passed through the generously wide stokehole. He was put in mind of the pictures of concentration camp crematoria that had lately appeared in the papers. This was business to get over quickly.

Wepper screwed up the incriminating documents and their covers, put his lighter to the ball of paper and chucked it inside. The wind sighed in the old chimney and the draught threatened to lift the still-burning papers and carry them out and onto the wind at the chimney cap. Wepper grabbed a rusting fire iron and held the glowing papers safely down until the flames had totally consumed them. With the iron, he agitated the remains on the bed of spent clinkers until they fell through the fire bars and into the ash pan. Whatever Dieter Gressler might tell the authorities could now gather no confirmation from the written testimony of Heinrich Daser, be that man dead or alive. Neither would Lance's verses portend death to the boy from Manchuria. The wind moaned more urgently in the chimney now and Wepper hastened to distance himself from that awful place; a place where grisly associations had lately displaced so many blissful memories.

But the peach house had yet to deliver up one more disconcerting secret. Wali had left a sign. A sign for Wepper? Wepper could only guess. For as he turned to leave the stove house, he noticed something wrong with the pipework. An L-bend had been displaced and had been left out-turned, looking for all the world like a cowl ventilator on its side. Intrigued and perturbed, Wepper went in closer to examine it. When he rotated it on the jointing it made no noise; it had been well greased, and that fairly recently. As had the short pipe length that led up to it. Wepper found he could move this pipe length along in the jointing. The sealing compound had long since decayed and had been replaced with lubricating grease. It would be short work to move the pipe along and release the L-bend from its collar for turning outwards — or to swiftly replace the pipework so that it looked undisturbed. But why? Wepper could only think of one purpose. Eavesdropping; the old-fashioned large bore pipework would carry sound most efficiently. Even now he could feel a draught coming through the pipe and could hear the sighing of the wind and the rattling of the panes in the peach house.

Before doing anything else he went and examined the hinges and latches of the other door that led outside and back towards the old bothy. All were similarly well greased — for silence. He walked back into the peach house to the area where the garden furniture had hosted the clandestine trysts of the blood-brothers. He went to the adjacent length of grating in the floor that covered the pipe trench. He found he could not lift it; it had been seized into place with industrial adhesive. He tried the two adjoining lengths; they both yielded to his pull. Returning to the critical length he looked down into the darkness. Impatiently he flicked his cigarette lighter to gain more light. Through the grating he could see the jointing collar of an upturned L-bend; an L-bend where no L-bend ought to be. The pipework had been severed and the L-bend inserted and left upturned, the better to catch sound. There could be no doubt now. The old heating pipes had been converted into an efficient eavesdropping system.

A number of questions now assailed Wepper. Indeed,

question begat question. For how long had Wali been eavesdropping on their trysts? And to what purpose? One thing Wepper was certain of, it could not have been mere prurience; Wali was not of that persuasion. Wepper could only conclude that Wali must have been under an extraneous compulsion of some kind. That he was reporting to someone. Instinctively he knew that the real author of this latest treachery to come to light could only be Peter Pynxcytte, Rector of Monsalvat. It must be that Pynxcytte had the same information on Wali that Heini intended to vouchsafe to Wepper. That he had known for long enough that he had been hosting the Beast of Natzweiler within his walls. But how had he become so apprised?

Of course Wepper had no knowledge of the midnight confession of Heinrich Daser some five years earlier. Nevertheless, it was common knowledge that Heini was — or had been — an active Catholic making regular confession — exclusively to Pynxcytte. It was also common knowledge that Wali affected a religiosity that ostensibly induced him to make periodic confession — also exclusively to Pynxcytte. Wepper could only conclude that in Wali's case, as with Foul Mouthed Frank Leport, the Seal of the Confessional had been used and abused as an avenue of intrigue and a necessary precursor to blackmail and treachery.

Then another thought struck him: if Heini had indeed been murdered by Wali, had it been at the behest of Pynxcytte? Pynxcytte would have a ready executioner in Wali if Wali knew that Pynxcytte was apprised of his history as The Beast of Natzweiler. And why would Pynxcytte come to want Heini out of the way in such a drastic manner? Wepper could only assume it was because of what Heini knew of his compatriot, combined with his increasingly erratic and drunken behaviour; that Heini had become an intolerable threat to the security of some clandestine operation, an operation of commanding importance to Pynxcytte.

And why had Pynxcytte set Wali eavesdropping on such trivia as the passing amours of silly schoolboys? While such dalliances might be of legitimate pastoral concern, they were hardly crucial to the running of a school. Unless of course the aforesaid prurience was directed from the upper echelons of the hierarchy. That would explain a lot of the goings-on at Monsalvat. Among other things it was proof, if proof were needed, that the eculeation of Alexander had been nothing other than a sadistic act and an opportunity to obtain graphic images of that act. Images that might have a market of sorts in the *demi-monde* of London and beyond. Wepper felt he had a better idea now of what that attaché case might contain...

It was also fairly common knowledge that Monsalvat was limping along on the brink of impecuniosity; that pupil numbers and hence revenue had fallen below fiscal feasibility. Wepper surmised that the deficit had been made up by the clandestine marketing of illicit images; images by which Pynxcytte and his cronies could indulge their proclivities and make money at the same time. But Wepper doubted that such sales alone would sustain Pynxcytte's squalid empire. There must be some corollary. It could only be blackmail. Wepper recalled the cockney spiv in the flashy American car. And as the affair at the station had confirmed, Pynxcytte had friends in low places; friends who were willing to travel. Just as he had had his enforcers within the walls of Monsalvat, so did he have his enforcers beyond those walls. Wepper could only conclude that Monsalvat was the centre of a web of intrigue that stretched far and wide.

Wepper resolved not to tell Lance of this latest treachery to come to light. It would only complex matters and serve no useful purpose. What he did do was arrange through the agency of Father Laskiva for Alexander and Lance to have their final meeting.

In the interests of propriety, the parting was to be in the

presence of the pastoral Fathers. Only Father Fillery would be absent. One of the guest chambers in the bell tower was set aside for the purpose.

* * *

At the appointed time Alexander appeared at the open door with Father Laskiva standing behind him. Alexander sensed that this was to be a decisive occasion. He glanced around apprehensively at the circle of Fathers standing there and looked to Lance for reassurance. As if it had been rehearsed, the Fathers discreetly withdrew to an adjoining room leaving only Father Laskiva and the two boys together. The connecting door remained ajar however.

Lance stood up. His face showed the anguish within. All was silence save for the ticking of a long case clock in the corner.

At last he spoke and his voice was soft: "It's all right, Alexander. They know about us. Come to me." He held out his arms. The child advanced into them and Lance gathered him in so that his face was buried against Lance's right shoulder. Lance's lips were pressed against the child's head, almost buried in the golden swirls; his eyes became closed.

"I want you to listen carefully to what I have to say. I want you to be brave. Will you do that for me, Alexander?

Only the ticking of the clock rived the silence. Then Father Laskiva saw the wheaten head nod to signal acquiescence.

Lance continued with a perceptible tremor in his voice: "Alexander, I want you to know that whatever happens now, whatever becomes of us, I love you most dearly and I always will; nothing in the whole world can alter that. And I know that you love me just as much. But the Fathers have pointed out that our love is not part of man's estate."

With that, Alexander lifted his face from Lance's lapel and

looked up and into Lance's eyes. "But we are not yet men," he shrilled, with the devastating logic of the innocent.

Lance continued in a soothing, velvet voice: "Quite so, quite so. But in the Fathers' scheme of things our great love is deemed inappropriate — they think it will lead to bad things. And they are right, although not in the way they think; already our love has got us into trouble and interfered with what you are here for — to get an education so that you may make your way in the world. Alexander, I am older than you. Your first friendships should be with your form mates. I have no right to take you away from the established order of things. And... it is not for me to come between you and the Faith of your mother and father. Now you have been punished for maintaining silence... trying to protect me. And as for me, I am to leave Monsalvat in disgrace. These things shouldn't be happening to chaps in the course of their education. These things are proof enough that our love, however pure and chaste we have striven to keep it, is surely destructive and cannot continue. Alexander, we live in the world and are judged by the world and the world decrees that our love must end. Look at it this way — a boy like you will quickly make other friends, friends of your own age, be invited into their houses in the holidays and some day soon I'm sure you will be adopted into a loving family."

The import of what Lance was saying was beginning to dawn on Alexander. Despite that attempt at reassurance all his hopes for the future, of another welcome into that warm and happy Cumberland home in which he had sojourned at Christmas, away from the austere walls of Monsalvat, were now falling away. All those memories of love and happy hours over the Christmas holidays were now becoming barbs to torment him. He returned his forehead to Lance's lapel. Incipient sobs began to convulse the little body.

"But what about Mark?" he asked plaintively.

The clock ticked ten times. The looks of anguish on the faces of the listening Fathers in the next room heightened perceptibly as Lance struggled for words.

"Mark will be unhappy too. We must do our best to find him other companions that he'll regard as highly as he did you — but that will be difficult, for he loved you unreservedly. Fate has dealt him a cruel blow. The family all know he's not long for this world. It was I who suggested you two should sleep together in the big bed. Usually he's on his own and only has a call bell. You brought him comfort during the long nights when he couldn't sleep because of the pain. He said you made the pain less. I couldn't ever be jealous of my little brother or grudging of the hours you gave him. I was content that you were under our roof and happy. Taking Mark out in the wheelchair; looking after the animals, walking the dog, fussing the cat... as long as you were happy. I know my parents could never take the place of your beloved mama and papa, or your dear little sister — but I hoped that we could go some way to mending your broken heart. But the world decrees it's not to be.

"Alexander, it's time for you and I to say our last goodbye. Some day, when we're grown up, I hope that somehow we shall meet again and be happy. Just now, we are children, but that state doesn't last for ever. Some day, God willing, we'll have children of our own, for that is truly man's estate; but for now, as children, we must part. Listen carefully, Alexander; are you listening?"

There was no immediate response. "Alexander?" prompted Lance ever so gently. The clock ticked ten times before once again Lance felt the cradled head nod against his shoulder.

"Father Laskiva is standing behind you. He understands what this means to you and he'll look after you. When I let you go I want you to turn and go to him and not to look back. Will you do that, Alexander?"

The clock ticked another ten times before the younger head

nodded assent. And the clock ticked a further ten times before Lance relaxed his arms, releasing the child from his hold.

"The time is upon us. Go now, Alexander. And remember — don't look back."

Alexander backed slowly away. His face, hidden until now, became upturned and revealed all the uninhibited manifestation of emotional devastation. It was doubtful if he could see anything at all through the tears stinging his eyes. As he backed away the two boys' arms remained outstretched, each towards the other. Lance's hands drifted slowly down the length of Alexander's arms until, slowly, inexorably, the fingertips parted. Only then, as bidden, did Alexander turn and run into the arms of Father Laskiva, burying his face in the cleric's cassock. The priest's arms enfolded him and conducted him from the room and out of sight.

Lance had spoken bravely and well beyond his years. He sank back onto his chair and buried his face in his hands. Out in the corridor, Alexander started to cry after the manner of a child half his age. Unabashed and unabated, the boy's loud, long, sighing sobs echoed back along the corridor, fading away until they became diminished by increasing distance and closing doors.

Of the Fathers in the ante-room, they stood like statues and none thought fit to break the clock-ticking silence. Eventually, one of them looked up towards a crucifix on the wall and fixed his gaze there for some time before speaking. Struggling to control his voice, the words came out convulsively: "What have we done? How many times must that boy's heart be broken?"

The clock struck the hour. It was three o'clock.

CHAPTER TWENTY-ONE

The Long Night Begins

As was expected, the task of taking William W. Wepper to the station for his final departure from Monsalvat had been delegated to Father Laskiva. Partly by way of a programme of rehabilitation the priest had recruited De Leapey, late of the Irish Gang, to assist him with Wepper's heavy baggage. It was when the priest was changing out of his cassock and into his street clothes of clerical black suiting that he came across Alexander's *Agnus Dei* which had lain forgotten in a pocket of the cassock since the cruel and fateful eculeation. The priest resolved to return it to Alexander as soon as was practicable, but at the moment he was preoccupied with speeding the departure of Monsalvat's Bold Contemner. Nevertheless, Father Laskiva did not like to think of the young Removite being deprived of the possession and the protection of the medallion that meant so much to him. Carefully he placed it in a secure inside pocket of his suit jacket to await a suitable opportunity.

* * *

It was gathering dusk when Yseult heard the faint patter of approaching juvenile footsteps. They stopped at the door of the old bothy. Upstairs Yseult waited expectantly. She guessed it would be Alexander. She had heard he was up and about again after his bruising encounter with authority. Sure enough, she heard him call up the stairs.

"Wali, Ist dass Sie? Sind Sie ess?

Yseult made no reply but Alexander sensed that somebody was up there. Gingerly he mounted the rickety stairs and duly found himself in the presence of Wali's girl-friend. She was sitting on one of the bunk beds and looking uncharacteristically unkempt. Alexander caught the heady aroma of schnapps. There was a half-empty bottle and a glass on the table top.

"Oh, it's you, is it? I was wondering when *you'd* turn up." The greeting was decidedly less than cordial. Alexander looked puzzled. Yseult had never addressed him like that before.

"Wali has gone. You'll never see him again. Although you might read about him in the papers. Look for the Beast of Natzweiler."

Understandably, Alexander was baffled; and disturbed. "Beast? Natzweiler? Yseult, whatever do you mean?"

"Here. Look at these. You'll see what I mean." Yseult was holding out an old jam jar towards him. It was lidded and it contained a sheaf of papers. They appeared to be small notelets. They were crumpled and sullied with what looked like ash from the boiler furnace. And so it proved to be.

Alexander took the jar from her, prised off the lid and took out the notes. He leafed uncomprehendingly through them, complying with what he thought was expected of him. Then his eyes lit on the ciphers. They were addressed to 'JD' and signed with a circled 'E'. They were written in violet ink. Alexander knew straight away the hand that had written them. They were from William Wepper to himself. But he had never seen them. Alexander was astounded.

By way of explanation Yseult told him: "Wali couldn't give you these notes."

"Why not? I don't believe you. Wali would never betray me."

"He had no option. He was being blackmailed. You know what blackmail is?"

Alexander looked up at her and nodded. He leafed through the notes again, this time reading their one-line legends. They were not dated but on reading them he could match them to the incidents that had occurred to him last term. They were advance warnings of the Irish Gang's intentions, viz.:

"Cabaret tonight, make yourself scarce."

and:

"I can't pull that one again. Didn't you get my earlier?"

Alexander knew that this last one could only refer to the fire alarm incident. There was more in similar vein.

Yseult continued with what seemed like malevolent relish: "Look at them again. See how they're crumpled and dirtied with ash. That's how Lance left them. He scruffed them up and chucked them in the boiler furnace for Wali to burn later. But Wali retrieved them and hid them away. Lance was blackmailing him and he felt he needed the notes as countervailing evidence. Lance has been your betrayer all along, young man. He's responsible for all the bad things that have happened to you. Whoever wrote you these notes was your real protector."

"I don't believe you. Lance would never betray me."

"Now you're beginning to sound like a busted gramophone record." Such was Yseult's unsympathetic response.

Incredulous now, Alexander returned to the sheaf of papers in his hand. Among them was an empty brown foolscap envelope with some handwriting on its face. It had been sealed but was now torn open. As before, the handwriting on it was in violet ink and it was addressed to 'JD'.

> *"Here's your 'Agnus Dei' back. Ask no questions. The clasp is OK, the only damage was to the meeting link which had been stretched out. It has been reset and left hanging on a replacement link, so nothing of it has been lost. I've had it sterilised with methylated spirit and shaken with jewellers' rouge to purge it of any residue of hands that sought to profane it."*

Like all the others, the note was signed with the circled 'E'.

The last sentence jumped out at Alexander and struck him to the heart. It was almost *verbatim* the words Lance had used when he was posing as the retriever of the medallion, placing it round his neck in the peach house. Now there could be no doubt. The Bold Contemner had indeed been his aspiring protector all along. The interceptor of Wepper's missives and the frustrater of Wepper's benign intentions had been Lance. His very blood-brother had betrayed him… had been betraying him ever since he had known him… had delivered him into the hands of those who would do him harm.

Lance had brought the *Agnus Dei* envelope to the peach house furnace, thinking it the only safe place in which it could be destroyed. But at the time it had been daylight and he had been afraid to put a match to it himself in case the charred fragments should go up the chimney and attract unwanted attention. Instead he had taken a chance and left it for Wali to burn in the fullness of time; as he thought Wali would do with the others that came to him via the old bothy *poste restante*. Lance was careful never to take them away to where they might fall within the probing gaze of the pastoral Fathers.

Yseult watched as Alexander backed away and seemed to shrink into a ball. Consumed with anguish, he turned his gaze upwards and railed against the empty air: "Why? Why?"

Yseult saw him stuff all the notes back in the jar and run out of the door with it. As she listened to his footsteps dying away into the night, Yseult began to realise the full import of what she had just done. The thought came to her of her own child, like Alexander, a boy, taken from her and placed somewhere out in the world with strangers, vulnerable and beyond her reach. She leapt up and ran down the stairs to the door, calling after him: "Come back, Alexander... Come back."

But the boy was out of sight and out of earshot. She knew he would be on his way to the bell tower to confront Lance. In her anguish at the fate of Wali, Yseult had thwarted the benign intentions of those who had conspired to protect Alexander from the truth. In drink and vengeful spite, she had taken matters beyond the point of no return. The drama must now run its course and fetch up whither it would.

She sank back onto the bench and put her head in her hands. Too late came the realisation that she had set Wali's self-sacrifice at nought and that she was now just another betrayer of the boy from Manchuria. Now it was her turn to rail. She gave out a great sob of remorse: "Oh Wali, Wali... what have I done?"

* * *

The distraught Alexander now ran from the old bothy towards the bell tower and the object of his animus. It was dark by this time and he could pick out the lighted windows of the guest rooms and could guess in which room Lance would be quarantined. He arrived under the windows of what he thought was the most likely room. Without more ado he hurled the jar, still full of notes, upwards and against the closed window. The leaded light yielded to the impact, the jar going right through and landing on the carpet in a shower of glass splinters. Beyond the broken window Alexander could see Geddington frantically waving somebody back into the safety of the room; it was Lance. Geddington flung open an adjacent window and called down, "What the hell's going on down there?"

Alexander's anguished response came up: "I must see William Wepper." On an impulse he had swerved from his object of seconds ago; he had no further use for Lance.

But it was Lance's silhouette that appeared behind the shattered leaded light. He opened the window frame, the better to look down upon his younger blood-brother. Upon seeing his betrayer silhouetted against the light in the room, Alexander pointed an accusing forefinger at him and, face screwed up and knees bent in pathetic juvenile emotion, he uttered a long, loud, anguished cry that echoed back from the surrounding walls of Monsalvat – *Ju—das!*".

Lance gazed down, seemingly impassive. He volunteered that The Bold Contemner had left for the station some ten minutes ago in Father Laskiva's car. Alexander stood transfixed for a split second until the whistle of a train echoing through the western headland tunnel jerked him back into action. He turned about and flew like the wind across the grand terrace then onto the great parterre, over the bridge and downhill towards the station. Lance called after him despairingly: "Alexander... some day you'll understand... some day you'll understand."

But the boy never looked back.

Along the corridor, a breathless Parry-Jones, delayed by a particularly difficult session with the local ladies' glee club, had laboured up the stairs to say a belated goodbye to Wepper, only to find that Wepper had already departed for the station. On hearing the breaking of glass he naturally felt compelled to investigate and burst through the door of the room where Lance was calling down to Alexander. Parry-Jones saw the broken window and the glass strewn across the carpet. Clearly the damage had been done from without. He demanded to know: "Who the devil did that?" He already knew the answer, because he had already recognised Alexander's anguished voice screeching up from below; perhaps he was entertaining a small hope that Lance might name another boy rather than his lyrical protégé.

For Lance, the entrance of the music teacher was fortuitous. Of all the priests and teachers at Monsalvat, the opera-loving Parry-Jones was uniquely qualified to interpret the import of Lance's response, for Lance chose not to identify the boy from Manchuria by any form of appellation by which a Monsalvation would be known to his fellows. The name he intoned was: "Lohengrin."

Thus did Lance speak the cryptic name, an enunciation that, in the concomitant mythology, would bring about the banishment of one lover and the death of another. Mythology or no, Parry-Jones instinctively knew that the disturbed boy was not trifling with him. The revelation was ominous — and Parry-Jones knew he was too late to intercept he knew not what.

Just then a hurriedly dressed Tycho Gyles-Skeffington arrived on the scene from his dormitory, seriously concerned for his form mate.

Lance called out to him: "After him, Tycho, he's in a bit of a state."

Sensing the urgency, Tycho sped off into the darkness after Alexander without waiting for further exhortations. By now Alexander had crossed the bridge over the ha-ha and was speeding downhill across the pasture on the track which led to the public road and the station frontage. Tycho's breathless shouts arrested him not at all. Nevertheless, Tycho was a good runner and had a fresher start and had begun to gain on Alexander. As he climbed over the cattle gate from the pasture land he could see over the station building rooftops that the signals on the 'down' line were at green. As they neared the dimly-lit station entrance, he was only about twenty paces behind Alexander. The two boys sprinted past Father Laskiva's car, which was parked on the station frontage. Standing idly near it was De Leapey, his baggage-handling duties duly discharged. He had hauled Wepper's cabin trunk onto the 'down' platform so that the duty porter could take it across the line. Surprised at the sight of the flying youngsters, he walked quickly after them towards the 'down' platform.

'The 'local' which was to convey The Bold Contemner away from Monsalvat for the last time was already pulling noisily in to the 'up' platform with much hissing of safety valves. These trains did not linger. It was touch and go whether any intercourse with Wepper was going to be possible. As Tycho cleared the ticket office and emerged onto the 'down' platform he saw that the baggage barrier which kept passengers away from the level crossing had been left open. It had been opened to make way for the hand-cart bearing Wepper's trunk and the hurrying porter had not stopped to secure it behind him.

As Tycho went to sprint up the footbridge steps he saw Alexander run through the open barrier and down the sloping platform end towards the level crossing. Mindful of the signals Tycho yelled out: "Not that way, Alexander, not that way!"

Tycho's treble shout rived the chill night air with a shrill urgency. At the same time he became aware of a rushing noise rapidly rising to a crescendo from some distant point over his right shoulder. As he arrived on the decking of the overbridge he became enveloped in a hot blast of sulphurous smoke and was hit by the shock wave of a speeding express thundering beneath his feet. The pounding wheels sent tremors up the footbridge piers and Tycho could feel the bridge shaking through the soles of his plimsoles.

CHAPTER TWENTY-TWO

In the Penmaenbach Tunnel

Porter Sam Rowlands slung William Wepper's trunk into the guard's van with deft practice while the man himself jumped into one of the many empty compartments. The late stopping train to Crewe was sparsely patronised on a midweek night. As was normal at the time with local services, the train was made up of obsolescent non-corridor stock. Wepper settled into a seat on the landward side, 'facing engine'. He intended to transfer to the seat opposite when the train had cleared the station. Doing this would change the visual aspect and prolong the fleeting uphill panorama and thus enable him to better savour the leaving of Monsalvat for the last time. There was no-one to see him off on the platform except Father Laskiva, who had brought him down from the college in the Super Snipe. De Leapey, who had come down to give a hand with the heavy trunk, had remained on the forecourt with the car. Wepper had purposefully arranged to say all his goodbyes back at the college. As for Rhiannon, the two betrothed had made an anguished lovers' parting that afternoon, secure in the knowledge that they would meet again in Paris in a few days' time. Neither of them wished to say their goodbyes in the necessary presence of the priest.

Wepper felt prompted to lean forward in his seat and look

back along the opposite platform, so as to see for the last time the station entrance and booking office with its 'left luggage' depository where, as far as he was concerned, it had all begun some three years before. He was musing on this when he saw a figure come onto the opposite platform and run towards the footbridge. It was only a glimpse, but he instinctively knew it was a college boy and, judging by the diminutive size and bare legs, that it was a junior. By leaning further forward in his seat, he was able to see the boy run up the footbridge steps then stop halfway and lean over the handrail as if to call out to another. What, he wondered, were such young college boys doing running about the station when they should be up the hill in bed? If it were mischief then such a public place as the railway station would not be the best place to be up to it. Concerned now, Wepper jumped up and fumbled with the leather window strap, intending to lower the window to get a better view. Just as he got it open the carriage shook with the shock wave as an express thundered through the station just a few feet away on the opposite line. He would see no more of the opposite platform until the rake of carriages had hurtled by. Wepper glanced at his watch and considered the time of year. It was the shoulder of the holiday season. A relief 'Irish Mail', he mused.

His own train had started to pull out and by the time it was safe to put his head out of the window the developing scene on the 'down' platform, whatever it was, was left behind and lost in the darkness. The tang of sulphur from the passing of the express was still hanging in the air and stinging his nostrils and the gathering slipstream of the accelerating 'local' was ruffling his hair. Whatever was happening was for others to sort out, he reflected; he was out of it now. The sloping platform ends fell away and he waited for the long panorama that was Monsalvat to slide into view as the spread of opulent villas on the outskirts of Pencadno gave way to open pasture land. He remained at the open window, the better to savour the scene. Up at the college he could see that a few windows in the presbytery were lit and he could make out the dim lights along the colonnade where it marched with the grand terrace. The blue night station light at the bell tower glimmered briefly before becoming extinguished by the shifting perspective. Beyond the old gym, all was darkness saving for the occasional flash of reflected light from the odd pane in the range of glasshouses. He could imagine the peach house, cold and silent, no longer a place for secret trysts...

Immersed in nostalgia, he remained at the open window until the chill night air gave him reason to close it. Monsalvat was gone now; gone from his gaze and from his daily routine. He pulled up the window on its leather strap and took the seat opposite so as to get a final view of the receding familiar landscape before the train entered Penmaenbach tunnel. In truth all was in darkness now, save for the lights of the few habitations that dotted the landscape east of Pencadno. He could only imagine the easternmost extremity of the cross-country course, the point round which the runners were customarily tallied by a duty prefect with a clip-board. Soothed now by the warmth of the steam heat he leaned back against the cushions. Just as he did so the train entered the tunnel under the Penmaenbach headland. The beat of the wheels over the rail joints echoed back from the dank walls of the tunnel. Wepper began to experience uneasy waves of claustrophobia as he thought of the thousands of tons of granite above his head. He had been through the tunnel dozens of time but this was the first time he had experienced such unease. He reassured himself that the transit would soon be over — the tunnel was less than half a mile long (actually 0.41 of a mile as he recalled from some half-remembered illustrative mathematics project) and the train would soon be out of it. Or so he thought, for the brakes came on and the train groaned to a halt in the depth and darkness of the tunnel. A sepulchral silence ensued, relieved only by the gentle hissing of the steam through the heating pipes under the seats. The only light came from the single overhead bulb and this had dimmed considerably when the train stopped. Flat batteries again, thought Wepper resignedly. Upkeep and maintenance were in chronic deficit on the railways at this time, particularly on local services. He was minded to go back to the window to see if he could see the night sky at one of the tunnel ends but he knew the tunnel followed the curve of the headland and he didn't care to contemplate that both tunnel ends might be out of sight. Instead he closed his eyes and pressed himself back into the cushions and tried to shut out the thought of the vast bulk of the headland enveloping the stationary train.

His troubled imagination became invaded by recollections of the Dickens' short story 'The Signalman'; a tale of tunnels and premonitions of disaster. Try as he might, he could not banish it from his reverie. Then his reverie became interdicted.

"Old Monsalvation, I presume?"

Wepper almost jumped out of his skin. He had assumed he was alone in the darkened compartment. In the faint diffuse light he could make out the shape of an adult male sitting diagonally opposite him against the far side of the compartment. Wepper noticed that the stranger was wearing a linen suit such as one might wear in the tropics. This new-found travelling companion was clean-shaven and well-presented. Wepper took him for a successful businessman or official of some rank.

Quickly recovering his accustomed composure, he responded to the stranger's inquiry in what he hoped were measured terms. "I'm sorry, I didn't know you were there." And then: "How did you guess?"

"Oh, it's not difficult. Your age, the time of year, the time of night. And of course your trunk being brought onto the platform. It was worth a punt that you were a ripe peach being unleashed onto the adult world."

The stranger's use of the insider term put Wepper on his guard. Perhaps this person was one of the disensconced 'dog walkers' still hanging around the periphery of the college. But Wepper quickly dismissed that; the man was too well-presented to be one of those.

Wepper decided to chance his arm with an exploratory ploy. "There are peaches — and then there are peaches," he ventured.

"Not in my day," retorted the stranger, rather explosively. "Neither Canon Drage nor the Fathers would have countenanced it." Clearly an old 'peach' himself. Wepper knew that Canon Drage had been Pynxcytte's predecessor. But this revelation did not entirely satisfy Wepper's curiosity; he thought it anomalous that the stranger should be aware of the term's later pejorative connotation. Wepper remained on his guard accordingly. The stranger's diction was precise and perfect, with no hint of a regional accent. Wepper decided to try a punt himself.

"I take it you live locally?"

"No I don't," came the response. "This is the first time I've been back in the locality."

"But you seem to have fairly recent local knowledge," ventured Wepper boldly.

The stranger made no reply on the point. Instead he changed the subject. "You were a prefect of course." The statement was impliedly interrogatory. Wepper had to admit that he had not been, knowing that this would put his interrogator on inquiry. Wepper's obvious seniority combined with his tall and comanding presence would in the normal course of events have attracted the office.

"Myself and the Fathers didn't always see eye to eye on matters of faith." And then: "They felt reluctant to accord me the office," he added guardedly.

To his relief his purporting fellow Old-Monsalvation did not pursue the matter. Instead he pointedly changed the subject. "It's unusual to stop in the tunnel, don't you think?"

Wepper paused perceptibly before responding. "I don't care for tunnels; the sooner we're out of here the better." Then, as if to transfer his palpable unease: "It can't be any fun for the locomen. All that smoke and fumes."

"Quite. Before I was at the school there was a rock fall into this tunnel. Thankfully some platelayers were working nearby and managed to stop all traffic short of the obstruction." Wepper had heard tell of the incident, which he knew had taken place in 1913. This would seem to put the stranger's age at about the mid-fifties, but this did not seem to fit in with his stature and pitch of voice. He was slim and fit and Wepper judged him to be at least fifteen years younger. Wepper glanced upward through the windows towards the great I-beams supporting the roof of the tunnel, notwithstanding he could not actually see them in the darkness.

After giving Wepper some time to contemplate the information he had just imparted, the stranger continued. He seemed to be on a mission to disconcert his young travelling companion: "It would have been about here that another platelayer tried to flag down an express freight," he mused. "It was on the night of the great storm of 1899. The sea had breached the seawall and sapped the track bed just beyond the tunnel mouth. The driver saw the platelayer's lamp and tried to stop but the locomotive and several wagons ran onto the breach and were pitched into the sea. They found his body the next morning, washed up on Conway sands." He paused perceptibly before adding: "The fire-man's body is out there still — somewhere."

A contemplative silence followed the imparting of this weighty intelligence. The train must have just passed over the spot where the sea had encroached back in 1899. An involuntary shudder passed down Wepper's spine as he thought of the power of the waves, unseen in the blackness of the night, washing hungrily against the seawall and sapping the foot of the headland; the headland round which Wali must have walked in the small hours of that September day when Heini was supposed to have absconded. He thought of the body of the fireman still out there somewhere, gone forever from the warmth of hearth and home. He longed for the train to get underway again, out of the tunnel and towards the lights of Conway.

Unbidden, the stranger launched into a peroration on the course of life and the chain that we forge as we make our way. The peroration was apposite to the relationship between a mature Old Monsalvation and a young man such as Wepper who had just succeeded to that status. All this profound mention of chains and life prompted Wepper to lighten the load by making a Dickensian interjection.

"You mean... like Marley's ghost?"

But his talkative companion did not rise to the bait. Instead he continued his musings. "Life is a looking glass. It is the nature of perspective that when you see yourself in a mirror your image hides the chain that trails out behind you. But it is there nevertheless. On rare occasions there seems to occur a refraction in the image; the obliquity brings the chain into view and we can see it as it recedes into our past. It's then that we can see what impact our passage has had on those whom we have left behind. Those familiar faces... are they happy faces? Or sad? Especially the young ones; how have we left those young ones who, in one way or another, have come within our charge? Have we left their faces bright and responsive and ready to face the world? Or are those faces apprehensive perhaps. Perhaps they betray fear or have become wet with tears in the darkness of the night. What have we done – or left undone – that we might reproach ourselves for?

Wepper shifted uncomfortably. This sermonising was echoing Lance Lapita's acerbic observations in the bell tower just a few hours previously. He decided to shift the onus.

"I take it you're not content with your own passage through life then?"

"We are each consigned to our bourne of time and space..."

"Tennyson, egad!" exclaimed Wepper, seeking to lighten the load again.

His fellow Old Monsalvation continued, leaving this interjection unremarked upon: "...and we must seek to fill it to advantage. To have achieved a contented maturity is to have developed a selective memory. One's chain of life contains constraining padlocks and caskets locking us inexorably into our past actions and forever caching the guilt of our acts and omissions." (Marley's ghost indeed, thought Wepper.) "Nor does our youth furnish exculpation. Perhaps in the eyes of our indulgent seniors, yes — but never in our own eyes. Nothing is more certain than that we will end our lives writhing in the fetters we have wrought. They grate and clink in the silence of the night. The chain of each is fastened to them with a padlock. Padlocks have keys. We would do well to contemplate the analogy of the key. You're familiar with the poem, I take it?"

He then launched into a recitation in measured and sepulchral tones. Wepper did indeed recognise the words. They were the words of Vudsen Senior, although why this person should assume his knowledge of such an obscure and esoteric poem, a poem that for long enough had remained secreted in an old edition of the college magazine in some obscure corner of Monsalvat's library, he could not fathom:

"I

am a key,
I tumble to secure or to release
and for my thrall excruciate —or ease,
for I hold precious liberty in fee
and pelf and intrigue, each hath need of me
my throw confoundeth questing for all three.
As when greater magnitudes encompass me
I be witless to sequester or set free,
my task but to remit mute custody
of cumbers waxingfortunate —or fell
to station you nigh paradise —or hell
before what hand,
my master;
turneth
me."

Wepper recalled the way the layout of the words resembled the blade of a typical key.

Having delivered himself of his literary burden, the stranger fell silent. It was with some relief that Wepper heard the brake shoes come off and the train start to roll forward again. He did not care to revive the stilted conversation and he pointedly relinquished eye contact with his enigmatic travelling companion.

The accelerating beat of the wheels echoed back from myriad tons of granite. Wepper heard it and felt thankful for the company of the stranger nevertheless. After what seemed to him an eternity, the infinite blackness of the Penmaenbach tunnel gave way to the starlit darkness of the night. Wepper remained gazing fixedly out of the windows to his left on the side away from the stranger. He thought to keep him under discreet observation by way of his reflection in the window glass; but somehow Wepper could not make out any such reflection. He defied curiosity and declined to turn his head.

A few minutes later the train pulled into Conway station. The sparse lighting on the platforms of the station relieved the darkness in the compartment. Still looking towards his left, Wepper found himself contemplating the wagons of an empty ballast train stationary against the far platform. Emboldened now that he was free of the claustrophobic confines of the tunnel, Wepper at last turned his head to look once more at his mysterious fellow-Old Monsalvation. He was hoping that the augmented lighting might reveal some sort of scrutable countenance.

An involuntary sigh escaped his lips when he became transfixed by an icy paroxysm of fear. He had found that he was quite alone in the compartment.

CHAPTER TWENTY-THREE

The Vigil

Down on the timber battens of the level crossing at the west end of Pencadno station the contest between boy and express train had been unequal. The right arm, outstretched in a futile attempt to fend off the pounding locomotive, was torn away, the right side of the body grossly abraded and the skeletal frame crushed within its tegument. The abdominal cavity was breached below the right rib cage and coelomic fluid escaped, although the cavity remained mercifully uneviscerated. The scant clothing was bloodily torn away and strewn down the track. The noble head, that much caressed and sacred treasured shell, that repository of an outreaching love, both familial and wider, of incisive empathy and a confounding intellect which had proved sufficient to shake the faith of his mentors, became dashed to pieces against the unrelenting buffer bar. The ejected brain, the very citadel of his being, landed on the line-side in two pieces. The crowning tumble of mischievous flaxen whirls which had captivated so many became cast into the cess as the nest of a sparrow displaced by a windstorm. This latter-day reincarnation of Polydeukion was struck suddenly, totally, absolutely, irretrievably and inexorably from the light of admiring eyes. In that instant, the lyric voice that had charmed congregations, that had stayed the bullies in their very tracks, became stilled and denied to posterity. Alexander Fragner Vudsen was suddenly, totally, absolutely, irretrievably and inexorably — dead. Absent from his person was his *Agnus Dei*. That fateful device was presently languishing some hundred yards away in one of Father Laskiva's jacket pockets.

"No, Alexander, no!"

The 'local' pulled out of the 'up' platform, its crew and passengers, including The Bold Contemner, oblivious of the drama unfolding at the west end of the station. As its red tail light diminished in the distance and the sparse straggle of alighted passengers made their way to the footbridge and the exit to the public road, the treble tones of a youngster's voice screeched out again and again into the smoky night air. The voice carried a strident note of undeniable desperation. This was not youngsters messing about. Clearly something was very wrong. Father Laskiva sprinted past the others and ran for the footbridge. When they caught up with him he was kneeling alongside Tycho. He had his hand under the distraught boy's chin so as to bring his face upward and keep his eyes away from the bloody wreckage strewn along the cess. The grisly debris was dimly visible in the faint light from the windows of the adjacent signal box. The alighting passengers grouped about priest and boy and two of them started to gently prise the quivering boy's fingers, one by one, off the lattice-work of the guard rail. This was to take some time.

Duty porter Sam Rowlands shone his lamp into the wake of the express and along the cess on the 'down' side of the level crossing. He swiftly changed to flicking the beam onto the windows of the signal box to alert the signalman, calling out: "Stop all traffic."

But the signalman already knew the worst. Alerted by the shrieks from the footbridge he could see the object of the commotion strewn below his very windows. He called back to Rowlands, "All traffic stopped — and I've telegraphed ahead to halt the mail at Bangor. You better call the police", and then after an ominous pause, "Better call Dewi Evans while you're at it. Don't bother with the ambulance." Dewi Evans was the local undertaker.

Tycho was escorted from the footbridge and conducted into the booking office. Here Father Laskiva and others, themselves shocked to the core, tried their best to comfort hirn. The boy kept repeating in a tremulous voice, "I told him not to go that way." He seemed to cling on to the phrase as he had clung on to the lattice-work of the footbridge, treating it as some sort of physic that would expunge from his mind the awful event he had just witnessed. A bowl of warm water was produced together with a bottle of antiseptic and some cotton wool and some kind person gently set about wiping clean the boy's bloodied and sooty hands where the metal of the lattice-work had cut into them.

Within minutes the police and the coroner's officer duly attended and Doctor Tulloch was called to certify death at the scene. There was no call for an ambulance; as the signalman had implied, it was clearly a job for Dewi Evans.

The man himself arrived with a hearse and some of his short-notice bearers in an accompanying car. They opened the back of the hearse and, in a trade of euphemisms, withdrew a long rectangular white-painted metal chest euphemistically referred to as a 'utility chest' from that discreet compartment that lies beneath the glazed funerary bier. The railway, the foreshore and the local quarry workings provided sporadic employment for the firm's utility cases. In the present case the coroner's officer of police had sent ahead that the juvenile size would be appropriate for the job at hand.

Tilley lamps were broken out and lit and a first aid party was assembled from the railway staff manning the quarry sidings.

These men and the undertaker and his bearers went forward down the line carrying tools, a bag of sawdust and the white metal chest.

When the doctor arrived at the station he was urgently referred to Tycho in the booking office, who was exhibiting all the signs of shock. As the doctor was preparing a hypodermic syringe with which to give Tycho a calming injection, he was told that the coroner's officer requested his presence down on the line. "Tell the coroner's officer my first duty is to the living," he responded petulantly, "what is it with the dead that can't wait a few minutes?"

The message bearer gave an answer. "There are certain injuries on this body which are not consistent with the accident." He was referring to the striations on the buttocks. The delinquencies of Monsalvat were coming to light.

While all this was going on Father Laskiva told an ashen-faced De Leapey to telephone Canon Pynxcytte with the fateful news. Shortly afterwards the Rector of Monsalvat and Father Fillery came down in the Delage. They and the civil functionaries held urgent council in the booking office. It was decided that Alexander's body should rest overnight in the school chapel rather than having it taken to the Bangor morgue. The hurried proposition was that the whole school would keep vigil throughout the hours of darkness. Releasing the body thus, might be a procedural irregularity, but it was mutually agreed that it would make no material difference in terms of time and, as Dewi Evans lugubriously observed, "It is after all a consecrated building and more priests than you can shake a stick at." He made arrangements to re-take charge of the body at daybreak. The utility chest was not a coffin but it was secure and would serve the occasion as a casket if suitably draped with a funeral pall. The next task was to get the hysterical Tycho back up the hill and into the sanatorium. Father Laskiva gathered him up in his arms and, assisted by willing hands, deposited him in the back seat of the Super Snipe. Within the half hour the boy was tucked up in a hospital bed and Geddington was put on watch over him. It was hoped that the sedation administered by Doctor Tulloch down at the station would take effect and that he would at least have a peaceful night despite the horror and mental trauma he had been subjected to. His fingers had been bandaged; the morrow would have to take care of itself.

Word was sent up to the school to make ready for the arrival of the corpse. The two caretakers, Bringsam and Bowker, were tasked to prepare the chapel by the setting out of coffin bearers, drapes and the four great free-standing candle holders. Handel Trefor, the head gardener, was able to make up vases of white lilies from the stock of ready blooms in the peach house. Instructions were sent round that all the boys were to be assembled in warm clothing on the great parterre. Bringsam and Bowker were set to issuing processional candles to all present. Despite the lateness of the hour the Rector of Monsalvat decreed that at an appropriate time a funerary peal should be sounded from the bell tower.

Urgent notice was telephoned to the Abbot of Basingwerk, who duly despatched a task force of Brothers in two charabancs. Their duties would be to escort the deceased into the chapel and thereafter to deploy to policing Monsalvat while its nucleus of priests and lay staff were otherwise engaged on matters contingent with the fatality.

It was now near midnight on a balmy June night. The body parts were recovered from the cess and assembled on a canvas sheet, which was gently lowered into the utility chest. Some further evidences had been retrieved from the locomotive at Bangor where the express had been halted. These were gathered by one of Dewi Evans' professional colleagues, consigned to a waterproof bag and sent along the coast road to Pencadno in a police car. The bag was also placed in the chest, the lid of which was then secured against a rubber seal by means of screw latches. Dewi Evans' four bearers then portered it up onto the 'down' platform where the coroner's officer placed a seal round it and handed it over into the temporary custody of Canon Pynxcytte, Rector of Monsalvat.

With the line now clear, traffic could begin to flow again and the signalman opened the section to cautionary passage. Soon the backed-up traffic began to pass through the station. On the passenger trains word had been passed that the delay was due to 'an incident on the line at Pencadno'. As the first trains passed through, the curious passengers looked out at the policemen and the unusual activity on the 'down' platform and guessed that the incident must have involved a fatality.

Under Dewi Evans's direction a melancholy impromptu procession formed up on the station forecourt and began to wind its way through the gate, onto the pasture land and up the hill to the bridge over the ha-ha. The chest was carried at the low port by Dewi Evans's bearers and a quartet of Tilley lamps, carried by the railwaymen, illuminated its progress. The Rector of Monsalvat himself walked ahead. He had ordered that the great processional cross should meet the chest at the bridge and precede it along the aditus maritimus and through the great west door of the chapel, which would stand wide open in readiness. The duty of bearing the cross, normally the prerogative of a junior, was assigned to one of the prefects so as to spare the sensitivities of the dead boy's distraught peers. The Rector had also ordered that the chapel *aspersorium* and *aspergillum* be taken to the bridge so that the chest could be anointed there with holy water. Father Fillery was left to take De Leapey back to the college in the Delage.

As the procession began its slow passage up the hill towards the bridge, Godred, at the bell tower, unlocked the hand wheel and stood by to let in the master clutch that drove the funerary carillon. By the time the procession had reached the bridge the whole school had been assembled in reverse order of seniority and deployed either side of the *aditus maritimus*. Each boy held before him a candle set in an upturned transparent conical shield that protected the flame from the wind. As was thought meet and proper, it was Alexander's form fellows who were arrayed to greet his corpse first and to fall in behind it on the way into the chapel. Their now-depleted roll-call is recorded for posterity as follows:

Michael Roger Brennan
Philip William Broke
Nigel Scott Catonsworth
Neil Francis Frankland
Raimo Haroldsen
Jean-Louis Jouvet
Laurence Marco Loxley
Maurice McGuckin
Harry Norton
Michael Polders-Leigh
Vicente Jaime Rivadavia
Barden Miles Sender
Geoffrey Charles Williamson

These were the boys who later would have to walk past Alexander's empty bed space to get to their own; who would see his precious things gathered up and taken away, to be put into store against the possibility of some future claim.

Absent from the array was Tycho Cotolay Gyles-Skeffington, by this time in the sanatorium, reputedly under sedation. Further along the *aditus maritimus* and up the scale of seniority, also conspicuous by his absence was Foul Mouthed Frank

Leport. Following the Great Purgation he had been withdrawn by his guardian at his own request. Rumour had it however that he had moved in with a local lady of ill-repute. Alexander had vanquished the Irish Gang; nevertheless Hogan, Rogan, Flynn, Fitzgerald, Regan and Begen were present alongside the *aditus maritimus*. Not necessarily in that order and no longer representative of any gang. They were soon to be joined by the badly-rattled De Leapey. Also present was Lance Lapita; with the death of Alexander the *raison d'etre* of his relegation to the bell tower no longer obtained and Geddington, who had the night station duty, had his hands full with Tycho. Lance had been left free to roam whither he would.

The quartet of gently swinging Tilley lamps coming up the hill heralded the approach of the corpse. The gaunt faces of the boys lining the *aditus maritimus* were eerily illuminated by the dim light of their lanterns. On the aditus itself, sixteen of the brothers of Basingwerk stood by in column of two, ready to precede the chest into the chapel with choral honours. The procession arrested briefly on the bridge. Scaffold boards had been placed over the bars of the cattle bridge, the better to ease its progress. It was at this point that the corpse came under the escort of the reception party. The chest was draped with a funerary pall and dashed with holy water from the *aspersorium*. The processional cross was stationed ahead of it and the censer was swung towards it. Under the direction of Dewi Evans, the bearers now raised the draped chest onto their shoulders. At a signal, the column of monks on the *aditus maritimus* turned about and processed towards the chapel, at the same time commencing a solemn antiphonal chant. There followed the Rector, the censer, the processional cross and the chest itself. Thus, was the broken body of Alexander Fragner Vudsen brought back within the walls of Monsalvat.

At a pre-arranged signal Godred in the bell tower let in

the clutch to start the carillon. Ponderously the four great bells began ringing out their tribute to the dead boy. Their message boomed out into the night in great dolorous metallic sobs that echoed back from the mountain and reverberated between the two headlands. Thus, were the townsfolk alerted to the tragedy that had taken place on the railway line below their town.

There were some three hundred and fifty boys at Monsalvat and even the most detached of them could not but have known Alexander. They had seen him serving Mass, had seen him carrying the processional cross and swinging the censer, had seen him heading the choral processions, had seen him expertly conning the racing shells on the Conway River. And they had seen the snow-white dove land on his shoulder at the Christmas service, had heard his sublime soprano voice reaching down to them from the heights of the dome. All could not but know that this was the gentle boy who had brought down the Great Purgation upon their late iniquities. Now he had been struck from them forever and they found themselves cast into the presence of death.

The broken body of the gentle and valiant boy from Manchuria was passing before them now; passing between the two files of boys as they waited to fall in behind it. The guttering flames of their lanterns shone upwards into their faces, casting them as grotesques and heightening their looks of anguish and distress. The chanting of the monks, the tolling of the carillon, the pungent incense on the chill night air, the lateness of the hour; all conspired to generate an atmosphere of pulsating dolour that weighed down each heart with an intolerable burden of grief and emotion. That burden was reflected in all their faces.

As was a frisson of horror. The boys of Monsalvat knew that death on the racing metals that snaked along Pencadno's foreshore would not have been kind to the fragile body of one of their number. Each was conscious of the bloody wreckage that must lie hidden in the chest that was passing before their eyes. All the panoply of high church now attending upon that box could not banish the horror from their thoughts. That the warm, bright, laughing, gambolling creature that they lately had lived, eaten, slept, bathed, joked, suffered, played and studied with, was now reduced to a grisly ruin that needst be hid from their gaze. Just a few had seen sudden death at first hand in the late war; most had been spared the experience. All imagined and shuddered.

The boys fell in, in column of two, and followed the chest across the great parterre and up onto the grand terrace. Here it was paused while the bearers regrouped to carry it up the chapel steps and through the great west door of the chapel. Beyond the confines of the college estate, the funerary peal had alerted the townsfolk to the drama unfolding at Monsalvat. Those staff members who lived in the little town could not but hear it and considered themselves summoned back to the stricken House in case their services might be needed.

On entering the chapel, the column of monks divided into two and filed into the side aisles still singing their antiphonal chant. Preceded by the Rector and the great processional cross, the chest was carried up the centre aisle and the procession stopped before the altar rail. Here the chest was placed upon the trestles and the four great candlesticks at each corner were lit. The tribute of white lilies, hurriedly made up by Handel Trefor from the pots in the peach house, was placed upon the chest. Padded kneelers were arrayed in a rectangle around it. As all this was being done the column of boys, each still bearing his processional lantern, waited in the aisle for a signal to file into their customary pews.

The monks ceased their antiphonal chant; the carillon fell silent. The scarcely suppressed sobs of some of the congregation filled the void. Canon Peter Pynxcytte, Rector of Monsalvat, left his place at the head of the procession and walked authoritatively over to the pulpit steps. A moment later he appeared at the lectern. With a wave of his hand he directed the boys to file into their pews. He waited until all were seated and their lanterns ensconced in the brackets on the backs of the pews. Then he commenced to address the array with his customary command.

"And so we have brought the broken body of Alexander Fragner Vudsen back among us." His intended panegyric got no further. He suddenly saw the eyes of his congregation deflected upwards over his head. The distraction was a snow-white dove swooping down from the dome. The dove glided silently down and along the nave. All heads turned to follow its flight. The lowest point of its trajectory coincided with Alexander's casket. From there it made a shallow ascent towards the great west door, continuing on an unerringly straight course to disappear into the night sky. The desultory beat of its wings caused the flames of the four great funerary candles to gutter. A great gasp of awed amazement echoed round the chapel.

All eyes now returned to the tall commanding figure in the pulpit. It was the obeisant flight of the snow-white dove that was to finally end the iniquitous charade for so long played out by Canon Peter Pynxcytte, Rector of The Roman Catholic College of St Michael Monsalvat. All could see that the blood had drained from his face and that he stood struck silent in the pulpit. The congregation began to be concerned for his wellbeing.

At last they saw him move. Slowly and deliberately he took off his biretta and put it down beside the lectern. He looked over to where Father Laskiva was standing, somewhat apart from the other Fathers. He beckoned him to come over. As Father Laskiva stood below the pulpit looking up at him, the Rector leaned over and whispered something clearly of import. Then he straightened up and began to address the congregation. It was clear he was in a state of great emotion and agitation.

"Boys, look upon me. As you are now, so once was I. As I am now, so you must never become. The road to perdition is taken in small steps. The presence of my unworthy person in the same holy place as the mortal remains of Alexander Fragner Vudsen is an abomination in the sight of the Lord. I must remove myself from this place forthwith and forever. I cannot bid you goodbye, for that would imply that I have in me some good to bid you. I discern none. The only good resides in my departure. I hereby relinquish the office of Rector and Headmaster of the Roman Catholic College of St Michael Monsalvat and all the privileges and responsibilities attaching thereto. Father Laskiva will take provisional control in all respects with effect from immediately. The good Brothers of Basingwerk will assist him in that for the time being. That is all."

With that he stepped down from the pulpit. It was the turn of the pastoral Fathers to be ashen-faced now — apart from Laskiva, that is. Pynxcytte's discarded biretta fell to the flags from the lectern. One of them picked it up and held it out towards him. It was upside down, whether by design or happenstance we are not to know. Pynxcytte slowly and deliberately removed his rosary, dropped it into the proffered hat as if it were largesse and moved on. As he did so, he hissed *sotto voce*, "Sauve qui peut" towards his six priests. His hitherto commanding presence had deserted him and the congregation saw him assume the stoop of a broken man. He had become assailed by too many uncanny coincidences. Their erstwhile chief confessor and arbiter of all their fortunes made his way to the south transept door. The six anxious priests shuffled after him. Father Laskiva watched from the foot of the pulpit as all seven passed through the south transept door into the ambulatory and out of the chapel for ever.

Pynxcytte's six lieutenants had known all along how fragile was their tenure; that some day would be a day of reckoning. For the greater part of a decade Monsalvat had been their bolt-hole; their deliverance from the consequences of the foibles, peccadilloes and indiscretions that had lost them their previous posts. For the greater part of a decade Peter Pynxcytte had been building up his empire. He had built up that empire in response not to logic but to a dark inner compulsion. Within the walls of Monsalvat he had progressively displaced worthy incumbents on a variety of pretexts so that he could gather about him a ragbag of rejects living on borrowed time. Furthermore, among the cohort of pupils he had instigated and nurtured a reign of terror and moulded it into a raiser of revenue. Under that reign of terror, pupil numbers decreased and Monsalvat necessarily began to subsist on immoral earnings. Beyond the cloistered confines of Monsalvat the slithering tentacles of Pynxcytte's empire extended beyond the peddling of dubious images into the even more shadowy world of blackmail and coercion. Not a few of his friends in high places lay in fear of his friends in low places.

It was an empire that contained the seeds of it own destruction; and destruction was now upon it. The emperor himself now felt the fires of hell licking at his heels. As for his viceroys, the death of one of their young charges had once more cast them as barks on a stormy sea fleeing before the winds of public opprobrium. All had laid plans towards their future bolt-holes. The inevitable hour was upon them and now they must fly.

Father Laskiva gazed after them for several seconds. Then he strode towards the pulpit. His footsteps rapped determinedly on the marble flags. Across the lectern his gaze swept over the array. He was acutely conscious of so many young faces turning towards him for guidance and words of comfort in the wake of sudden and violent death. He could see fatigue and grief in their candle-lit faces. For the moment at least he appeared to the boys as composed and confident. Then he began to speak. His opening words were a virtual repeat of those used by Pynxcytte.

"And so we have brought the broken body of Alexander Fragner Vudsen back among us. He has no mother, no father, no sisters or brothers to mourn his passing. Tragic happenstance on the other side of the world cast us as his only family. His only home, for better or worse, was within these walls; with us." Then he added in a lower tone: "Would that it had been for the better."

From the boys in the pews not a few audible sobs answered that opening. The priest continued: "We shall keep vigil until dawn. Water is being made available. Otherwise, we shall fast until dawn when we will break our fast as normal. I have sent instructions for a hearty breakfast to be made ready." Then his voice dropped to a more conversational tone: "I am sure Alexander would wish that for you." As he said that, the ghost of a smile fleeted across his gaunt expression. Then, with renewed vigour: "There will be no lessons tomorrow. All staff members whose duties do not require them to be elsewhere are invited to join the boys in this vigil. Any boy who wants to go to his bed may do so. If you wish to go to your bed please leave now; I can assure you no shame shall attach to you." Then his voice dropped to his previous tone: "Alexander would understand."

Not a boy stirred from his pew.

"Then we are all committed." With that, he held out his right arm towards the pews as if to draw in the congregation and said: "Paramount among the things I must say to you is this: within these very walls we saw Alexander return all the boys of Monsalvat to a state of grace. Those of you who purposefully set out to do harm to him — and you know who you are — can rest secure in the knowledge that you had his unconditional forgiveness. As his confessor I can vouch for that. Alexander was content — indeed was adamant — that excoriating remorse was not to be your lot. You are absolved. Peace of mind is yours. Sufficient for him that you carry forward, from this time and place, that precious forgiveness unabated and undiminished.

Make it so and you will surely and commendably continue the work that Alexander started in this place. Do that and you will not be found wanting. "Then he paused before continuing, arms akimbo: "Boys... Alexander has not left you. From this night on... wherever the winds of fate may take you... your bodies, your minds, your souls... Alexander will be with you. He will be with you to the end of your days. He will be your guide and your inspiration in the opportunities and adversities of life. Whatever your wont, he cannot be denied."

He had spoken commandingly. Now he swallowed hard and his voice took on a less composed timbre: "The scales have only lately fallen from mine eyes. Too late I fear to save this gentle boy who lies among us now in fatal distress. If there is an unabsolved penitent here tonight it can only be myself. For, to my eternal shame, I lately stood by and watched as he was being cruelly used. I did not intervene because I had allowed myself to be duped into believing that what was happening was the lesser of two evils. After becoming one of many to secure his trust I was the last of many to betray him — and, being the last, there was not time for me to ask his forgiveness. Ah! Unlike all of you who had his forgiveness in life, that omission will follow me to my grave. All I can do now is beg forgiveness over his mortal remains and hope that he will heed my implorations in heaven."

The priest was visibly struggling to continue now. His strangulated tones gave ample witness to the anguish and emotion under which he laboured. He now waxed indignant.

"Alexander endured the slights and injuries that were heaped upon him without making complaint and without seeking redress via authority. Why? Because no less a person than our late Rector..." (Here he shot an accusatory glance over his shoulder in the direction of the departed Pynxcytte and his cronies) "... gave him to believe he had to live up to a compact with his father to that effect. That he had to be tested according to the mores and tenets of Monsalvat, its pastoral Fathers and its community of boys. It was a lie. There was no compact. The tenets had been usurped. This vulnerable little boy was not to know that Monsalvat had become a very different place to what it had been in his father's day. His father thought he was delivering his son to *secura nidificat* — the safe nest." The priest's voice rose now to a vituperative crescendo. "Little did he know he was delivering him to... a nest of vipers."

That acerbic phrase echoed round the chapel. The priest paused now while he struggled to bring his voice back under control somewhat. After a while he was able to continue in a more composed and deliberating manner: "The purported compact was a manipulative fabrication. He was duped by those in whom he thought he could trust. Their intention was to exploit him for their own evil ends." He then swept his arm over the congregation and continued: "As many of you were similarly exploited. I can assure you, boys, all that is now at an end. In life we saw Alexander begin the Great Purgation of Monsalvat. In death he has completed it. This house is indeed purged — albeit at a terrible cost. He has driven out the vipers. He has returned Monsalvat to that benign condition that obtained in his father's day. You are the inheritors of that deliverance." Then his voice rose to a crescendo: "Alexander truly is the Redeemer of this House."

The climactic utterance echoed back down from the dome. The priest continued in quieter vein: "Yes, you boys are the legatees of that deliverance. Happenstance has cast me into the role of custodian of that legacy. Henceforth, unceasing vigilance will be my lot. Rest assured, boys, henceforth I shall be argus-eyed in my duties. And I shall set up an argus-eyed regime of propriety that will be its own audit. My awareness of my own fleshly failings makes me uniquely fitted for this task. Make of that what you will."

He paused to let his audience contemplate that fateful admission. Such a public confession could only fix him in his declared course.

"No more during my tenure of office, or my posterity, shall fear and violence stalk the corridors of Monsalvat. No more will these cloistered surrounds harbour secret societies in defiance of our Faith. The *trophimoi* and the Irish Gang and their ramifications have been exposed and extinguished." This was the first time the boys had heard any voice in authority utter those two esoteric appellations. The priest continued his verbal crusade: "No more will the lustful predator make free with the bodies and images of our young fledglings. Your bodies are the temples of your soul, and those temples must be inviolate. Rest assured, as long as I live and breathe, and as long as my posterity holds sway, Monsalvat will be fit to receive your own sons in the fullness of time."

Having done with his own shortcomings, Father Laskiva thought fit to address another outstanding matter. "And for good measure, no more shall we see the likes of our lately departed Bold Contemner making free with the benefits of a Catholic education. With the dark secrets of this House now laid bare there can be no more cuckoos in the nest."

The analogy seemed complete; but Father Philip Joseph Laskiva was not yet done with William Wesley Wepper, for three long and troubled years the Bold Contemner of Monsalvat.

"Logic tells me that The Bold Contemner must have held the key to those dark secrets ever since he accrued his opprobrious title. That same key could have been the key to a much earlier redemption. Had he acted virtuously and sacrificially, instead of in his own self-interest, all those terms ago, then Monsalvat would have been all the earlier purged — and we would have been able to walk and talk with Alexander today. The Bold Contemner was the antithesis... the stayer... of redemption. With his vested interest in the evil status quo, he was the ultimate betrayer. Of Monsalvat. Of you boys. Of the dead boy now before the altar."

The terrible indictment was complete. That Wepper had been much younger when the iniquitous arrangement had been set up — or that it had been set up not by him but by his guardian — the priest declined to adduce. He felt such mitigating considerations irrelevant to the lesson implicit in the indictment.

The priest had one last telling item to impart: "Alexander was much challenged in this place but still we can thank God that he died in his innocence — ah yes, innocence, *mes enfants;* that all-redeeming, but oh-so-fragile, domain of the young. You who are growing up should cherish it; cherish it, I say, in others if not in yourselves. Do not be too impatient to relinquish it."

* * *

If Father Laskiva had anything more to say, it was not to be. The proceedings were curtailed by a commotion at the north transept door. Once again, a hysterical treble voice could be heard and the voice of an adult remonstrating urgently. The transept door banged open and a junior ran in, his bare feet pattering on the marble flags. He was wearing only pyjama bottoms and there were bandages on his fingers. It was Tycho Gyles-Skeffington and his face bore a look that should never be seen on the face of a young child. He was closely pursued by Geddington, who fetched up abashed in the transept before the whole congregation.

"There's no holding him, Father. He says he's got to be with Alexander."

Doctor Tulloch's sedating injection had clearly been inadequate to stem the boy's anguish. Father Laskiva came down from the pulpit and gently led him to the kneeler at the foot of the bier. After settling him down on his knees he called for blankets to shield the half-naked boy from the chill night air but there were none to be had in the immediate vicinity.

Just then a man stepped forward from out of the shadows of the north side-aisle. It was a big rough fellow, a workman from the quarry sidings who had come up from the station carrying one of the Tilley lamps. He came across to where Tycho was kneeling. The man took off his donkey jacket and draped it around the boy, taking care that the hem of the garment covered the boy's bare feet. The diminutive kneeling figure quite disappeared into the all-enveloping garment. The onlookers could now only see the little hands clasped in prayer. Having performed this service, without a word, the man returned to the side-aisle, leaving the boy to keep his lonely vigil. But he was not to be lonely for long. As stated, padded kneelers had been placed all round the bier and the boys of Monsalvat were being called forward in rota to occupy them. Tycho was soon joined by the rest of his form fellows and it was intended that after half an hour had elapsed these should give way to those senior to them so that by the end of the vigil every boy would have had the opportunity to make close obeisance at Alexander's bier.

Father Laskiva had one more momentous gesture to make. He opened the gates of the altar rail and stepped up into the sanctuary. The congregation saw him walk up to the high altar. Here he opened the doors of the tabernacle and withdrew a vessel with both hands. When he turned with it to face the congregation, it could be seen that the vessel was the Great Grail of Monsalvat-Pencadno. The priest had arranged to have it brought out from its august repository in the sacristy. Walking down from the high altar, he stopped at the altar rail and ceremoniously raised the Grail. With it he then made the Sign of the Cross. All promptly knelt and returned the Sign. Then he walked forward and placed the Grail on Alexander's casket. Finally, reaching into his jacket pocket he withdrew something that glistened on its chain in the candlelight. Gently he lowered it into the Grail. Thus was Alexander reunited — too late — with his treasured *Agnus Dei*. The priest then knelt at the foot of the bier, alongside the praying Tycho. It was sufficient; the vigil could commence.

* * *

But again it was not to be. Less than an hour into the vigil the great 'E' bell, the greatest of the bells in the carillon, rang out into the night. It gave a clear initial stroke but this was followed by a disordered quivering of the clapper that tailed off into silence. Clearly something was wrong at the bell tower.

It was Tycho who first realised what was happening. In an instant he had sprung up from his nest in the donkey jacket and was running towards the north transept door by which he had entered. As he ran, his voice rived the silence of the vigil: "No, Lance, no... Alexander wouldn't have wanted it". He grasped the great ring-bolt of the door and flung it open. It was his quickest route back to the bell tower. As he sped on his way he could be heard calling out tremulously: "Alexander wouldn't have wanted it... Alexander wouldn't have wanted it."

CHAPTER TWENTY-FOUR

The Darkest Hour?

In Lance's scheme of things, the Immanent Will which had revealed itself to him at Liverpool landing, stage was now fulfilled. Alexander's life had been closed off before boyhood's end. The convergence of events proved that Earth had been only a temporary and an unfit repository for such a divine creature. Decay was Earth's revenge upon transitory perfection. Lance had seen his beloved younger brother, Mark, succumb to premature decay. But such decay could not have Alexander now. He had died in his perfection. Nor would decay have Lance. The two of them had been rendered immune. He could now join Alexander in death. And he could do so with clean hands! Could it not be said that he had not so much as lifted a finger to facilitate the boy's demise (apart, that is, from lifting a pen to plagiarise a poem)? That burden now fell upon those who had thought fit to intervene in the inevitable cascade of events. Especially the unfortunate Wepper. Was it not he who had presumed to swerve the stars in their very courses? And had not the stars held steady?

And had not the boy been delivered to him nestless and free from familial burdens? And had it not been the kiss of a serpent that had delivered him, as if in mockery of Lance's own inept machinations? Surely the Immanent Will had shown Its hand and could not be denied. The Spinner of the Years had cut the timely thread. Inexorably, the Twain had Converged.

As to where God stood in Lance's scheme of things — or Lance in God's — he drew comfort in the presumption that the Almighty must surely look with forbearance upon the deranged mortal mind, much as the law here on Earth ameliorates its sanctions towards the afflicted offender. And again, Lance had not so much as lifted a finger to facilitate the boy's demise. Were any guilt to be adduced, if not from acts against others then from the sin of *felo de se,* Lance would take his chances in a plea of insanity before the Ultimate Bar.

It remained for him to complete the fateful tableau. Thus did he snatch up a Sabatier knife from the kitchen and repair with it to the bell tower. His facility with knots would do the rest.

Lance had not been under restraint of lock and key at the bell tower; there were no feasible facilities for such a drastic process. Instead he had been placed under the supervision of the duty male nurse. On the evening of the fatality, that had been Geddington, but Geddington had run after Tycho and thereafter had remained in the chapel with him. In any case his responsibilities regarding Lance had surely now ended with the death of Alexander. Alexander was clearly beyond further harm. Consequently, Lance had been left free to roam, which indeed he had done. He had joined the rest of his form fellows on the grand parterre, had taken up a processional taper and had followed Alexander's casket into the chapel. If Tycho's intuition was right Lance had returned from thence alone to the bell tower for the last time. Tycho had remembered Alexander confiding in him that Lance had shown him how to fashion a hangman's noose.

* * *

"After him, Geddington!"

It was Father Laskiva calling out. He had leapt to his feet but Geddington was already sprinting out through the north transept door after the fleeing boy. Both realised now what Tycho would find at the end of his flight and both wanted to spare him further trauma. Father Laskiva gathered his wits; he was in charge now and must act resolutely.

"Boys, stay where you are. Brother James... take over here please. Staff members... follow me."

With that he ran over to the north transept door and sprinted after Geddington. Less adroitly, Handel Trefor, Bringsam, Bowker and Godred left their places in the pews and ran after the priest. The depleted congregation could hear their shouts echoing back through the still-open transept door.

Geddington caught up with Tycho just as the boy was trying to turn the great handle of the door to the bell tower itself. Geddington flung the half-naked boy aside and bellowed a warning to him: "Stay there... don't come in". Tycho cowered down in the shadows alongside the door and watched the goings-on. Geddington entered into the stairwell of the campanile.

In judicial process a hangman's noose is a sacrificial device; it goes to the grave with the felon, severed by a blade from the length of rope from which it has been fashioned. Indeed, the remaining length of the rope itself is discarded, it being considered too stressed for further use. Attempted suicide is a different matter. Clearly some effort must be made by would-be rescuers to relieve the pressure on the neck. The primary function of the noose in the judicial process is to sever the spinal cord, using that weight of the body which lies below the head, rather than to act as a choking ligature.

Lance had done his homework meticulously. He had tripped the 'E' bell rope from its snatch block, thus taking the tension off it. Thus, he could cut it without it flying from his grasp. It was this releasing, causing the hammer to fall free against the bell, that had sent the initial stroke booming out into the night. Then he had carried the fall end just two flights up the stair well. Here he had stopped and had fashioned the noose which was to end his life. It remained for him to step out into the void, his last conscious action in this world. It was the jarring of his body weight on the rope that had shivered the hammer against the bell and alerted Tycho to its dread import.

Looking up into the shadows, Geddington could just make out a dark object desultorily bobbing up and down on the bell rope. If it was what he thought it was, it was going to be a difficult job getting it down. Taking summary charge, he rapped out orders: "Get ladders. Call the fire brigade. Call an ambulance." Father Laskiva, having brought up the rear, relayed these demands to staff members as he thought fit. Geddington retained the initiative: he quickly tripped the remaining three snatch blocks. This slackened off all the ropes and sent further solemn booms out into the night.

"Father, grab that fire hose and run up after me with it. Let it run off the reel." Then to Godred: "Stand by and let go the fall end." With that he ran up the spiral staircase to a point above where the object was hanging. By dint of impinging a span of the fire hose against the four now-slack bell ropes over the stairwell, priest and male nurse managed to swing Lance's body over towards the spiral staircase where it could be grabbed. Lower down the flight, willing hands tried to bring it in over the handrail — but staircase and body were at disparate levels. They were desperately heaving down on the bell rope against the counterweight of the hammer up above in order to relieve the rope of the weight of the body.

As they struggled on the narrow stairway with the precariously canted body, somebody came sprinting up the stairs. This new arrival squeezed past thc struggling rescuers and carried on up to the bell platform. It was William Wesley Wepper, Monsalvat's erstwhile Bold Contemner.

Wepper had got as far as Colwyn Bay. When his train had arrived in the station he heard an announcement to the effect that all traffic towards Holyhead was subject to delay "due to an incident on the line at Pencadno". He had been labouring under a premonition of impending doom ever since his strange encounter in the Penmaenbach tunnel. Acting on impulse, he had jumped out of the 'local'. His baggage was still on the Crewe-bound train but he seemed not to care. He ran towards the station entrance, commandeered a waiting taxi and told the driver to make for Pencadno. Arriving at the college, he had paid off the taxi and, alerted by the strokes, had run towards the bell tower — but it was very evident from all the activity that he was arriving too late to save his blood-brother from himself.

Wepper could see the difficulty the rescuers were having in getting the body onto the staircase. On the bell platform he had strength enough to haul upwards against the weight of Lance's body so that he could lift the thimbled eye of the rope off the heel of the hammer. Then, enlisting the aid of friction by impinging the rope against the lip of its hole in the timber platform, he gingerly paid it out until he felt the weight go off it. They had brought the body onto the staircase.

Wepper let go the upper end and it fell away down the stairwell. On the staircase they eventually managed to slacken the noose and manoeuvre it over Lance's lolling head. It was left to its own devices and the weight of the discarded length already hanging in the stairwell pulled it over the handrail. Thus, all of the rope, with its now-contorted noose, fell to the floor of the stairwell.

In the presbytery, Pynxcytte and his six priestly accomplices were throwing things into suitcases, frantically wondering what had to be packed and what was safe to leave behind. They saw the commotion between chapel and bell tower as an opportunity to make a discreet getaway. The Super Snipe was still parked at the bell tower where Father Laskiva had left it. Father Quedda commandeered it and brought it round to the rear of the presbytery. Here, five of them piled into it and headed towards the entrance gates with Quedda at the wheel. Only as he left the college grounds did Quedda switch the car's lights on. He turned right and accelerated away onto the Holyhead road. There was still time to catch the night mailboat to Dun Laoghaire.

Fillery had taken the wheel of the two-door Delage once more. He now reversed it, silently and unlighted, along the grand terrace and into the *porte-cochère,* level with the main doors of the presbytery. Here he got out, opened the boot of the car and waited for Pynxcytte.

According to plan, Pynxcytte emerged from the main entrance with two suitcases, which he threw into the boot. Fillery stood holding the passenger door open for him. But Pynxcytte now withdrew a jerry-can from the car's boot and ran with it back into the presbytery. Fillery moved to close the boot and was now looking about him nervously. Upstairs in his office chambers the erstwhile Rector of Monsalvat frantically opened all the drawers of his filing cabinets and went about feverishly pouring petrol over the contents of the drawers and then onto the carpet. He then retreated to the door. From there he grabbed a votive lamp and flung it towards the open drawers. He banged the door shut and held it to. The room exploded in flames and the closed door shook and rattled against his hand.

* * *

In the bell tower someone had switched on the emergency lighting in the well. It was obvious to Geddington by the way the head flopped that Lance's neck was broken and the spinal cord fatally severed. Thus had Lance Lapita achieved his final objective of joining his exquisite blood-brother in death. Like two golden gods, it was in perfection that their fortunes had converged and it was in the perfect union of death that they were now forever locked. That their liaison in life had contained the seeds of its own destruction was now manifest. The love between them had sprung from different directions and needs; nevertheless, it was as one in intensity. And, irrespective of the censure of authority, their love had been pure and chaste. Whatever dark and carnal impulses might have lain in the interstices of Lance's mind as far as his younger blood-brother was concerned, he had not, and never would have, given way to them.

That such impulses may have posed irresolvable conflicts which lay at the root of his irrational behaviour can only be conjectured. Be that as it may, Lance had lately, publicly and genuinely, abnegated his dangerous lien upon Alexander; following which, worldly censure notwithstanding, both must surely have been content for their love to be judged by the all-knowing Being in which they both believed.

The urgency of the situation at the bell tower now received a new fillip. In the presbytery the sensors had reacted to the heat and fire gongs had started sounding throughout all the buildings of Monsalvat. General evacuation was mandatory in accordance with fire drill.

His would-be rescuers struggled to strap Lance's body into a canvas stretcher on the narrow stairway. Laboriously, they portered it down to the ground floor. The Bold Contemner could only stand by haplessly while the body was loaded into an ambulance. It was destined for the Bangor morgue. There was to be no all-night vigil for this erstwhile blood-brother.

* * *

In the open drawers of the filing cabinets in Pynxcytte's

chambers, thousands of highly flammable photographic plates were adding to the conflagration. As were thousands of incriminating documents. As also were the several questing letters of the Edgars, letters the purpose of which had been frustrated, letters the knowledge of which had been withheld from Alexander.

Pynxcytte turned to go back down to the main entrance door but at the last second he decided to run back along the corridor and into his private chambers. As he re-passed his office door he could hear the roar of the fire inside and could see the door buckling and its varnish bubbling with the heat. In his private chambers he flung aside a heavy tapestry curtain and tore a picture from the oak panelled wall of an inner recess. The picture was glazed on both sides; even in its seclusion it had a public and a private face. Pynxcytte tucked it under his arm. By now the corridor and stairwell were pulsating with smoke and heat. Rather than returning to the main door Pynxcytte thought it more prudent to turn about and make for another staircase leading down to a smaller door nearer the garth and also leading out onto the grand terrace. He knew it would be locked but he also knew there was an emergency key in a glass fronted box alongside it. By now Pynxcytte was aware that the fire gongs were ringing out all over the college. Panicking now, he smashed the glass with a corner of the picture frame. In grabbing the key he cut his hand but paid no heed to the injury. He fumbled frantically with the lock on the door. At last the lock gave and the door flew open. Pynxcytte stepped out into the colonnade and took a great gulp of the cool night air.

But combustible gases from the burning apartments had crept down the stairs with him. Fed by a fresh supply of oxygen, the gases took fire explosively. The resultant blast propelled him bodily out of the colonnade, across the grand terrace and over the balustrading. Pure happenstance deposited him upright on the great parterre as a screaming, running human torch. He dashed across the great parterre, leaving a trail of sparks and shreds of glowing burnt clothing floating on the night air. All this was under the appalled gaze of the onlookers spilling out from the chapel in response to the fire alarms. They saw the fiery apparition run diagonally across the *aditus maritimus* and pitch headlong into the ha-ha. The terrible screaming ended in a ghastly gurgle. Down in the declivity his very body seemed to combust. Those braver onlookers who had run to the lip of the revetment in some forlorn hope of rescue recoiled in horror from the flames and the greasy smoke. They could only stand and stare and hold their kerchiefs to their noses as Monsalvat's erstwhile Rector was reduced to a heap of glowing bones before their eyes.

* * *

At the bell tower it was William Wepper who next came across Tycho Gyles-Skeffington. The distraught boy clad only in pyjama bottoms was still cowering alongside the entrance door. He had been there ever since Geddington told him to stand fast. Wepper gathered him up. The boy was shivering violently and the skin of his bare torso was icy cold to the touch. Wepper groped for words of comfort.

"Steady now, Farmer old fellow. We'll soon have you warmed up. We'll clean up those feet of yours and put you back into bed. You'll be as warm as toast."

But Tycho had been watching the ominous glow of the burning presbytery through the clerestory windows of the chapel; had seen the sparks spiralling upwards into the night sky; seen them landing on the chapel roof. He wriggled in Wepper's arms, freed his right arm and extended it towards the chapel.

"The chapel roof is on fire. Alexander's in there. We've got to get him out."

"But the alarms are going, Tycho. Nobody can go inside."

There seemed no answer to that, but just then Father Laskiva came face to face with Wepper and his precious burden. Wepper changed his tack.

"Don't worry, Farmer, I'm your man. I'll get him out." And then to Laskiva: "Here, Father, can you take him? Get him some blankets from the san. I've got to see to Alexander."

With that he summarily deposited Tycho into the arms of the priest. Wepper did a quick computation, recalling one of Calthrop's half-remembered illustrative maths lessons; the height of the shaft of the bell tower was equivalent to the length of the nave. In disregard of the fire alarms, he ran back into the bell tower to retrieve the discarded bell rope. Having gathered it up, he then tried to re-enter the chapel via the north transept door but was repulsed by falling debris. Still holding the rope, he ran with it round the side of the building and onto the grand terrace. Tycho saw him run off and his concern for Alexander's body was assuaged somewhat. He had always taken Wepper to be the man of action he indeed was. As for Wepper, he considered he had one last duty towards his dead half blood-brother...

Also disregarding the fire alarms, Geddington went up to the sanatorium and grabbed some blankets so that Father Laskiva would have some cover for the shivering boy. The priest began to carry him, now swathed in the blankets, over to the grand parterre where the rest of the college were by now mustered to emergency stations. As he crossed the grand terrace and went down the steps onto the parterre he could see the seriousness of the situation. The presbytery was blazing fiercely and the light night airs had carried the sparks onto the roof of the chapel where they had taken hold. Laskiva gathered his new-found lieutenants about him to assess the situation. The classroom and dormitory blocks were safe enough but desperate efforts were underway to save the chapel. The fire brigade had sent just one appliance in response to the call for assistance in getting the body down from the bell tower; it had taken another call to initiate a general call-out to a fire situation. By the time reinforcements arrived the chapel roof was well alight. The glasses in the lantern had blown out and the dome was acting as a great chimney, spouting flames high into the night air.

Out on the great parterre a small group of adults and prefects stood on the lip of the ha-ha. They were dutifully waving the curious younger boys away from the horror below. They were also pressing handkerchiefs to their noses and cringing away from the acrid greasy smoke. In the ditch a glowing skeletal hand protruded grotesquely upwards from the frightful embers. The ornate rings, the badges of Pynxcytte's office, hung limply from the now fleshless fingers. A few still-glowing flakes of skin eddied up in the convection currents. Peter the Painter was indubitably beyond the sanction of any temporal law.

An appalled Fillery, who had seen Pynxcytte's nemesis from the *porte-cochère,* got back in the Delage and eased it nervously towards the town gate. The gates now stood wide open for emergency vehicles. Like Quedda before him, Fillery intended to keep the car unlighted until he gained the public road. As the Delage neared the gate another automobile, a dark green Rover, turned in off the public road and blocked its exit. It was closely followed by another dark green Rover. Fillery thought it prudent to switch his car's lights on. The headlamps illuminated a burly fellow in an overcoat getting out of the passenger door of the leading Rover. Instinctively Fillery knew who these people were and he felt an ice-cold hand reach in and close around his heart. He could see that besides the driver there were two other men in the rear seat of the leading Rover. The burly fellow came up alongside the driver's window and flashed a police warrant card. Fillery perused it dutifully and decided a little bluff was needed. This policeman could not have failed to notice his clerical collar.

"What is it, officer? I'm in rather a hurry."

The man who flashed the warrant card seemed singularly unimpressed. The clangour of fire engines and a burgeoning glow told their own story.

"What, the place is afire and you're leaving? I find that rather strange. Nobody's going anywhere until we've had a word... Father."

The delay in appending the title and the tone of voice in which it was appended seemed to convey an intentional lack of respect. Fillery took another tack.

"But your people are already here about the accident," he volunteered querulously.

"Oh, we're not the local constabulary We're the vice squad." Then he indicated the following car and added: "The people behind us are 'Forensics'. They're on a different mission. I understand they want to examine the boiler furnace of your peach house in the matter of the disappearance of one Heinrich Daser."

The delinquencies of The Roman Catholic College of St Michael Monsalvat were indeed coming to light.

* * *

On the grand terrace and at a safe distance from the great west door of the chapel, a hurried conference was taking place. The fire chief and the coroner's officer had been joined by Dewi Evans. Having been roused from his bed, first by the funerary peal then by the clangour of the fire engines, the dutiful funeral director was now expressing some urgent professional concerns.

"We've got to get that chest out. That boy's body is subject to a post mortem examination. We took custody of it in a mutilated state. There'll be hell to pay if it's gets incinerated as well."

But the fire chief was adamant. "Nobody goes in there. The roof's already well alight and it could go any second. It's no use, I've told my men to knock off here and deploy to the buildings downwind."

These deliberations were ended by the approach of a figure out of the night from the direction of the bell tower. It remained now for Monsalvat's erstwhile Bold Contemner to perform one last service for his half blood-brother — or, as Wepper had ruefully dubbed him, *nobody's fool but God's*. Wepper was staring straight ahead and giving no recognition to any who attempted to arrest his progress. He ran past the point where the conferring officials were gathered and fetched up level with the great west door.

They saw him flake out the bell rope and bend it on to the nozzle of a fire hose some firemen were in the process of disconnecting from a hydrant on the *aditus maritimus*. Dragging the length of hose behind him he continued through the great west door and into the fiery maw of the chapel. He called over his shoulder: "Heave on the hose when I give the shout."

"No, Will, no. Alexander wouldn't have wanted it."

This was Rhiannon's voice now, shrieking out hysterically over the noise of the flames and destruction. She had come forward from the burgeoning throng of townsfolk who by now were joining the Monsalvations on the great parterre. She tried to join her lover, struggling against two of the fire crew who were holding her back. But Monsalvat's Bold Contemner only had ears for higher things now. He had to shout to make his voice heard over the roar of the conflagration. It was clear his characteristic urbanities had deserted him.

"He ran to me in time of need and perished in so doing. Now I must go to him. If I perish in so doing, then so be it. He has been betrayed too many times. Whatever happens, Rhiannon, I'll always love you."

He turned to continue into the nave of the chapel.

"Come back, come back you silly bugger!" So roared the fire chief.

Wepper stood momentarily in the void of the great west door, his figure silhouetted against the swirling flukes of flame inside. He would have continued upon his fateful way but just then another figure came flying in from the direction of the south transit port. Whoever it was took Wepper down in a flying rugby tackle. With seeming superhuman strength this interloper retained his grip on Wepper's lower limbs, lifted him up and pitched him headlong back down the chapel steps. Wepper landed at Rhiannon's feet. He was slightly concussed and much cut and bruised during the descent but was fortunately without permanent injury. (Not that any could know it at the time, but in that one violent act of deliverance, a future Alexander and a future Sabine were plucked from the brink of oblivion and delivered to posterity.)

The figure, whoever it was, then turned and made to re-enter the nave. They saw him snatch up one of the occasional tables from the porch and hold it over his head to shield him from the falling sparks as he ran towards Alexander's bier. He had picked up the bell rope and was dragging it behind him. Overhead the burning roof crackled and groaned ominously and the glass in the windows was popping and flying everywhere. Through the smoke and sparks they could barely see this interloper reeving the bell rope through the grab handle on the end of the casket. He tied it off and called out: "Heave away". Some now recognised the voice and were able to match it to the stature of the unknown figure.

Five firemen took up the trailing hose and ran with it across the great parterre, scattering those onlookers who had ventured too near for safety. Their action dragged the casket off its trestles, down the aisle and out past the transit ports. From there it bucketed down the steps and onto the safety of the *aditus maritimus.*

The Great Grail of Monsalvat-Pencadno did not come out with it. The heavy ornate pall was still on casket but it was askew and smouldering ominously. Dewi Evans snatched it off and smothered the incipient fires. Thus, were the mortal remains of Alexander Fragner Vudsen delivered from the flames on the end of his blood-brother's suicide rope.

All now waited — hoping against hope — for the deliverer to emerge from the fiery maw that lay inside the great west door. They were still waiting when the dome caved in. A welter of swirling debris, sparks and flame advanced along the nave. Those near the great west door ran for cover. The thunderous roar of destruction shook the very ground beneath their feet. As it died away, a great column of smoke went up into the night sky from the drum of the dome. Still, the interloper might have made it to the north transept door...

* * *

"Water here... water quick!" The action now was on the north side of the chapel and the exhortation was to the firemen playing cooling jets onto the roof of the bell tower. Unseen by those on the grand parterre, a figure trailing sparks and smoke had run out from the north transept porch and had collapsed in a flower bed. The clothing was largely burned off and the person was clearly *in extremis*. One of the hoses was played on him but it was too late to save him. His eyes stared wide in death from a mask of blackened flesh that had been a face. One arm lay outstretched into the flowerbed, the hand grasping an object. The object was sullied with ash but was otherwise undamaged. The object was the Great Grail of Monsalvat-Pencadno which lately had graced Alexander's bier. In it glistened Alexander's

Agnus Dei. Thus did Francis Dominic Leport, formerly foul of mouth and fouler of deed, expiate and purge his unspeakable trespasses against Alexander Fragner Vudsen.

* * *

Out on the great parterre Father Laskiva was still cradling the blanketed Tycho in his arms. By now, Barden had left his muster station and was in solicitous attendance, rearranging the blankets from time to time to keep the trembling boy warm. The priest was partially resting his precious burden on one of the piers of the bridge balustrading. Some of the seniors were standing attentively by. There was little else anyone could do now except watch the fire crew's efforts to preserve the rest of Monsalvat. The residential blocks had not been affected and it was hoped to re-occupy them in a matter of hours and get the boys to their beds once the fire chief had declared the site safe. As to what state the boys could be expected to be in after no less than four grisly and very public fatalities was another matter. Father Laskiva was glad to have Sisters Gloria and Henrietta and the brothers of Basingwerk standing by to render pastoral care.

The darkness of the long night was now receding and the fire-blackened path of the flight of Peter the Painter across the great parterre could now be made out. One of the boys picked up the picture that had fallen from his hand. The boy brought it over to Father Laskiva. He gingerly held it out and just as gingerly the priest took hold of it. He perceived unmistakable slivers of burnt skin sticking to the frame. The glasses had broken and the back-to-back plates were far too mottled and scorched by the heat to be able to determine what they had depicted. Clearly, even in its private alcove in Pynxcytte's chamber it had been deemed prudent for the picture to have both a public and a private face. Both plates fell out of the frame. On the reverse of one could still be made out the college date stamp and the ostentatious legend in Pynxcytte's own florid hand: *"The Apotheosis of Polydeukion* as depicted by Master Alexander Fragner Vudsen". It was Pynxcytte's private memento of Alexander's induction into the *trophimoi*. It was surely the ultimate ignominy heaped upon Alexander via the agency of Pynxcytte's fictitious and infamous 'compact', a constraint no father would ever have inflicted upon his son.

Father Laskiva put the ruined plate down on the coping stone and wiped the black ash from his fingers on the corner of one of the blankets that cosseted Tycho. Unheeded, a slight gust of wind lifted the plate and carried it into the ha-ha. It would later be retrieved by the vice squad as evidence. The *trophimoi* of Monsalvat were no more.

Dawn was beginning to break. Grey daylight was now flooding the great parterre and driving out the blackness of this longest of nights. The smoke column from the drum of the chapel dome towered into the air until it seemed to hit an atmospheric inversion. The top of the column spread out horizontally and the watching throng on the great parterre saw it beginning to take the form of a cross. There was much pointing and incredulous murmuring among the watchers.

Then, to much acclaim from the watching throng, the rays of the morning sun rising over the mountain struck the cross, suffusing it with a spectacular fiery glow. Some fell to their knees and returned their own sign of the cross. Others stood transfixed. All felt instantly comforted. For the believers among them the horrors of that longest and darkest of nights became banished. Here was the ultimate evidence, as if more were needed, that a Greater Hand was guiding the events of that momentous night of purgation and redemption. The unbelievers were left to conjure with a most remarkable cascade of coincidences.

* * *

"See, Tycho. See..." It was Father Laskiva exclaiming ecstatically and pointing upwards with his free arm. "A sign... It must surely be a sign".

The boy lifted his head in its cosseted nest and looked up at the forming shape. Father Laskiva looked down into the boy's face, as a cradling mother might look down into the face of her child. He saw the face bathed in the golden glow from the fiery cross that now hovered over Monsalvat. And he saw all the anguish of that long night drain away from that face. The look that should never be seen on the face of a child was driven out, to be replaced by an expression of serene contentment. The eyes, for so many hours now, stark and staring, became the untroubled eyes of a natural boy once more. The pernicious trembling that had for so long racked the boy's body became stilled at last. His lips moved and both Barden and Laskiva strained to catch the words:

"Holy smoke!"

The jest might well have withered on the death-charged air.

Laskiva was incredulous. Such an impious remark — and in such circumstances! Was not Pynxcytte's blackened, skeletal hand still clutching at the empty air just a few feet away? And was not the chest containing Alexander's broken body lying within sight along the *aditus maritimus?* And alongside the shell of the chapel, were not gloved hands gingerly prising the Great Grail from the fire-reddened fingers of Francis Dominic Leport? And in an ambulance on the Holyhead road, on the way to the Bangor morgue, was not the warmth of life and love ebbing from the corpse of Lance Lapita?

Then it dawned on both Barden and Laskiva; the old Tycho, Tycho the jester, was back. Both found themselves unable to stifle a laugh. It was a painful laugh, an involuntary laugh, a convulsive laugh, a laugh born out of hours of cold, fatigue, fasting and shock — but a laugh nevertheless. The solicitous prefects standing around were incredulous — until Laskiva managed to relay Tycho's remark to them. Then they too began to laugh; first nervously, then hysterically. The incongruity! It had taken an eleven-year-old to put the horrific events of the last few hours into a perspective of decades. Others on the great parterre not privy to the jest looked over with concern at the laughing group gathered about the balustrading of the bridge. They could see them looking up at the fiery cross, the tears rolling down their cheeks. How Alexander would have approved!

The eyes of Alexander's steadfast friend remained fixed on the cross for some time. Then physical and emotional exhaustion took charge; the eyelids came down and the precious young head lolled back against the priest's shoulder. The fiery cross was the last thing he saw before falling into a long and restorative sleep. Henceforth the horrific events which that longest and darkest of nights had so cruelly inflicted would weigh not so much as a feather on that young and fertile mind.

The fiery cross hung in the air over the college buildings for some time, keeping its shape as it drifted slowly out to sea in the light morning airs. The watchers on the great parterre saw it as a sure sign that Alexander's work at Monsalvat was now complete.

THE END